RESCUING SOPHIA

Charlie Team

Guardian Hostage Rescue Specialists
Book 5

ELLIE MASTERS

JEM Publishing

Dedication

This book is dedicated to my one and only—my amazing and wonderful husband.

Without your care and support, my writing would not have made it this far.

You pushed me when I needed to be pushed.

You supported me when I felt discouraged.

You believed in me when I didn't believe in myself.

If it weren't for you, this book never would have come to life.

Also by Ellie Masters

The LIGHTER SIDE

Ellie Masters is the lighter side of the Jet & Ellie Masters writing duo! You will find Contemporary Romance, Military Romance, Romantic Suspense, Billionaire Romance, and Rock Star Romance in Ellie's Works.

YOU CAN FIND ELLIE'S BOOKS HERE: ELLIEMASTERS.COM/BOOKS

Military Romance

Guardian Hostage Rescue Specialists

Rescuing Melissa

(Get a FREE copy of Rescuing Melissa

when you join Ellie's Newsletter)

Alpha Team

Rescuing Zoe

Rescuing Moira

Rescuing Eve

Rescuing Lily

Rescuing Jinx

Rescuing Maria

Bravo Team

Rescuing Angie

Rescuing Isabelle

Rescuing Carmen

Rescuing Rosalie

Rescuing Kaye

Cara's Protector

Rescuing Barbi

Charlie Team

Rescuing Rebel

Rescuing Stitch

Rescuing Mia

Jenna's Protector

Rescuing Sophia

Delta Team (Coming Soon)

Rescuing Ember

Military Romance

Guardian Personal Protection Specialists

Sybil's Protector

Lyra's Protector

The One I Want Series

(Small Town, Military Heroes)

By Jet & Ellie Masters

EACH BOOK IN THIS SERIES CAN BE READ AS A STANDALONE AND IS ABOUT A DIFFERENT COUPLE WITH AN HEA.

Saving Abby

Saving Ariel

Saving Brie

Saving Cate

Saving Dani

Saving Jen

Rockstar Romance

The Angel Fire Rock Romance Series

Becoming His Series

THIS SERIES MUST BE READ IN ORDER.

The Ballet

Learning to Breathe

Becoming His

Dark Captive Romance

A STANDALONE NOVEL.

She's MINE

To My Readers

This book is a work of fiction. It does not exist in the real world and should not be construed as reality. As in most romantic fiction, I've taken liberties. I've compressed the romance into a sliver of time. I've allowed these characters to develop strong bonds of trust over a matter of days.

This does not happen in real life where you, my amazing readers, live. Take more time in your romance and learn who you're giving a piece of your heart to. I urge you to move with caution. Always protect yourself.

Grab the First Book in The Guardian Hostage Rescue Specialists Series for Free

https://elliemasters.com/RescuingMelissa

ONE

Blake

──────────

THE FAMILIAR SCENT OF GUN OIL AND SWEAT HITS ME AS I STRIDE
into Guardian HRS headquarters. My boots echo on the polished
floor, matching the pounding of my heart. Another day, another
mission. I live for this.

I spot Gabe and Walt near the coffee machine, heads bent close
in conversation. Gabe's shoulders shake with silent laughter at something Walt said—probably another terrible joke.

"Morning, ladies. Gossiping already?" I stroll in with a smirk.

"Well, if it isn't the pretty boy of Charlie team." Gabe's head
snaps up, grinning. He clasps my hand in a firm shake that turns
into a quick, one-armed thump against my back. "Thought you
might be too busy admiring yourself in the mirror to grace us with
your presence."

"Unlike some people, I don't need hours to make this look
good." I shove him playfully, gesturing to my face as Walt rolls his
eyes.

"Yeah, yeah, we get it. You're God's gift to women." Walt hands
me a steaming cup of coffee. "Drink up, Casanova. We've got a big
day ahead."

The bitter liquid burns down my throat, grounding me. I savor the moment, this easy camaraderie forged through blood and bullets. These men are more than teammates; they're brothers.

Hank and Rigel join us. Rigel, a seasoned Navy SEAL new to our team, is eager to prove himself and earn his place among us.

"Any idea what this meeting's about?" Rigel's gaze darts between us.

"Probably another milk run. Rescuing kittens from trees, that sort of thing." I shrug, feigning nonchalance despite my burning curiosity.

"Don't let Blake fool you. He's as eager as a virgin on prom night to find out what's going on." Hank claps Rigel on the shoulder, snorting.

Our laughter ceases as Ethan, our team leader, rounds the corner. His face displays its usual stoic mask, but a glint in his eye sends a shiver of excitement down my spine.

"Alright, children," Ethan's voice carries the weight of command, "playtime's over. CJ wants us in the briefing room. Now."

We fall in line behind Ethan, our steps in perfect sync. The playful atmosphere evaporates, replaced by focused intensity. This is what we're made for. This is who we are.

The briefing room buzzes with activity when we enter. CJ stands at the head of the table, his presence commanding even in stillness. Sam and Mitzy flank him, their faces unreadable, but it's the fourth person who catches my attention: Forest Summers, the big boss himself.

This must be serious.

My gaze sweeps the room, cataloging details out of habit: tension in CJ's shoulders, a slight furrow between Mitzy's brows as she taps her tablet, and Sam's fingers drumming an impatient rhythm on the table.

We take our seats, the scrapes of chairs piercing the loaded silence. I lean back initially, projecting casual indifference even as every nerve in my body stands at attention. The presence of these heavy hitters tells me this is far from our usual op. Sensing the gravity of the situation, I shift forward, elbows on the table, giving CJ my full attention.

"Gentlemen, let's recap what we know about Sentinel." CJ's voice cuts through the quiet like a knife. His gaze sweeps over us, a reminder of our mission's gravity.

"As you're all aware, Sentinel is more than just a simple organization," Forest says, his massive frame dominating the space. "It's a network that's been giving us hell for months now."

My pulse quickens. Sentinel. The boogeyman of the underworld. We've brushed up against their operations before, always coming away with more questions than answers.

Mitzy taps her tablet, and a holographic display springs to life above the table. The familiar web of connections, names, and locations floats before us, now grown with new threads connecting pieces of the puzzle we've been struggling to solve.

"Let's go over the structure again," Mitzy says, manipulating the display. "We're dealing with nine distinct entities, each headed by an individual we're calling a Sentinel."

The hologram shifts, highlighting nine figures. Eight remain frustratingly blank, but one face stands out in sharp relief: Jonathan Greaves, the bastard we cornered on that yacht rescue, the one who slipped through our fingers.

"Thanks to the intel gathered during the Jenna Marlowe case," Sam continues, "we've identified the Ninth Sentinel, Jonathan Greaves. His specialty, as we know, is human trafficking."

My jaw clenches, a familiar rage burning in my gut. Human trafficking. The lowest of the low. Memories of the yacht op flash through my mind—the terrified girls, the stench of fear and desperation. Jenna clinging to my brother when he rescued her. The way Sophia looked at me, her expression bouncing between hope and distrust. I rescued her, and I still can't get the way she clung to me out of my head.

Sophia. The name echoes in my mind, stirring up feelings I've been trying to bury. Focus, Jackson. This isn't the time.

"Unfortunately," Forest's deep voice pulls me back to the

present, "Greaves is still in the wind after the yacht raid. Finding him is our top priority."

"Any new leads on the other Sentinels?" Ethan leans forward, his eyes sharp.

"That's where we need to step up our game." CJ's expression hardens. "We need to put faces to the other eight Sentinels, uncover their specialties, and figure out how they're all connected. Until further notice, Charlie team's primary mission is to get Greaves. Find out who these other eight are. How they're connected—"

"They're connected through Malfor," I interject, rolling my eyes. "We all know he's the kingpin."

"Shut your trap and let CJ finish." Ethan's glare pins me down, his tone delivering a verbal beatdown.

"Just saying, it's obvious how they're connected." I smirk, leaning back slightly.

This is big. Bigger than anything we've tackled before. Energy crackles in the air, radiating off my teammates until the entire room buzzes.

"Mitzy and her team will provide tech support. The other Guardian teams—Alpha, Bravo, Delta—will assist as needed, but this is your baby." Sam addresses that last comment to Ethan.

"There's one more thing." Forest's deep, rumbly voice causes us all to snap to attention. "An asset we have…"

My breath catches. No way. They're not…

"Sophia Reeves provided us with invaluable information after the yacht rescue," Forest continues, his gaze sweeping over us. "We've decided to grant her protection at Guardian HQ."

My gut twists at the news. They're going to use her.

I lean back, trying to mask my reaction. Every muscle in my body tenses, my mind racing through scenarios, each ending with Sophia and me in a situation I shouldn't be imagining.

Sophia. The woman who's been haunting my dreams and fueling heated fantasies since I first laid eyes on her is going to be a permanent resident of Guardian HQ?

My pulse quickens, heat creeping up my neck. I can't stop the flood of images—her soft skin, the way she looked at me, the unspoken connection between us.

Every night since the rescue, she's been in my thoughts, my dreams. My fantasies.

Now, she'll be *here*, within reach, but off limits. The intensity of my attraction doesn't make sense. For her safety and mine, I need to do whatever it takes to never be alone with her. The thought of having her close, yet untouchable, is maddening. My mind conjures images of her—her body pressed against mine, her breath warm on my skin.

I grit my teeth, trying to banish the fantasies springing to life in the middle of the briefing. My body betrays me, arousal stirring and making it hard to concentrate. My fingers dig into the armrest as I struggle to maintain composure.

The temptation to be near her, to let my guard down… It's unbearable. I can't let this mess with my head or be a distraction. I have to distance myself, no matter how hard it gets.

She's been through hell, a victim of sexual slavery, and doesn't need some horn dog Guardian drooling over her.

Get it together. Focus. She deserves better.

Trying to regain composure, I focus back on the meeting, but my mind is already spiraling, fueled by fantasies I have no business pursuing.

I can't get away from those haunted eyes and her siren's call.

Kidnapped, captured, sold like livestock, she's been through hell and back, endured unimaginable trauma at the hands of animals, and all I can think about is fucking her.

I've done it in my sleep every night since I first saw her, and I'm not proud of it. I'm deeply ashamed. Deeply aroused.

Deeply fucked ten ways 'til Sunday.

"Blake," CJ's voice slices through my spiraling thoughts. "You'll be assigned as Sophia's primary point of contact."

I do a double take. "What?"

"She latched onto you after the rescue," Forest explains. "No need to start with someone new when there's already a connection. You're the one she trusts."

My mind races back to the rescue mission on the Ninth Sentinel's yacht. We were there for Jenna, but we found Sophia, too. She clung to me like I was her lifeline.

"Your job is to keep her safe, help her get settled, and make her feel comfortable enough to share any more information she might have about Sentinel."

"After everything she's been through, you want me to interrogate her?" I glance around the table, searching for any sign that I heard wrong.

"Not interrogate." Mitzy shakes her head. "Gain her trust. She needs someone she feels safe with."

"And how am I supposed to do that?"

"Just show her around the place. Make sure she gets what she needs. Be a friend. Get her to open up to you, and hopefully, she'll share more about Sentinel so that we don't have to interrogate her."

"Wouldn't someone else be better?" Anyone else?

"There is no one else," CJ says.

"What about Jenna? She and Sophia know each other. Now that Jenna is staying on HQ grounds, that seems the best fit."

I do not want to babysit Sophia. I want nothing to do with her.

"Jenna isn't trained for this. Not to mention, she's not a Guardian HRS employee." Forest doesn't mince words. "Until further notice, Sophia is your responsibility."

"Understood." I force myself to keep my expression neutral even as my insides churn.

The meeting continues, and I'm completely distracted, flooded with the details of that mission. All I can think about is Sophia—her haunted eyes, her trembling body, the way she looked at me with something that made my heart race and my palms sweat.

None of it makes sense. The intensity of it makes no sense. It twists my thoughts and stirs desires I've never felt before.

Sophia changed something in me. She awakened a need that refuses to be ignored. No matter how much I try to push it aside, it keeps coming back, stronger and more insistent. She's different from any other woman I've known—or rescued—and that difference is dangerous.

I can't get her out of my head, and I don't know if I ever will. Why her? Why now?

I've rescued countless women, all in similar situations, but none of them affected me like this. None of them crawled under my skin and lodged themselves in my brain like Sophia.

This isn't attraction; it's something else. Something confusing. Something inherently dangerous.

I'm stuck in an endless loop of wanting her, needing her, and knowing I must stay away—if only to protect her from myself.

And now, she's my assignment. Totally fucked.

As we file out of the briefing room, the excited chatter of my teammates fades into the background. They have a new mission. A chance to take down Sentinel. But I get Sophia, the woman who's literally in my dreams—very dark, very X-rated dreams.

I take a deep breath, squaring my shoulders. Suck it up, buttercup. Nothing you can do about it. Let the games begin.

TWO

Blake

____

THE MEETING ADJOURNS. CHAIRS SCRAPE AGAINST THE FLOOR. Ethan motions for us to gather, his face set in its usual stoic mask.

"Alright. You heard the brass. We're going all-in on Sentinel." Ethan's voice is low, meant for our ears only. "For now, we wait while Mitzy and her team track down Greaves. I'm sure she's tracking that yacht. All leaves are canceled, not that any of you ever ask for time off. We're on training duty until the techies build out a mission packet."

I wait for the other shoe to drop. I know what's coming but hearing it out loud makes it real.

"Blake, you've got Sophia." Ethan's gaze lands on me. "She latched onto you, so she's yours now. Make her comfortable. Show her around. Get her settled in and see if you can get her to open up about anything she might have left out in her initial debrief."

I open my mouth to protest, to suggest someone else. "Hank or Rigel would be better suited for this. I—"

Ethan's stern gaze locks onto mine, unyielding. "She needs someone she feels safe with. That's you. You handle her and do it right. No arguments."

"Copy that." I keep my face carefully neutral.

As the team disperses, I linger, my thoughts churning.

Sophia.

Just the thought of her name sends a rush of heat coursing through my veins. I make my way out of the briefing room, my feet carrying me automatically through the familiar halls of Guardian HRS. My mind, however, is far away, lost in memories of that night on the yacht.

Sophia huddled on that bed, barely dressed.

Her eyes wide with fear and desperation.

The way she flinched when I approached.

How her expression softened when she realized we would be rescuing her as well.

Sophia's presence of mind, directing us to the safe and insisting we grab the documents, hard drives, and thumb drives with crucial information on the Sentinels, was impressive.

It was impressive, especially given the chaos.

Nor will I forget the way her body pressed against mine. The way she clung to me. The way she felt when I held her in my arms during the boat ride back to shore. So light, as if years of abuse had whittled her down to nothing but skin and bones. Yet she clung to me with surprising strength, her face buried in my chest.

The memory sends another wave of heat through me, followed immediately by self-loathing.

What kind of man gets turned on by a trauma victim's desperate grab for safety?

I've rescued many women, but none ever got under my skin like Sophia. I'm fucked in the head. That's what I am. Stay away. Keep my distance. Get through this fucked up assignment.

For her sake and mine.

But that's not happening.

Fuck me.

I drag a hand down my face and grimace.

Each small interaction replays in my mind—a highlight reel of moments I've tried—and failed—to forget.

Sophia's hand gripping mine as we led her to safety. Her body fitting perfectly against mine when I carried her off the yacht. Her voice, trembling yet clear, directing us to the safe and the critical information inside. The fleeting look in her eyes filled with gratitude and something more. Leaning on me for support during the boat ride back, her breath warm on my neck.

These moments refuse to fade, playing repeatedly, pulling me deeper into dangerous attraction. The truth is impossible to resist: I'm intensely attracted to Sophia Reeves.

Deeply, irresistibly, irrefutably attracted.

It's more than just her physical beauty, though. God knows she's gorgeous. Long, dark ringlets cascade down her back. Eyes the color of storm clouds, gray and intense. High cheekbones and full lips that beg to be kissed. Her body, slender yet strong, every curve draws me in.

No, it's more than that. I am impressed by the strength and resilience that allowed her to survive unspeakable horrors. The intelligence shining in her eyes, choosing each word carefully to minimize any retribution, as if every word might be turned into a weapon to use against her, intoxicates me.

Lost in these thoughts, my feet carry me on autopilot. Suddenly, I find myself outside Medical, the familiar surroundings snapping me back to reality.

Sophia is here…

Already, my blood heats as desire stirs.

I'm a fucking monster.

How am I supposed to do this?

How can I be the Guardian she needs when every part of me aches to hold her close and never let go?

I lean against the wall, taking deep breaths to center myself. This isn't about me. This is about the mission. About taking down Sentinel and making sure no one else has to go through what Sophia did.

I can do this. I have to do this.

Squaring my shoulders, I push off from the wall and head toward the reception desk. Time to find out exactly where they put Sophia and get this show on the road.

"Can I help you?" The receptionist, a pretty young woman, eyes me as I approach.

"I'm looking for Sophia Reeves." I'm proud of how steady my voice sounds.

She taps at her computer for a moment, then nods. "Room 217."

"Thanks." I turn to go, but her smile widens.

She leans forward, exposing just enough cleavage to let me know she's interested. Her voice drops a notch, becoming sultry.

"Is there anything else I can help you with? Maybe grab a drink later?"

Usually, I'd consider it. My bed's never empty for long, and it's no secret I have a healthy appetite for sex. My urges are carnal and raw. Aggressive and dark.

Fuuuuuck… Stop thinking about sex!

But right now, all I can think about is Sophia. Her face, her voice, the way she looked at me.

"Thanks, but I've got my hands full today." I give her a polite nod, moving down the hallway.

"You sure? I promise I don't bite—unless you ask nicely." Her pout is almost comical.

"Maybe another time." I shake my head. A different day, and I'd be all on board.

"I'll hold you to that." Her disappointment is palpable, but she recovers quickly.

Walking down the hall, my heart races with each step. 215… 216… 217. I stop outside her door, hand poised to knock—frozen in place.

Get it together, Jackson. You've faced down terrorists and drug lords. You can handle one woman.

But that's the problem.

Sophia isn't just a woman. She's the one who haunts my dreams—the one I have to face every day while pretending I don't want to lose myself in her completely.

But I do.

I desperately do.

I cut that thought off before it can fully form.

Professional. Be professional.

Taking a deep breath, I knock on the door. The scent of antiseptic mingles with the faintest lavender perfume. There's a moment of silence, and a soft voice calls out.

"Come in."

I turn the handle, the cool metal grounding me before I step into the room. The dim lighting casts a warm glow, creating a small oasis in the otherwise harsh medical ward. Sophia Reeves sits on the edge of the bed, her head bowed, those storm-cloud eyes hidden behind a curtain of dark lashes.

For a moment, I forget how to breathe.

The room feels ten sizes too small, the air too thick to breathe. The faint hum of the air conditioning and the distant murmur of voices in the hall fade away, leaving only my heartbeat thundering past my ears.

A few seconds pass in heavy silence, and then she gives a slow, languid blink. Her gaze lifts, meeting mine, and my skin tingles under the intensity of her stare.

"Is there anything I can do for you?" Her voice is a whisper, like the rustle of silk, sending shivers down my spine. The warmth of her breath and the gentle cadence of her words wrap around me, pulling me in.

I'm so fucked.

I clear my throat, trying to find my voice. "Do you remember me? From the yacht?" My words sound hollow compared to the storm of emotions raging inside me.

"Of course, I remember you." Her eyes widen slightly, and a small, almost shy smile plays on her lips. "How could I forget the man who saved me?"

She shifts slightly, the movement causing a strand of dark hair to fall across her face. The urge to reach out, to brush it aside, and feel the silky softness of her hair slip through my fingers consumes me.

Her storm-cloud gaze pierces through me, reading every thought and desire I'm trying to suppress.

The room's atmosphere shifts, the air thickening with an undeniable chemistry. Her eyes lock onto mine, and the spark of interest in her gaze mirrors my intense attraction. The tension between us crackles, electric and palpable.

"How are you doing?" My voice is rough.

"I'm okay, considering the circumstances." Sophia sighs softly, her shoulders lift and fall. The subtle scent of lavender wafts toward me. Her gaze locks onto mine, and she bites her lower lip gently. "I don't know what happens next."

"Uh, yeah." I try to clear the haze clouding my thoughts. "I'm here to talk to you about that. Guardian HRS is concerned about your safety. We'd like to offer you quarters and protection."

"Really? For me?" Her brows arch in surprise, lips parting slightly, drawing my attention. She leans forward, her fingers grazing the bedspread, creating a soft rustle.

That and more.

It's the *more* part which is the major fucking problem.

"It's the least we can do, considering how you helped us." I shift on my feet, trying to appear nonchalant, but the room feels smaller with her so close.

"What did I do? You rescued me." She tilts her head, dark hair cascading over one shoulder, releasing a subtle hint of her floral shampoo. Her eyes remain fixed on mine, a playful curiosity in them.

"The safe and the drives. We want to ensure you're safe." My voice falters, remembering her bravery as she guided us to the crucial information cutting through the chaos.

"Thank you." Sophia's gaze softens, and she offers a small, appreciative smile. "For everything." Her voice is warm and sincere.

"We'll take care of you, Sophia. You can count on that." I swallow hard, my senses overwhelmed by her presence and the intensity of her gratitude.

"We?" She tilts her head, a playful glint in her eyes. "What about you?"

A hint of flirtation laces her voice, and the question hangs between us. The heat between us intensifies; the chemistry undeniable as she waits for my response.

"I've been assigned to oversee your needs. To take care of you." My voice comes out huskier than I intend, thick with desire.

Her eyes widen, the playful glint growing sharper. The air between us crackles with electricity. My heart pounds as I catch the subtle parting of her lips, an unspoken invitation, and the faint hitch in her breath.

"Take care of me? Well, that's a wonderful surprise." Her voice is soft and flirtatious. "Exactly what does overseeing my needs entail?" Her eyes lock onto mine with a dangerous mix of curiosity and desire.

"Anything you need," I whisper, my voice barely holding steady. "I'll make it happen."

My pulse races, palms damp, as I fight to keep my composure.

"Anything?" Her eyes sparkle with a hint of mischief, testing the limits of what anything might mean.

I swallow hard, forcing myself to stay focused. "Anything we would do for those in your situation." I steer away from the dangerous territory we seem to be stepping into. "We have a place called the Facility where we take the women we rescue. It's a halfway house that helps them recover from their trauma and get back on their feet, but with Jonathan Greaves still out there, we think it's safer for you to remain on Guardian HQ grounds."

At the mention of Greaves, Sophia flinches, her face paling.

"He's a monster, a truly terrible human being. I can't believe I'm finally free of him, but it doesn't feel real. This feels like a dream. I'll never be able to repay you for what you did."

"It's my job."

"Your job?" She tilts her head, giving me a slow, deliberate once-over.

Her curious gaze sweeps over all six-foot-three of me, and I can't help but imagine her lingering below my belt as her eyes make a languid journey down to my boots, then back up again.

Did she lick her lips?

Fuck. Now I'm hallucinating shit.

She glances around the sterile hospital room, her gaze lingering on the plain white walls and the uninviting bed. A flicker of disappointment crosses her eyes.

"I'm so tired of hanging out in this hospital room, but beggars can't be choosers."

She thinks she's stuck here indefinitely.

"No. Not at all." I rush to her, my hand instinctively reaching out to touch her shoulder. The instant spark of connection sizzles through me, a rush of heat and desire that nearly takes my breath away. "You're not staying *here*. We have quarters for you, a place where you can be comfortable."

Her eyes widen, fear giving way to relief and gratitude that softens her features. With a simple touch, the connection between us deepens, the air now charged with undeniable electricity.

"This is a dream." A smile brightens her face, filled with hope and a touch of uncertainty. "I'm grateful and blown away. Please tell me this isn't a dream."

"Not a dream, sweetie. This is real."

"Wow. I want to kiss you right now." Her gaze lingers on my lips, sending my pulse racing. A flood of warmth shoots straight to my groin.

Nope. Not headed down that path.

Be professional.

I clear my throat, forcing a casual tone. "How about we bust you out of this joint, and I show you to your new quarters?" As I reach out to help her, a fresh jolt of awareness surges through me.

"I'd love that." She rises slowly, her movements naturally sensual. As she loops her arm through mine, her fingers lightly brush my bicep, sending a shudder through my heart.

"Wow, muscles on top of muscles." She squeezes my arm, then trails her fingers from my shoulder down to the back of my hand. "Quite impressive."

I swallow hard, my pulse quickening.

Be professional.

Yeah right. I'm giving myself ten-to-one odds this won't stay professional at all.

THREE

Blake

We leave Sophia's hospital room and make our way outside. She stays close, clinging to me, her hand wrapped around my arm, her body pressing against me with every step.

"Tell me more about the Facility." Her voice fills with genuine curiosity. "It sounds amazing."

"It's a secure place where we help those we rescue to recover. We offer counseling, medical care, and a safe environment to start rebuilding their lives. There's even a school."

"A school?"

"Yeah, some of them are kids. Too many." I clear my throat, trying to shake off the weight of my words. "I'll get you whatever you need—clothes, food, anything. Just tell me, and I'll make it happen."

"Wow, like my own personal protector."

"Just someone to help. We find it's easiest if you have one person to turn to, but don't feel obligated—"

"Not feeling obligated. I'm feeling all kinds of grateful. It still doesn't feel real."

As we exit Medical, I steer her toward a waiting golf cart.

"You'll find these all over HQ." I gesture to a cart. "The carts are for anyone's use and are handy to have around."

Sophia stops, her eyes wistful as she looks around.

"Do you mind if we walk? Is it too far?"

"It's a good ten-minute walk. The cart is much faster."

"It's been years since I've been allowed outside without a guard. Years since I've been able to walk free. If it's not too much of a bother, I'd rather walk."

Her words tug at something deep inside me. I swallow hard at the reminder of her trauma.

"Of course. Let's walk."

The magnetic pull between us grows stronger as we stroll through the expansive grounds of Guardian HRS.

Our bodies brush together with each step, heightening the chemistry between us. Her grip tightens slightly, and I savor the sensation, even though it's risky to let this attraction deepen.

"I can't get over how beautiful it is here." Her voice is low and soft, almost sultry. As we walk, her eyes widen with wonder.

"It is." I agree, though my mind isn't on Guardian HRS. I'm completely captivated by the beauty beside me. "And it's safe." She needs to remember that she's not just free but safe from men like Greaves.

"Thank you for everything. I don't know how I'll ever repay you."

"There's no need for that. It's my pleasure, but if you want to repay me, focus on your healing. What you've endured… I hate that you suffered like that. While you won't be at the Facility, we have amazing counselors when you're ready."

"Thanks. That's incredibly kind and generous. I'm not sure I'm ready for—something like that." Her voice softens. "It's hard to forget everything that's happened. Even harder to believe it's really over." Her fingers curl around mine, a spark of electricity shooting through me, and her eyes glisten with tears. "Thank you so much."

Her vulnerability is going to be the death of me.

We arrive at the dormitories, a set of clean, functional quarters meant for part-time personnel. I lead Sophia to her new apartment.

"This will be your place." I gesture toward the small but well-appointed apartment. "It's got a living room, a full kitchen, a small dining area, and of course, a bedroom."

Sophia steps inside while I remain in the hall. Her eyes widen in surprise. "This is so much more than I expected." She turns to me, a joyful glint in her eye.

I hesitate, determined to stay in the hall where it's safer.

Her excitement radiates, arms lifting as she spins around, a squeal of delight escaping her lips. For a brief moment, the haunted look in her eyes is replaced by pure happiness. It's a rare, beautiful sight, and I can't help but smile. She suddenly halts mid-spin, realizing I'm still in the hall.

"Stop being silly and come in." She playfully tugs me inside.

So much for staying in the hall.

The door clicks shut behind us, and I stand awkwardly in the middle of the room as she begins to explore. She moves through the small space, opening the fridge, checking every drawer and cupboard. Then she heads into the bedroom—a place I'm not about to enter. More squeals of delight echo as she tests the shower and inspects the walk-in closet. Guardian HRS certainly knows how to take care of its people.

Sophia reappears from the bedroom, her mouth agape and eyes wide, before she turns to me.

"I could use some food." Her voice drops to a husky whisper. "And clothes. But maybe we start with food? How does a girl get food around here? I'm starving."

"There are several dining facilities on the grounds. We've got cafeterias, a burger joint, and a dine-and-dash. If you make a list of things you want, I'll get them delivered."

"You have all of that? Here? On the grounds?"

"Yeah, and more. What stimulates—um, interests your tastebuds the most? We can grab anything you want." My voice is rougher than it should be.

The sooner I can get her out of here, the sooner I can rid myself of my intrusive thoughts, like how much I want to fuck her on that bed.

This is my personal version of hell.

"Perfect." Her eyes lock onto mine. "Lead the way, my gallant hero."

We leave the apartment, and she stays close, her body pressing against mine with every step. My mind races with desire, determination, and disgust. I have to stay professional. I cannot, and will not, take advantage of her.

In the cafeteria, she picks at her food, her eyes never leaving mine.

"So." Her voice is silky smooth. "Tell me about yourself. How did you end up with the Guardians?"

I take a deep breath, trying to steady my racing heart. "I used to be in the Navy. After I got out, I joined Guardian HRS. It's a good fit for me. I like the work we do."

"I bet you do." Her eyes gleam. "You seem like the kind of man who enjoys helping people."

"Something like that." My gaze lingers on her rosebud lips, drawn to them for a moment too long. The urge to close the distance and taste her is almost overwhelming.

She smiles, slow and seductive, the kind of smile that makes my pulse race and my blood burn. "Well, thank you—for everything." Her fingers curl around mine, her touch sparking a fire that threatens to consume my self-control.

Every instinct urges me to lean in, to close the distance between us, but I force myself to stay steady. I can't let this happen, no matter how much I want it. The battle inside me rages, desire clashing with duty. I must keep my distance and protect her from myself.

As we finish our meal and return to her room, the tension between us intensifies. She moves close, her fingers brushing my arm, sending jolts of electricity through me. When we reach her door, she turns to me, her eyes shining with gratitude.

"Thank you." She lifts on tiptoe and gently kisses my cheek.

My skin burns, and my groin heats.

"Goodnight, Sophia." I swallow hard, my pulse racing. As I turn to leave, her voice and a gentle hand on my arm stop me.

"Would you mind staying a bit longer? I'm scared to be alone in this strange place."

Kill me. Just kill me now. I will not survive this torture.

But I'll do it—fuck me—I'll do whatever it takes to keep her safe. Even if it means fighting my desires every step of the way.

"I'll stay." I force a smile.

"Unless you have somewhere to be, or someone to see?" Her voice is tentative, probing for information.

She's fishing for clues about my personal life, whether I'm married, attached, or have a girlfriend. Still, her tone also shows genuine nervousness about staying alone in an unfamiliar place.

"There's no one waiting for me, Sophia." My voice softens. "I'd enjoy the company too."

Her shoulders relax slightly, and she offers a small, grateful smile. It makes me want to stay close to her, not out of duty but because I genuinely enjoy her presence.

I step into Sophia's new apartment for the second time, my heart pounding. The familiar scent of lavender mingles with the faint smell of fresh paint. The soft, incandescent light casts a warm glow on her features, accentuating the delicate curve of her jaw and the intensity of her stormy eyes.

My gaze shifts to a package on the coffee table that wasn't there before—a distraction, a welcome one—but the electric tension between us is impossible to ignore. Her nearness stirs desire and trepidation, a battle raging within me.

"Looks like someone left you something." I gesture to the package. My voice is steadier than I feel; each moment with her tests my self-control.

Sophia's eyes light up as she tears into it, pulling out comfortable-looking pajamas, toiletries, and other necessities. At the bottom, a handwritten note catches her eye. She reads it silently, a soft smile spreading across her face.

"It's from Jenna." She clasps the note to her chest, her eyes shining with unshed tears. "She's happy I'm here and can't wait to see me once I'm settled in." Her voice wavers slightly, the joy in her expression tempered by guilt. "I can't believe I'm free, that I get to see my friend again. But—I feel horrible for what I did to her. It's my fault she was taken. If I hadn't…" Her voice trails off, the guilt and relief mingling in her eyes as she looks up at me, seeking reassurance.

My chest tightens at the vulnerability in her eyes. I clear my throat, searching for words that won't betray the storm of emotions inside me.

I step forward, closing the distance between us. Without thinking, I wrap my arms around her, pulling her into a tight embrace.

"It's okay," I murmur into her hair. "Jenna doesn't blame you—none of us do. You had no choice, and we understand how horrible that was."

The hug lingers—two seconds, three—five long seconds. She relaxes into me, her body slowly melting into the embrace. Her arms wrap around my waist, clutching me like I'm her lifeline.

I breathe in, catching the subtle blend of her perfume and lavender, and for a moment, the world narrows to just the two of us, bound together in this intimate, comforting embrace.

Fuck emotions. This is a raw, visceral *need*.

"Um, I think I'll take a quick shower if that's okay?" Sophia gathers up the toiletries, her movements graceful despite her exhaustion.

"Of course." I keep my voice neutral, even as my pulse quickens. The slight flushing of her cheeks and the way her hands tremble as she collects her things says far too much. "I'll be right out here if you need anything."

She gives me a small, almost shy smile before turning away. The bathroom door closes softly behind her, and I sink onto the couch, dropping my head into my hands. The sound of running water fills the apartment, a reminder of her presence just a few feet away.

My imagination runs wild, picturing her in the shower, and I groan, forcing myself to think of anything else—mission reports, weapon maintenance, literally anything but Sophia naked in the next room.

But the way she looked at me, the way her body responded

during that hug—it's impossible to ignore the chemistry between us. The tension is undeniable, and she feels it too.

When she finally emerges, wrapped in a fluffy robe with damp hair curling around her face, I stand abruptly, my body on edge. Time to make a quick exit and end this torment.

"I should get going." I head toward the door, eager to escape the temptation she poses.

Sophia's eyes widen, a flicker of panic crossing her face.

"Actually… Would you mind staying? Just until I fall asleep?" She twists the belt of her robe between her fingers, her voice trembling slightly. "I know it's a lot to ask, but this place still feels unfamiliar."

"Alright." I should leave, but I'm unable to refuse her. "I'll stay until you're asleep."

She disappears into the bedroom, and I take off my boots, bracing myself for what's ahead. My hands tremble as I set them aside, and I take a deep breath to steady myself.

"Blake?" Sophia's voice calls softly from the bedroom.

I step in cautiously. She's wearing the pajamas from the care package—soft flannel pants and a loose T-shirt. The sight of her like this, so vulnerable, makes my throat tighten as I swallow hard against the lump forming there.

"Could you… If it's not too much to ask, do you think you could hold me until I fall asleep?" Her voice is timid and unsure, and her eyes are wide with vulnerability.

"Of course." I take a step closer, my heart pounding.

I sit beside her, gently pulling her into my arms. She nestles against me, her body fitting perfectly against mine. The warmth of her skin, the soft scent of her hair—everything about this moment feels both right and dangerously intoxicating.

My pulse races, but I force myself to focus on being a comforting presence for her. She gradually relaxes, her breathing slowing, fingers clutching my shirt. Each second stretches into an eternity.

"I never thought I'd be free of him." Sophia's breath is warm against my neck. Her fingers trace idle patterns on my chest, sending shivers down my spine. "I'll always be grateful to you for saving me."

My arm tightens around her involuntarily. I want to tell her how strong she is, how much I admire her resilience. But I stay silent, not trusting myself to speak.

As Sophia's breathing evens out and she drifts off to sleep, I lie there, hyperaware of every point where our bodies connect. It takes every ounce of willpower not to stroke her hair or press a kiss to her forehead.

Once I'm sure she's deeply asleep, I carefully extricate myself from her embrace. I pause at the bedroom door, looking back at her peaceful form. Something tightens in my chest, but I force myself to leave the room. I settle onto the couch, bracing for a long, uncomfortable night. My body aches with unfulfilled desire, but even more, my mind races with conflicting emotions.

I want to protect Sophia, to help her heal, but I also want her in ways I shouldn't—ways that would complicate everything. As I stare at the ceiling, I curse Forest Summers and this assignment.

The night drags on endlessly. I toss and turn, struggling to find a comfortable position on the too-small couch. At some point, I must have dozed off, because I suddenly jerk awake to the sound of soft whimpers coming from the bedroom. Instantly, I'm on my feet, moving silently toward Sophia's room.

She's tangled in the sheets, her face twisted in fear as she mumbles incoherently. A nightmare. My heart aches for her as I approach the bed.

"No... Please... Not again... Master, please... I'll be good... Don't hurt me..."

"Sophia." I gently nudge her shoulder. "Wake up. You're safe."

Her eyes fly open, wild with terror. She doesn't recognize me and shrinks away.

"It's okay." I keep my distance. "It's Blake. You're safe. You're at Guardian HQ. No one can hurt you here."

Recognition flickers in her eyes, quickly followed by relief. Without warning, she throws herself into my arms, sobbing against my chest.

I hold her close, murmuring reassurances as I gently stroke her hair. As her tears begin to subside, the reality of our position becomes impossible to ignore—Sophia in my lap, her curves pressing against me, my hands resting on her back.

Things are stirring that shouldn't.

I should put her back to bed and return to the couch, but I can't bring myself to let her go.

"Stay," Sophia whispers, her lips brushing my neck. "Please. I don't want to be alone."

God help me. Will the torment never end?

I gently shift us back onto the bed, keeping her close. As we settle in, Sophia curls against me like she belongs there, her warmth and trust igniting something deep inside me.

I'm playing with fire, but for tonight—for her—I'll risk getting burned.

FOUR

Sophia

THE SIZZLE OF BACON IN THE HOT PAN FILLS THE SMALL KITCHEN AS I crack eggs into a bowl. My movements are precise, almost ritualistic —designed to be flawless.

The rich scent of coffee brewing mingles with the savory aroma of the bacon, wrapping me in a warm, comforting cocoon that almost makes me forget where I am.

Almost.

I steal a glance at the closed bedroom door, my heart quickening. Blake is still asleep, and I'm determined to make everything perfect for when he wakes up. It's the least I can do to show my gratitude for everything he's done. But deep down, this gesture means more. I need to make him see me as more than *just* an assignment.

Because he's been assigned to me.

No big mystery there.

Guardian HRS wants something out of me.

Everyone wants something out of me.

There's no such thing as true freedom when everyone wants something.

Whatever. I roll my eyes, the thought almost reflexive.

I'm used to being used. I turn back to the skillet with a frown. The only good thing about any of this is that I get to play pretend.

Pretend I'm free.

Pretend I can be loved.

Pretend I have a future worth fighting for.

And, if I'm going to pretend, I might as well have a little fun.

Blake is super-hot, and guys like him know their way around a woman's body. For once, I could enjoy intimacy without fear or force. Maybe, just maybe, I could find out what it's like to be with someone because I want to, not because I have to. I've never felt the thrill of mutual desire before, but just thinking about it sends a shiver of excitement down my spine.

The omelet slides easily onto a plate, steam rising in delicate wisps. I've added extra cheese, hoping it'll mask any imperfections in my cooking.

It's been years since I've cooked anything. Slaves aren't allowed near kitchens where weapons might be within reach. My hands tremble slightly as I arrange the plate on the small dining table, the memories of captivity and powerlessness flooding back, a reminder of the years I spent stripped of even the smallest freedoms.

A soft groan from the bedroom makes me freeze.

Is he awake?

I quickly pour a cup of coffee, adding a generous amount of cream and sugar. Men like their coffee sweet. At least my master does.

I shake my head, banishing those thoughts. This is different. Blake is different.

The bedroom door creaks open, Blake emerges, his dark brown hair tousled from sleep, a wild mane against his otherwise disciplined persona.

He's shirtless, every inch of his athletic, muscular frame catching the soft morning light. His presence fills the room like a primal force, raw and untamed.

My gaze travels slowly from the small scar above his left eyebrow, a remnant of some childhood mishap, down to his piercing-blue eyes that see straight through me. He moves with the grace of a predator, each step deliberate and powerful, his muscles rippling under his skin.

Heat floods my cheeks as I watch him, my breath catching in my throat. The air crackles with his raw, intoxicating energy, making my heart race and my skin tingle. The sight of him is exhilarating, a heady mix of excitement and danger that makes my pulse quicken.

My gaze lingers on the defined lines of his chest and the subtle dip of his abdomen, leading to the waistband of his low-slung pants.

He pauses, his eyes locking onto mine, and the room seems to shrink around us. The intensity of his gaze sends a shiver down my spine. It's like staring into the eyes of a wild animal, unpredictable and thrilling.

My body reacts instinctively, a wave of desire crashing over me as I take in the sheer virility of him, every inch the embodiment of untamed masculinity.

I openly savor each inch of his physique, how his muscles ripple with the slightest movement, and how his powerful presence commands my attention. A blush creeps up my neck when I finally meet his eyes again.

Sleeping with him is going to be fun.

At least, I have that to look forward to.

Blake smirks, catching the way my eyes roam over his body. "Like what you see?" His voice is a low, teasing rumble that sends another shiver down my spine.

I raise an eyebrow, refusing to be embarrassed. "Of course." I let my gaze travel over him again, making no effort to hide my appreciation. "You're the whole damn feast, and I'm an appreciative person."

"Glad to know I'm appreciated." His smirk deepens, and he steps closer.

I meet his gaze head-on, my heart pounding but my composure intact.

"Very much so." My voice is sultry, hinting at the playful promise of more to come.

"Hmmm…" Blake's eyes darken with desire, the tension

between us electric. "What do I smell? Did you make breakfast for me?"

"I did. I can't say what it tastes like. My kitchen skills leave much to be desired." My voice comes out higher than intended—squeaky even.

"You didn't have to do that." Blake blinks, surprise evident on his face.

"I wanted to. Not that there was much to choose from in the fridge, but whoever stocked it for me, please tell them thank you for me."

"I had it stocked."

"Then thank you very much." I gesture to the table, suddenly unsure. "It's a simple omelet, but I thought… Well, I hope you like it."

"It smells great. Thank you." A small smile tugs at his lips.

I stand there, twisting my hands together, watching as he sits down, my heart pounding. He takes a sip of the coffee first, and I hold my breath. When his eyes widen, and he sputters, nearly spitting it out, my stomach drops.

Oh no! He hates it.

Why did I even try?

But despite the mishap, I can't help but admire how he handles it, wiping his mouth with the back of his hand, his expression more surprised than annoyed. He's so effortlessly composed, even in moments like this. I suddenly feel self-conscious, wondering if I'll ever measure up, if I can ever truly be the kind of woman who fits into his world.

"I'm sorry." I reach for the cup, my hands trembling. "I'm sorry. I thought… I mean, I can do better. I can make it again." My voice quivers, my mind racing, desperate to fix this, to make him happy, fearing the worst.

Every fiber of my being screams to fix this, to make him happy, to ensure his satisfaction at all costs. The old, ingrained fears surface, the ones that tell me a mistake like this could have severe consequences.

The desperation to please him overwhelms me, and I can barely breathe as I wait for his reaction, praying I haven't ruined everything.

Blake holds up a hand, swallowing with visible effort. "It's fine," he croaks. "I just—usually take it black."

Embarrassment floods through me. *Of course you do. How could I be so stupid?*

"I'll make a new pot." I turn away to hide the trembling of my hands.

"Sophia." He suddenly stands, and I shrink back, expecting a blow, but he grabs my arms and makes me look at him.

His gaze locks onto mine.

"Stop." He's firm but kind. "I'm not upset, and I'm not going to take it out on you."

His steady gaze and reassuring words soothe my frantic heart. His touch grounds me, and the fear recedes, though the old instincts are hard to shake.

"I'm sorry, I just..." My voice falters as I struggle to find the right words. "Mistakes were never tolerated. I don't know how to react. I'll do better next time."

"The omelet looks delicious. Why don't you sit down and join me?"

I hesitate, glancing back at him. Blake's eyes are soft and kind, and his posture is open and inviting. Slowly, I turn, my heart still racing but soothed by his sincerity.

He gestures to the seat beside him, and I take a tentative step. He reaches out, lightly touching my arm, grounding me in the moment.

"You don't have to be perfect. Just be here with me."

I swallow hard and finally take the seat next to him. My body is still tense but beginning to relax. His smile is reassuring, and for the first time, I allow myself to believe that maybe, just maybe, I don't have to please him at all costs.

I can simply be me.

Whoever that is.

We eat in silence for a few moments, the only sound the scrape of forks against plates. The omelet is decent, if a bit overcooked, but I can hardly taste it, let alone swallow past the lump in my throat.

"So," I say, desperate to break the awkward silence. "What's on the agenda for today?"

Blake looks up, surprise flitting across his face. "Well, I have to report in and go over some intel. You can stay here and rest if you'd like."

The thought of being left alone in this strange apartment sends a shiver of panic through me. The silence is too loud.

"Stay here? All day?" I try to keep my voice light, but fear creeps in at the edges. My fingers twist together *again*; a nervous habit I can't control. "By myself?"

"Is that a problem?" His brow furrows, but there's concern in his piercing blue eyes.

I force a smile, leaning forward slightly, my agitation barely contained.

"I was hoping you might show me around. I'd love to see more." My voice wavers slightly, betraying my attempt at nonchalance.

And spend more time with you.

"You don't have to wait for me. You can go out and look around if you want." Blake shrugs, his tone casual.

"You mean I can... I can leave the apartment by myself?" I blink in surprise.

"Of course you can." His expression softens. "You're not a prisoner, Sophia. You can come and go freely."

Can I?

I'm here because Guardian HRS fears Jonathan Greaves will try to take me back. They're not wrong about that. Well, it's not Greaves who wants me back, but that's another story.

"I—I've never been allowed to walk around on my own." I look at him, the weight of his words sinking in.

Blake's hand hovers above the table, fingers twitching like they have a will of their own. His jaw clenches, muscles tightening beneath his skin, and his eyes flash with something raw and unguarded.

He shifts in his seat, shoulders tensing, betraying his internal battle. He looks at me, his gaze torn between the restraint of duty and the undeniable urge to offer comfort.

"I just don't want to be alone," I confess, my voice trembling slightly.

Blake's resolve wavers and he finally gives in, taking my hand in his. The contact sends a shiver down my spine.

"You don't have to stay if you don't want to." His gaze heats. "I'll make time to show you around. We can do it together."

"Thank you. Thank you. I'd really like that." Relief and a hint of triumph wash over me.

My first genuine smile breaks free after years of captivity. I catch his eye, drawing on every ounce of vulnerability I can muster. "And thank you for staying with me last night. You went above and beyond, and I'm grateful for it." My voice is steadier now but still soft. "I—I felt safe."

"I'm glad it helped." His expression is warm and reassuring. "You've been through a lot, and it can feel strange in a new place. You'll get used to it soon enough."

"I appreciate everything you're doing to help me." I let my voice shake slightly, my eyes wide with calculated vulnerability.

Men love vulnerable women; it makes them feel powerful. Even if I genuinely crave Blake's touch, a part of me remains guarded, wary of his power.

"Any time, and it's my pleasure." His blue eyes soften even more.

It's a small victory and a good start. I lower my gaze demurely, hiding the small, secret smile that threatens to reveal my true intentions. I plan on many nights with Blake in my bed.

If I have to do this, I might as well enjoy it. There's no reason to deny myself pleasure with a man who looks like Blake.

As he finishes his breakfast, I carefully craft my next move.

"Everything here is so new and—overwhelming. I hate to take you away from your work." I look at him through my lashes, knowing it's too soon to do the flutter thing.

Seduction is an art.

Less is best.

"But I do really appreciate it." My voice is soft and sincere.

"How about we ride around in one of those golf carts? It would be a fun way to see everything. And maybe, if it's not too much trouble, you could take me to where you work? I'd love to see more of what you do."

"Sounds like a plan." His eyes flicker with consideration.

Relief and triumph swirl within me as I clear the dishes and place them in the sink. I'm good to let them stay there, but to my surprise, Blake grabs a sponge and cleans everything.

"Blake, you don't have to do that. I'll get it done. Don't worry about it." I reach out to take the sponge from him.

He stops me, his grip gentle but firm. "Sophia, you don't have to do the dishes. Let me do this for you."

His words floor me. I've spent years serving and pleasing others, but having someone care for me like this is beyond anything I've known. His insistence and kindness are too much to process.

I stand there, watching him finish the task, my heart swelling with gratitude and something deeper... Something I can't quite name.

FIVE

Sophia

___

WHEN WE FINALLY HEAD OUTSIDE, I STOP TO TAKE A DEEP BREATH. Crisp, fresh morning air fills my lungs, bringing with it a sense of freedom I haven't known in years. My chest tightens, and tears prick at the corners of my eyes.

Standing here without a guard feels like an impossible dream come true, yet the weight of captivity remains a heavy burden to bear. I dare not let it be replaced by tentative hope, but it's hard not to want to believe.

For the first time in a long while, the sun warms my skin without fear. The gentle breeze carries the scent of flowers and freshly cut grass to flood my senses. I soak it all in, every detail, every sensation.

I close my eyes and let the moment wash over me, savoring the simple act of standing here, free and unshackled. A small, genuine smile spreads across my face, a rare and precious gift I allow myself to enjoy.

This is what it feels like to be free.

To have choices.

To have a life that is mine to live.

I embrace the emotion fully, letting it seep into my soul, even as a cautious voice in the back of my mind reminds me this moment is fleeting. For now, however, I choose to live in the moment, soaking up the sun's warmth, the gentle whisper of the breeze, and the sweet scent of flowers and freshly cut grass.

Opening my eyes, I find Blake standing there, watching me. His gaze is gentle, filled with understanding, and something deeper, something that makes my heart flutter.

"Ready to see more?" His voice is soft, his hand reaching out to me.

He pulls me to him, his arm wrapping around my shoulder. The warmth of his touch is reassuring, a silent promise that he's here for me and that I'm not alone.

Together, we walk into this new world, side by side, with hope tentatively blossoming in my heart.

I keep close to Blake, making sure I'm always touching him at some point. As we walk, my fingers brush against his arm and then linger on his back, a constant reminder of my presence as I develop a connection between us.

Today will be interesting, and I intend to make the most of every moment.

I turn to Blake, a mischievous grin spreading across my face. "Can I drive? I've never driven a golf cart before."

"You've never driven a golf cart?" Blake raises an eyebrow, a smile tugging at the corner of his mouth.

"Actually, I've never driven anything before."

His eyes widen in surprise, but he laughs and steps out of the driver's seat, gesturing for me to take his place.

"Alright, let's see what you've got."

I slide into the seat and grip the steering wheel with excitement and nervousness. As soon as I press the pedal, the cart lurches forward, and I let out a delighted squeal.

"Careful." Blake chuckles, holding onto the handrail.

We zoom along a path, the wind whipping through my hair as I navigate the twists and turns. My laughter fills the air, giddy and unrestrained. The sense of freedom is exhilarating, and I feel truly alive for the first time in years.

Blake's laughter joins mine, and he points out different landmarks as we pass by.

"That's the training field… And over there is the gym."

I make a sharp turn, and he grabs onto the rail, his eyes wide with mock fear.

"Hey, take it easy, speed racer."

"Sorry. This is just so much fun." I slow down, trying to suppress my giggles.

"Just keep your eyes on the road," he teases, still smiling.

We continue our joyride, the scenery blurring as we zip along. The weight of the past starts to lift, replaced by the simple joy of living in the moment.

"This place is huge." My eyes are wide as I take in the sprawling campus. "How many acres did you say it was?"

"Several thousand. It's a secure facility, so we need the space."

"And it's all Guardian property? Right up to the coast?" I file away the information.

"Not quite," Blake replies, his tone measured. "There's a road and some private properties along the cliffs, but we have agreements to ensure security."

As we cruise the winding paths, I marvel at the contrast between the rugged landscape and the sleek, modern buildings that dot the property. People in various uniforms and casual wear walk, bike, or drive by in other golf carts, all seeming to have a purpose, a place to be.

"Where to next?" I lean slightly into Blake. It's not overt, but the cart isn't very wide. I take advantage of every opportunity to brush against him.

"How about the tech facility?" He points toward a cluster of impressive buildings. "That large glass and steel structure is our tech center. It's where most of our intelligence and communications work happens."

I whistle appreciatively.

"Impressive. Do you spend much time there?"

"Not personally, no. That's more Mitzy's domain, but it's crucial to our operations." Blake shakes his head.

We continue, passing by several other buildings. Blake points out the cafeteria, a surprisingly upscale-looking establishment, and a more casual burger joint and pizza place.

"You guys eat well here." I try to keep the envy out of my voice. After years of meager rations and whatever scraps I could scrounge, the idea of such abundance is overwhelming.

"We believe in taking care of our people. You're welcome to eat at any of these places, by the way. Your Guardian ID will cover all your meals." Blake's expression softens slightly.

"Guardian ID?"

"Everyone has one. It's one of our stops."

The next stop on our tour leaves me speechless. The gymnasium looms before us, a colossal structure that rivals any professional sports arena I've ever seen.

"*This*—is a gym?" It's impossible to keep the awe from my voice. "It's the size of a football field."

"Go large or go home." Blake's laughter is a thing of beauty. "It's where we do most of our physical training. There are various training areas set up. A track around the perimeter, sparring mats, and weight training equipment. We have a rock wall that spans the entire length and scaffolding overhead to practice our rope skills."

"Rope skills?"

"Like rappelling out of a helicopter... Stuff like that."

I spin slowly, taking it all in. The sheer scale of the place is mind-boggling. He's right about the climbing wall. An entire wall is devoted to a massive structure while scaffolding and obstacle courses fill other areas.

"And all of this is just for Guardian use?" My mind can barely take it all in.

"Primarily, yes," Blake confirms. "Though sometimes we host joint training exercises with other agencies."

As we exit the gym, a row of smaller, more utilitarian buildings catches my eye. "What are those?"

"Those are the team bullpens," Blake explains. "Each Guardian team—Alpha, Bravo, Charlie, and Delta—has its own dedicated space. It's where we store our gear, plan missions, and other such activities."

"So, that's where you work most of the time?" I try to appear casual as I file away this information.

"When we're not in the field, yeah." He glances at his watch. "Speaking of which, I need to check in with my team soon."

"Could I come with you?" My heart races at the thought of being left alone. "I'd love to see where you work."

"Non-team members aren't allowed inside the bullpens," he says slowly. "But… There's a conference room nearby where you could wait. If you want."

"That would be perfect. Thank you." I beam at him, relief flooding through me.

I spot a familiar face in the distance as we approach the building. My old friend Jenna—the woman I betrayed—stands outside an empty storefront, gesturing animatedly to a man who looks exactly like Blake.

"Blake, look." I point toward Jenna and Carter. "It's Jenna. Do you think we could stop and say hello?"

"Absolutely."

As we approach, Jenna's face lights up with recognition.

"Sophia." She waves enthusiastically. "I was hoping I'd run into you soon."

We climb out of the cart, and I'm immediately enveloped in a warm hug. The familiar scent of Jenna's perfume—a light, floral fragrance—brings back a flood of memories, both good and beyond painful.

"It's so good to see you." I'm suddenly blinking back tears.

"You look amazing." Jenna pulls back, her hands on my shoulders as she looks me over. "How are you settling in?"

"It's a lot to take in," I admit. "Blake's been showing me around."

"That's great." Jenna's gaze flicks to Blake. "Blake's one of the best."

"So, what's all this?" I gesture to the empty building behind her.

"Oh, it's wonderful." Jenna's excitement returns in full force.

"Guardian HRS is letting me open a coffee shop here at HQ. Since I had to give up my old place for witness protection, they thought this would be a good way for me to keep busy and feel useful."

The words hit me like a slap in the face.

While I was enduring years of captivity and abuse, Jenna was living a normal life, running a successful coffee shop. And now, even in hiding, she's given opportunities I can only imagine. I push the bitter thoughts aside, forcing enthusiasm into my voice.

"That's amazing. I'm so happy for you."

"Thanks." Jenna beams. "Maybe you'd like to help out? Once we get things up and running, of course. It could be fun."

"That's really sweet of you to offer," I say slowly. "Let me think about it, okay? I'm still getting my bearings here."

"Of course, no pressure." Jenna's smile dims slightly. "Just know the offer's open if you want it."

We say our goodbyes and I climb back onto the golf cart.

"Jenna seems really happy." I smooth my hair back, trying to keep my voice casual.

"We're glad we can give her a chance at a normal life." Blake hops into the driver's seat, glancing at me with a playful grin.

"Hey, I thought I was gonna drive," I protest, a mock pout forming on my lips.

"You've abused this poor cart enough today." He winks as he starts the engine.

As we approach the Guardian's building, a growing sense of isolation wraps around me. Despite the tour and seeing Jenna, my outsider status is glaringly apparent.

I don't belong here, not really. I'm a guest at best and a burden at worst.

But as Blake helps me out of the cart, his hand is warm and steady on mine. I push the ugly thoughts aside. I have a purpose here, a mission of my own, and I'm determined to see it through, no matter what it takes.

"Are you ready to meet the team?" A hint of a smile plays on his lips.

"Lead the way." I square my shoulders, summoning every ounce of confidence I can muster.

SIX

Sophia

———————

The Guardian building looms before me, a utilitarian square structure that screams efficiency. As we step inside, the scent of gun oil and sweat fills my nostrils, a sharp contrast to the crisp ocean air outside. The underlying tang of metal adds a final touch to the overtly masculine atmosphere.

Each corner houses a bullpen for the different teams—Alpha, Bravo, Charlie, and Delta. My attention is drawn to the center, where a massive conference room stands, brimming with high-tech equipment that makes my fingers itch to explore.

"Wait here while I change into PT gear. Won't be long." Blake's hand on my lower back sends a shiver up my spine as he guides me to the conference room.

The moment he disappears down a hallway, I'm on my feet, circling the room. My heart races as I take in every piece of technology. It's mind-blowing.

Computers with multiple screens, communication devices I've never seen before, and access points that could lead to who knows what kind of information. It's a goldmine, and I'm standing right in the middle of it.

Footsteps echo down the hall, and I quickly return to my seat, arranging my face into a mask of innocence as Blake re-enters.

His PT gear—a snug T-shirt and shorts—clings to his muscular frame, emphasizing every chiseled feature. His sharp jawline contrasts with his piercing-blue eyes, which seem to see straight through me. Broad shoulders lead to powerful arms, each bicep bulging impressively.

My gaze trails down to his thighs, like sculpted tree trunks, every muscle clearly defined and rippling with each step. I force myself to look away, my pulse quickening despite my best efforts to remain composed.

"Enjoying the view?" Blake smirks, catching my wandering eyes.

"Just appreciating the, uh, scenery." I laugh, trying to play it cool.

"You know, you don't have to be so subtle about it." He chuckles, stepping closer.

"Oh, really?" I arch an eyebrow, feeling a spark of playful defiance. "Obviously, I wasn't trying to be subtle."

"No, you weren't. You should wipe the drool from your mouth."

"I'm not…" I swipe at my chin, which makes Blake laugh.

The man is virility on steroids, a walking, talking embodiment of raw, masculine power.

"Sweetie, you're more than welcome to check me out anytime you want." His eyes glint with amusement. "But fair is fair."

"What does that mean?" I tilt my head, intrigued.

"If you're checking me out," he leans in, his eyes twinkling with mischief, "then I get to check you out, too."

"I'll keep that in mind." A playful blush creeps up my cheeks, and I bite my lip to hide my smile.

"Good," he grins, "because I'm definitely keeping an eye on you.

"Ready to join the team?" A hint of a smile plays at the corners of his mouth.

"Absolutely." I stand, smoothing my hands over my clothes, suddenly aware of how I must look.

Five men enter the conference room behind Blake, their faces breaking into welcoming grins that ease some of the tension in my shoulders. The heady power of testosterone clots the air, thick and palpable.

Blake's raw masculinity is impressive, but the combined presence of his teammates is overwhelming, a symphony of strength and power. Each man radiates a fierce, commanding presence, making Blake's singular intensity seem almost modest in comparison.

It's like standing in the eye of a testosterone-infused hurricane. I'm both intimidated and fascinated by the sheer force of their collective presence.

"You might remember the guys, but I'll do reintroductions. Sophia, this is Charlie team. Guys, this is Sophia." Blake's voice carries a note of pride that sends warmth blooming in my chest.

"My name is Ethan." A tall, rugged man with piercing eyes steps forward first, his voice carrying the weight of authority. "Team leader."

The others follow suit: Walt, stocky and solid, with laugh lines crinkling his eyes, Hank, tall and lean, with a quiet intensity that reminds me of a coiled spring, Gabe, whose easy smile makes me feel instantly at ease, and finally, Rigel, who practically vibrates with barely contained energy.

"Nice to meet you." I'm surprised by the steadiness in my voice.

Standing before the men who rescued me off my master's yacht is overwhelming. Surreal.

These men risked their lives for me.

And how am I going to repay them?

Best not to think about that.

Technically, the rescue was for Jenna. I was just collateral. But still, they didn't know me, yet they risked so much to save me.

"Alright, ladies." Ethan claps his hands together, the twinkle in his eye belying his tone. "Today's focus: hand-to-hand and knife skills. To the gym." His gaze shifts to me, eyebrow raised. "You coming with us?"

"Yeah, she's hanging with me all day long." Blake steps in, placing a reassuring hand on my back.

"Sounds like a plan. Come on, ladies, time to show Sophia what we can do." Ethan adjusts his stance, his eyes gleaming with enthusiasm.

The men's banter washes over me like a warm wave. It's so different from what I'm used to—my former guards' cold, formal demeanor. These men are close friends, and their camaraderie is evident in every joke and playful shove.

Gabe nudges Rigel with his elbow. "Hope you're ready to eat mat today, rookie. I've been practicing my throws."

"Rookie? In your dreams, old man. I may be new to Charlie team, but I know my shit." Rigel scoffs, a cocky grin spreading across his face. "I'll have you tapping out in five minutes flat."

"*Oh ho!*" Walt slaps Rigel on the back. "Big words from the baby of the team. Care to put your money where your mouth is?"

"How about this—loser buys drinks for the whole team tonight?" Hank jumps right in, not missing a beat.

A chorus of agreements and whoops follows this suggestion.

"Don't let them fool you." Blake, walking beside me, leans in close. His breath tickles my ear as he whispers. "Hank's the real shark here. He always cleans up on these bets."

I suppress a shiver at Blake's proximity, forcing myself to focus on the conversation around us.

"And the overall loser has to run the obstacle course in full gear —backward." Ethan's unable to hide his amusement.

This announcement is met with a mix of groans and laughter.

"Better start stretching, Gabe," Walt teases his teammate. "Those old bones of yours aren't going to like running backward."

Gabe responds with a rude gesture that makes everyone laugh again.

As we enter the gym, the playful atmosphere lingers, starkly contrasting the intense training I'm about to witness. I can't help but smile, caught up in their infectious energy.

The gymnasium is even more impressive up close. The polished floors gleam under the bright lights, and the air is thick with the scent of rubber mats and determination. The team spreads out, pairing off for sparring. I settle on a nearby bench, my eyes drawn immediately to Blake.

He steps onto the mat, squaring off against Hank. They exchange a nod, a silent agreement to give it their all. A moment later, they begin, their movements a blur of precision and power.

It's like watching a deadly dance, each strike and block flowing seamlessly into the next. Blake's style is aggressive, constantly pushing forward, while Hank relies more on counterattacks.

"That's Krav Maga." Walt sits beside me on the bench, his voice warm and friendly. "It's an Israeli fighting style. Brutal but effective."

I startle, surprised. Too engrossed in watching Blake, I missed Walt's approach, but my attention snaps back to the mat. Blake executes a flawless throw, sending Hank flying through the air. Hank recovers swiftly, sweeping Blake's legs out from under him.

They grapple on the mat, a tangle of limbs and muscle. Blake counters with a deft twist, using Hank's momentum against him. Hank rolls, trying to leverage Blake's arm, but Blake anticipates the move, slipping free and flipping Hank onto his back.

The intensity of their sparring is mesmerizing, every move calculated, every counter executed with precision. Blake finally gains the upper hand, pinning Hank to the mat, his powerful frame commanding the scene. Their heavy breaths underscore the sheer exertion and skill woven into their combat.

"Wow." The word slips out, mesmerized by the display of strength and technique before me.

"Impressive, isn't it?" Walt chuckles softly beside me, leaning closer. His eyes follow the action. "Blake's one of the best. He's not just strong, he's smart—always thinking three steps ahead."

"You're slipping, old man." Blake wipes the sweat from his brow, his voice tinged with amusement.

"Just setting you up for a false sense of security." Hank grins, a playful glint in his eye.

The display of raw power and skill leaves me in awe, a flutter of excitement and admiration stirring within me. My gaze stays fixed on Blake as he helps Hank to his feet, their camaraderie clear in the exchange of grins and pats on the back.

I glance around the room, noticing the other pairs. Gabe and

Rigel are focused on knife defense techniques, their movements swift and precise. Ethan watches intently, offering corrections and praise in equal measure.

"This is so different," I muse aloud, the words escaping before I can stop them.

"How so?" Walt's eyebrow arches, curiosity written across his features.

I hesitate, then decide honesty is the best policy. "The guards I'm used to… There was never any warmth between them."

Walt's expression softens with understanding, his eyes gentle. "Yeah, we're a different breed here. More like family than co-workers."

Family. The word lodges a lump in my throat, stirring memories and long-buried emotions.

"Hey, wanna learn some moves?" Walt's voice is gentle and inviting.

The scent of sweat and mat cleaner fills the air, mingling with the distant hum of voices and the faint clang of metal weights. The place feels alive, charged with energy and camaraderie, a polar opposite to the cold, sterile environments I'm used to.

Family.

It's been so long since I've had anything like that.

"Sure."

"Nothing too fancy." Walt guides me onto a nearby mat. The rubber surface is firm yet forgiving under my bare feet. "Just some basic self-defense."

We start with simple blocks and strikes. Walt's a patient teacher. His hands are warm and steady as he guides me through each movement. His touch is gentle but firm, ensuring I understand the mechanics of each move.

He positions himself behind me, his chest lightly pressing against my back as he helps me perfect a defensive stance.

The closeness is steady and professional, lacking the spark that ignites when Blake is near. It doesn't send heat coursing through my veins like Blake's does.

"Like this." His hands are on my hips, adjusting my position slightly. "You want to keep your center of gravity low." Walt's hands move to my arms, guiding them into the proper blocking position. He knocks the back of my knee, forcing me to lower my center of gravity.

"Keep your elbows in tight." His voice is low and encouraging. His fingers brush my skin as he corrects my form.

"Now try a strike." He steps back, watching as I execute the move.

When I falter, he steps in close again, his body aligning with mine as he demonstrates the technique. The solid strength of his frame presses against me, providing both support and a sense of safety.

"Hey, Walt, getting a bit handsy with my girl, aren't you?" Blake's voice cuts through the air, sharp and cold.

I startle, turning to see Blake standing there, his presence commanding and tense.

Walt steps back immediately, hands raised in a placating gesture. A sheepish grin spreads across his face, but the tension in the air thickens as the powerful men square off.

"Just teaching her some moves. She shouldn't have to sit on a bench and watch us fight. Gotta learn some self-defense skills, brother." Walt's voice carries a hint of challenge, his eyes sparkling with mischief.

"That may be, but there's no need to get all touchy-feely." Blake steps closer, his eyes narrowing.

Walt chuckles, shaking his head. "Why'd you bring a woman to practice and force her to watch from the sidelines like a second-string player? I just thought I'd teach her some moves. She needs to learn."

The other guys stop their activities and turn to watch the interaction. A few snickers and whistles break the silence, adding a layer of camaraderie to the scene.

"Don't be such a caveman, Blake," one of them calls out. I'm not sure which one.

"She's got spirit," another one adds with approval. "Let her learn."

"Blake's getting protective of his girl," Gabe calls out, earning a round of laughter.

Blake's jaw tightens, but he doesn't deny it. Instead, he sighs, running a hand through his hair.

"Alright, fine. But keep it professional."

"Professional it is." Walt straightens and gives a mock salute. "Alright, Sophia, ready to try again?"

"Yes, let's do it." I glance at Blake, noting his protectiveness and the irritation in his eyes.

Walt steps in, guiding me through a couple more moves. His hands are firm yet gentle as he positions my arms and adjusts my stance, bringing us closer.

"Good, now try this." Walt demonstrates a throw, stepping in close. His chest brushes against my back as he shows me the movement.

Blake steps forward, eyes blazing with possessive jealousy. Without a word, he physically separates us with a light shove, his presence dominating.

"Walt, stop being an asshole. If anyone trains her, it's going to be me." A hint of a grin plays at the corners of Blake's mouth, but the intensity in his gaze leaves no doubt about his feelings.

"All yours, brother." Walt raises his hands, feigning surrender, stepping back with a laugh.

Blake takes Walt's place, his body so close that the heat radiates off him. His voice is low and intense.

"Let's work on some throws." His hands grip my shoulders firmly, guiding me through the motions with precision and care.

The room fills with the men's banter and camaraderie. Their support and good-natured teasing create a surprisingly comforting environment. Despite the intensity of the training, a sense of belonging begins to take root within me.

Blake's hands on my hips send a jolt through me, like a live wire sparking to life. His touch is firm and commanding, a noticeable difference from Walt's calculated guidance. Every movement we make together is charged with a raw, kinetic energy that reverberates through me, intensifying our connection.

As we move, Blake's strength complements my agility, and the rhythm of our synchronized steps feels natural. Each successful throw earns a murmur of approval from him, his voice a deep, resonant timbre that sends warmth blooming in my chest. The heat mingles with the electric sensation, creating a potent mix of exhilaration and desire.

"You're a natural." His breath is hot against my ear.

"I have a good teacher." I turn to face him, our bodies mere inches apart.

Something flashes in Blake's eyes—a potent blend of desire and frustration—but then he steps back and clears his throat.

"Let's try that again. This time, I'll be the attacker."

He lunges at me, his movements deliberately slow. I react on instinct, using the techniques he just taught me. The world narrows to just us—the feel of his body against mine, the sound of our labored breathing, the faint scent of his sweat mingling with mine.

I sweep Blake's legs out from under him in a move that surprises us both. He goes down hard, pulling me with him. We land in a tangle of limbs, my body pressed flush against his.

For a moment, we're frozen, staring into each other's eyes. I'm acutely aware of every point of contact between us—his muscled chest heaving against mine, his powerful thighs tangled with my own. The press of his hard length against my belly.

The air is charged, electric. Blake's pupils dilate, and his breathing slows. His grip on my waist tightens slightly, and for a heartbeat, I think he might pull me in for a kiss.

"Nice move." His voice is rough and thick, while his gaze fills with desire.

I allow myself a small, victorious smile as a shiver ripples down my spine.

Someone clears their throat nearby, breaking the spell. It's Ethan, looking down at us with amusement.

"I think that's enough fiddling around for today, lovebirds." He extends a hand to help me up.

As I get to my feet, I catch the poorly concealed smirks of the other team members. They're clearly relishing the sight of Blake being taken down a peg, their barely restrained laughter hinting at the teasing he's bound to face later.

Heat rises to my cheeks, but I lift my chin, refusing to let embarrassment take hold.

"Thanks for the lesson." I look at Blake, who's now standing and pointedly avoiding my gaze.

"Anytime." He runs a hand through his sweat-dampened hair, his expression carefully neutral.

The team disperses, heading for the showers, their voices carrying playful taunts.

"Man, you've got it bad." Rigel claps Blake on the shoulder, giving him a little shake.

"Never seen you so distracted, Blake." Hank smirks, glancing between us.

"Guess we know who the real knockout is here." Walt winks at me, a playful smile filling his face.

More heckling follows, adding to the light-hearted teasing aimed at Blake.

"Our boy's all grown up and in love." Gabe claps his hands over his chest, mimicking a heartbeat with a pseudo-serious expression.

"Sorry about them." Blake's ears turn red, but he doesn't deny their accusations. Instead, he turns to me, his expression apologetic and something else I can't quite decipher. "I'll walk you back to your quarters." His voice is gruff as he steps closer, a protective edge to his posture.

As we leave the gym, the cool air of the hallway shocks my overheated skin. Every step beside Blake heightens the tension between us, the space charged with unspoken emotions. My skin tingles in his presence, the closeness making my heart race.

Frustration bubbles up inside me. I'm getting under his skin; that much is clear, but he's still fighting it, still clinging to that professional distance.

It's maddening.

When we reach my door, Blake hesitates. His hand hovers near my arm but not quite touching.

"Sophia, I…"

"Yes?" I turn to face him, hope rising in my chest.

Lifting a finger, I place it gently on his chest, trailing it down slowly over the soft notch of his throat, down his broad chest, slipping down to his washboard abs, letting it linger suggestively at the waistband of his shorts.

"Do you want to come in?"

"I need to take a shower." He swallows hard, his eyes darkening with desire, but he shakes his head slightly.

"You could take a shower here. A shower for one is lonely." I let my finger trail back up to his chest.

It looks like he might give in for a moment, but then he steps back, breaking the contact.

"I, uh, left something in the gym. I should go get it."

"Up to you." Frustration bubbles up inside me, but I force a smile.

"I'll pick you up for dinner later, okay?" His voice is gruff, and he seems to struggle with himself.

"Looking forward to it." I hide my disappointment behind a smile.

As I shut the door behind me, I lean against it, closing my eyes. The memory of Blake's body against mine, the heat in his eyes, and the tension in his voice swirl in my mind, leaving me frustrated and longing for more.

SEVEN

Sophia

THE SUN DIPS LOW ON THE HORIZON, PAINTING THE SKY IN VIBRANT oranges and pinks as I stand before the mirror in my new apartment. My reflection stares back at me, a stranger in borrowed clothes. I smooth down the simple blouse and jeans, wondering if I look normal enough.

Whatever that means these days.

A knock at the door sends my heart racing.

Blake.

I take a deep breath, steeling myself. Tonight, he'll see me as more than just an assignment.

I open the door, and there he stands, all six-feet-plus of chiseled perfection. His blue eyes sweep over me, lingering with an unmistakable flicker of appreciation that sends warmth rushing to my cheeks.

"Ready for dinner?" His voice is gruff, his gaze still locked on me as he takes a step closer.

"Absolutely. I'm starving." I step out into the hallway. As we walk, I intentionally let my arm brush against him, relishing the brief contact. "What are our options?"

Blake clears his throat. "We've got the cafeteria, a burger joint, or a pizza place. Your choice."

"Pizza? I haven't had that in… I can't even remember." Excitement bubbles up in my voice.

A flicker of something—pity?—crosses Blake's face before he schools his features back to neutrality. "Pizza it is then."

The pizza place is cozy, with checkered tablecloths and the mouthwatering aroma of melted cheese and tomato sauce. We settle into a booth, and Blake takes a seat facing the door, his back to the wall. He's always vigilant—even when on Guardian HQ grounds.

"What do you recommend?" I lean forward, deliberately giving him a view down my blouse.

"The Margherita is good. Classic." Blake's eyes flick down for a millisecond before snapping back to my face. He's interested, but something holds him back.

I need to fix that.

"Kind of boring for my first pizza in years. Can't we spice it up a bit?" I reach across the table, letting my fingers brush his as I point to an item on the menu. "What about this one?"

"Also good." He pulls his hand back as if burned.

"Good evening and welcome." A waiter arrives, a charming smile playing on his lips. "Is there anything I can get for you? Maybe a special recommendation?" His gaze lingers on me, not subtle in the least.

"Just water for now, thank you." I smile politely, sensing his flirtation.

"Are you sure? We've got some amazing cocktails, and I'd love to recommend one just for you." The waiter leans in slightly, his eyes never leaving mine.

Blake's eyes narrow, his attention shifting between me and the waiter, growing more intense with each passing moment. As the waiter continues, Blake's agitation becomes palpable. His jaw tightens, and he leans forward slightly, a muscle ticking in his jaw.

"Water and a supreme pizza." Blake's tone is firm, pushing the waiter off with his words. The waiter's smile falters as he steps away.

Blake's eyes stay on me, the flicker of jealousy unmistakable as he takes a deep breath, trying to mask his frustration.

"That was a little rude." I raise an eyebrow.

"He deserves it for looking at you like that." Blake's jaw remains tight, tension evident in his voice.

"There's nothing wrong with that." I try to keep my tone light.

"There is when you're with me." His voice is low and dangerous, a growl beneath the words. "I don't want anyone else looking at you like that." Blake leans forward, his gaze intense, burning with a possessiveness that makes my pulse race.

My heart pounds, but I force myself to hold his gaze. I let a seductive smile curl my lips. Perfect. I'm finally getting to him.

"I'm not yours. At least, not yet. You haven't claimed me, and until you do, the waiter has every right to look."

"My job is to keep you safe, not complicate things with—more." His tone is clipped, irritation seeping through as he struggles to maintain his professionalism.

I let his words hang in the air, the unspoken challenge between us thick with tension. The intensity of his possessiveness, the way he struggles against it, stirs something profound within me. Heat rises in my cheeks, the thrill of his barely restrained desire making my pulse quicken.

"What's wrong with more?" My voice comes out low, almost challenging.

Blake's eyes flash, frustration and desire warring within them. "I'm here to protect you, not to sleep with you." His tone is firm, but the raw edge of longing betrays him.

"I don't see the problem." I let my fingers brush lightly against his arm. "Why can't we have both?"

Blake takes a deep breath, trying to regain control. "We barely know each other, and it wouldn't be right, considering everything you've been through. You're a victim, and I won't take advantage of that."

His words ignite a fire within me.

"A *victim*?" Anger flares as I snap. "I'm perfectly capable of making my own decisions about who I want to be with. Don't you dare assume otherwise."

An awkward silence envelops us, thick and suffocating. The air grows heavy with unspoken tension, each second dragging on like an eternity.

The waiter arrives with our pizza, his cheerful demeanor faltering as he senses the tension. He carefully places the pizza down, his smile wavering.

"Here you go. Enjoy." He steps back quickly, giving us a wide berth.

The air remains charged, the silence stretching out as we grapple with our thoughts.

Desperate to break the tension, I smile brightly and grab a slice of pizza. The first bite is heaven—gooey cheese, tangy sauce, crisp crust. A moan escapes me before I can stop it.

"Oh my, this is amazing."

Blake shifts in his seat, his eyes never leaving my face. "Good?"

"Better than good. It's decadent." I lick the sauce from my lips, savoring the burst of flavor.

His eyes follow the movement of my tongue, darkening with a smoldering intensity. I suppress a triumphant smile.

Throughout the meal, I brush my foot against his under the table. Each time, he tenses but doesn't pull away. The brief contact sends little sparks of electricity between us.

The aroma of melted cheese and baked dough fills the air, mingling with the faint tang of tomato sauce. The bustling sounds of the pizzeria—clinking cutlery, soft chatter, the hum of conversation—create a cozy backdrop to our private tension.

"That was incredible. Thank you." I lean back, patting my stomach.

"Glad you enjoyed it." A small smile plays at the corners of his mouth, a brief moment of softness that makes my heart flutter.

I take a deep breath, letting the warmth and satisfaction of the meal settle over me. "So, about the tour this morning, I enjoyed seeing where you work. I'd love to see more. Maybe the tech building?"

"I'm sure I can make that happen."

We walk back to my apartment in comfortable silence. The night air is cool against my skin, and I shiver slightly. Without a word, Blake shrugs off his jacket and drapes it over my shoulders. The gesture, so simple and yet so intimate, makes my heart skip a beat.

I'm not used to a man taking care of me. Not even close. Quite the opposite. I've been conditioned to serve, to cater to every whim. My needs were always secondary, barely acknowledged. Is it wrong to wish for a bit of comfort, for once? To spend a night of pleasure with a man I choose?

The thought of Blake caring for me, even in small ways, stirs something deep inside. I've always been the one to give, to sacrifice, to endure. The idea of someone tending to me, looking out for me, feels like a forbidden luxury.

Am I allowed to crave that? To yearn for the warmth of his embrace, not out of obligation, but out of genuine desire? The thought of spending a night with him, wrapped in his strong arms, free to explore the connection between us, sends a thrill through me. It's more than physical attraction; it's the possibility of choosing, of having a say in my pleasure.

Is it wrong to dream of a moment where I can be vulnerable and safe at the same time?

Blake represents that chance.

At my door, I turn to face him, my heart pounding. "Would you like to come in? Maybe have a drink?"

"I don't think that's a good idea." Blake hesitates, his eyes flickering something I can't quite grasp.

"Just one drink. To say thank you for today." I step close enough to feel the heat radiating from his body. My voice is low and inviting.

Irresistible.

He swallows hard, his Adam's apple bobbing. For a moment, I think he'll refuse, but then he exhales slowly.

"One drink."

Inside, I pour each of us a glass of water—the only beverage I have. We sit on the small couch, and I deliberately position myself close to him, our thighs almost touching. The air between us feels charged, electric.

"Blake..." I turn to face him. My hand finds his knee, and he tenses under my touch. "I appreciate everything you've done for me."

"It's my job, Sophia." His eyes meet mine, a storm of conflicting emotions swirling in their tumultuous depths.

"Is that all it is?" I lean in, my lips mere inches from his. "Is that all I am? A job?"

For a heartbeat, he looks like he might close the distance between us. His gaze drops to my lips, and his breath catches audibly, but then he stands abruptly, putting space between us.

"We can't do this." His voice is rough, strained with effort.

"Why not? We both want to." Hurt and rejection wash over me like a cold wave.

Blake's hands clench into fists at his sides, his muscles taut with the struggle to rein in his desire. His eyes darken, and his jaw tightens. He takes a deep breath, forcing himself to step back, creating a wider gap between us.

"You have no idea how much I want you." His voice is low and raw, as if every word costs him monumental effort. "But we can't."

"I'm not some fragile thing. I know what I want."

"You've been through a traumatic experience. You need time to heal. Not…" He backs away, maintaining the distance between us.

"Don't tell me what I'm thinking or what I need. You have no idea what I need." My anger flares, and I step closer, my hands clenched at my sides.

"It's not about want. It's about what's right. You're under my protection. It would be taking advantage." Blake puts distance between us.

"Taking advantage?" I laugh bitterly. "I'm not some delicate flower you need to protect."

Blake's expression hardens, his jaw clenching. "I know you think you want this, Sophia. But this—us—it can't happen. Not now. Not like this."

"Why?" I blink furiously to keep my tears from falling. "So that's it? You're just going to push me away? Because you're protecting me? From who? Myself? Or you?"

He hesitates, the silence between us crackling with tension. "I'm protecting you from me," he finally admits, his voice a mere whisper.

"What do you mean, from you?"

His gaze darkens, and he takes a deep breath. "I'm not gentle, Sophia. I'm afraid I'll be too rough with you. You've been through so much already; the last thing I want is to hurt you. I'm going to do the sensible thing and walk away." He moves toward the door, his hand on the knob. "I'm sorry, but this is how it has to be."

"You have no right to tell me what I want. Or that what I want is wrong. You know what's funny? You may have rescued me, but I'm still not free to do as I please." I close the distance and poke a finger at his chest. "You don't get to tell me how to feel. You don't get to tell me what I want."

"You sure about that?" His voice is hard and challenging.

"Damn sure."

"You sure you're not using me to feel safe?"

I am using him, but not for that. I don't have the luxury of *feeling safe*.

I stagger back, speechless. "Where the hell do you get away saying that?"

"Aren't you?" Blake's eyes are cold now. "Isn't that what you've been trained to do? Use your body to get what you want?"

His words hit with the force of a punch, knocking the wind out of me.

"Is that what you think? This is different."

"How? How is *this* any different?"

"Because for the first time, *this* is what I want." My voice rises, trembling with outrage. Anger and hurt swirl inside me, burning hot. "For the record, I wasn't trained, I was forced…" Fury rises within me, white-hot and cold as hell. "Repeatedly. I learned how to survive and endure what was done to me."

It was only after that—once I was broken—that I was trained in the art of seduction, but there's no reason to mention any of that to Blake.

I stare at him, daring him to say anything.

Blake's eyes widen as the gravity of his mistake sinks in. His face pales, the coldness in his expression giving way to horror. He steps back, his mouth opening to speak, but no words come out.

Anger drains from his eyes, replaced by guilt and remorse. He reaches out a hand, trembling slightly, and his voice breaks as he finally speaks.

"I'm so sorry. I didn't mean…" His voice trails off, and he stands there, helpless, realizing the full weight of his mistake.

"Get out." I shove him, fury bubbling up. "You don't get to tell me what I'm thinking or how I feel. You have no idea what you're talking about."

"Sophia, please—" He stumbles back, his face a mask of regret.

"No, don't 'Sophia' me. You think I don't know what I want? You think I don't know how to make my own decisions? I know exactly what I'm doing. But you… You see me as some broken thing that can't even think for herself."

Blake's shoulders sag, the weight of my words hitting him hard. "I don't see you that way. I just… I can't stay because—"

"Because you'd be too rough. You said that already, but you never asked what I like. You could never be too rough with me, but I guess you'll never know." I point to the door. "I'll find someone else."

Blake's expression hardens instantly, his remorse giving way to a flash of anger. His jaw tightens, and his eyes darken with a possessiveness I've never seen before.

"There will be no one else."

"I think that's up to me."

"No other man is going to touch you, Sophia," he growls, his words sharp and final. "No one. And that includes me." His voice is rough, laced with frustration, as if it pains him to say it. "I won't touch you because I refuse to exploit your vulnerability.

His anger flares again, but beneath it is a fierce protectiveness, a determination to keep me safe—even from himself.

"Exploit?" My anger flares. "It's not about that—you just don't want to be with someone who's been used. As if I'm filthy, unworthy of your affection because of what was done to me. Is that what you see when you look at me? Something dirty and damaged?"

My voice trembles with the weight of my words, the accusation cutting deep. By holding back, he's hurting me in the worst possible way, telling me I can't think for myself—or worse, that he sees me as something broken beyond repair.

"No. Not at all." He holds out a hand, pleading, but I'm too far gone.

"Get out." Tears sting my eyes.

"Sophia, I'm sorry. I didn't mean to hurt you." Blake's expression softens, regret flashing across his face.

Too fucking late for that.

"Get. Out." My voice is steel now.

When he doesn't move, I shove him toward the door. Blake's nearly twice my size, but he doesn't resist. He backs up toward the door.

Opens it.

I shove one last time.

He nods once, then turns and leaves without another word. The moment the door closes behind him, I collapse onto the couch, sobs wracking my body.

I'm left alone with my frustration and hurt. How dare he assume he knows what's best for me? But beneath the anger, a small voice whispers a painful truth: maybe he's right.

But then my anger returns—white hot and inescapable.

How dare he?

How dare he assume he knows anything about me, about what I want?

I curl into myself, confusion and hurt swirling inside me.

If not Blake, I'll be forced to move on to another.

EIGHT

Blake

THE DOOR SLAMS BEHIND ME, THE SOUND REVERBERATING THROUGH the empty hallway and straight into my bones. I stand frozen, fists clenched at my sides, every muscle in my body coiled tight with tension. Sophia's perfume still lingers on my clothes, a sweet, haunting reminder of how close we were just moments ago.

I pace the narrow corridor, my steps quick and uneven, tension coiling through me like a tightly wound spring, ready to snap.

I can't stay here.

I can't leave.

I stop mid-stride, pressing my back against the cool, unforgiving wall, trying to ground myself. My breath comes in ragged gasps, and I rake a hand through my hair. The sensation of my fingers against my scalp does little to calm the storm raging inside me. I close my eyes, but all I can see is Sophia's face, her eyes filled with hurt and rejection.

My body betrays me, arousal building painfully. I'm furious, disgusted by how badly I want her. This primal need clashes violently with my sense of duty, tearing me apart from the inside out.

Goddammit.

I want her.

I push off the wall, taking a few steps away from her door, my fists clenched at my sides. The hallway stretches out before me, an endless path leading away from temptation. Each step feels like I'm losing her—abandoning her—when she needs me the most.

Fuck.

I take a step toward the elevator, then stop. My heart hammers against my ribcage, a frantic rhythm that matches the chaos in my mind. I should leave. I need to leave. But my feet refuse to move.

I turn back, my feet dragging me toward her door, driven by a force I can't control. My hand twitches at my side, already imagining the feel of her soft skin beneath my fingertips. The memory of her lips on mine sends a jolt of electricity down my spine.

My hand lifts, trembling violently as I bring it closer to the door. The weight of my emotions—desire, guilt, fear—threatens to crush me.

I can't do this.

I shouldn't.

She's been through so much already, and the last thing she needs is me complicating her life.

I let my hand fall to my side, frustration bubbling up inside me. The heat of my desire clashes with the cold reality of the situation. She deserves better than this—better than me.

"Dammit." I run a hand through my hair.

I walk away again, but the pull is too strong. I'm denying a part of myself that I can't ignore. I pivot, turning back once more, my resolve crumbling.

My arousal and frustration mix into a potent cocktail, clouding my thoughts. I can't think straight, can't focus on anything but the overpowering need to be near her. My body and mind are at war, and I'm losing on both fronts.

The hallway is quiet; the only sound is the soft hum of the building's ventilation system. The scent of lavender lingers in the air. I take a deep breath, trying to steady my racing heart, but the scent brings back memories of her—memories I can't push away.

Fuck this.

I pause at the window at the end of the hall, pressing my forehead against the cool glass. The night sky stretches before me, stars twinkling innocently, oblivious to my inner turmoil. I close my eyes, trying to center myself, to find some semblance of the control I've always prided myself on.

But all I can see is Sophia: the way her eyes darkened with desire, the soft gasp she made when I pulled away, and the hurt and confusion on her face as I stammered out pathetic excuses.

My body responds to the memories, a rush of heat flooding through me. I grit my teeth, furious at my lack of control. This isn't me. No matter how beautiful or tempting, I don't lose my head over a woman.

But Sophia isn't just any woman. She's my responsibility, my charge. Someone who's been through hell and back, who needs protection and support, not another man taking advantage of her vulnerability.

The thought is like getting doused by a bucket of ice water. I straighten, shame washing over me. What kind of man am I to consider crossing that line?

I turn away from the window, determined to put as much distance between myself and temptation as possible. As I pass Sophia's door again, a muffled sound draws me up short, makes my breath hitch, my heart clench.

Is she crying?

My hand rises of its own accord, hovering inches from the door. I should knock, ensure she's okay, and apologize for my behavior. But if I knock, I'm not sure I'll have the strength to walk away.

I lower my hand, conflict tearing me apart. The need to comfort her wars with the knowledge that I'm the last person who should be offering that comfort right now.

In the end, duty wins out over desire. I force myself to take one step, then another, toward the elevator. Each step feels like I'm moving through molasses, every fiber of my being screaming at me to turn back.

As the elevator doors open, I pull up short.

Fuck professional boundaries.

I stride back to her door, resolve tightening in my chest. This time, I'm going to knock. I'll make her understand. My hand lifts, muscles taut with tension.

Before I can knock, the door swings open, and she stands in the doorway, eyes wide in surprise. We lock eyes, the air thick with a storm of unresolved emotions.

"Sophia." Her name escapes my lips, a desperate whisper.

She stays rooted in place, silent, those stormy eyes of hers brimming with a mix of hope and hurt. The silence between us stretches, heavy and suffocating, as we stand there, trapped in this moment.

In a sudden, uncontrollable surge of emotion, I close the distance between us, my arms wrapping around her waist, pulling her to me. My lips crash against hers, the kiss fierce and primal, a release of all my pent-up desire and frustration.

Her body tenses, but then she melts into me, her arms snaking around my neck, pulling me closer. Her sweet and intoxicating taste fills my senses, and I lose myself in the sensation.

The hallway fades away, the world narrowing to just the two of us. My hands roam her back, feeling the warmth of her skin through the thin fabric of her blouse. Her fingers tangle in my hair, tugging gently, sending shivers down my spine.

I pull back, gasping for breath, my forehead resting against hers.

I'm about to make the biggest mistake of my life, but I don't fucking care.

"You need to understand something." My voice is rough and strained.

"What?"

"I like it rough and dirty." I struggle to keep my voice steady. "I don't want to hurt you."

She doesn't flinch or pull away. Instead, her eyes darken. "Good thing that's exactly what I need—someone who won't treat me like I'm made of glass." She steps closer, her breath warm against my skin.

Her words send a jolt through me. I search her face, looking for any sign of hesitation or fear.

"Are you sure? Because once we start, I don't know if I'll be able to stop."

I search for any sign of hesitation, but all I see is determination and need.

"I want this. I want you." Sophia's hands slide up my chest, her touch searing through my shirt. "The good. The bad. The ugly. The rough and the dirty. All of it." She rises on her tiptoes, her lips brushing my ear. "I won't break. Show me how much you want me."

"Sophia." My voice is a whisper, barely audible.

She leans in, her lips brushing against mine, a soft, tantalizing touch. "Please." Her fingers trail down my chest.

The last threads of my control snap. I growl low in my throat and spin us around, pressing her against the wall. My hands grip her hips, hard enough to bruise, but she doesn't protest. Instead, she arches into me, a soft moan escaping her lips.

"Last chance to back out," I warn, my voice barely recognizable.

Her fingers trail down my abdomen, stoking the fire burning inside me. "Show me every inch of the darkness you keep hidden from the world."

The realization hits me like a lightning bolt, searing through my veins and awakening every nerve ending in my body. For the first time, I'm with a woman who can handle all of me—the depths of my desire, the intensity of my passion, the darkness that lurks beneath the surface. It's a terrifying thought, one that sends a shiver down my spine. But it's also exhilarating; like standing at the edge of a precipice, ready to jump into the unknown.

"Then prepare to be consumed." The final thread of my restraint shatters. I can't hold back anymore.

I capture her lips in a brutal kiss, all teeth and tongue, pouring every ounce of my bridled aggression and lust into it. She meets me with equal fervor, her nails raking down my back, urging me on.

I break away from her lips with a growl, trailing hot, open-mouthed kisses down her neck and onto her collarbone. Her pulse races beneath my tongue, fueling my lust.

I break away, panting. "Bedroom. Now."

Her pupils blow black, wild with desire. A small part of my brain screams this is a terrible idea, but with Sophia looking at me like that, wanting me like this, I can't bring myself to care.

I point toward the bedroom, my command clear. As she turns, I smack her lightly on the ass. She gasps, then looks over her shoulder at me, eyes sparkling with mischief and desire.

"That all you got?" Her voice is husky and challenging.

I break away, panting, my eyes wild and dark. "Strip." It's less a request and more a command. "Now."

Sophia's breath catches, but she doesn't hesitate. Her fingers move to the buttons of her blouse; her gaze never leaves mine as she slowly begins to undress.

I watch, transfixed, as more of her skin is revealed. My hands itch to touch her, but I force myself to wait, savoring the anticipation.

"Beautiful," I murmur, drinking in the sight of her. "You're perfection," I rasp, my hands stroking the soft lines of her body reverently. "Absolute perfection."

Sophia blushes but stands tall, confident under my gaze.

"Your turn," she says softly.

"Oh no, sweetheart. I'm in control."

"Promise?" Her eyes darken, a shiver running through her—not from the cold, but from the promise in my words.

"Yes." I step closer.

I circle her slowly, drinking in every curve and contour. My fingers trail lightly across her shoulders, down her spine, barely touching. Goose bumps rise in the wake of my touch.

"On the bed," I order, my voice low and gravelly.

Sophia complies, moving with a grace that takes my breath away. She settles on the edge of the mattress, her eyes filled with anticipation.

I cup her face in my hands, my thumbs stroking her cheekbones. "If anything becomes too much, you tell me to stop. Understood?"

"Yes, sir." Her hands rest lightly on my wrists. "And when it's not enough, I'll tell you that too."

Her words hit me hard. She's playing right into my deepest, darkest fantasies. Is it possible that I won't have to hold back with her as I have with other women?

"Fuuuuuck…" I grit my teeth as her words send a rush of heat to my groin. "You're going to be the death of me."

"Don't hold back. I can take it. I want to take it—from you."

Her boldness stuns me for a moment. Then, a primal growl escapes my throat.

"You have no idea what you're asking for, sweetheart." I pull back, searching her face for any hint of hesitation. There is none. Only desire, trust, and a challenge that sets my blood on fire. "Last chance," I warn, my voice barely recognizable.

In response, Sophia grabs my shirt, pulling me closer. "Stop talking and start showing. Command me, control me… Make me yours." Sophia's lips curl into a seductive smile.

Her words send me into a frenzy of need. Desire courses in my veins. I capture her wrists in one hand, pinning them above her head. My other hand traces the curve of her jaw down her neck, feeling her pulse race beneath my fingertips.

I push her back on the soft sheets and take in every inch of her body with hungry eyes.

"God, you're stunning," I growl, trailing kisses along the column of her neck. Sophia's fingers thread through my hair, and she arches into me, moaning softly. "I've wanted you since the night we met." The words send electricity coursing through my veins.

"You have me." Her reply is instantaneous.

Our lips collide with almost violent force. Our mouths move together with a dizzying ferocity, our tongues tangling and teeth clashing in a passionate battle. Our heavy breathing fills the room, accompanied by our passionate frenzy.

My hands roam over every inch of exposed skin, memorizing the shape and feel of it all. I break away from our kiss to trail hot, open-mouthed kisses down Sophia's neck and onto her chest. She gasps when my lips close around one nipple while my hand massages the other breast.

"Blake," she moans, writhing beneath me.

Her essence, a delicate mix of flowers and vanilla, fills my nose as I breathe her in deeply. The musky scent of desire and arousal fills the air around us.

Her hands wander over my chest and shoulders, tugging at my shirt. Without breaking our kiss, I quickly remove the offending fabric before returning my attention to Sophia's lips.

I'm lost in the sensation of our bodies pressed together, skin on skin. Her hands trail down my chest and stomach, reaching the button of my jeans. With practiced ease, she undoes it and slides her hand inside.

My breath hitches as she wraps her hand around me, stroking me slowly. Our tongues dance together as I reach down to return the favor. Sophia gasps into my mouth as I cup her between her legs.

She runs a finger along my length, making me gasp.

She leans in close until our noses are almost touching. "Tell me how to serve you."

As we lose ourselves in each other, a harrowing truth hits me: this may be the first time I'm with a woman who can handle all of me. The realization is a potent cocktail that pushes me over the edge.

NINE

Sophia

When I wake, Blake's arm is draped over my waist, his steady breathing tickling the back of my neck. I inhale deeply, savoring his scent—an intoxicating blend of cologne and something uniquely him.

I turn in his arms, studying his face. In sleep, the lines of worry that usually crease his forehead are smooth. My fingers itch to trace the curve of his jaw, but I resist, not wanting to wake him.

As if sensing my gaze, Blake's eyes slowly open. A smile spreads across his face.

"Morning, beautiful." He pulls me closer, nuzzling into my hair.

I press a soft kiss to his collarbone. "Sleep well?"

"Better than I have in years." His fingers trail lazily up and down my spine, leaving goose bumps in their wake.

"I want to talk about last night." I prop myself up on one elbow, meeting his gaze.

"Having regrets?" His body tenses slightly.

"No." I shake my head emphatically. "The opposite. You held back—I want more."

"More?"

"More."

His eyes darken, but uncertainty flickers across his face. "Sophia, after everything you've been through…"

I press a finger to his lips, silencing him. "This isn't about my past." I cup his face in my hands. "It's about us, here and now. I don't want you to be afraid to take what you need."

He captures my hand, pressing a kiss to my palm. "I don't want to hurt you."

"You won't, but pain and pleasure…" How do I tell him what I need? I shift closer, eliminating the space between us. "This is my choice."

A low rumble escapes his throat. "Do you know what you do to me when you talk like that?" Blake's free hand cups my cheek, his thumb tracing my lower lip.

"You could show me." I meet his gaze unflinchingly.

A rough sound rumbles from deep in his chest, and then he yanks me into his lap, where it's abundantly clear what my words do to him. "We need to set some boundaries first. Safe words. I must know you'll tell me if anything's too much."

"Of course." Warmth blooms in my chest at his concern.

He doesn't know how dark I can go. Last night was child's play compared to what I've endured. Not that I want that with him. I'm not insane, but I am a masochist. I always have been, and I crave the control of a dominant man.

His hands settle on my hips. "Promise you'll be honest. No holding back. If you're uncomfortable, you tell me."

"I promise." Tears prick at the corners of my eyes. I wrap my arms around his neck, overwhelmed by the depth of emotion I feel for this man.

"I'm going to push you."

"I hope so." My breath catches.

Blake pulls back slightly, his gaze intense. "Good. Now, tell me what you want." His voice is low, commanding.

I take a deep breath, gathering my courage. "To serve. However, you need."

"Are you sure this isn't because of your past?" Blake's expression softens. "You can always say no. There's no judgment."

"I'm sure." I silence him with a kiss, pouring my certainty into it. When I pull back, we're both breathless.

"And if I tell you to kneel?" His grip on my hips tightens.

"Then I kneel." A shiver runs down my spine.

He holds my gaze for a long moment, then nods. His voice drops, taking on the edge of command. "On your knees."

Without hesitation, I slide off the bed and kneel before him.

For the first time, this is something I want—something I choose, not something forced upon me. The realization washes over me, bittersweet and powerful. Yet, even as I revel in this newfound freedom, a shadow of unease flits across my mind. Unseen strings exist, forces I can't escape. I push the disquiet away, focusing on Blake's heated gaze.

This moment is real. My desire for him is genuine, even if the circumstances that brought us together are more complex than he knows.

Blake slips from the bed, standing before me. His broad hand grips his rigid and engorged cock. He reaches out, cupping my face in his hands. The tenderness in his touch nearly undoes me, but the steel of his command ignites a firestorm within me.

"Open your mouth."

I lean into his touch, savoring the connection. Yes, there are complications I can't share, burdens I must bear alone, but with him, I allow myself to believe in the possibility of something untainted by my circumstances.

I'm ready to explore every bit of it while I can, hoping that the genuine feelings growing between us might ultimately outweigh the deceptions I'm forced to maintain.

I part my lips obediently, eager to please him, feeling my heart race as he leans in to press the head of his cock against them. His taste is intoxicating—something unique to Blake. I inhale deeply, taking in his scent as he presses forward slowly.

My tongue darts out to explore the veins on the underside of his shaft. He groans softly, a deep rumble that vibrates against my tongue and resonates through my body. His hands grip my hair gently but firmly as he thrusts deeper, stretching my mouth with each powerful stroke. He grips my jawline, holding me in place as he experiments with the depths of my mouth.

The musky scent of arousal fills the room as his cock slides in and out, hitting the back of my throat with each thrust. It's intense and overwhelming.

His hips move faster, picking up pace as he loses himself to the sensations I'm creating. The rhythm is hypnotic, almost trance-like; it forces me to focus on nothing but the feel of his cock sliding in and out of my mouth.

His other hand rests possessively on the back of my head, a controlling and commanding presence. His fingers intertwine with my hair, caressing gently before tightening their grip to guide my movements with precision. His cock slides in deep, filling my mouth with his heat, and he withdraws slowly, a soft groan escaping his lips —a sound that sends shivers down my spine.

Every vein in his shaft pulsates against my tongue as he thrusts deeper, the rhythm growing more insistent. My throat constricts around him, a primal reaction that I fight, fiercely determined to take all of him. The overwhelming heat of his body radiates, wrapping me in an intoxicating haze that urges me to please and serve him tirelessly.

My free hand wanders between my thighs, seeking solace from the molten ache building there, the slickness betraying my desperate need. I'm sure I appear like a wanton slut, kneeling with hungry eyes and an eager, bobbing head wholly devoted to his pleasure. To be used by him, to earn his gaze filled with such intensity, is an exquisite torment I crave more than anything.

Abruptly, he pulls out, leaving me gasping and whimpering in protest. My hand reaches for him instinctively, driven by an uncontrollable desire to reconnect, but he raises a stern finger in warning.

"Remove your hand from your clit," he growls, a low, commanding whisper that reverberates with power. His cock twitches in anticipation, his hand running through his tousled hair. "The privilege of touching yourself is mine to give or take. Your pleasure—every ounce of it—belongs to me now." He grips my wandering hand and delivers a sharp slap.

The light sting spreads through me, igniting a ripple of pleasure that tingles every nerve.

He grabs a fistful of my hair again, this time with more force, and directs my mouth back to his still-throbbing cock. His demand is clear—longer, deeper strokes that push me past my limits.

My gag reflex protests, but the intensity of the act feels both dirty and exquisitely decadent, forbidden yet thrilling beyond belief. He thrusts deep, holding himself inside me for what feels like an eternity, before a low, primal growl signals his release, sending shivers cascading down my spine.

The air is thick with lust as he pulls me to my feet. My legs feel weak and unsteady beneath me, but my eyes remain locked on his. He pushes me back onto the bed, his motions commanding and forceful, spreading my legs apart at the knees as he kneels between them.

His large hands rest on the outside of my thighs, caressing them with a mixture of gentleness and possession before slowly sliding upward, claiming every inch of my skin.

He leans down and nips at my inner thigh, a rough bite that makes me gasp as pleasure mingles with the sting. His hands are gentle yet insistent as they spread my folds, revealing my swollen and sensitive clit. His eyes devour the sight hungrily before he leans in. He starts with soft, teasing sucks that have me moaning, then increases the intensity when my reactions spur him on.

I arch my back off the mattress as he flicks his tongue skillfully, tracing intricate circles around my most sensitive nub while his fingers part my folds below with expert precision. His other hand finds my throat, gripping it loosely, a subtle reminder of his control that sends further shivers down my spine, making me feel both dominated and cherished.

"You're so wet for me," he murmurs against my flesh, his voice a blend of desire and appreciation. He licks up a bead of moisture that has gathered there, savoring the taste, before pushing two fingers inside me with a slow yet firm motion.

A thick groan escapes his throat as he fills me, his fingers moving rhythmically, seeking out that special spot that makes my body convulse with pleasure.

His relentless touch launches me over the edge. My legs tremble uncontrollably as waves of ecstasy course through every inch of my being. My scream of pleasure fills the room, a raw expression of the intense release he coaxed from me.

As the final tremors of my orgasm subside, Blake wastes no time. With a confident motion, he moves on top of me, his eyes dark with lust and determination. His cock, more than recovered from the blowjob, now stands erect and eager, pressing insistently against my entrance.

Heat radiates from him, a tangible expression of his desire that makes my breath hitch. His hands grip my hips firmly, lifting me slightly to align our bodies perfectly. With a deliberate thrust, he enters me, filling me completely.

The sensation overwhelms me—his thick length stretching me, pushing deeper with each driving motion. He sets a rhythm, slow and intense at first, letting me feel every inch of him sliding in and out, the friction sending sparks of pleasure through my oversensitive core.

Blake's eyes lock onto mine, holding my gaze as he moves inside me. Our physical and emotional connection intensifies the experience, melding our bodies and desires into a singular, pulsating dance. His thrusts grow more urgent, and I respond with equal fervor, matching his movements, lost in the primal rhythm we create together.

The bed creaks beneath us with the force of his thrusts, and the sound mingles with our moans and gasps, creating a symphony of pleasure that fills the room. His hands roam over my body, one coming up to grasp my breast, squeezing and kneading, while the other slides to my clit, circling it with skilled precision. My body reacts instinctively, arching into him, seeking more.

The intensity builds, and another orgasm coils deep within me, ready to explode. Blake senses it. His movements become erratic, driven by the raw need to claim and possess. With a final, deep, shuddering thrust, he pushes us both over the edge.

We come together, a shared climax that sends waves of ecstasy crashing through us. My walls clench around him, milking his release as he spills into me with a guttural groan. The sensation is almost too much, a blissful overload that leaves me gasping and quivering beneath him.

Blake's hands gently rest on my hips, the firm grip now tender as he slowly pulls out and lowers himself beside me, grounding me in the moment with the warmth of his body pressed against mine. I catch my breath, feeling the lingering aftershocks of our intimacy resonating through every part of me.

Blake's hands gently rest on my hips, grounding me in the moment with the warmth of his body against mine. I catch my breath, feeling the lingering aftershocks of our intimacy.

"Are you okay?"

"I'm more than okay." A genuine smile brightens my face for the first time in years.

The feeling of Blake's warm body against mine, still intimately joined, creates a profound sense of rightness, like the shattered pieces of my soul are beginning to knit back together. Blake's fingertips trace idle patterns on my skin, soothing and grounding.

I take a fortifying breath. "This is the first time I've ever had sex without fear, force, or dread."

Comprehension dawns in Blake's expressive eyes. He cups my face tenderly, thumbs caressing my cheekbones.

"I'm honored to give you that," he whispers fervently. "I want nothing more than to worship this exquisite body and make you feel cherished."

Blake presses a soulful kiss to my lips, pouring heartfelt emotion into the intimate touch. Tears prick my eyes, overwhelmed by the depth of care and gentleness he shows me.

"I could use a shower." I sigh contentedly, then shift, feeling the delicious soreness in my muscles.

"Mind if I join you?" His playful grin is hard to resist.

"Not at all." I wink, and together, we make our way to the bathroom, the steam enveloping us as we step under the warm spray.

The water cascades over our intertwined bodies, washing away the remnants of sleep and intensifying our connection.

"Ready for some breakfast?" After we've cleaned up, Blake wraps me in a soft towel, his touch lingering on my skin.

"Absolutely." My stomach growls in response, making us both laugh.

TEN

Sophia

Hand in hand, we leave my new quarters, the lingering warmth of our morning still electrifying the air between us. The early sunlight bathes the corridor in a soft glow as we make our way to breakfast.

The cafeteria buzzes with morning activity. The scent of fresh coffee and sizzling bacon greets us as we enter, mingling with the hum of conversation and the clatter of dishes. My stomach growls again, louder this time, drawing an amused glance from Blake.

"Starving after our vigorous morning activities?" he teases, his eyes spark with mischief.

"Famished." I grin, feeling a blush creep up my cheeks. I lean up on tiptoe to whisper in his ear. "And ready for more *vigorous* activities. You took it easy on me."

"I'll take note of that." His lips twist into a cocky grin. "Sweetie, we've barely begun. Trust me when I say, I've barely scratched the surface of what I want."

"Oh, I hope so."

"Dammit, if you get me hard in front of my team, I'm going to swat that pretty ass of yours and keep you on your knees for hours."

"Hmmm… Now that sounds tempting."

"Tempting?" He looks down at me, his pupils dilating with intense, unbridled desire. "Don't try to manipulate me, sweetie, or I'll turn you over my knee and redden that ass of yours."

"There's no playing involved. Only obedience."

"Obedience?" He tilts my chin up with a finger, searching my eyes. "Baby, you don't have to obey me. I'm not your master."

"Not yet." The loaded words hang between us.

"I'll never be that."

It's a letdown. He doesn't understand the deep-seated reasons driving my behavior.

Blake pulls me aside, his voice low and filled with earnest intensity. "I want equalty in this relationship. Mutual respect and care. Domination and submission without coercion—nothing like what you've experienced before."

His gaze holds mine firmly, and I can see the depth of his sincerity. "I enjoy being dominant," he continues, his voice softening yet remaining authoritative. "I crave the kink, the power exchange, but not because I want to be your master or to control you through fear. I want to guide you, help you explore your submission in a way that's empowering for you, free from the shadows of your past."

The words resonate deeply, sinking into the very core of my being. He promises a different kind of intimacy, one where my desires are acknowledged and respected. A place where my past doesn't define the dynamic but rather offers a foundation for something healthier and more profound.

Blake's touch is tender and reassuring. "This is about mutual consent, trust, and genuine connection. You're safe with me, and I want us to build something real together. No fear, no manipulation —just us, finding our way."

A knot in my chest loosens, and I exhale, feeling the weight of my past begin to lift. In his eyes, I see not a promise of dominance for the sake of control, but an invitation to explore and reclaim my pleasure and submission on my terms.

"What if I can't escape my conditioning?" My voice wavers, betraying my emotional turmoil.

The reasons behind my actions are a tangled web of true desires and the brutal conditioning I've endured. The line between the two is so blurred that sometimes, I can't tell where one ends and the other begins.

"That's abuse, not love." His tone is gentle but resolute.

I lift my gaze to meet his, silently conveying the depth of my longing. He understands. This isn't just about desire or control—it's about finding something real amid the chaos that can anchor us both.

Blake's thumb strokes softly against my skin. The gesture is tender and intimate, and it reassures me that he sees beyond the surface, that he, too, seeks the same genuine connection.

"Do you trust me?" Blake asks, gazing into my eyes earnestly.

"With my life." I cling to him desperately, trembling. "But what if my pleasure comes from—from coercion? What if that's the only way I know how to feel good?" I desperately search his eyes, fearing he'll reject me and my broken desires.

"It's important to unpack that," Blake notes patiently. "Your body and mind have endured unimaginable trauma. What you crave might be scar tissue response as much as real preference. Understanding which is vital."

He squeezes my hand reassuringly. "I'm a Dominant, yes, but a loving one. I push boundaries out of care and consensual exploration. Not cruelty or coercion. I want to help you heal and reclaim your right to agency and consent. I want to explore submission with you in a way that prioritizes your safety and pleasure above all."

"That's a tall order." I shudder at the enormity of the path ahead, but Blake's steadfast belief in me bolsters my courage.

"This journey starts and ends with you." He brings my trembling fingers to his lips. "You lead, I'll follow. No demand without consultation. No punishment without cause. Mutual trust, mutual respect."

He embraces me fiercely. "Let me show you a different way of being intimate—a way that meets both your needs and mine."

In this moment, the boundaries blur, not just between our bodies but between our hearts, as we forge a bond that transcends mere physicality, reaching into the depths of our souls.

I bury my face against his chest and make a solemn vow to myself. I choose Blake's love over the comforting numbness of submission. I choose to heal despite the crushing stigma and self-doubt I'll undoubtedly face.

"Deep thoughts for the cafeteria, and I'm interested in exploring this further." Blake's hand tightens around mine, grounding me in the present. "But how about we continue that in private?" He searches my eyes, his gaze softening as if he understands the weight of what we've just shared.

He shifts the conversation back to something lighter, something easier to handle for now. "So, what are you in the mood for?" His voice is warm and comforting.

"Anything and everything." I laugh, feeling a wave of happiness wash over me. "But coffee first."

We move through the serving line, selecting our food while exchanging light banter. The scent of fresh coffee and sizzling bacon fill the air, making my stomach growl in anticipation. With our trays full, we weave through the bustling cafeteria, searching for a quiet corner.

Just as we find a cozy booth, a familiar voice calls out.

"Morning, lovebirds. Sleep well?" Ethan, the team leader, grins at us from a nearby table where the rest of the team is gathered.

We approach the table where Charlie team sits. Ethan's face breaks into a wide grin. "Well, look who finally decided to grace us with their presence. Come on, plenty of room."

Blake pulls out a chair for me. His fingers brush my shoulder as I sit, a barely-there touch that steadies my nerves. He takes the seat beside me, a solid presence at my side.

Gabe leans forward, his eyes twinkling with mischief. "Good to see you, Sophia. We were starting to think Blake was keeping you locked away in a tower."

Heat rushes to my cheeks.

Blake's jaw tightens, but there's no real heat in his voice when he says, "Watch it, smartass."

The team chuckles, a warm, familial sound. Walt tosses a

wadded-up napkin at Gabe's head. "Ignore him, Sophia. We don't let him out in public often."

"You're just jealous of my charm." Gabe catches the napkin mid-air.

"Is that what we're calling it now?" Hank drawls, sipping his coffee.

Rigel, practically vibrating with energy, pipes up. "Sophia, what do you think of Guardian HQ? Pretty cool, right?"

The easy banter washes over me. These men seem…human. Approachable.

Ethan's expression softens, his tone gentling. "How are you settling in, Sophia? Is Blake taking good care of you? Getting you everything you need?"

I glance at Blake, finding strength in his steady gaze. "He's been... very kind." My voice barely rises above a whisper.

"Kind, huh?" Walt waggles his eyebrows. "That's not a word I'd usually associate with Blake."

Blake's hand finds mine under the table, a silent reassurance. "Alright, enough. Let the woman eat in peace."

The conversation shifts, the men falling into an easy rhythm of jokes, banter, and tall tales of their prowess. I listen, picking at my food, marveling at how these dangerous men can also be so... normal. And how, despite the noise and unfamiliarity, I feel safe.

Protected.

Blake's thumb traces circles on my palm, grounding me in the moment. For the first time in years, I allow myself to relax in the presence of men.

"Everyone's been very kind." I twist a strand of hair around my finger, my heart racing. "It's a lot to take in, but I'm grateful for... everything."

"Speaking of… Any news from Mitzy's team on Greaves?" Gabe leans forward, his expression turning serious.

I flinch, my body instinctively curling inward. Blake's hand finds mine under the table, a steady anchor.

"You okay?" His voice is low, meant only for me.

I nod, forcing myself to breathe. To listen.

"The last ping put the yacht somewhere in the Pacific." Ethan's voice drops as he leans in, his expression tense. "They're having trouble getting a solid lock."

Walt shakes his head, frustration etched on his face. "Bastard's slippery."

"How... how does Mitzy's team track people like that?" My mind races. I need to know more. "It must be complicated."

The team exchanges glances. Blake gives me an encouraging nod.

"It's a combination of satellite imaging, financial tracking, and intelligence work," Hank explains carefully. "Mitzy's got some tricks we don't fully understand."

"Satellite imaging? Financial tracking? What do you mean exactly?" I lean in, my curiosity piqued.

Hank hesitates, then elaborates. "Well, we use advanced satellite tech to scan large areas. As for financials, we track suspicious transactions, offshore accounts, that sort of thing."

"Like those new micro-drones," Rigel blurts out. "Did you see the demo? They're practically invisible."

"Easy, rookie," Ethan warns, but there's pride in his voice.

"Drones?" I ask, trying to keep my tone casual. "What kind of drones?"

Rigel's eyes light up. "They're tiny, like insects. Perfect for surveillance in tight spots."

"It sounds incredible." I file away every scrap of information. My stomach churns with conflicting emotions. "I'd love to learn more about how it all works."

Blake squeezes my hand. "One step at a time, okay? You've been through a lot."

I don't push—it's not worth arousing any suspicion—and lean back, letting the conversation flow around me.

The men shift to lighter topics, but my mind races with what I've already learned. As I listen to the team's easy banter, guilt hits hard. These men trust me and make an effort to include me, yet here I am, gathering information to use against them.

I push the thought away, focusing instead on Blake's warm presence and the tantalizing smell of my neglected breakfast.

The eggs are cooling, the toast growing stale, but I can't bring myself to eat. My stomach is too knotted with anxiety and guilt.

I force a smile, joining in the laughter at one of Gabe's jokes, and allow myself to pretend, just for a moment, that I could genuinely be a part of this.

This could be my life, free from the chains of my past and the threats that loom over my future.

"Well, if it isn't my uglier half and his merry band of misfits." A familiar voice cuts through the cafeteria chatter as we finish our breakfast.

ELEVEN

Sophia

Blake's twin brother, Carter, approaches with a protective arm wrapped around Jenna's waist. Beside them, a large German Shepherd pads along, alert eyes scanning the room. Max's slight limp, the aftereffects of a bullet wound, catches my eye.

Guilt twists in my stomach; Max took that bullet because of me. He was protecting Jenna, but it never would have happened if I hadn't arranged her abduction.

"Speak for yourself, pretty boy." Blake stands, pulling his brother into a brief, tight hug. "Some of us work for a living."

The team chuckles at the twins' banter. Jenna catches my eye, offering a warm smile that sends another pang of guilt through my chest.

"It's good to see you." She steps forward, arms open for an embrace. How can she be so kind after everything I did? "How are you settling in?"

"Pretty good. I'm a little in shock, honestly. I never would've expected such generosity."

As we talk, Max settles at Carter's feet. His watchful gaze never leaves Jenna.

"Yeah, they're something else. Where did they put you up?" Jenna's tone is warm and friendly.

"One of the dorms. It's a whole apartment."

"Have you thought about helping out at the shop?"

"I don't know if I can help. I know nothing about coffee."

"She's right about that." Blake chuckles. "Her coffee is foul, with a capital F."

Jenna laughs. "I'll teach you everything you need to know. I thought it might give you something to do rather than sitting around all day twiddling your thumbs." She pauses, her expression softening. "Not that you have to, of course. I just… I thought it might be nice. For both of us. We could hang out and catch up."

Her smile falters slightly, a shadow passing over her face as she realizes what she said. The memories I'd share aren't pleasant ones.

"Thanks. I'd like that. Maybe we can make new memories instead of revisiting the past." I force a small, reassuring smile, hoping to ease the tension.

"Then it's done." Jenna beams at me, relief evident in her tone. "Wonderful. Oh, and I wanted to invite all of you to the grand opening next week." She turns her attention to the men.

"Guardian HRS moves fast." Blake raises an eyebrow in surprise. "One week? You've only been here a few days."

"This place does move fast, but Jenna moves faster." Carter grins, reaching down to scratch Max behind the ears. "Once she sets her mind to something, there's no stopping her."

"It'll be nice to have decent coffee around here for a change," Gabe quips. "Any chance you'll be serving your amazing blueberry muffins?"

"Blueberries have no business being in muffins," Walt argues good-naturedly. "Do you make any with chocolate chips?"

"I do," Jenna replies, her smile widening at the team's enthusiasm. "They're just as good as the blueberry ones, but I make scones, not muffins."

The table erupts in laughter, and Max's tail thumps against the floor, picking up on the jovial mood. As Jenna interacts with the team, her resilience amazes me.

A part of me aches for the life I could have had and the friendships I could have formed if my life had turned out differently—if I had been able to escape the way Jenna did.

As the conversation flows, I sit back and observe the group dynamics. Blake and Carter, so similar yet so different, share a shorthand language born of a lifetime together. Jenna, once a victim like me, radiates a quiet strength. And Max, ever-vigilant, is a constant reminder of the dangers lurking around the corner.

Max's ears perk up at the mention of food as the conversation circles around favorite pastries and coffee blends. Carter slips him a small treat, earning a gentle nudge from the dog's nose.

I lean back, taking it all in. The warmth of community, the easy affection between friends, even Max's loyal presence—it's everything I've ever wanted.

It's the worst form of torture—showing me what my life could be like while knowing it's something I can never have.

Ethan stands, clapping his hands to gather everyone's attention. "Alright, folks, time to wrap it up. We've got a training exercise at the range. Let's get moving."

The team responds with groans and laughter. Everyone gathers their plates and busses the table. The camaraderie is palpable, the playful banter underscored by a shared sense of purpose.

"I've got to head out." Blake's hand finds the small of my back, his touch both comforting and unsettling. "We're training at the range today."

A flicker of disappointment crosses my face before I can hide it. Blake's brow furrows with concern.

Rigel's eyes light up. "Hey, if you're interested in checking out some of that tech we mentioned, you could always drop in on Mitzy. She loves showing off her cool toys."

Blake scratches his head, furrowing his brow. "I guess I could take her there, maybe after lunch?"

"She can come with us," Carter says. "Jenna and I are headed there."

Blake's eyes find mine, searching. "What do you want to do?"

I pause, the question hanging heavy between us. The weight of making my own decision, a simple choice, is as thrilling as it is terrifying.

For so many years, every decision, every movement, was dictated by someone else. Blake waits, giving me space to think. The reality of being *allowed* to decide is monumental. I glance at Blake, his supportive eyes encouraging me. A small, nervous smile forms on my lips as I take a deep breath.

Finally, I meet his gaze. "I'd like to go with Jenna and Carter if that's okay." My voice grows stronger as I continue.

A mix of emotions flashes across his face—pride, concern, and something darker, more primal.

"Are you sure?" He steps closer, his voice low.

"I'm sure." My heart races at his proximity.

Blake's eyes darken, a silent conversation passing between us. His hand finds the small of my back, fingertips pressing ever so slightly. He leans in, his breath warm against my ear.

"I can't wait to see you later." His voice is husky.

As he pulls back, raw desire flashes in his eyes, quickly masked. His thumb traces small circles on my lower back, promising things to come.

"Already, I miss you." Blake leans in for a kiss, his lips brushing my cheek. He lingers there, his breath warm against my skin.

My heart skips a beat at his words. Blake pulls back slightly, his eyes locking with mine. The intensity in his gaze makes my breath catch.

"We'll talk more when we're alone. And Sophia…" He leans in again, voice dropping to a husky whisper.

"Yes?" My voice trembles slightly with anticipation.

His hand tightens on my waist, fingers digging in just enough to remind me of his strength. A thrill runs through me, equal parts excitement and trepidation.

Blake's eyes darken, a predatory gleam flickering in their depths.

A low growl rumbles in his chest. "You're doing great." His approval washes over me like a warm wave. "Enjoy the freedom to make your own choices now. Later... you're mine."

My breath catches. The promise of surrendering control to

Blake, of letting go completely, is intoxicating. So very different from the fear that accompanied every moment of my previous life.

Images flash through my mind—Jonathan Greaves' cruel smile, the constant terror, the pain of disobedience. His command to call him *Master*, to bow and scrape, and serve. I shudder, pushing the memories away.

This is different.

Blake is different.

With Blake, submission is a choice—a gift I give willingly, not something ripped from me. The trust between us is fragile and new, but it's there, growing stronger with each passing moment.

As thrilling as exploring Guardian HRS might be, a part of me is already counting down the hours until I can lose myself in Blake's arms and surrender to his need.

It's a heady feeling, this power to choose. To say yes, knowing I could say no. To give myself over to Blake, not out of fear, but by a choice born out of desire and trust.

Yet a small voice in the back of my mind whispers.

Can you truly trust anyone after what you've been through? Aren't you trading one form of control for another?

I push the thoughts aside.

This is different.

I am different.

With Blake, I'm not a thing to be used, abused, and put away until it's time to do it all over again. I'm an equal partner, cherished and protected. I say *equal* as if I know what that means, but for the past few years, I've been anything but.

I've been subjugated and forced. Yet, with Blake, I believe someday I'll truly understand what it means to be equal.

"Sophia?" Blake's deep voice pulls me from my thoughts.

"Yes?"

"Are you okay? You zoned out for a minute."

"I'm good. Just deep thoughts." Anticipation and submission color my tone, but there's something else there, too—a hint of wonder at my own capacity to heal, trust another, and actually desire physical intimacy with a man.

Blake's eyes soften as if he can read the complex swirl of emotions behind my words. His thumb brushes my cheek, a tender gesture that speaks volumes.

"So am I, sweetheart," he murmurs. "So am I. Have a good tour. I look forward to hearing all about it… *later*." Blake steps back, his professional demeanor sliding back into place, but the heat in his eyes promises so much more.

The word later hangs between us, loaded with anticipation. As Blake leaves, the charged atmosphere in his wake makes my skin tingle in every place he touched me.

"Look at the lovebirds." Gabe leans back with a grin.

Blake crosses his arms, growling, "Knock it off."

"Our boy's growing up so fast." Walt shakes his head with a smirk.

Blake flips them off. "Mind your own business and play with your guns."

As Blake leaves with his team, I fall in step with Carter, Jenna, and Max. The German Shepherd's nails click against the polished floor, his watchful gaze never leaving Jenna.

"So, Sophia," Carter's voice is warm, "are you excited about helping at the coffee shop?"

"I think I am, but I'm nervous. I don't think Jenna realizes how helpless I am, but having something to do will be nice." I'm surprised by my enthusiasm.

"I can't wait for you to start, and you're going to do just fine." Jenna beams at me as if it's settled. "I'm thinking of calling it 'Guardian Grounds.' Too cheesy?"

"Definitely too cheesy." Carter groans playfully.

"I don't know. I kind of like it." I shrug, and Jenna's smile widens. "How about The Guardian Grind?"

"Perfect. I like that." Jenna leans forward, her eyes bright with interest.

"Has anyone talked to you about the programs available here?" Carter turns to me, genuine concern evident in his expression.

"Not really." I shake my head. "Blake mentioned the Facility and what they do there, but I'm not allowed to leave HQ…"

"Well, it's true that you can't leave the grounds," Carter says, leaning against the counter, "or rather, you shouldn't, but that doesn't mean you can't take advantage of their services. Therapists who can come talk to you are on site if that's something you're interested in."

"Maybe. I'll think about it." The idea of therapy makes my stomach churn, but I force a nod.

"No pressure. Just know it's an option." Carter's expression softens.

We approach the Tech building, a towering structure of glass and steel that gleams in the morning sun. Security checkpoints line the entrance, each more advanced than the last.

"Wow," I breathe in, taking in the array of scanners. "How does all this work?"

"Everyone has access cards." Carter pulls out a sleek card from his pocket. "They're encrypted with our biometric data and clearance levels." He swipes the card, and a green light blinks. "Different areas require different levels of clearance."

We pass through a series of scanners—retinal, palm, full-body. The air hums with unseen energy, making the hair on my arms stand on end.

As we enter the central atrium, a blur of color and energy comes barreling toward us.

"Welcome to my playground." A petite woman with psychedelic rainbow hair rushes us. Glitter shimmers in her pixie cut as she bounces on her toes.

No introduction is needed, as I remember Mitzy from the briefing when I explained the nine Sentinels to the Guardians.

"Blake asked if you could give her the tour." Carter chuckles at Mitzy's boundless energy.

"Yes, he did. Texted me, too. Told me to show you everything." She wraps an arm around my shoulders. "Come on, let me show you the cool stuff."

She leads us down a corridor, chattering a mile a minute. We stop at a large room filled with strange equipment. Hexagonal platforms cover the floor, each with a harness and headset dangling above it.

"What is this?" I stare at the room, confused by what I see.

"This is our VR suite," Mitzy announces proudly. "State-of-the-art training simulations. It's Forest's love child. He's a freak when it comes to VR, and we're finding all kinds of new applications every day."

"How do they work?" I step closer, examining the sleek headsets.

"Put one on and find out." Mitzy's grin widens.

With trepidation, I slip the headset over my eyes after Mitzy gives me a brief 'how-to.' Instantly, the world around me disappears, replaced by a startlingly realistic cityscape. I take a hesitant step forward, and the platform beneath me moves, allowing me to "walk" through the virtual environment.

"This is incredible." I turn in a slow circle. "How do you make it so realistic?"

"We use schematics when we can." Mitzy's voice comes through the headset's speakers. "For places we can't access or don't have the architectural schematics for, we send in our bumblebee drones to map everything out."

"Bumblebee drones?" I remove the headset, blinking as my eyes readjust.

"Oh, you've got to see these." Mitzy practically vibrates with excitement. She leads us to another lab, this one buzzing—literally—with activity. "They're great for getting covert intel on the ground. No one pays attention to bugs. Beyond that, we've found applications for them in search and rescue."

"Search and rescue?"

"Oh yes, we just used them recently for one of our own. Bumblebees can search debris better than humans. They can move through the tiniest openings, locate survivors, and radio back to rescuers. We've already put them into production in the civilian sector specifically for that."

Tiny, insect-like drones flit about the room. Some are no bigger than my thumbnail, while others are the size of my palm.

"Look. This is one of our bumblebees." Mitzy holds out her

hand. A tiny black bumblebee drone lands on her palm. "Perfect for recon and surveillance."

"And the bigger ones?" I lean in, marveling at the intricate design.

"The dragonflies are a bit bigger. They can operate autonomously or with the help of a human. We developed them first but are finding the hive is superior."

"Hive?"

"Bumblebees come in hives." She doesn't provide any further explanation, and before I can ask, she flits over to a four-legged robot that looks like a large dog or a small sheep. "This is one of our greatest successes: RUFUS."

"RUFUS?"

"Robotic Ultra Functional Utility Specialists." Carter supplies. "They work with the Guardian teams."

Between Mitzy and Carter, I learn more about robots than I ever knew or wanted to know. However, I catalog and memorize everything… for later.

As we move through the building, I take in every detail. The layout, the security measures, the glimpses of restricted areas behind frosted glass. My heart races with a mixture of genuine fascination and calculated observation.

We pass by another lab, this one filled with rows of computers. A woman looks up as we enter.

"Hey, Mitzy, what's up?" A striking woman with flowing, jet-black hair that cascades down her back in glossy waves, her beautiful eyes, dark and expressive, draw me in with their captivating depth.

"This is our cryptology division," Mitzy announces. "And this is Jinx. Jinx, meet Sophia, Jenna, and Carter. Carter's new to the Guardians, assigned as Jenna's Protector, but he comes to us with a strong background as a detective."

"Nice to meet you." She shakes our hands while complex algorithms scroll across her screen before we move on.

Max pads along silently throughout the tour, his watchful gaze never wavering. Carter and Jenna exchange occasional glances, their fingers intertwined. A pang of envy and longing tugs at me, stirred by their easy intimacy.

As we near the end of the tour, guilt gnaws at me. These people have been nothing but kind. Mitzy's enthusiasm is infectious, Carter's quiet strength reassuring, and Jenna's warmth inviting.

For a moment, I imagine what belonging here might be like. It's easier to think about that than the reality ahead of me.

I glance at my watch. Blake is probably back from working with his team by now.

"Wow, I didn't realize how much time has passed. Thank you so much for taking the time to show me around." My words are sincere. "This was fascinating. There's just so much to take in. I'd love to come back if that's allowed… If only to drool at all the marvelous tech."

"I get that a lot around here, and you're more than welcome to visit anytime you want."

As we leave the building, I take one last look around, cementing every detail in my mind. I've done what I came to do. Now comes the hard part.

TWELVE

Blake

Over the next few days, a new rhythm settles in—a routine that feels strangely domestic, almost comforting. Each morning, I head off to work, the hours consumed with strategy meetings and security briefings.

Meanwhile, Sophia spends her days with Jenna, learning the ins and outs of making coffee as the shop slowly takes shape. Construction on The Guardian Grind hums along, transforming the empty building into something warm and inviting.

Each evening when I return home, there's a lightness to Sophia that wasn't there before, a small victory with every skill she masters. It's as if she's reclaiming pieces of herself, one cup of coffee at a time.

The weight of everything she's been through still lingers, but with each passing day, I see new signs of healing—small steps as she starts to figure out who she is and what she truly wants from life.

We've also been cautiously exploring our dynamic, testing the waters of power exchange. It's a slow, delicate process woven into our routine like a thread of understanding and trust. With each conversation and every subtle shift in control, we discover new depths in ourselves and in each other, finding a balance that feels right for us.

"Honey, I'm home." I push open the door, arms loaded with boxes. The scent of garlic and herbs fills the air, though there's a hint of something… Burnt?

Sophia peeks around the kitchen doorway, a smudge of flour on her cheek. When she sees me, her eyes light up, and I can't help but smile back. "Welcome home, darling. How was your day at the office?"

Her playful response brings a smile to my face.

I set the boxes down, drinking in the sight of her. The domesticity of it all sends a warmth spreading through my chest.

"Oh, you know, same old, same old. Saved the world, stopped a few bad guys, bought my woman clothes at the store, all before lunch."

She rolls her eyes, brandishing a wooden spoon at me. "My hero. Now make yourself useful and unpack while I finish dinner."

I snap a mock salute, grinning as she disappears back into the kitchen.

The clattering of pots and pans fills the air as I start unpacking. A timer dings, followed by a muffled curse.

"Everything okay in there?"

"*Fine! Everything's fine!*" Her voice is slightly higher than usual.

I chuckle, imagining her frantic attempts to salvage whatever's in the oven.

I saunter into the kitchen, wrapping my arms around her waist from behind. The heat from the stove warms my skin as I nuzzle her neck, inhaling the scent of her shampoo mixed with cooking spices.

"What's on the menu tonight, chef?"

Sophia leans back into me, her body soft and pliant.

"Trying my hand at chicken parmesan. No promises on edibility."

I squeeze her hips gently, pressing closer. The fabric of her dress is thin, and every soft curve presses against me.

"I'm sure it'll be delicious, but you know…" I trail kisses along her neck, feeling her shiver. "We could always skip straight to dessert."

"Down, boy." She squirms in my arms, her breath hitching. "This might taste good, and I won't have you ruining my hard work."

"It would be worth it." I growl playfully, nipping at her earlobe.

"Behave, you can punish me for saying no later, but I want to try this dish." Sophia turns in my arms, eyes sparkling with mischief.

I freeze. We haven't incorporated punishments into our dynamic yet. The possibilities send a thrill down my spine, but she worries me. I tread exceptionally carefully in my role, navigating my way through the trauma of her past, looking for any landmines I might inadvertently set off.

I cock my head, studying her face. I take all my cues from her. She may be sublimely submissive, but she's still in recovery following her trauma. As far as I'm concerned, she takes the lead in defining the limits of our budding dynamic.

I wouldn't have it any other way.

"Punishments, huh? That could be... interesting." I test the waters, watching her closely.

"I thought you might like that." She blushes, the pink in her cheeks rivaling the sauce on the chicken.

That blush is my green light, but if her face ever pales, that's my stop sign.

"Oh, I do." I lean in, my voice dropping to a husky whisper. "I like it very much."

"Hand only. No..." The timer dings again, saving us from the growing tension, but the color just drained from her face.

Sophia rises on her tiptoes, pressing a quick kiss to my lips. The taste of her, mixed with a hint of tomato sauce, makes me hunger for more.

"Can you set the table while I rescue dinner?"

While she takes care of dinner, I process what I witnessed. Punishments may be on her list, but I take them off mine... for now.

"I love my kinky girl." I step back, watching as she bends to pull a slightly charred chicken parmesan from the oven. The sight of her, flushed from cooking and our flirting, stirs something primal inside me.

"Hush, you. Less talking, more table setting." She throws a playful glare over her shoulder.

Grinning, I grab plates from the cupboard. The ceramic is cool against my heated skin.

"Yes, ma'am. Whatever you say, ma'am."

"'Ma'am'? Why are you calling me ma'am?" Sophia's brow furrows in confusion.

"Fair's fair, don't you think?" I chuckle, setting the plates down on the counter.

"Huh?" She tilts her head, still not understanding.

"It only seems fair, considering you'll call me 'sir' when dinner's done." I step closer, nuzzling her neck. My breath is hot against her skin.

Sophia squirms at my words, her breath catching. She turns in my arms, looping hers around my neck and pressing tight against me.

"I look forward to it." Her voice turns husky. "But the ma'am thing makes me feel old."

"Christ, Sophia. You're killing me." I take a step back, drinking in the sight of her flushed cheeks and bright eyes. I adjust my stance, acutely aware of how hard and aching I've become. "Now I'm hard."

"You're always hard around me. Completely insatiable." She cuts me off with a playful shove, pushing me toward the dining area. "But later, big guy. It's food time now. Playtime later." Her eyes sparkle with mischief and promise.

I groan dramatically but comply, heading back to finish setting the table.

As I set the table, stealing glances at Sophia bustling around the kitchen, I'm struck by how far we've come in such a short time.

As for dinner, the burnt edges of the chicken add a smoky flavor that works. I make a show of savoring each bite, delighting in Sophia's proud smile.

"This is delicious, babe. You're getting better every day."

"Thanks. I've been practicing." She preens under the praise, her fork scraping against the plate as she takes another bite.

"I'm proud of you." I reach across the table and take her hand. Her skin is soft against my calloused palm.

Sophia's smile softens, her eyes misting slightly. She squeezes my hand; her thumb tracing patterns on my skin.

"It's all thanks to you. You've given me a chance at a real life."

"You did that yourself." I shake my head, marveling at her strength.

We eat in comfortable silence, exchanging soft smiles and lingering looks. The clink of cutlery and the gentle hum of the refrigerator create a soothing backdrop to our meal.

My mind keeps drifting to her earlier comment about punishments. Excitement bubbles beneath the surface, but I need to navigate with the utmost care.

"So, what's the verdict?" Sophia speaks up, her voice tinged with a hint of uncertainty.

"Well, the food's decent, and the company's not bad..." I pretend to consider it, tapping my chin thoughtfully.

"Jerk." She kicks me playfully under the table, her laugh ringing like music.

"Seriously though, it's good."

"Just good?" Her smile slips.

"Better than good. It's extraordinary, and there's nowhere else I'd rather be than sitting across the table from you, eating this fantastic meal." I capture her foot between mine, grinning. The warmth of her skin seeps through my socks.

Sophia's smile softens, her eyes taking on a faraway look. She pushes a piece of chicken around her plate, suddenly lost in thought. The comfortable silence stretches for a moment, broken only by the soft clink of cutlery against the plate.

"Blake," she says quietly, her voice barely above a whisper. "Can I ask you something?"

The sudden change in her tone makes me sit up straighter. "Of course, Soph. Anything."

She takes a deep breath as if steeling herself. When she meets my gaze again, her vulnerability catches me off guard.

"How can you..." she starts, then stops, swallowing hard before continuing. "After everything that's happened and everything I've done, how can you want to be with me?"

The abrupt shift in conversation throws me for a moment, but I lean forward, ready to reassure her. The vulnerability in her eyes makes my heart ache.

"How can I not be fiercely and utterly attracted to you?" I meet her gaze steadily. "Your past does not define you. You're so much more than that."

"I don't deserve you." She blinks rapidly, emotion clouding her eyes. A tear slips down her cheek.

"Hey." I move around the table to kneel beside her chair. The hardwood floor is unforgiving against my knees, but I barely notice. I brush away her tears with my thumb, cupping her face. "None of that. You deserve the world, Soph. And I intend on giving it to you."

"Sorry, I'm an emotional mess today." A strangled laugh escapes her. She leans into my touch, her skin warm against my palm. "I didn't mean to ruin dinner with my insecurities."

"Dinner's not ruined. It was amazing." As I clear the table, the clatter of dishes fills the air, and Sophia comes up behind me. She wraps her arms around my waist, pressing her cheek against my back.

"Thank you," she murmurs, her breath warm through my shirt.

"For what?" I turn in her embrace, setting down the plates to cup her face in my hands. Her skin is soft, a contrast to the roughness of my palms.

"For being you." Her voice is barely above a whisper, filled with emotion.

I lean down, pressing my forehead to hers. Our breath mingles, the taste of dinner still lingering.

"I'm all in, Soph. I want this… with you. Whatever comes next, we face it together."

"Together." A small smile plays on her lips. "That sounds nice."

I kiss her then, soft and sweet, pouring all my feelings into it. She tastes of tomato sauce and hope, of new beginnings and second chances. When we part, both slightly breathless, I can't help but grin.

"Now, about that punishment…"

"What punishment? I didn't do anything wrong." Sophia's eyes widen, and a hint of sass enters her voice.

"Well, you did leave me hard and aching. I think that deserves some… correction, don't you?" I cock an eyebrow, glancing pointedly down at my obvious arousal, then back up to meet her gaze.

We both pause, the air between us electric. Sophia's lips curl into a smirk, her eyes darkening with desire. The shift is palpable as she slips into her submissive role.

"Yes, Sir," she purrs, her voice low and sultry. "How would you like me to make amends?"

"Oh, I have a few ideas…" The sudden switch in her demeanor sends a jolt of arousal through me.

I take a deep breath, steadying myself. Punishments can be fun, but I have no intention of using my hand on her… ever.

I have better things in mind—like a night of delicious torment.

The world fades away. The apartment becomes our private paradise with its lingering warmth from the oven and the soft glow of the evening sun filtering through the curtains.

THIRTEEN

Blake

—————

The next morning, I prop myself up on one elbow, admiring the way the morning light plays against Sophia's face. She stirs, her eyes fluttering open to meet mine.

"Morning, beautiful," I murmur, leaning down to press a soft kiss to her forehead.

Sophia stretches, a contented sigh escaping her lips.

"Morning," she replies, her voice still husky with sleep.

As we go through our morning routine, the scent of fresh coffee fills the apartment. I wrap my arms around her waist, pulling her close. Sophia leans into me, her body warm against mine.

We finish getting ready, and I take her hand in mine as we leave the apartment. The woman beside me, confident and smiling, is a far cry from the broken soul I first met.

"Let me walk you to work?"

"My knight in shining armor." She laughs, and the sound is light and carefree.

As we approach Jenna's café, the rhythmic pounding of hammers, the whine of power tools, and the shouts of workers create a cacophony of activity. The scent of fresh-cut wood mingles with the aroma of paint and coffee.

Jenna stands in the middle of it all, a bright yellow hard hat perched on her head, clipboard in hand. She directs workers with the precision of a seasoned general, her voice carrying over the din.

"No, no, the espresso machine goes there," she points emphatically. "We need to maximize counter space."

Sophia squeezes my hand, nerves and excitement radiating from her. I give her a reassuring smile and wrap my arm around her shoulders.

Jenna spots us, her face lighting up. "Blake, you're here." She navigates through the chaos to meet us, narrowly avoiding a worker carrying a large piece of drywall.

"Malia's around here somewhere. My partner in caffeinated crime. I want you to meet her."

"You must be Blake." A petite woman with warm brown skin and a mass of curly hair approaches, her smile wide and welcoming. "Jenna's told me all about you."

"All good things, I hope?" I take her hand, returning the smile.

"The good, the bad, and the ugly. Sophia just can't stop talking about you."

"At least her coffee is getting better." I can't help myself and huff when Sophia smacks me in the gut.

"You deserve that." Sophia gives me a look. "It's not that bad."

"It really was *that* bad." I turn to Malia and press my hands together, begging. "Thank you for teaching the woman how to brew coffee."

"*Oaf.*" Sophia smacks me playfully in the gut again.

"I'm teaching her everything I know." Malia pulls Sophia away from me.

The three women fall into easy conversation, and I hang back, content to watch Sophia integrate seamlessly with Jenna and Malia. The construction continues around us, the air thick with sawdust and possibility.

A worker passes by, carrying a large beam of wood. The metallic scent mingles with the earthy smell of fresh wood and the chemical tang of paint. It's a heady mixture, a physical representation of new beginnings.

"We're going for a modern industrial look." Jenna's excitement is palpable as she outlines her vision for the café. She gestures to the exposed brick walls and steel beams. "But with warm touches to make it cozy, it will be beautiful.

Sophia listens intently, her eyes wide as she takes it all in.

"We're just getting the coffee bar set up," Malia chimes in. "We're getting top-of-the-line equipment." She turns her attention to Sophia. "You're going to love learning on these machines."

I'm struck by how natural it all seems. Sophia, laughing and engaged, looks like she belongs here. It's a far cry from the withdrawn, fearful woman I first met.

A worker calls for Jenna's attention, and she excuses herself with an apologetic smile. Malia takes the opportunity to steal Sophia from me.

"Come on." She leads Sophia toward a partially set up counter. "Let me show you the basics of our espresso machine."

Not wanting to intrude on this moment, I hang back. Sophia glances over her shoulder, her eyes shining with excitement. I raise my hand and give her a thumbs up, feeling a swell of pride in my chest.

"This is the group head." Malia points to a part of the gleaming machine. "It's where the magic happens."

"And this part?" Her brow furrows in concentration. She indicates another component.

"That's the steam wand. We use it to froth milk for lattes and cappuccinos."

Their voices blend with the ongoing construction noise, creating a symphony of new beginnings. The rhythmic pounding of hammers is a steady backbeat to Malia's lesson and Sophia's questions.

With Sophia in good hands, it's time for me to head to work. I go to where she and Malia huddle around the espresso machine.

"Sorry to interrupt." I place a hand on the small of Sophia's back. "I've got to head out."

"Already?" Sophia turns to me, her eyes bright with newfound knowledge.

"Duty calls. But it looks like you're in good hands." I glance at my watch.

"Don't worry, I'll take good care of her. By the time you return, she'll be a coffee maestro." Malia gives Sophia a playful nudge.

"I think that might be a bit optimistic." Sophia rolls her eyes good-naturedly.

I can't resist anymore. I pull Sophia close, one hand cupping her face as I kiss her deeply. It's probably inappropriate for a workplace, but I don't care. Her taste, mingled with the scent of coffee and sawdust, is intoxicating.

When we part, both slightly breathless, Malia looks on amused. Sophia's cheeks flush, and her lips are slightly swollen from our kiss.

"I can't wait for tonight. I have a few things I want to try." I lean in close, my lips brushing her ear as I whisper.

"Is that a promise?" Sophia shivers in my arms, her fingers tightening on my biceps.

"You bet it is." I squeeze her ass, relishing her sharp intake of breath. "Be good today. I'll see you tonight." With a final peck on her cheek, I step back. "Ladies." I nod to Malia and Jenna, who's made her way back over. "Take care of my girl, will you?"

"Don't worry, Blake. We've got this." Jenna grins, throwing an arm around Sophia's shoulders.

Malia stage-whispers to Sophia. "Girl, you've got to tell me everything later."

Sophia's laughter follows me onto the street, the sound warming me from the inside out.

The walk to Guardian HQ is short, but my mind still buzzes with the morning's events. The contrast between the chaotic energy of the café construction and the ordered efficiency of HQ is distinct.

As I enter the bullpen, I'm greeted by the familiar sights and sounds of my team at work. Computer screens flicker with data, the low hum of conversation punctuated by the occasional burst of laughter.

"Well, well, look who finally decided to grace us with his presence." Gabe looks up as I approach, a grin spreading across his face.

"Some of us have lives outside of this place, you know." I roll my eyes, dropping into my chair.

"Oh, we know. How's the little woman settling in?" Walt chuckles from his desk.

"She's good. Things are moving along at Jenna's café." The term 'little woman' grates on me, but Walt doesn't mean any harm.

This piques everyone's interest. Ethan looks up from his computer, eyebrows raised.

"No kidding? That's great."

"Yeah, she's excited about working there. Nervous but excited." I can't suppress the pride in my voice.

"Good for her," Rigel chimes in. "It'll be nice to have decent coffee around here for a change."

This sparks a debate about the merits of various coffee shops in the area, and I sit back, letting the familiar banter wash over me. As I boot up my computer and start reviewing the day's intel, a profound feeling of contentment settles over me.

Sophia is finding her place and building new friendships, but the threat against her remains. Jonathan Greaves is still out there, threatening our happiness.

As the team settles into work, discussing strategies and analyzing data, my mind drifts back to Sophia. I picture her at the café, learning the intricacies of coffee-making, laughing with Jenna and Malia. The image brings a smile to my face.

"Earth to Blake." Gabe's voice cuts through my thoughts. "You with us, lover boy?"

I snap back to attention, clearing my throat. "Yeah, sorry. What were you saying?"

As Ethan outlines our latest lead, I knuckle down and focus. There'll be time for daydreaming later. Right now, I have a job to do, but even as I immerse myself in the work, a part of me counts down the hours until I see Sophia again.

The day stretches ahead, full of potential and promise. Sophia is experiencing new beginnings, the team is facing ongoing challenges, and I am facing the exhilarating task of balancing it all.

FOURTEEN

Blake

THE WEEK LEADING UP TO THE GUARDIAN GRIND'S GRAND OPENING flies by in a blur of anticipation and routine. Each morning, I walk Sophia to work, our hands intertwined as we navigate the bustling streets of Guardian HQ.

The air grows cooler with each passing day, autumn subtly making its presence known along the Northern California coast. The scent of salty ocean breeze mingles with the earthy aroma of damp soil and coastal flora, creating a serene, refreshing atmosphere.

Sophia's excitement builds with each step closer to opening day. Her chatter becomes more animated, her gestures more expansive as she describes the progress at the café.

I'm swept up in her enthusiasm, marveling at the transformation not just of the space but of Sophia herself.

"You should see the espresso machine." Sophia's eyes light up one morning, her breath fogging in the cool air. "It's like something out of a sci-fi movie. All gleaming chrome and flashing lights."

I chuckle, squeezing her hand. "Sounds impressive. Are you getting the hang of it?"

"Malia's a great teacher. I think I've finally mastered the perfect foam for cappuccinos." She nods vigorously, her ponytail bouncing.

"That's my girl." Pride swells in my chest.

As we approach the café, the sounds of final preparations reach us. The whine of power tools and the shouts of workers create a feeling of anticipation. Sophia's steps quicken, her eagerness palpable.

"I'll see you tonight." She rises on tiptoe to plant a quick kiss on my cheek. The scent of her shampoo, floral and fresh, lingers as she pulls away.

I catch her hand, pulling her back for a proper kiss. Her lips are soft against mine, tasting faintly of the mint toothpaste we share. When we part, her cheeks are flushed, and not just from the chill in the air.

"Tonight," I agree, my voice husky. "Have a great day, sweetheart."

This routine repeats itself, with slight variations, each day. By the end of the week, Sophia's nervous energy is tangible. That morning, she's practically vibrating as we walk, her fingers drumming an erratic rhythm against my palm.

"Hey." I tug her to a stop. We're a block away from the café, the morning crowd parting around us like a stream around a boulder. "You okay?"

Sophia takes a deep breath, her shoulders rising and falling with the motion. "Just nervous. What if I mess up? What if I can't handle the pressure?"

I cup her face in my hands, my thumbs stroking her cheekbones. Her skin is cool from the morning air, but the warmth of her blush rises beneath my touch.

"You've got this." My voice is firm, filled with conviction. "You've been working hard all week. Jenna and Malia believe in you, and so do I."

She leans into my touch, her eyes closing briefly. When she opens them, there's a new resolve in their depths.

"You're right. I can do this."

"Damn straight." I lean in to press a kiss on her forehead. "Now go show that espresso machine who's boss."

Her bright and clear laughter follows me as I head to work.

Saturday dawns clear and crisp, the autumn day that begs for warm drinks and cozy conversations. Perfect weather for a coffee café opening. The team and I agreed to meet at the café at 10 AM, an hour after the official opening. We want to give them time to work out any initial kinks before descending en masse.

As we approach, the first thing that strikes me is the transformation of the exterior. Gone is the chaotic construction site of the past week. In its place stands a welcoming storefront, all warm wood and gleaming glass. A hand-painted sign proclaims "The Guardian Grind" in elegant script, with "Grand Opening Today!" written on a chalkboard easel below.

The scent of fresh coffee and baked goods wafts out each time the door opens, mingling with the crisp autumn air. The sidewalk is bustling with people, some leaving with steaming cups, others queuing to enter.

"Looks like Jenna and Malia have a hit on their hands," Gabe comments as we join the line.

I nod, a mixture of pride and nervousness churning in my gut. "Let's hope so."

The line moves quickly, and soon, we step into a warm cocoon of aromatic bliss. The café's interior is even more impressive than the outside.

Exposed brick walls are softened by local artwork and lush plants. Edison bulbs hang from the ceiling in artistic clusters, casting a warm glow over the space. The countertops are polished wood, their rich grain complementing the industrial-chic aesthetic of the metal and leather chairs.

But it's not just the visual aspects that captivate. The café is a melody of sensory experiences. The hiss and gurgle of the espresso machine provide a bass line to the melody of quiet conversations and the occasional burst of laughter.

Fingers tap against ceramic mugs, spoons clink against saucers, and the rustle of pages turning from those lost in books or newspapers add texture to the auditory landscape.

The air is thick with the rich aroma of freshly ground coffee beans, underscored by the sweet scent of baked goods. As we approach the counter, I catch whiffs of cinnamon, chocolate, and something citrusy.

And there, in the midst of it all, is Sophia. She wears a forest green apron over a white button-down shirt and her hair pulled back in a neat bun. Her cheeks are flushed from the heat and activity, but her movements are sure as she crafts drink after drink.

Our eyes meet across the crowded space, and her face lights up with a smile that steals my breath. She says something to Malia, who nods and takes over her station.

"Hey, stranger," Sophia greets us as she approaches the register. A smudge of flour dusts her cheek that I ache to brush away. "What can I get for you guys?"

The team places their orders—a variety of coffees and pastries that will let us sample a good portion of the menu. When it's my turn, I lean in, pitching my voice low. "Surprise me."

"You got it, boss." Sophia's eyes sparkle with the challenge.

As she rings us up, I marvel at the change in her. The nervous energy of yesterday is gone, replaced by quiet confidence. She moves with purpose, her interactions with customers warm and professional.

We find a table large enough to accommodate the team, positioned perfectly for me to watch Sophia as she works. The chairs are surprisingly comfortable, and the leather is supple against my back.

"What do we think?" Ethan leans back in his chair. "Did Jenna and Malia pull it off?"

"I'll reserve judgment until I taste the coffee." Rigel glances around, taking in the exposed brick and steel beams. "But I have to admit, the place looks great."

Walt drums his fingers against the polished wood of the table, a satisfied smile spreading across his face. "It's got a good vibe. Cozy, but not cramped."

We continue to chat, our conversation a mix of work talk and casual observations about the café. My attention is divided, half engaged with the team and half watching Sophia as she navigates the busy morning rush.

Finally, Malia appears with a tray laden with our orders. The pastries look divine: flaky croissants and scones studded with berries. No muffins.

The drink she sets in front of me captures my full attention. It's served in a large, hand-thrown ceramic mug with a deep blue glaze that reminds me of the ocean. A delicate design—a stylized guardian angel—is traced in the foam on top.

The aroma that wafts up holds complex notes of chocolate and something spicy, mingling with the rich coffee scent.

"Sophia's special creation." Malia winks, then flashes the prettiest smile at Walt. "She's been working on it all week."

I lift the mug, the warmth seeping into my palms. The first sip is... surprising. There's the expected bite of espresso, but it's smoothed out by what I think is dark chocolate. Then a hint of heat blooms on my tongue—chili, maybe? It's followed by a subtle sweetness that balances everything perfectly.

"Damn." I take another sip. "This is good."

The team's reactions to their drinks are similarly positive. We dig into the pastries, which are just as delicious as they look.

The croissant practically melts in my mouth, buttery layers giving way with a satisfying crackle. Walt and Gabe argue over the scones.

As we enjoy our treats, the café continues to buzz around us. I keep one eye on Sophia, watching as she efficiently manages the steady stream of customers. Her movements are graceful, almost choreographed, as she pulls espresso shots and steams milk.

Then, amid the pleasant hum of activity, a voice rises above the rest. "This is unacceptable. I asked for soy milk."

I tense, my hand automatically moving to where my weapon would be if I were on duty. A middle-aged man's face turns red as he gestures with his cup.

Malia moves toward him, but Sophia beats her to it. I half-rise, ready to intervene, but Ethan's hand on my arm stops me.

He gives me a reassuring nod. "Let her handle it. She's got this."

Reluctantly, I sink back into my chair, every muscle coiled tight as the scene unfolds.

Sophia approaches the man, her posture open and calm. "I'm so sorry for the mix-up, sir." Her voice is rock steady. "Let me remake that for you right away." She takes the cup from him and lightly touches his arm with a flutter of her fingers.

The man continues to bluster, but Sophia doesn't flinch. She listens attentively, nodding at appropriate moments. Her hands are relaxed at her sides, not fidgeting or clenched.

"I completely understand your frustration." Sophia's voice is smooth and soothing as she steps closer to the man. "We pride ourselves on getting orders right and failed you this time. Please allow me to remake your drink and offer you a complimentary pastry for the inconvenience." Her eyes meet his, radiating empathy and calm.

The change in the man is almost comical. His anger immediately dissipates, replaced by a sheepish expression. "Oh, well, that's very kind of you. Thank you."

"It's our pleasure." Sophia smiles, genuine and warm. "What kind of pastry would you like?"

She expertly navigates the interaction, using every skill she's honed to diffuse the situation. Trained to please men and manipulate them if needed, she sways him effortlessly with a touch and a few kind words. It's unsettling to see how easily she controls the exchange.

Her ability to handle the situation gracefully is a harsh reminder of what she's endured and the skills she developed. My admiration for her strength is mixed with a protective instinct that surges to the forefront, making me want to shield her from ever having to use those skills again.

As she leads the now-placated customer to the pastry case, a swell of pride surges within me, so intense it's almost painful. The Sophia I first met would have crumbled under such confrontation. Sophia handled this gracefully and professionally, which I wouldn't have thought possible a few weeks ago.

"Well, I'll be damned," Gabe mutters beside me. "Girl's got skills."

The rest of the team shares similar sentiments. The rest of our visit passes without incident. We linger over our drinks, savoring the excellent coffee and the warm atmosphere. I catch Sophia's eye a few times, exchanging smiles across the busy space.

As the morning rush tapers off, Sophia finally comes over to our table. She looks tired but happy, and a light sheen of sweat on her brow attests to her hard work.

"So," she says, a hint of nervousness creeping into her voice, "what's the verdict?"

The team doesn't hold back, showering her with genuine praise. Sophia blushes at the attention, but I can see how much it means to her.

When the others have had their say, Sophia turns to me, her eyes seeking mine. "And you? What did you think of your drink?"

I finally indulge my earlier impulse to brush the smudge of flour from her cheek. Her skin is warm beneath my fingers, and I let my touch linger.

"It was perfect," I tell her, my voice low and sincere. "Just like you."

Her answering smile is radiant, lighting up her entire face.

As the team gathers their things, preparing to return to work, I pull Sophia aside. We find a quiet corner, partially hidden by a large potted plant.

"I'm so proud of you." My hands rest on her hips. "The way you handled that customer… You were amazing."

"Thanks." She ducks her head, a pleased smile playing on her lips. "It was nothing."

I tilt her chin up, meeting her gaze. "You did that all on your own. Don't sell yourself short."

Sophia leans into me, her body fitting against mine in a way that feels like coming home.

I press a kiss to her forehead, then to her lips. It's brief, mindful of her still being on the clock, but filled with all the emotions I can't put into words.

"I'll see you at home later?" I ask as we part.

"I can't wait." Her smile is soft.

Back at HQ, my mind is still in the café. The taste of Sophia's exceptional coffee lingers on my tongue, a reminder of the morning's sweet success.

Sophia is flourishing, growing into herself in ways I never could have predicted, and I—lucky bastard that I am—get to witness it all.

More importantly, I'll be damned if I let anyone take it away.

FIFTEEN

Blake

The Guardian Grind hums with the afternoon lull, the earlier chaos of the grand opening settling into a more manageable rhythm. The aroma of freshly ground coffee mingles with the sweet scent of baked goods, creating an atmosphere that's both invigorating and comforting. I lean back in my chair, the supple leather creaking slightly, and take a moment to appreciate the warm glow of the Edison bulbs overhead. They cast a gentle light over our table.

Gabe clears his throat, drawing my attention back to the matter at hand. "So, fearless leader, what's our next move on Greaves?"

"That's the million-dollar question, isn't it?" The mention of Greaves' name is like a splash of cold water, jolting me from my momentary contentment. I lean forward, elbows on the polished wooden table, and lower my voice. "How did he slip away from us? He was on the fucking yacht."

"That's the million-dollar question." Ethan's fingers drum a restless tattoo on his mug, the ceramic clinking softly with each tap. "We've hit a wall. Every lead has turned up dry."

"It's like chasing a ghost," Walt adds, his usual jovial tone tinged with frustration. "The bastard's always one step ahead."

The rich taste of my coffee suddenly seems bitter on my tongue. "I know. It's like he's completely dropped off the grid."

Rigel leans in, his voice barely above a whisper. "What if he has? What if he's gone to ground so deep we can't dig him out?"

A heavy silence falls over the table, broken only by the whir of the espresso machine and the muted conversations of other patrons. I look around at my team, seeing my frustration mirrored in their faces.

"That's not an option." My voice is firm, even as doubt gnaws at the edges of my resolve. "We can't let him slip away. Not after everything he's done."

Gabe nods, his jaw set in determination. "Blake's right. We've got to keep pushing. There's got to be something we're missing."

Before anyone can respond, a familiar voice cuts through our tense discussion. "Refills, gentlemen?"

Sophia approaches our table, a tray balanced expertly on one hand. The sight of her cheeks flushed from work and a smudge of flour on her forehead momentarily pushes thoughts of Greaves from my mind.

"You're a lifesaver." Walt grins, already reaching for a fresh mug, his eyes lighting up with appreciation.

She sets down our refills with practiced ease, the aroma of fresh coffee wafting up and momentarily dispelling the heavy atmosphere. As she leans over to place my mug before me, I catch a whiff of her perfume—something light and floral—mingling with the scent of coffee and vanilla.

"Everything okay?" Her gentle gaze meets mine with a hint of concern.

I force a smile, not wanting to burden her with our troubles. "Just shop talk. Nothing to worry about."

Sophia raises an eyebrow, clearly not buying it, but doesn't push. "If you say so. Enjoy your coffee, boys."

As she walks away, her hips swaying just enough to distract me, I catch the guys exchanging glances. One of them lets out a loud, exaggerated cough, barely disguising the words, *"pussy-whipped,"* while another chuckles under his breath. I roll my eyes, but the corner of my mouth twitches—yeah, I'm not even going to pretend they're wrong.

"She's settling in well here." Ethan leans back, a knowing smile playing on his lips.

"Yeah, she is. It's... It's good to see." I cross my arms, a hint of pride creeping into my voice.

Gabe opens his mouth to respond when all of our phones buzz simultaneously. I pull mine out to see a message from Mitzy.

Briefing in 15. HQ. Don't be late.

The tone shifts instantly, the casual banter dissolving as we exchange looks. This can only mean something serious has come up.

"Looks like we might get some answers," Walt mutters, already standing.

We quickly finish up and head back to Guardian HQ. The tension builds as we walk, each of us mentally preparing for whatever Mitzy has to share.

When we enter the briefing room, Mitzy is already there, along with Stitch and Jeb. The map of the last known movements of Greaves and his yacht is projected on the wall, casting a faint glow over the room. We all take our seats, the air thick with anticipation.

Mitzy doesn't waste any time. "Here's what we know. The yacht docked in Bucharest, but there's no record of Greaves disembarking. Since then, the yacht has been moving erratically, and we've lost visual confirmation of his location."

Stitch jumps in, typing rapidly on her laptop. "We've been monitoring all major transportation hubs, but so far, nothing concrete. There's been a lot of digital chatter, but it's all noise— nothing we can pin down."

Jeb crosses his arms, his expression grim. "It's like he's gone to ground, or he's deliberately throwing us off."

Rigel leans forward, his brow furrowed in concentration. "Could he have slipped off the yacht unnoticed? Maybe using a smaller craft?"

"It's possible," Mitzy acknowledges, "but unlikely without us catching some trace of it. The fact that we haven't suggests he's either still on the yacht or he's found another way to stay hidden."

Gabe taps his fingers on the table, clearly frustrated. "So, he's keeping us chasing our tails. Spreading misinformation, throwing us off his trail."

"Smart move," Ethan grudgingly admits. "If we don't know where to focus our efforts, we can't pin him down."

"Hell, he could be dead for all we know. That's one way to disappear." I take a deep breath, thinking about the problem.

The room falls into a heavy silence as we all absorb the situation. We're no closer to finding Greaves than we were before, but the determination in the room is palpable.

"Unfortunately, that's impossible to prove. We have no body." Mitzy tugs at her ear. "I'm working on the theory he's still alive and kicking. We're going to shift our focus, going old school. Watch his known associates. They might be helping him stay hidden."

Stitch's fingers pause over the keyboard, her expression thoughtful. "We've already started digging into their backgrounds, but these people are careful. They know how to cover their tracks."

"Someone's bound to slip up." Gabe leans back in his chair, crossing his arms over his chest, his gruff tone matching his rugged demeanor.

"It's not much," Ethan admits, "but it's a start."

For the next hour, we dive into the details, refining our strategy and piecing together what little information we have into a plan. The frustration of the unknown is still there, but now it's tempered with a clear direction.

As the meeting wraps up, chairs scrape against the floor, and everyone begins to gather their gear. Gabe grunts something about needing a stiff drink, while Walt claps Rigel on the back, muttering about the long hours ahead. Stitch and Mitzy exchange a few last words, their heads bent over the tablet, before heading out with Jeb in tow. The team disperses, each of us heading out into the night, focused on the tasks ahead.

We may not have solved the problem, but we've taken a step forward.

The walk back to my apartment is filled with thoughts of our next moves. The cool evening air nips at my face, carrying the scent of fallen leaves and wood smoke.

It's fully dark by the time I reach home, the streetlights casting pools of warm light on the sidewalk.

As I open the door, the mouthwatering aroma of garlic and herbs envelops me. Sizzling fills the air, punctuated by the soft clink of utensils. A low hum of jazzy, mellow music sets the scene.

"Sophia?" I call out, shrugging off my jacket.

"In the kitchen." Her voice rings back, warm and welcoming.

The sight that greets me in the kitchen stops me in my tracks. Immediately, my tension melts away.

Sophia stands at the stove, her hair piled in a messy bun atop her head, wisps escaping to frame her face. She's wearing one of my old T-shirts, the hem hitting her mid-thigh, and she's swaying slightly to the music as she stirs something that smells divine.

She looks up as I enter, her face breaking into a radiant smile. "Hey, you. Dinner's almost ready."

I cross the room in three strides, wrapping my arms around her from behind and burying my face in the crook of her neck. She smells of garlic and rosemary, underlaid with her unique scent that never fails to center me.

"Missed you," I murmur against her skin, feeling her shiver slightly.

She leans back into me, her free hand coming up to tangle in my hair. "Missed you more. Tough day?"

I sigh, not wanting to burden her but also craving her understanding. "You could say that."

Sophia turns in my arms, her eyes searching my face. "Want to talk about it?"

I hesitate, torn between my instinct to protect her and my need for her support. "Let's eat first, then we'll talk."

She nods, stretching up on her tiptoes to press a soft kiss to my lips. "Go set the table. This'll be ready in five."

Dinner is a sensory experience that momentarily removes all thoughts of work from my mind. The chicken is perfectly cooked, tender, and infused with herbs. The roasted vegetables provide a satisfying crunch, and Sophia's chosen wine complements everything beautifully.

As we eat, Sophia regales me with stories from the café—a regular who insists on ordering in rhyme, a dog who's developed a taste for biscotti, and the ongoing saga of the temperamental espresso machine. Her laughter is infectious, and my shoulders slowly unwind, the knot of tension easing with each of her joyful anecdotes.

But as we finish our meal, the weight of the day settles back over me. Sophia must sense the shift in my mood because she reaches across the table, her fingers intertwining with mine.

"Okay, spill," she says softly. "What's going on?"

I take a deep breath, gathering my thoughts. "It's Greaves. We're… We're stuck. Every lead we follow turns into a dead end. It's like he's just vanished into thin air."

Sophia's grip on my hand tightens slightly. "But that's not possible, right? No one can disappear completely."

I shake my head, frustration creeping back into my voice. "You'd be surprised. With enough money and the right connections, you can come pretty damn close."

She's quiet for a moment, her thumb tracing soothing circles on the back of my hand. "What does this mean for... for us?" The question is hesitant, tinged with a fear that makes my heart clench.

I meet her gaze, my expression resolute. "Hey, this changes nothing. You're safe here. I promise."

She tightens her grip on her mug, worry still lingering in her eyes. "I know. I trust you. It's just... sometimes it feels like we're living in this bubble, you know? Like the rest of the world can't touch us. And then something like this happens, and it seems I'll never be free of my past."

"I know it can feel like that, but what we're building together is real. And I'll be damned if I let Greaves or anyone else threaten that."

A small smile tugs at her lips. "My hero," she says, only half-joking.

I bring her hand to my lips, kissing her knuckles. "Always."

We fall into a comfortable silence, the weight of our conversation settling around us like a heavy blanket. But it's not oppressive. Instead, it feels like a shared burden, lighter for being carried together.

Finally, Sophia speaks again. "So what's the plan? To find Greaves, I mean."

I lean back in my chair, running a hand through my hair. "Back to basics. We're going to start with his known associates and work our way up. Someone has to know something, and eventually, they'll slip up."

Her brow furrows in thought. "That makes sense. And, Blake?" Her voice takes on a determined edge that captures my full attention. "You'll get him. I know you will."

The absolute faith in her voice hits me like a physical force. At that moment, looking at her across our dinner table, backlit by the soft glow of our kitchen lights, I'm struck by how far we've come. This woman, who's been through hell and back, is offering me comfort and support.

"Come here," I say, my voice rough with emotion.

Sophia stands, moving around the table to settle into my lap. I wrap my arms around her, breathing in her scent, letting her presence ground me.

"Thank you," I murmur into her hair.

She pulls back slightly, her hand coming up to cup my cheek. "For what?"

"For being you. For this." I gesture vaguely at our surroundings. "For giving me something to come home to."

Sophia's eyes soften, a smile playing at her lips. "Well, when you put it that way…" She leans in, her lips meeting mine in a kiss that starts soft but quickly deepens.

As we lose ourselves in each other, the day's worries fade into the background. There will be time for strategizing, chasing leads, and facing the dangers that lurk in the shadows. But for now, in this moment, there's just us.

And it's enough.

The weeks that follow settle into a rhythm that's both comforting and energizing. I walk Sophia to the café each morning, our hands intertwined, sharing quiet conversations or comfortable silences. The air grows crisper as autumn deepens.

I watch with pride as Sophia blossoms in her new role. Her confidence grows with each passing day, her smile brighter, and her laughter more frequent. She comes home with stories of charming difficult customers, mastering complex orders, and forming friendships with regulars.

One evening, as we're curled up on the couch, the soft glow of lamplight creating a cozy atmosphere, Sophia looks up at me with a contentment that takes my breath away.

"I never thought I could be this happy." Her fingers trace idle patterns on my chest, her voice barely above a whisper.

I pull her closer, pressing a kiss to the top of her head. "You deserve all the happiness in the world, Soph."

She hums contentedly, nestling further into my embrace. The scent of her shampoo mingles with the aroma of the herbal tea she favors in the evenings, creating a fragrance that I've come to associate with home.

These moments of domestic bliss are interspersed with the ongoing challenges of the mission. We make slow but steady progress, each lead bringing us incrementally closer to our goal.

But we're still grasping at straws. Sooner or later, reality will crash in.

It's just a matter of time before everything unravels.

SIXTEEN

Sophia

Steam curls up from the espresso machine, mingling with the rich aroma of coffee and freshly baked pastries that fills The Guardian Grind. I wipe down the counter, the steady hum of the café's activity creating a comforting rhythm. The soft chatter of customers blends with the clinking of cups, offering a soothing backdrop to my thoughts.

"One vanilla latte and a blueberry scone, coming right up." My voice is cheerful despite the melancholy tugging at my heart.

As I prepare the order, my hands move with practiced ease, and thoughts of how much I've come to love this life swirl in my mind. The rhythm of the work, the joy of crafting the perfect cup of coffee, the satisfaction of a customer's smile, and the sense of belonging among my coworkers—it's precious to me.

Beneath the surface, constant anxiety lurks, ready to crash down at any moment. I expected only days, maybe a week at most. Instead, I've had precious, beautiful weeks of falling in love, becoming part of a family, and finding a sense of belonging I never thought possible.

I'm destined to destroy all of it.

The day progresses as usual. I take orders, steam milk, pull espresso shots, and clear tables. Each interaction is tinged with a bittersweet awareness of its fleeting nature.

Nothing good ever lasts, and I hate that.

Something catches my eye as I approach a recently vacated table to clear the dishes. A manila envelope sits innocuously among the empty cups and crumb-strewn plates. My heart leaps into my throat at the sight of my name scrawled across its surface in harsh yet familiar handwriting.

My hands tremble as I reach for the envelope, quickly pressing it to my chest to conceal it from view. I glance around nervously, but no one pays me any attention. Swiftly, I tuck the envelope into my apron pocket, its weight a ticking time bomb against my hip.

"Sophia? Are you okay?" Jenna's concerned voice breaks through my panic. "You look like you've seen a ghost."

The room spins, making me feel lightheaded and fearful. The envelope burns against my side like a brand, a stark reminder that this beautiful illusion is officially shattered.

"I-I don't feel well. Do you mind if I take off early?" I force a weak smile, avoiding her gaze, and lean against the table for support.

"Of course not. Go home and rest. I've got things covered here." Jenna's brow furrows with worry.

Gratitude and guilt war within me as I thank her and hurry out of the café. Instead of heading home, I find a secluded bench in a nearby park. With shaking hands, I open the envelope.

Inside, there's a flip phone, a small USB drive, and a note that says *Call me*.

My stomach churns as I power on the phone. There's only one contact listed—a capital M.

Taking a deep breath, I press the call button. It rings once before a familiar voice answers, sending chills rushing down my spine.

This is it.

The moment I've been dreading since that night on the yacht. My heart races as Malfor's oily, corrosive voice slithers through the line.

"Hello, my dear. I trust you've been well?"

"Yes, sir." My voice barely rises above a whisper, trembling with fear.

"I hope you've enjoyed your little vacation."

"Yes, sir." The words slip out automatically, and I cringe, realizing my mistake.

"Yes?" His voice tightens, the sadistic pleasure evident. *"I hope you're not getting too comfortable settling in with the enemy. Did you forget our little arrangement?"*

"No, sir. I have not forgotten. Forgive me, I misspoke." The lie catches in my throat, and its weight sits heavy on my chest.

Memories flood my mind—laughter with Blake during stolen moments, the warmth of his hand in mine, the sense of safety I feel in his presence. Quiet days during the week, sharing stories with Jenna over coffee. Each memory is a dagger, reminding me of the fragile happiness I've built, happiness that Malfor is ready to destroy.

"Good." His voice carries a sharp edge, disbelief lingering beneath the surface. *"You have work to do. Don't forget why you're there."*

His words wrap around me like a serpent, squeezing the air from my lungs and making it impossible to breathe. My hands shake so violently I nearly drop the phone.

"Do you have access to all the necessary areas?" His dark and menacing laughter crackles through the speaker.

"Yes, sir." I swallow hard, my mouth dry as sandpaper. "I only need his ID."

"Very good." His tone is smooth, almost seductive, sending a shiver down my spine. *"Now listen carefully. Go to the server room within the technical building. Call me once you're inside. I'll give you further instructions then."*

"Yes, sir." I pause, not entirely sure of his expectations. My mind races, searching for any way out of this nightmare. "When?"

"Now, you silly fool." His voice cracks like a whip, the sadistic pleasure in his tone unmistakable.

"Sir, I'm sorry, but I don't have his badge. I'll have to get it." My voice cracks. Tears prick at my eyes, but I force them back, my heart pounding in my chest like a drum.

There's a pause, and in that silence, my thoughts race to Luke—sweet, innocent Luke with his gap-toothed smile and unruly hair—Luke, who depends on me. Before I can stop myself, the words tumble out.

"How... how is Luke doing? May I speak with him, please?"

The moment the question leaves my lips, I regret it. The silence on the other end stretches, heavy and oppressive. Malfor's anger radiates through the phone like a palpable force. When he finally speaks, his voice is low and dangerous.

"You forget your place. You have no right to make demands of me."

It wasn't a demand. I asked nicely. Not that it matters to Malfor. He twists every word into an affront, a personal challenge to his authority. His mind, coiled and ready to strike, sees rebellion in the simplest request and treachery in everyone.

Tears stream down my face as I listen, shame and fear coursing through me. I know better than to ask, but Luke...

God, Luke...

"I'm sorry, sir." I hate how weak I sound. "I just... I miss him."

"Miss him?" Malfor's laugh is cold and mirthless. *"How touching. Let me give you some motivation. The sooner you complete your mission, the sooner you can come home. Then we may discuss whether you will or will not see your son."*

I gasp, the air catching painfully in my throat. A sob escapes before I can stop it, tears streaming down my face.

"And, Sophia? I have plans for when you return. Big plans."

A chill runs down my spine at his words. I think of Jonathan Greaves, of the life I escaped, and horror grips me—there might be worse fates waiting for me.

"Do you understand?" His voice cuts through my spiraling thoughts.

"Yes, sir." I choke on the words.

"Good. Now stop your sniveling and pull yourself together. You have work to do."

"I understand." I hang my head in defeat.

"Excellent. I'll be waiting for your call. Don't disappoint me."

"I won't."

"Good girl." The mockery drips from his voice like venom. *"Until your mission is finished, you will not see Luke. You will not talk to him. You will do nothing but what I tell you. Is that clear?"*

"Yes, sir," I choke out the words.

"Don't forget what's at stake. One wrong move, one hint of betrayal, and Luke will pay the price. It seems as if you've forgotten who you belong to?"

"Forgive my impertinence, sir," I whisper, hating how weak I sound. "I overstepped."

"Oh, you'll be forgiven, my dear. Forgiven at the end of my whip."

"Your whip?" I choke at his words.

"Why yes, my dear. You'll serve me directly upon your return. Aren't you excited?"

The world tilts beneath me. Serve Malfor? My mind races with the implications, each possibility worse than the last. I struggle to find my voice, knowing he expects a response. Not returning to Jonathan Greaves should be a relief, but how Malfor speaks fills me with dread.

"You should be grateful." His voice cuts like a blade, laced with sadistic glee.

"I-I'm honored, sir." The words taste like ash in my mouth.

"Good girl." The smirk in his voice is unmistakable, dripping with satisfaction.

"Thank you, sir." I swallow hard, fighting back tears.

"With all this freedom you've enjoyed these past weeks, you'll need… reeducation upon your return."

A chill runs down my spine at his words. I think of Jonathan Greaves, the life I escaped, and realize with horror that a worse fate awaits me.

"Thank you for your graciousness in helping me to serve you better. I will atone for everything."

"Everything?" His voice drips with disdain. *"We'll see about that. Your real test is just beginning. Don't disappoint me, Sophia. You know what happens when you disappoint me."*

"I won't disappoint you, sir. I promise." Fear claws at my throat.

"Excellent, because failure is not an option." His voice drips with venom. *"I'll be waiting for your call."*

The line goes dead, leaving me with the weight of his threats and the magnitude of what I must do. I sink to my knees, overwhelmed by fear and despair. Sobs wrack my body as the full extent of my captivity reveals itself; even in this place I've come to think of as home, I am still not free.

Luke's face swims before my eyes—his trusting gaze, his infectious laugh. Then Blake's face joins it—his warm smile, the love in his eyes when he looks at me. Two worlds, impossibly far apart, both dependent on my subsequent actions.

I take a shuddering breath, trying to calm myself. With trembling hands, I wipe away my tears. It's time to destroy everything I've come to love. Each step from here leads me further from the life I've grown to cherish and closer to a future I can barely bring myself to contemplate.

There's no choice, not really.

Luke needs me.

That night, I chop vegetables for dinner. The rhythmic sound of the knife against the cutting board steadies my thoughts. Blake stands nearby, sipping a glass of water, his presence grounding me in the moment.

"You're quiet tonight." He leans against the counter. "Everything okay?"

"Just thinking, that's all." I force a smile, focusing on the task at hand.

He steps closer, brushing a strand of hair behind my ear, his touch sending a shiver through me. I linger in the moment, committing the warmth of his hand and the intensity of his gaze to memory.

After dinner, we retire to bed, the familiar comfort of our routine wrapping around us. I sink deep into my submission, seeking the solace and security it brings. Blake's arms, strong and reassuring, envelop me as we make love—a tender, quiet connection that leaves me aching.

In the darkness, I trace the lines of his face with my fingers, memorizing every angle and detail. He catches my hand and presses a kiss to my palm.

"You sure you're okay?" Concern fills his voice.

I swallow the lump in my throat and offer a soft smile. "I'm fine. Just… happy to be here with you."

He holds me close, his breath warm against my skin as sleep takes him. I lie awake, fighting back tears, knowing these moments are limited, that soon, I'll betray the man who has shown me nothing but love and kindness.

Blake will never forgive me, but at least he'll be alive to hate me.

But the thought of Luke, alone and scared, steels my resolve. I have no choice.

The next morning, the alarm on my phone vibrates silently under my pillow, rousing me from a fitful sleep. Blake's arm drapes over my waist, his breath warm on my neck. For a moment, I allow myself to sink into his embrace, savoring the comfort and safety I feel in his arms.

But duty calls, and with it comes a familiar knot of dread in my stomach.

Carefully, I extricate myself from his hold, my movements slow and deliberate to avoid waking him. As I pad over to the dresser, the hardwood floor is cool beneath my bare feet.

I find Blake's ID badge where he always leaves it. The metal is smooth and innocuous in my hand, but it feels as heavy as lead.

I slip the badge into the pocket of my robe and make my way to the kitchen. As I go through the motions of making coffee, my mind races with the tasks ahead. The invigorating aroma of coffee fills the air, a cruel mockery of the regular morning routine I've come to cherish.

By the time Blake stumbles into the kitchen, sleep-rumpled and adorably confused, I've hidden his badge in a book on the bookshelf. Guilt churns in my stomach as he searches for his badge. His frustration grows with each passing minute.

SEVENTEEN

Blake

"Sophia?" I call out, my voice tinged with frustration. "Have you seen my ID?"

Her voice drifts in from the kitchen, amusement clear in her tone. "Did you check the dresser? You know, where you always leave it?"

"Of course I did," I grumble, running a hand through my hair. "It's not there."

I never misplace my badge. Never.

"Are you sure?" Sophia's footsteps approach, growing louder with each step. "You're usually such a creature of habit."

I check the dresser—again—pulling open drawers with increasing urgency.

"I'm telling you, it's not here."

The contents of each drawer—neatly folded clothes and organized accessories—mock me as I search. My movements become more frantic, and I toss items aside with growing frustration.

Dropping to my knees, I peer under the dresser, hoping to see the glint of my badge. Nothing but dust bunnies greet me.

"Come on, where are you?" I move to the bed and yank back the sheets. Pillows go flying as I search every inch of the mattress.

Sophia appears in the doorway just as I'm emptying the contents of the bedside table onto the floor. Her eyebrows shoot up at the chaos I've created.

"Wow." A laugh bubbles up from her. "I've never seen you like this. It's cute."

I glare at her, but there's no heat behind it.

Her smile fades as she takes in my distress. "Hey." She steps into the room and places a hand on my arm. "We'll find it, okay? Let's think about this logically."

Together, we methodically search the apartment. Sophia checks the laundry hamper while I scour the living room. We look under couch cushions, in kitchen drawers, even in the refrigerator—stranger things have happened.

After ten minutes of intense searching, we both stand in the middle of our now-disheveled apartment, defeated.

"Shit, I can't believe this." I run a hand through my hair for what feels like the hundredth time. "I never misplace my badge."

Sophia wraps her arms around me, resting her head on my chest. "It's okay. These things happen. You'll get a temporary one made, right?"

"Yeah, I guess." I sigh, my chin brushing the top of her head.

"First time for everything, right? Maybe the universe is telling you to shake up your routine a bit." She pulls back, looking up at me with affection.

"Maybe you're right." Despite my frustration, I can't help but smile.

"It's just a badge. I'm sure they go missing all the time."

"Maybe. But it's a big deal—like huge."

"Why?"

I meet her concerned gaze, the gravity of the situation clear in my voice.

"My badge grants access to highly restricted areas of Guardian HQ. Server rooms, weapons caches, classified document storage—everything. In the wrong hands…"

"What happens if you can't find it?"

I let out a humorless laugh. "I face Mitzy's wrath. She's going to tear me a new one for this security breach. Not to mention, the guys will never let me hear the end of it."

"It's just misplaced. Not lost."

"No. I distinctly remember putting it on the dresser last night."

"I'm sure we'll find it." Sophia tenses. "What happens if we don't?"

"The moment I report it missing, they'll deactivate it and reset all the systems it had access to. It's going to be a nightmare."

"Maybe you should hold off on reporting it just yet." There's an odd note in her voice that I can't quite place. Desperation? Fear? But before I can analyze it, she continues.

"Think about it. If you report it now and then find it in an hour, you'll have caused all that trouble for nothing. You'll have to face the team's teasing and Mitzy's anger."

"I don't know, Soph. It's pretty serious…" I hesitate, torn between protocol and the logic in Sophia's words.

"Just give it until tomorrow morning. You're human. Mistakes happen. If it doesn't show up by then, you can report it. Give it a chance to, I don't know, magically reappear?"

Her urgency is puzzling, but I agree with her logic.

"Okay, you're right. I'll wait until tomorrow, but I must report it if it doesn't turn up. No exceptions."

"Of course. That's reasonable." Relief floods Sophia's face. "But think of all the trouble you'll avoid when you find it."

I can't shake the nagging feeling that something isn't quite right. I walk her to The Guardian Grind. It's part of our daily routine. Her hand is uncharacteristically cool in mine. Halfway there, she stops, tugging gently on my arm.

"I can make it the rest of the way." She stretches up to kiss me. "You're already running late."

"You sure?" I hesitate, torn between duty and desire.

"It's not far. Go. I'll see you tonight." She kisses me again. "Try to have a good day, and don't worry about the badge. It'll show up."

A genuine smile spreads across my face. "Yes, ma'am. You have a good day, too."

"I told you not to call me that." She playfully punches at my chest. "If you keep it up, you'll force me to do something I don't want to do."

"And what is that?"

"Stop going to my knees when I call you *Sir.*"

"*Fuuuuck*… Do you know what that does to me?"

Instant, fucking hard on.

"I know exactly what it does." Her voice turns sultry and seductive. "So, if you want to keep me on my knees, you might want to let up on calling me *ma'am.*"

I pull her close, and our bodies press together. The heat between us is undeniable.

"I guess we'll just have to see how the rest of the day goes, won't we?"

"Tonight is going to be… unforgettable." She smirks, eyes glinting with mischief.

A thrill courses through me at her words, anticipation building. The promise of a night filled with fire and passion lingers between us, making it hard to think about anything else.

I'm struck by how much has changed in such a short time. Months ago, I focused solely on the mission—on bringing down Greaves and his organization. Now, I have a warm goodbye, a place to come home to, and someone to share my life with.

I wouldn't trade this for anything. The mission remains crucial, a driving force in my daily life, but it's no longer my only purpose. Now, I have someone to protect and come home to.

Sophia makes me not just a better Guardian but a better man. The missing badge is a minor setback, nothing more.

As I stride into work, the bullpen buzzes with activity, the familiar hum of muted conversations washing over me.

Gabe spots me first. "Well, well, look who finally decided to join us." He checks his watch, leaning back in his chair with a cheeky grin plastered all over his face. "Over an hour late? What do you get up to in the mornings?"

"Can it, Gabe." I roll my eyes, already bracing for the inevitable ribbing.

"Oh, I bet something was *up.*" Walt chuckles, shaking his head.

"The great Blake Jackson… Never thought I'd see the day you'd be pussy-whipped."

"Maybe he's getting soft," Rigel chimes in, his usually serious expression cracking with amusement. "Too much domestic bliss clouding that razor-sharp mind."

"Soft?" Gabe laughs. "I think you meant to say something *hard* is clouding that razor-sharp mind of his."

A flush creeps up my neck, equal parts embarrassment and something else I can't quite name. "Are you three done? We have actual work to do, you know."

"Oh, we're just getting started." Gabe laughs, winking at Walt. "How's Sophia? Keeping you busy, I assume?"

"Busy? More like hard and exhausted," Walt adds, grinning. "You look like you barely survived the night."

"And morning." Gabe taps his watch. "Bet that's why he's over an hour late to muster."

"Cut the guy some slack," Rigel says, smirking. "Sophia might be able to handle your… stamina, but we're starting to wonder if you have any energy left for actual training. Or did you forget you're a Guardian?"

"You guys are impossible." I can't help but laugh, shaking my head at their antics.

"Come on, Blake. Just admit it. She's got you wrapped around her little finger." Gabe claps me on the back, his grin widening.

"Alright, alright." I hold up my hands in mock surrender. "You got me. Now, can we please get to work?"

As we dive into the day's tasks, the playful banter fades, replaced by the focused intensity that defines our team. Still, the lingering smiles and occasional jabs remind me that, despite everything, these guys are my family. And for that, I'm grateful.

EIGHTEEN

Sophia

BLAKE'S BROAD SHOULDERS RETREAT INTO THE DISTANCE, EACH STEP tearing a piece of my heart away. My chest tightens painfully, the weight of what I'm about to do crushing me from within.

How can I possibly let go of this amazing, virile man who has been my strength, my protector? The thought of never feeling his touch again, never hearing his voice, rips through me like a knife. I'm going to miss him so much it physically hurts.

As soon as he disappears, I reach into my pocket, fingers closing around his badge. My steps are quick and purposeful as I change direction, heading not toward the café but to the technical building.

The flip phone Malfor gave me feels like a lead weight in my hand. I dial with trembling fingers.

"What?" His voice, cold and irritated, grates against my ear.

"There's a problem." I force the words out. "The badge. It'll be deactivated as soon as Blake gets a replacement."

A string of curses crackles through the line, followed by a long pause. Then Malfor's oily voice slithers toward me again. *"Did those idiots give you a badge?"*

"Yes, sir. Everyone has one."

"Good. We'll clone it. Now, listen carefully. Do exactly as I say. First thing, get to the tech building. Call me the moment you're inside."

"Yes, sir." I nod, forgetting he can't see me.

The line goes dead. I swallow hard, pocketing the phone and quickening my pace.

Guardian HQ sprawls before me, a maze of buildings separated by manicured lawns, walking paths, and the ever-present golf carts as people move around.

The technical center looms ahead, all glass and steel, familiar yet suddenly foreboding. My steps falter as I approach the entrance, my heart pounding against my ribs.

I reach for Blake's badge, then freeze. The weight of my own badge around my neck is a glaring reminder of my deception. Sweat beads on my forehead as I push Blake's stolen badge deeper into my pocket. The cold metal against my flushed skin sends a shiver through me, amplifying the guilt that gnaws at my insides.

Two guards flank the entrance, their postures alert despite the early hour. I force a smile, praying they can't hear the frantic beating of my heart.

"Morning, Sophia," the taller guard greets me, his smile genuine.

"Hey," I manage, my voice steadier than I feel. "How's it going?"

"Going great," he replies. His partner nods in agreement. "Love The Guardian Grind, by the way. Best coffee on the planet."

"Oh, thanks so much." The words taste like ash in my mouth.

The shorter guard tilts his head, curiosity flickering in his eyes. "Aren't you working at the Grind today?"

My stomach lurches. "Oh, no," I lie, the words tumbling out. "Mitzy's giving me another tour. I'm supposed to meet her inside."

"Do you know where you're going?" he asks, concern evident in his voice.

I offer a quick smile, perhaps too quickly. "Yeah, yeah, I know where I'm going. Don't worry about me."

They wave me through, and I swipe my badge with trembling fingers. Green light. I'm in.

The interior hums with technology. Fluorescent lights cast harsh shadows, making the corridors seem longer and more ominous. I walk quickly, head down, avoiding eye contact with the few early workers I pass.

Finding an empty corridor, I duck into a small alcove. My fingers fumble as I pull out the flip phone, blood rushing in my ears.

One call and there's no going back.

I dial, each beep echoing in the empty hallway.

"I'm in," I whisper as soon as the line connects. "But I'm not sure where to go. What am I looking for?"

"The server room, you idiot." Malfor's irritation crackles through the phone. *"Tall black cabinets, lots of blinking lights. Probably cold. Mitzy never showed you?"*

"She did, but there are so many divisions…" I trail off, remembering the tours through cryptology, robotics, and virtual reality.

"It'll be labeled 'Server Room' or 'Data Center,'" Malfor snaps. *"Hurry up."*

"Okay, I think I know where you're talking about."

Pocketing the phone, I step out of the alcove. The hallway stretches before me, suddenly alien and threatening. I move quickly, trying to look purposeful.

A group of techs rounds the corner. I duck my head, veering to the side. Their chatter fades as they pass, oblivious to my presence.

I pass the robotics lab, glancing through the glass at half-assembled machines. My eyes linger, remembering Mitzy's swarm of bumblebee drones inside. She was always going on about how no one cares about bugs, how they can slip in and out of places unnoticed.

I never fully understood how they stayed powered up or what all they could do, but the thought crosses my mind—if no one notices bugs, maybe Malfor won't either.

Maybe, just maybe, one of those tiny drones could be a lifeline back to Guardian HRS… If they still want me after what I'm about to do.

I slow my pace, looking to see if anyone's inside. The lab is empty. My heart pounds as I push the door open and step inside, the soft hum of machinery the only sound in the room. I scan the room, trying to remember where Mitzy kept the hive.

There. In the far corner, nestled between a pile of parts and a stack of manuals, I spot the small, inconspicuous container. I move quickly, hands shaking as I open it and carefully take one of the tiny drones. It's lighter than I expected, barely more than a speck in my hand.

I slip it deep into my pocket, the cold metal barely noticeable against my skin. With one last glance, I exit the lab, hoping this tiny piece of tech might be the lifeline I desperately need.

My pulse races as I slip out of the Robotics lab. I head down the corridor, and just a few steps later, I reach the VR suite.

The large glass windows offer a view of the darkened room, the equipment still and silent, but memories rush back, vivid and overwhelming.

My eyes are drawn to the center of the room, where the VR rigs stand like sentinels of the digital age. Headsets dangle from ceiling-mounted harnesses, their visors dark and waiting. Below each headset is the real marvel—the omnidirectional treadmill. It's not the linear track I'm used to at the gym, but a smooth, circular platform rigged with sensors.

I hesitate, the familiar tangle of wires and headsets reminding me of the countless hours I spent here—playing with the tech, losing myself in virtual worlds, finding a brief escape from reality.

For a moment, I'm back there, trepidation turning to exhilaration as Mitzy helped me suit up. The weight of the headset, the strange sensation of walking without moving, and then... A new world pops up around me, so real I could almost touch it.

I shake off the memory.

Stop wasting time. Still not where I need to be.

I wrack my brain, trying to remember the rest of Mitzy's whirlwind tour. That woman has boundless energy, her words tumbling out faster than her feet can carry her. I can almost hear her rapid-fire explanations, see her gesticulating wildly as she...

Wait.

A memory surfaces of Mitzy practically bouncing on her toes.

She led me to an elevator. *"And now, for the coolest part—literally. Our server room is in the basement. It's like a high-tech igloo down there."*

The basement. Of course.

I approach the elevators, my heart racing. Just as I reach for the button, the doors slide open. A group of techs spills out, chattering about some code breakthrough. Inside, two more wait, holding the door. They look at me expectantly.

I freeze, cold realization washing over me. I can't be seen heading to the server level—it's not a place I'd ever have a reason to go.

"Sorry, forgot something." I back away. Their puzzled looks follow me as the doors close.

Panic rising, I scan the hallway. There—a stairwell. I push through the heavy door, grateful for the sudden silence. The stairs wind downward, my footsteps echoing in the empty stairwell. With each floor I descend, the weight in my chest grows heavier.

At the bottom, I pause, ear pressed to the door. Silence. Slowly, I ease it open, slipping out into a dimly lit corridor. Empty, thank God. I creep forward, trying to remember Mitzy's tour route.

A heavy door looms ahead, "Server Room" stenciled in stark white letters. This is it. I tuck my own badge under my shirt, fingers trembling as I pull out Blake's. The stolen badge feels hot in my hand, a burning reminder of my betrayal.

I swipe it, holding my breath.

A soft beep.

A green light.

The lock disengages with a click.

Breath quickening, I slip inside, closing the door behind me. The room envelops me in a world of technology. Rows of black cabinets stretch into the distance, a digital forest of massive computing power. The air is cool, almost frigid, yet sweat still beads on my forehead.

Pulling out the phone again, I whisper, "I'm in. What now?"

"Look for a terminal," Malfor snaps through the phone. *"It'll have a monitor, keyboard, and probably some USB ports. Should stand out from the servers."*

My heart sinks. "There are just—servers everywhere. Row after row."

"Then look harder," he growls. *"It has to be there somewhere. Find it."*

I swallow hard, terror clawing at my throat. Disappointing Malfor isn't an option. Not with what's at stake.

I weave through the maze of humming machines, each aisle looking identical to the last. Blinking lights and whirring fans surround me, a digital jungle that seems to close in with every step. Sweat trickles down my back despite the chill.

One aisle. Two. Three. Nothing but towers of sleek black metal.

Panic rises. What if I can't find it? What will Malfor do?

Then, at the end of the fourth aisle, I spot it. A soft glow catches my eye.

There, nestled between two server banks, stands a small workstation. A monitor hums quietly, its screen visible in the dim light. A keyboard waits below, a scatter of USB ports visible.

Relief floods through me, so intense my knees nearly buckle.

"I found it," I breathe into the phone, my voice shaky.

"About time. Now, insert the drive."

My hands shake as I plug it in. The screen flickers to life.

"Input exactly what I tell you."

Malfor begins dictating a string of commands. My fingers tremble over the keys, fear making each stroke uncertain.

"Colon, backslash, backslash..." His voice crackles through the phone.

"Wait," I stammer, "is that two colons or one colon and two backslashes?"

"One colon, two backslashes," Malfor snaps. *"Pay attention."*

Sweat beads on my forehead despite the chill. I type carefully, then read it back.

"Wrong," he snarls. *"It's a forward slash, not a backslash. Start over."*

Tears prick at my eyes. My fingers shake as I delete and retype.

The process continues, each mistake ratcheting up Malfor's anger and my terror. My heart pounds so hard I'm sure it's audible over the phone. I'm alternately flushed and chilled, my shirt sticking to my back.

"S-sorry," I choke out after another error. "I'll get it right, I swear."

"You'd better," Malfor warns, his voice low and menacing. *"Or your son will pay the price."*

The threat sends a fresh wave of panic through me. I force myself to breathe, to focus.

Finally, mercifully, I input the last command correctly. Lines of text scroll by in a dizzying blur, meaningless to me but significant to Malfor.

"Excellent," he says smoothly, his mood shifting instantly. The sudden approval does nothing to calm my frayed nerves. *"Now, we need to—"*

The door handle jiggles. Voices approach.

My blood turns to ice. I'm trapped.

"Someone's coming," I whisper urgently into the phone. "What do I do?"

"Hide, you idiot." Malfor snarls. *"Don't get caught."*

NINETEEN

Sophia

I yank out the thumb drive, my heart thundering in my chest. Eyes darting wildly, I search for a hiding spot. The server banks offer no cover, just endless rows of blinking lights.

Footsteps echo closer. Panic rises in my throat.

There—a maintenance closet. I lunge for it, wrenching the door open. I squeeze inside. The space is tiny, crammed with cleaning supplies. The door clicks shut just as I hear voices enter the room.

"Did you see the game last night?" A man's voice, casual and unaware.

"Nah, missed it. How'd it go?" Another voice responds.

I curl into myself, willing my breathing to slow. The closet is stifling. The scent of chemicals burns my nostrils. Sweat trickles down my back, my shirt sticking uncomfortably to my skin.

Minutes crawl by like hours. My muscles cramp, protests ignored. I dare not move.

In the darkness, faces flash before my eyes. Luke, my beautiful boy, his future hanging by a thread. Blake's trust is a warm blanket I don't deserve. Jenna's friendship is a lifeline I'm slowly severing.

Guilt twists my stomach. I'm betraying them all, every moment, every breath.

The voices drone on, oblivious to my presence. I check my watch. Fifteen minutes. Thirty. An hour ticks by.

The Guardian Grind will be bustling now. Jenna will be wondering where I am. Another betrayal to add to my growing list.

Finally, after what feels like an eternity, the techs leave. I wait another agonizing five minutes before creeping out, muscles screaming in protest.

I retrace my steps and climb the stairs. Each footfall is a countdown to discovery. At the ground floor, I pause, taking a deep breath before pushing the door open.

The guards from earlier are still at their post. The taller one spots me, waving cheerfully.

"Enjoy your tour?" he calls out.

I force a smile, praying they can't see how I'm trembling. "Yeah, it was… illuminating."

"You look a bit flushed," the shorter guard observes. "Those VR sims can be a real workout, right?"

I laugh weakly. "Something like that. Thanks again."

I hurry past, the weight of their gazes heavy on my back. Outside, the fresh air does little to calm my nerves.

The flip phone buzzes. I answer with shaking hands.

"Are you out?"

"Yes, sir."

"Took long enough," Malfor snarls. *"Get to the HR building. Now."*

I scan the sprawling Guardian HQ campus. The HR building sits at the far end, impossibly distant.

A row of golf carts catches my eye. I approach one, Blake's badge still clutched in my hand from earlier. Without thinking, I swipe it over the cart's sensor. It chirps to life, the display lighting up. I hop in, my movements jerky with unease.

I shove Blake's badge deep into my pocket and grip the steering wheel.

The cart hums beneath me as I set off, buildings blurring past—the training center, the mess hall, the dormitories. Agents and staff move about their day, oblivious to the betrayer in their midst. Each familiar face I pass is another knife twist in my gut.

I park at the HR building, its imposing facade looming over me. I've only been here once before—Blake took me to get my badge.

Taking a deep breath, I square my shoulders and approach the entrance. Before I step inside, I pull out the phone.

"I'm at HR," I whisper.

"Good," Malfor's voice is cold. *"We're going to clone that badge."*

"Clone it?"

"Yes, you idiot. We're going to copy Blake's access onto your badge. It'll be in their server room. You should know how to do this by now."

"Okay." His arrogance and cruelty make me flinch.

Inside, a bored receptionist looks up. "Can I help you?"

"I-I need to update my employee information," I stammer, forcing a smile.

"Down there. Forms are on the desk." She waves vaguely toward a hallway.

I head in the direction she indicates. Once out of sight, I scan for stairs. The server room must be in the basement, like before.

I find a stairwell and descend, each step heavy with dread. The basement is quiet and dim. I wander, searching for anything that looks like a server room.

There—a heavy door with a card reader. I pull out Blake's badge, swiping it with trembling fingers.

Nothing.

Another swipe of the badge. Green light. The lock disengages. I slip inside, surrounded once again by humming machines and blinking lights. My heart races as I pull out the phone.

"I'm in the server room," I whisper.

"About time." Malfor's tone is sharp, impatience dripping from every word. *"Find a terminal. I'll give you the code to input. This will prepare the system for the clone."*

My vision blurs as I stare at the screen, the characters swimming before my eyes. How long have we been at this? Minutes? Hours? Time seems to stretch and warp around me.

My shoulders ache from tension, and my fingers cramp from the careful keystrokes. Each mistake sends a jolt of panic through me, and Malfor's impatience is a constant threat.

"I-I'm sorry," I stammer after another error. "Let me try again."

"You're trying my patience, girl. Better get it right this time."

The pressure builds with each passing moment. My breathing becomes shallow, and my chest is tight with anxiety. I force myself to focus, to shut out everything but the code and Malfor's voice.

Finally, after an eternity, I input the last character correctly. I slump, utterly drained. My hand shakes as I reach for the phone, awaiting the next command.

"Good." Malfor's approval does nothing to ease the knot in my stomach. *"Now, onto the next step. You need to demagnetize your badge. Hold it against the server tower for ten seconds. The electromagnetic field will do the job."*

My hand shakes as I press my badge against the cool metal of the server. One Mississippi, two Mississippi…

"Done," I whisper.

"Good. Now go back upstairs to HR. Tell them your badge isn't working. Say it's demagnetized. They'll reissue it, and when they do, that code will clone Blake's access onto yours."

The plan clicks into place. My stomach churns. "I understand."

"Don't screw this up." Malfor's voice cuts through the line, cold and final, before he hangs up.

I take a deep breath, pocketing both badges. Straightening my clothes, I head back upstairs, rehearsing my lie.

At the HR desk, a different person greets me. "Can I help you?"

I feign frustration, holding out my badge. "My card's not working. I think it got demagnetized somehow."

The HR rep nods sympathetically. "No problem, happens sometimes. Let's get you a new one."

I watch anxiously as they swipe my badge through a machine. A few keystrokes, a whir of electronics, and then they hand me back a seemingly identical card.

"There you go. All set."

I force a smile. "Thanks so much."

Walking away, the weight of what I've just done settles over me. In my hand, I now hold the key to all of Guardian HQ—and take another step deeper into betrayal.

"It's done." I grip my new badge tightly, feeling every bit the traitor.

"Good. Now get to work before they notice you're late," Malfor says, satisfaction coloring his tone.

Late? It's nearly two in the afternoon. I'm way past late, but the line goes dead. He has no further use for me today.

I hope.

I hurry across the grounds to The Guardian Grind. The lunch rush is in full swing. Jenna's eyes widen as I burst through the door.

"There you are." Relief and concern war in her expression. "I was worried sick."

I force a smile, tying my apron with trembling hands. "Sorry, I-I had some paperwork to fill out. HR stuff."

The lie tastes bitter. As I move behind the counter, the weight of what I've done settles over me. Each smile I give and each order I take feels like a betrayal of everything I hold dear.

And always, always, the fear for my son's life drives me forward. I'm trapped, a puppet dancing to Malfor's cruel tune. With each passing moment, the strings only tighten.

The day stretches endlessly, a blur of coffee orders and forced smiles. By closing time, exhaustion weighs on me like a physical thing. I drag myself home, knowing Blake will be waiting.

The thought of facing him, of lying to his face, twists my stomach in knots. But what else can I do? There's no way out.

When I walk in, Blake's face lights up when he sees me. That smile—so open, so trusting—hits me like a knife to the heart.

I'm Sophia, the betrayer.

Sophia the liar.

Sophia the traitor.

I take a deep breath, ready to play my part once more.

"Rough day?" He pulls me into an embrace.

I nod against his chest, not trusting my voice. His warmth surrounds me, and for a moment, I let myself pretend. Pretend this is real and that I'm not betraying him with every breath.

But as we settle in for the evening, Malfor's voice echoes in my head. *"Remember, you belong to me. Always."*

As we lie tangled together in bed that night, I cling to Blake tighter than usual. His hands roam my body, igniting a fire that momentarily burns away the guilt and fear.

"You okay?" Blake murmurs, his voice husky with concern and desire.

"I'm good. Just tired." I kiss him, pouring all my conflicted emotions into the gesture.

I curl closer to Blake, seeking comfort even as guilt gnaws at me. How long can I keep this up? How much more can I betray before it destroys me completely?

When he takes control, his commands soft but firm, I surrender gladly. For a little while, I forget the weight of my betrayal and lose myself in the safety of his dominance.

Once Blake's breathing evens out, I carefully disentangle myself from his embrace. The warmth of his skin lingers on mine, a bitter-sweet reminder of the connection we've just shared. Quietly, I slide out of bed, every movement deliberate and cautious, as if afraid the air might betray me.

I retrieve his badge from where I hid it earlier. The cool metal bites against my palm as if it carries the weight of my guilt. With a silent breath, I crouch down beside his side of the bed.

I hesitate for a fraction of a second.

But there's no going back. I've already committed the worst sin.

I slide the badge under the bed, pushing it just far enough so it's not immediately visible but easy to find. My heart pounds, each beat a countdown to when Blake will discover it.

When he'll wonder why we missed it before.

I straighten slowly, taking one last look at the hidden badge, my heart aching with the weight of my deceit.

The night deepens around me, wrapping me in its cold embrace as I slip back under the covers beside Blake. Sleep, however, remains elusive, chased away by the gnawing guilt and the ever-present fear for my son's life.

Tomorrow only brings more lies and more betrayal.

The following day, I wake early, the weight of yesterday still pressing down on me. I slide out of bed carefully, trying not to disturb Blake. I need a moment to clear my head, so I head to the bathroom and start the shower, letting the steam fill the small space.

The water is warm against my skin, but it does little to wash away the anxiety clinging to me.

As I stand under the spray, Blake stirs in the bedroom. The soft rustle of sheets tells me he's getting up, and my heart skips a beat.

Suddenly, he mutters, "What the hell…" His voice is low, laced with confusion.

My stomach tightens, knowing he's found the badge.

I quickly finish, wrapping myself in a towel, and step out of the bathroom just in time to see Blake holding his missing badge. His expression is one of confusion mixed with a hint of suspicion.

"Morning, sleepyhead." My tone is light, but there's a flicker of nervousness I try to hide. "Is that your missing badge?"

"Yeah," he replies, still staring at the badge. "It was under the bed. We must have missed it somehow."

My pulse races as I force a smile. "I told you it would turn up eventually."

He looks at me, his eyes searching mine for something, but I can't tell if he's found what he's looking for. There's a tension in the air, a moment of doubt that I can't quite shake off.

I step closer, placing a hand on his arm. "It's a relief you found it."

He nods slowly, but I can see the uncertainty lingering in his expression. "Yeah, I guess so."

I lean in and kiss his cheek, trying to push away the growing fear that he knows more than he's letting on. "Let's not think about it too much. It's just a badge, right?"

Blake's arms wrap around me, and for a moment, I relax into his embrace. But the knot in my stomach remains.

I hate lying to him—deceiving him like this.

TWENTY

Sophia

Autumn firmly settles over Guardian HQ, bringing a chill that mirrors the dread in my heart.

The usually vibrant California sun seems to recoil from my traitorous activities, shrouding itself behind a thick veil of gray clouds, turning its face away from my betrayal.

Day after day, the sun struggles to break through, its weak rays barely penetrating the ashen sky. When it does manage to peek through, it feels accusatory, its harsh light exposing my every move. I shrink from its gaze, seeking the shadows as I go about my clandestine tasks.

Even the usually temperate climate has turned against me. An unseasonable chill permeates the air, seeping into my bones. The cold is a constant reminder of the warmth I'm betraying, of the heat of Blake's embrace that I'll soon leave behind.

As I move through Guardian HQ, planting devices and inputting codes, the damp mist clings to me, much like the guilt that refuses to let me go. Fog rolls in, obscuring familiar landmarks, making the place I've come to call home feel alien and hostile.

In this dreary, sun-starved world, I've become a shadow myself —a traitor moving unseen, my actions hidden by the gloom that seems to judge me. In its relentless gray misery, the weather is both my accomplice and my accuser, covering my misdeeds while constantly reminding me of the brightness I'm leaving behind.

Each day blurs into the next, a haze of coffee orders and stolen moments of sabotage. The drizzle that has become near-constant feels like nature's silent weeping for my betrayal.

Every time my phone buzzes with new instructions, my stomach clenches, but I obey. I call in sick to work, my voice hoarse as I lie to Jenna. Then, I sneak into various buildings across the Guardian HQ complex—the damp air clings to me, as suffocating as the guilt weighing me down.

I plant devices and input codes as directed; each act is another nail in the coffin of the life I've come to love.

My instructions appear as if by magic—in my locker at work, slipped under the apartment door, and once even tucked into my apron at The Guardian Grind.

I don't know who's passing them to me, but the thought that Malfor has other operatives here sends a chill down my spine. I wish I could warn Blake about this security breach, but the irony of my position—the biggest breach of all—keeps me silent.

Each night, I return to Blake's arms, hating myself for the lies, but unable to give up the warmth and love I've found with him. As we cuddle on the couch, the throw blanket wrapped around us against the autumn chill, I try to memorize every detail—the sound of his heartbeat, the feeling of his arms around me, the way his laugh rumbles through his chest.

With each act of betrayal, these precious moments slowly slip away, replaced by the cold reality of my true purpose.

The next day dawns gray and misty, matching my mood as I head to work at The Guardian Grind. As I tie my apron, my fingers brush against something tucked in the pocket. My heart sinks as I discreetly pull out a small envelope. Inside are several tiny devices—listening bugs—and a handwritten note with instructions.

Throughout my shift, I move around the café, planting the bugs in inconspicuous places. Under tables, behind picture frames, and even in the potted plants.

I slip into the cafeteria during my break, continuing my clandestine task. The constant chatter and clinking of dishes mask the sound of my movements as I strategically place the bugs around the room.

As I'm finishing up, my phone buzzes. I duck into an empty hallway to answer it.

"*Is it done?*" Malfor's cold voice slithers through the line.

I swallow hard. "Yes. I placed the devices in The Guardian Grind and the cafeteria as you instructed."

"*Excellent.*" His tone shifts, a hint of glee creeping in. "*You've done well, my pet. Tomorrow's your last day there.*"

The words strike me hard, nearly knocking me off balance. My legs buckle, and I have to brace myself against the wall to keep from collapsing.

"T-tomorrow?" I choke out, my voice barely a whisper.

"*Did you think you'd get to play house forever? It's time to come home, where you belong.*" Malfor's cruel laughter echoes through the phone. "*I can't wait to see you again. I bet you're excited to come home to me, aren't you?*"

The thought makes my skin crawl. "Of course," I lie, my voice barely above a whisper.

"*Good girl.*" Malfor's voice drips with satisfaction. "*I have so many plans for you when you return. You've pleased me greatly.*"

I want to ask about Luke, to beg for confirmation that my son is safe, but the words stick in my throat.

"Thank you, sir."

His words send a chill down my spine. I know what awaits me—pain, torture, manipulation. An existence so bleak that, for a fleeting moment, I consider ending it all right here. One final act of defiance.

"*Sleep well, my dear.*" His voice drips with false tenderness. "*Tomorrow, you'll be back where you belong.*"

I take a deep breath, steeling myself for what's to come. Luke needs me. As long as he's in danger, I have to endure. I have to survive.

The world spins around me.

Tomorrow.

My last day of freedom, of happiness, of love.

The last day I'll see Blake's smile, feel Jenna's friendly pat on the shoulder, or hear the laughter of the regulars at The Guardian Grind.

For a moment, a wild impulse seizes me. I could run to Blake right now and confess everything. Beg for his protection, for his forgiveness. Tell him about everything I've done, even the parts I don't understand. Surely he could help, could save me from this nightmare.

But then Luke's face flashes in my mind. My beautiful boy held hostage by this monster. The thought of him suffering because of my weakness is unbearable.

"I'll be ready." I'm surprised by the steadiness in my voice.

As I end the call, I slide down the wall, hugging my knees to my chest. Tears stream down my face as the full weight of my situation crashes over me. Tomorrow, I will lose everything. Everything except the crushing responsibility of keeping my son safe.

I allow myself this one moment of weakness, of despair. Then, wiping my eyes, I rise, squaring my shoulders and standing tall. I have one day left. One day to memorize every detail of the life I'm leaving behind. One day to gather strength for the ordeal ahead.

For Luke, I will endure.

For Luke, I will survive.

For Luke, I will destroy any chance of happiness I may have had.

Bile rises in my throat. I wish I could tell Blake. That I could let him know the truth without putting Luke in danger.

Slowly, an idea takes root. I can't come out and tell him everything—Malfor would destroy Luke in an instant. But maybe... Maybe I could leave subtle hints, breadcrumbs he could follow to unravel everything I've done.

It's a risk, a dangerous game, but it might be the only way to lessen the damage I've caused without tipping Malfor off.

TWENTY-ONE

Blake

———

The next few days pass in a blur of activity. We make slow but steady progress on the Greaves case, each small lead bringing us incrementally closer to our goal. But there's an undercurrent of unease running through HQ.

It starts with small things. A door that should be locked is found open. A security camera glitches for a few seconds. Nothing major, nothing that can't be explained away by human error or technical hiccups, but it's enough to set my teeth on edge.

Everyone senses something's off, even if we can't quite put our finger on what it is.

By Friday morning, the strain is starting to show. Dark circles under eyes, shoulders hunched with invisible weight, nerves frayed to breaking point.

It's Gabe who finally breaks the silence as we're gearing up for another day of chasing shadows.

"You know what we need?" he announces, slapping his locker shut with more force than necessary. "Coffee. Real coffee, not the swill from the break room."

Walt grunts in agreement, rubbing his temples. "Guardian Grind?"

The suggestion is met with unanimous nods. Even Ethan, usually all business, perks up at the idea.

"Fifteen minutes." He checks his watch. "Then we hit the ground running."

The short walk to The Guardian Grind is a welcome respite from the oppressive atmosphere of HQ. The crisp morning air clears some of the fog from my mind, and I take deeper breaths, savoring the hint of autumn in the breeze.

The tension in my shoulders eases with each step toward the Guardian Grind. My steps quicken involuntarily, a spark of excitement igniting in my chest.

It's a rare treat, getting to see Sophia during the day like this. With the relentless operational tempo at Guardian HQ, our schedules rarely align outside of our evenings together.

The thought of her smile, of catching a glimpse of her in her element, sends a warmth through me that has nothing to do with the promise of coffee. It's these stolen moments, these unexpected intersections of our lives, that make everything else feel more bearable.

I straighten my shirt, running a hand through my hair. Gabe notices, of course, a knowing smirk playing on his lips. But I can't bring myself to care about the ribbing I'm sure to receive later. The prospect of seeing Sophia is worth it.

It's still a marvel to me how she affects me like this.

I push open the door to The Guardian Grind, and immediately, the rich aroma of freshly brewed coffee floods my senses. The chime above the door mingles with the soft hum of conversation and the rhythmic whir of the espresso machine.

"Well, if it isn't Charlie team." Jenna glances up from behind the counter as Gabe strides over, claiming our usual corner table with a cocky grin.

"Hey, aren't you going to order?" I trail after him, unable to resist calling out.

"They know what I like." Gabe doesn't even bother turning around. He just lifts a hand, waving off the question with a flick of his fingers.

"Guess that means the usual for you guys too?" Jenna raises an eyebrow, amusement dancing in her eyes as she wipes her hands on a towel.

"Exactly. That's what happens when you tip well." Gabe drops into his seat, leaning back like he owns the place.

"Or maybe we just feel sorry for you." Jenna chuckles, already moving to the counter.

"Nah, it's my cheery disposition you love." Gabe smirks, not missing a beat.

"You're something else, man." I shake my head, exchanging glances with the rest of the team as they start filtering in.

"What can I say? You get what you give." Gabe crosses his arms, grinning as he watches Jenna prep our drinks.

"One day, we're going to surprise you." Jenna sets Gabe's drink down first.

"Liquid gold." Gabe picks up his cup, raising it in a mock toast. He takes a sip. "Yup, best cup of Joe in the world."

I glance around the café, a nagging thought pulling at me. "Where's Sophia? She usually runs the front counter."

Jenna's smile falters for just a second before she recovers. "Oh, she wasn't feeling well today. Took off early to rest."

"That's not like her. I'll check in on her later." A flicker of concern settles in my gut, but I nod, trying to brush it off.

"I'm sure she's fine, just needs a little rest." Jenna busies herself with the next order, her movements just a bit too quick, too practiced.

The words are meant to be reassuring, but something about them doesn't sit right.

I slide into the seat across from Gabe, the worn leather of the chair creaking slightly under my weight.

"You two gossiping like old ladies again?" Walt joins us, his heavy footsteps announcing his arrival before he even speaks.

"You're just jealous you weren't invited to the tea party," Gabe quips, dodging the sugar packet Walt tosses at his head.

The playful banter is interrupted by the arrival of our drinks, carried by a familiar face I haven't seen in a while.

"Rebel?" I blink in surprise. "When did you start working here?"

Rebel sets down our drinks, a small smile playing on her lips. "Just started this week. Jenna needed the help, and I needed… Well, something to do."

Ethan appears behind her, his hand coming to rest on the small of her back. The gesture is casual and intimate, speaking volumes about their relationship.

Rebel's story isn't so different from Sophia's—both were rescued, and both are trying to find their place in this new world.

"The Grind's been good for both Sophia and Rebel. It's given them something meaningful, you know?"

Ethan waits until Rebel is out of earshot before leaning in, his voice low. "She's frustrated. Nothing new on her sister's kid, but she hasn't given up hope."

Rebel's sister, Violet, was forced into surrogacy, but after delivering the child, she managed to escape. She called Rebel for help, but before she could say much, Rebel heard a commotion over the phone—Violet was recaptured and killed. She's been searching for her sister's kid ever since.

We all know the odds, the grim reality of what happens to girls who disappear into the world of human trafficking, let alone any children they might conceive. Hope is a powerful thing, and sometimes it's all we have.

Rigel strides over, a rare spark of excitement lighting up his usually stoic face, cutting through the tension like a breath of fresh air.

"You guys have got to try the new cinnamon roll. It's like heaven in pastry form." His enthusiasm is almost contagious as he waves the plate in front of us.

"High praise coming from our resident robot," Gabe teases, but he's already signaling Rebel for an order.

As we settle into our usual rhythm of conversation and caffeine consumption, it's funny how quickly The Guardian Grind has become an integral part of our routine. It's more than just a coffee shop—it's a haven, a place where we can forget the weight of our responsibilities and just be.

The rich, spicy scent of cinnamon fills the air as Rebel brings over Gabe's pastry. The conversation flows easily, punctuated by laughter and the occasional good-natured insult. For a moment, it feels like any other day.

But the illusion is shattered by the sudden, insistent beeping of our pagers. Ethan pulls his out first, his face growing serious as he reads the message.

"All Guardian teams are being called in for a briefing." His voice cuts through the chatter. "Looks urgent."

TWENTY-TWO

Blake

The relaxed atmosphere evaporates instantly, replaced by a tense alertness that's become all too familiar.

The bright morning sunshine contrasts with the somber mood as we make our way back to HQ. The usual banter is subdued, and each of us is lost in our own thoughts about what this urgent briefing could mean.

As we make our way through the building, the familiar security protocols feel more oppressive than usual. The weight of my recovered badge seems heavier in my pocket, a constant reminder of the unease plaguing me.

When we reach the conference room, the air buzzes with tension. I take my seat among the other Guardians. Alpha, Bravo, and Charlie teams are all present, an unusual gathering that speaks to the seriousness of the situation. Delta team would be here, except they're out on a mission with the FBI.

Sam stands at the front of the room, his posture rigid. CJ paces behind him, his usual jovial demeanor replaced by a grim frown. Mitzy's fingers blur across the keyboard, her focus unbroken, while Forest leans against the wall, his arms crossed.

"Alright, let's get started." Sam's voice cuts through the murmur of conversation. The room falls silent. "As you're all aware, we've been experiencing some irregularities in our security systems."

Mitzy looks up from her laptop. "Irregularities is putting it mildly. We're talking about a potential full-scale breach."

A collective intake of breath sweeps through the room. My muscles tense, the weight of the situation settling on my shoulders.

"What kind of breach are we talking about?" Max, the leader of Alpha team, leans forward in his chair.

"That's the thing. It doesn't look like any breach we've seen before. It's... subtle. Almost undetectable." Mitzy's hands move swiftly over the keyboard, her gaze locked on the screen.

"But you did detect something." Brady, Bravo team's leader, points out.

"Barely," Forest chimes in, his voice grave. "And only because we've been expecting it."

CJ stops his pacing. "We've had doors unlocking themselves, security cameras glitching, and some odd data transfers that we can't account for."

"Why were you looking for a breach in the first place?" Max leans back in his chair, frowning.

"We've been on high alert since we rescued Mia," Sam says. "That's why we initiated Protocol Zero—it's not just about locking down Guardian personnel, but also reinforcing security measures across our systems. We've taken every precaution to protect against any potential breaches."

"We noticed a sudden increase in data requests." Mitzy doesn't miss a beat, pulling up a graph on the screen. "At first glance, they looked legit, but the volume and timing didn't sit right. That's when we knew something was up.

"And then there was a network traffic spike." Mitzy pulls more data. "We couldn't trace it back to scheduled activities, which made us dig deeper."

"All of this happened while we had issues with a security system update." Forest's gaze sweeps across the room as he folds his arms. "It failed to install properly, and we were worried it might have been compromised during the process."

My mind races, thinking back to my missing badge. Could it be connected?

"Any idea who's behind it?" Ethan asks, his fingers drumming a restless rhythm on the table.

"That's what we're here to figure out." Sam shakes his head. "We need ideas, theories, anything that might help us understand what we're dealing with."

"Could it be an inside job?" The question slips out before I can stop it. The room falls silent, all eyes turning to me.

"That's a heavy accusation, Blake. What makes you say that?" CJ's eyebrows shoot up.

I swallow hard, aware of the weight of my words. "Just—the level of access they seem to have. The subtlety of it all. It feels like someone who knows our systems."

Mitzy nods slowly. "He's not wrong. The intruder navigates our security like they built it themselves."

"But who?" Walt from my team speaks up. "We all go through rigorous background checks. And the loyalty of everyone in this room is beyond question."

"Is it?" Brady's quiet voice carries clearly across the room. "We've been infiltrated before."

Rigel shifts in his seat, his brow furrowed. "I remember Protocol Zero being activated when we rescued Mia, but that whole mission was a blur. Can someone remind me what exactly was involved? I wasn't fully briefed afterward, and it feels relevant now."

CJ's expression softens, understanding the chaos Rigel must have experienced during that time. "Sure thing, Rigel. Protocol Zero is more than just a lockdown. We isolated key personnel, scrambled communication lines, and rebooted the system from a clean backup."

Mitzy nods, picking up where CJ left off. "We also cut off all external contact and ran every team member through psychological evaluations, looking for any signs of coercion or manipulation."

Forest leans forward, his voice steady. "Behavioral audits, asset freezes, financial monitoring—we tore everything apart looking for breaches. And when we rebuilt, we didn't stick to a predictable layout or routine. Access routes were changed, key areas were relocated, and entry points were reassigned."

Sam adds, "We also enhanced physical security—biometric access, armed patrols, random schedules. Every piece of equipment was wiped and reprogrammed. We didn't just change the locks; we built an entirely new house."

Forest's gaze sweeps the room. "And for the most critical missions, we activated Ghost Protocol. Operatives went completely off-grid. Their identities were erased from every system. Only a handful of us knew they even existed."

Rigel nods slowly, the reminder settling in. "Got it. So if someone's breached us now, they've either found a way around all of that… or were never fully locked out in the first place."

The tension in the room ratchets up a notch.

Rigel leans forward, the concern evident in his voice. "Why not just activate Protocol Zero again? If we've been breached, shouldn't we lock everything down like before?"

Mitzy shakes her head, her fingers tapping lightly on the table. "We've considered it, but activating Protocol Zero now is like waving a giant red flag. Whoever's behind this will know we're onto them. Right now, we're monitoring the situation, minimizing data leaks, and trying to trace their movements. If we lock down, we lose the element of surprise—and any chance to catch them in the act."

I frown, trying to piece it all together. "What about the pattern of the breaches? Is there any rhyme or reason to which systems are being hit?" My gaze shifts from Mitzy to Sam.

"That's the odd thing." Mitzy turns back to her laptop, pulling up a series of diagrams on the large screen at the front of the room. "The intrusions seem... random. Almost like they're testing our defenses, probing for weaknesses."

"Or creating distractions," Gabe mutters beside me.

I turn to him. "What do you mean?"

He shrugs. "Just thinking out loud. But what if all these small breaches are meant to keep us looking in the wrong direction while something bigger is happening?"

The room falls silent as we consider this possibility. It's a chilling thought that makes a disturbing amount of sense.

"If that's the case," Max says slowly, "what's the real target?"

"Or who." CJ runs a hand over his face. "That's the million-dollar question, isn't it?"

"Okay, let's break this down." Sam's deep voice cuts through the tension. "What do we know for certain?"

Mitzy ticks off points on her fingers. "We've had unauthorized access to multiple secure areas. Data transfers that we can't account for. And a series of small but persistent glitches in our security systems."

"And it all started when?" A nagging feeling grows in the pit of my stomach.

Forest consults a tablet. "The first anomaly was detected a few days ago, but it could have been going on longer without us noticing."

Right around the time I lost my badge. The coincidence is too glaring to ignore, but I can't bring myself to voice my suspicions.

Not yet.

"What about external factors?" Brady asks. "Any unusual activity from known hostile entities?"

Sam shakes his head. "Nothing out of the ordinary. If anything, it's been quieter than usual on that front."

"Which could be suspicious in itself," Ethan points out.

The discussion continues, theories flying back and forth. Each possibility seems more far-fetched than the last, but none of them feel quite right. It's like we're all dancing around the edges of something, unable to see the full picture.

I clear my throat, drawing everyone's attention. "What if..." I hesitate, feeling the weight of their stares. "What if this isn't about stealing information or sabotage? What if it's about planting something?"

"Like a virus? Or a backdoor?" Mitzy's eyes widen.

"Something that would give them ongoing access. Or worse, control."

The idea that someone could be laying the groundwork for a

larger attack is concerning. Cyber warfare isn't my thing, but Mitzy and her crew are experts when it comes to battling it out in the digital realm.

"It fits," Forest says slowly. "The random pattern, the subtle intrusions. They could be setting up multiple points of entry."

"Or exit," CJ adds grimly.

Sam straightens, his face set in determination. "Alright, this gives us something to work with. Mitzy, I want your team to start looking for any unauthorized additions to our systems. Forest, work on strengthening our firewalls and intrusion detection. Something connects everything. We have to find it."

"We're already on it." Mitzy tugs on the tips of her psychedelic hair. "Right now, it's random. Nothing connects."

"As for the rest of you," Sam addresses the Guardian teams. "I want increased patrols. Physical and digital. Anything out of the ordinary, no matter how small, gets reported immediately."

"What about ongoing missions?" Max asks. "Do we pull back?"

"We can't afford to. Whatever this is, we can't let it disrupt our operations." CJ shakes his head. "That might be exactly what they want."

Sam leans forward, his voice steady. "Maintain your current assignments but be on high alert. And absolutely no discussion of this situation outside this room. We don't know who we can trust."

As the meeting breaks up, I hang back, my mind whirling. The timing of my lost badge and the start of these intrusions can't be a coincidence. The possibility Sophia might be involved gnaws at me, but it's a truth I'm not willing to consider—not yet.

"Blake?" Ethan's voice breaks through my thoughts. "You okay?"

"Yeah, just processing." I force a smile.

"It's a lot to take in. But we'll figure this out. We always do."

Before I tell the team anything, I need to talk with Sophia. It has to be a coincidence, and I trust her.

I have to trust her.

Because if I can't, everything we've built together is a lie. That's a possibility I'm not ready to face. Not yet.

I'm wound as tight as a spring when I make it home that evening. Sophia immediately picks up on my mood, her brow furrowing with concern as I shrug off my jacket.

"Tough day?" Her voice is soft and cautious.

Words stick in my throat, and I nod.

Sophia approaches slowly like she's dealing with a wild animal, her movements careful and measured. When her hands come to rest on my chest, the warmth of her touch seeps through my shirt, grounding me.

Calming the storm inside me.

I need to talk to her. I need to clear this gnawing doubt eating at me.

But I'm not ready. Not yet.

"What do you need?" Her eyes search mine, filled with concern and something more profound—trust, maybe.

Love, even.

The question lingers between us, heavy with unspoken fears. I take a deep breath, feeling some of my tension drain away under her steady gaze.

"You," I say simply, the word barely a whisper. "Just you."

I'll wait until morning. There's no rush. I need time. One more night before everything changes.

There's no going back once I ask the questions burning in my mind. So tonight, I'll hold her close, savor the feeling of her warmth, and enjoy her presence beside me.

Something shifts in Sophia's expression, a mixture of understanding and anticipation. She takes a step back, her posture changing subtly.

"Then take what you need." Her voice drops to a husky whisper. "I'm yours, Sir."

The honorific sends a jolt through me, igniting something primal and possessive. My fingers thread into her hair, pulling her close. The heat between us sparks to life.

"Say it again." My voice is low, a demand wrapped in dark desire.

"I'm yours, Sir," Sophia repeats, her breath hitching. "Always."

What follows is a dance of dominance and submission, a give-and-take that we've been perfecting over the weeks. I guide Sophia to the bedroom, my commands soft but firm. She follows willingly, and her trust in me is absolute.

We don't need elaborate scenes or equipment. It's all about the energy between us, the power exchange that happens with a look, a touch, a whispered word. I push Sophia, watching in awe as she surrenders control, finding freedom in her submission.

Afterward, we lie tangled together, the sweat cooling on our skin as the remnants of our passion linger in the air. Sophia's head rests on my chest, her fingers drawing lazy, soothing patterns on my stomach.

The quiet is heavy, filled with our breaths gradually slowing down, echoing our satiated hunger. Beneath that, the weight of my suspicions presses down, making the silence unbearable.

TWENTY-THREE

Sophia

Finally, the morning I've been dreading arrives.

I wake earlier than usual, my heart heavy with what I have to do. For a long moment, I sit on the edge of the bed, watching Blake sleep. In the soft, gray morning light filtering through the rain-streaked window, he looks younger, unburdened by the weight of his responsibilities. I want nothing more than to curl up beside him and pretend that this life we've built is real, that I'm not about to shatter it all.

But I can't. I have my orders.

I go through my morning routine mechanically, my mind elsewhere. When Blake stirs, I'm already dressed, perched on the edge of the bed with a forced smile.

"Morning, sleepyhead." I lean down to kiss him, trying to memorize the feeling of his lips against mine. "I've got to open the shop early this morning."

Blake nods, still half-asleep. "Okay, be safe."

Those words, so casually spoken, nearly break me. I want to confess everything, to beg for his protection, but the fear of what might happen if I do keeps me silent.

As Blake drifts back to sleep, I wander through the apartment. My heart breaks with each step. There's nothing to pack—anything I take with me will be removed and discarded.

Still, I can't help pausing over certain items. The sweater Blake bought me on our first real date still carries the faint scent of his cologne. The photo of us at the Guardian Grind's opening, our smiles frozen in a happier time.

Each one is a memory I want to cling to but have to leave behind.

I pick up the framed photo from the dresser, my throat tight as I look at our smiling faces. With a shaky hand, I place it face down. I can't bear to see it as I leave.

My phone buzzes, a stark reminder of why I'm doing this. I check the message, my heart sinking at the instructions.

It's time to go.

I take one last look around the apartment, trying to memorize every detail. The coffee mug Blake always uses is still in the sink from last night. The throw blanket on the couch where we spent so many evenings cuddled up together is neatly folded. His favorite book, dog-eared and worn, rests on the nightstand.

Tears blur my vision as I clutch the doorframe, my heart shattering with every passing second. My legs feel like lead, and I fight the urge to collapse onto the floor. I trace my fingers over the doorframe, the familiar grooves a painful reminder of our time together. With every ounce of strength, I take a deep breath, feeling my chest constrict.

With a trembling hand, I walk out, closing the door softly behind me. The click of the lock feels like the slamming of a coffin lid, sealing away a part of my soul. I linger for a moment, my heart breaking, unable to move forward but knowing I must. The emptiness swallows me whole as I step into the cold, harsh reality waiting on the other side.

I take a golf cart and drive toward the front gate of Guardian HQ. The drizzle turns into a steady rain, mirroring the turmoil in my heart, as if the sky itself is mourning my departure. Tears blur my vision, and I choke back a sob, my hands gripping the steering wheel so tightly that my knuckles turn white.

Memories flood my mind, each one a stab of pain. Jenna, who became a true friend, always there with a comforting word or a shared laugh. The regulars at The Guardian Grind, whose orders I memorized, their familiar faces now a part of my routine. And Blake…

God, Blake.

I will never forget his smile, his touch, and the way he made me feel safe and cherished.

A deep, wrenching sob escapes my throat, and I struggle to see through the torrent of tears. My chest heaves with the effort to breathe, each sob tearing through me like a jagged blade. The rain pounds against the golf cart's roof, drowning out the sound of my cries, but does nothing to soothe the ache inside.

I barely maintain control of the cart as I drive, my vision clouded by the relentless downpour and an endless stream of tears. The gate looms ahead, a stark reminder that I'm leaving everything behind.

Another sob shakes me, and I pull over, unable to go any further. I bury my face in my hands, the weight of my actions crashing down on me with unbearable force.

The thought of never seeing Blake again is too much to bear, and I let the grief consume me, the rain mixing with my tears in a symphony of sorrow and loss.

At the gate, I abandon the golf cart as instructed. The guard barely glances at me as I pass through, with no idea that he's letting a traitor walk free.

Outside the gates of Guardian HQ, a nondescript car waits for me, its windshield wipers fighting a losing battle against the rain. The driver's face is unfamiliar, but the cold efficiency with which he ushers me into the back seat is all too familiar.

As we drive away, I allow myself one last look. Through the rain-streaked window, Guardian HQ blurs and fades like a dream slipping away upon waking. The realization that I might never return hits me like a punch to the gut.

"I'm sorry," I whisper, though there's no one to hear my apology. "I'm so, so sorry."

I draw my arms and knees up to my chest, curling into a ball on the seat. Rocking myself gently, I try to find some semblance of comfort in the self-embrace. Each sway is a silent attempt to soothe the storm raging inside me, but the tears keep falling, mingling with the rain that drums against the window.

The car turns a corner, and Guardian HQ disappears from view. With it goes the life I'd dared to dream I could have; the happiness I'd foolishly thought I'd earned.

Ahead lies raw fear and the crushing weight of what I've done. I know exactly what's waiting for me—abuse, manipulation, punishment, and a return to invisible chains.

Every turn of the wheels brings me closer to the men who abducted me, to a life where freedom is a distant memory.

I close my eyes and allow myself one last moment of weakness. In my mind, I see Blake's smile and feel the warmth of his embrace. I lock those memories away, deep in my heart, where they can't hurt me—where Malfor can't use them against me.

It's time to become an empty shell again. To bury Sophia and extinguish any trace of humanity they could exploit. I must be nothing—a hollow vessel—to survive the dehumanization awaiting me. However, a small part of me that learned to love and be loved in return will always belong to Blake and the life we almost had.

The car speeds on, carrying me away from everything I've come to cherish, but the echo of Blake's voice, the ghost of his touch, the memory of the life we shared—these will stay with me, a bittersweet reminder of what could have been.

I vow—someday, somehow—I'll make this right.

The rain continues to fall as we drive, blurring the landscape into a watercolor of grays and greens. The sun tries to break through the clouds, a weak attempt at dawn, but for me, this is the end of everything.

The end of Sophia.

The end of happiness.

The end of love.

But deep down, there's still a flicker of grit and determination. I've been beaten, broken, and forced to betray those I love, but I'll do whatever it takes to endure and outlast the torment that awaits me. Beneath it all, I'm a survivor.

But more importantly, I'm also a mother.

TWENTY-FOUR

Blake

____

THE BELL OVER THE DOOR OF THE GUARDIAN GRIND CHIMES AS I push it open. The rich aroma of coffee envelops me. The warm, inviting atmosphere wraps around me, a world away from the tense, charged air back at HQ.

"Blake. What a nice surprise." Jenna's cheerful voice carries over the hum of conversation and the hiss of the espresso machine.

The counter is cool under my palms as I lean against it. "Hey, Jenna. Just needed a quick caffeine fix."

"The usual?" Her hands are already moving toward the espresso machine; the familiar clinks and whirs a soothing soundtrack.

"Please." The word comes out more like a sigh than a response.

As Jenna works, I scan the café, a habit born of years of training. It's busy, but not unusually so for this time of day. Regular customers hunch over laptops, and a group of techies animatedly discuss something in the corner.

But no Sophia.

"Here you go," Jenna says, sliding a steaming cup across the counter. "You look like you could use it. Rough day?"

A non-committal grunt escapes me, and my shoulders roll in an attempt to release some tension.

"Where's Sophia?"

"What do you mean?" Her question catches me off guard.

"Is she working in the back?"

"Blake…" Jenna's movements slow, confusion evident in her expression. "She called out sick the last couple of days. I assumed you knew."

"She's been at work every day this week." My heart races, blood rushing in my ears.

The whir of the milk steamer fills the sudden silence between us. Jenna's eyes widen, her mouth opening and closing without sound.

"Blake, what's going on?"

The cup trembles in my hand, coffee sloshing dangerously close to the rim.

"I don't know." My voice sounds distant, even to my own ears. "But I'm going to find out."

My hand moves to my pocket, fingers closing around the familiar shape of my badge. The badge I found tucked under the bed as if it had been there all along.

Jenna's words echo in my mind.

Sophia calling out sick when she was supposedly at work. The missing badge reappearing as if by magic. The security breaches escalating over the past week.

A picture forms in my mind.

"It can't be."

But even as I try to deny it, I know. Deep in my gut, I know.

With shaking hands, I pull out my phone and dial Ethan's number. Jenna watches me intently, concern etched on her face.

"Ethan," I start, my voice steadier than I feel. "I know the source of the breach."

"What do you mean? What have you found?" Ethan's voice is tense on the other end of the line.

I take a deep breath, steeling myself for the conversation I never thought I'd have to have. "It's… it's Sophia. She's behind the breaches."

"Sophia?" By the tone of Ethan's voice, he doesn't believe me. "That's a serious accusation. What makes you think that?"

I run a hand through my hair, pacing as I speak. "A few days ago, I lost my badge. I didn't report it because…" I pause, embarrassment coloring my words. "Because Sophia told me it would probably show up, and I didn't want to get ripped by the guys. The very next day, it showed up under the bed."

"And you're just telling me this now?" There's an edge to Ethan's voice.

"I know, I know. I screwed up. But that's not all." I swallow hard, forcing myself to continue. "I just found out from Jenna that Sophia's been calling out sick from work for the past couple of days. But she's been leaving the apartment with me every morning like normal."

The silence on the other end of the line is deafening. When Ethan speaks again, his voice is low and serious. "Blake, are you absolutely sure about this?"

"No." The word tastes bitter in my mouth. "But there are too many coincidences. The timing of the breaches, her lying about being at work, my missing badge... It all adds up to something I don't want to believe but can't ignore."

Ethan takes a deep breath. "Okay. Here's what we're going to do. I'm calling Mitzy right now. We need to track every place your badge has logged access during those 24 hours."

"Agreed. I'm heading back to the apartment. Sophia's not at work, and I have a feeling... I need to check if she's there."

"Be careful, Blake," Ethan warns. "If your suspicions are correct, we don't know what we're dealing with. Don't confront her alone if she's there."

"I won't." I run a hand down my face, feeling like shit. "I'll call you as soon as I know anything."

I'm off the call before he can say anything else. The need to confirm my suspicions, to find some evidence that I'm wrong, drives me forward.

"I'm coming with you." Jenna steps around the counter, determination in her stance.

Before I can protest, she's already on her phone. "Carter? It's

Jenna. I need you to meet us…" She pauses, then continues. "Me and Blake. It's about Sophia."

I turn to leave, nearly colliding with a customer entering the shop. The bell chimes again as I push through the door, the cool air hitting me like a physical force after the warmth of the café.

Jenna and I leave The Grind, the cheerful atmosphere now feeling like a distant memory. Jenna fills me in as we walk.

"Carter's going to meet us halfway," she says. "He was already in the area."

True to her word, we spot Carter about halfway to the apartment. His face is a mask of concern as he jogs up to us.

"Blake? What's going on?" Carter's eyes search mine, worry evident in his expression.

I give him a quick rundown as we continue toward the apartment. By the time we reach the building, Carter's face is a mixture of disbelief and shock.

"There has got to be more going on." He shakes his head, trying to figure this shit out. "Sophia would never—"

"I no longer know what she may or may not have done."

My hands shake as I fumble with the keys, the lock finally gives way with a soft click.

"Sophia?" My voice echoes in the quiet apartment, hope and dread warring in my chest.

But there's no answer. No sound of the shower running, no smell of food cooking. Just silence.

We move through the rooms, each space untouched and eerily normal. The bedroom is tidy, the bed made as if Sophia just left for work. Nothing seems out of place except for one thing: on the bedside table, a framed photo of Sophia and me lies face down.

The undisturbed state of the apartment is almost more unsettling than if the place had been ransacked.

It's as if Sophia simply vanished.

"Blake." Jenna's soft voice draws my attention. She's standing by the dresser, holding something in her hand. As I move closer, my heart sinks. It's Sophia's Guardian HQ badge.

On HQ grounds, everyone carries their badge at all times—it's more than just identification; it's a lifeline, a key to every door. For Sophia to leave it behind…

I take the badge from Jenna with trembling hands, its weight unbearable. This small piece of metal cements the horrifying truth I've been trying to deny.

"Sophia isn't coming back."

She's gone, deliberately severing her connection to Guardian HQ and to me.

And with her disappearance, who knows what secrets of Guardian HQ were compromised in the process?

Carter's hand lands on my shoulder, a grounding weight. "What the hell is going on?"

I sink onto the edge of the bed, the events of the day crashing over me.

"I think… I think Sophia might be behind the security breach at HQ."

The words hang in the air, heavy with implication. Jenna gasps, her hand flying to her mouth. Carter's grip on my shoulder tightens.

"Are you sure?" Carter's voice is low, tension evident in every syllable.

I shake my head, running a hand through my hair. "No. But there are too many coincidences. The timing of the breaches, her lying about being at work... And now this."

Jenna sits beside me, her presence a silent comfort. "What are you going to do?"

The question echoes in the quiet room. What am I going to do? How do I even begin to untangle this mess?

"This needs to be treated as a full-scale security breach."

"I'm so sorry." Jenna turns to me, her eyes filled with sympathy. "I don't know what to say, but whatever you need, we're here for you."

"Thank you. I appreciate that."

The next hour passes in a blur of phone calls and hurried explanations. By the time we leave the apartment, a full investigation is already underway.

"As for next steps, we regroup." My voice comes out steadier than I feel. "We figure out exactly what's been compromised and plug the holes. And then…"

I pause, the next words sticking in my throat. Saying them out loud will make this real.

"And then we find Sophia."

TWENTY-FIVE

Blake

————

THE READY ROOM DOOR SWINGS OPEN UNDER MY TOUCH, THE familiar click of the latch echoing in the sudden silence. Every eye turns to me, with disappointment and something harder to define.

Ethan stands at the head of the table, his posture rigid. "Glad you could join us, Blake."

The sarcasm in his voice is unmistakable. My throat tightens as I sit, the weight of their stares pressing down on me like a physical force.

Mitzy's fingers dance across her keyboard, the soft tapping a counterpoint to the tension thrumming through the air. The large screen at the front of the room flickers to life, displaying a map of Guardian HQ crisscrossed with a web of colored lines.

"We've been tracking your badge's movements," Mitzy's eyes never leave the screen. "At first, just for the day it went missing, but…"

"But what?" I glance around the table with trepidation.

"The activity continues well past that initial 24-hour period." Mitzy's fingers dance across the keyboard, and the display shifts. My stomach drops as the timeline extends beyond the day my badge went missing.

"That's impossible." I lean forward, squinting at the screen. "I've had my badge with me every day since."

"Then who's been accessing restricted areas with your credentials?" Sam's sharp gaze cuts through the room.

A ripple of murmurs sweeps through everyone gathered. I scan the data, my heart racing as her movements tell a disturbing story. Server rooms, restricted areas, places I've never even seen.

"This can't be right." I point to a specific time stamp. "It shows my badge accessing the server room last Tuesday at 1400 hours, but I was at the firing range with Gabe."

Gabe's usual smirk is replaced by a grimace. "He's right. We were working on his grouping all afternoon."

Another inconsistency catches my eye. "And here, Wednesday at 0900. The log shows me entering the tech lab, but I was in the gym with Walt."

"Yeah, I remember. You were bitching about that new leg press machine." Walt's gravelly voice confirms,

"There's more," Mitzy interjects, highlighting another section. "Your badge was used to access The Guardian Grind's back office at 2200 hours last night, well after closing."

The implications hit me like a ton of bricks.

"She cloned it." Ethan's voice is tight, barely controlled anger simmering beneath the surface. "Somehow, Sophia made a copy of your badge."

The words hang in the air, heavy with accusation. My fingers dig into the arms of my chair, the leather creaking in protest.

"How is that possible?"

Mitzy pulls up schematics and lines of code. "It's not easy, but with the right access and knowledge—it's doable. Especially if she had help."

"Help? How would she have had any help?"

The map on the screen shifts again, now showing two distinct sets of movements—mine and Sophia's. Some overlap, others diverge wildly. The branching paths seem to mock me, a visual representation of the trust I've misplaced.

"We need to separate your actual movements from Sophia's."

Sam's deep voice cuts through my spiraling thoughts. "Blake, we need you to go through your whereabouts step by step."

Sophia's betrayal settles over me like a lead weight. I struggle to reconcile the woman I love with these actions. The soft smile that greeted me each morning, the warmth of her body against mine at night—were they all just part of her cover?

For the next hour, I painstakingly identify my locations. The gym, the cafeteria, mission briefings—all normal Guardian activities. But Sophia's movements tell a different story. Server rooms, restricted areas, places I'm not sure where they're at. With each revelation, the knot in my stomach tightens.

"How did none of us notice this?" Walt's question breaks the tense silence that's fallen over the room. "Wouldn't there be an alert if our badges were used simultaneously in two separate locations?"

Mitzy pulls up a new screen. "That's where it gets interesting. The system did flag these discrepancies, but..."

"But what?" Ethan's voice is sharp, and his patience is wearing thin.

Mitzy takes a deep breath, her eyes darting nervously around the room. "The alerts were suppressed."

A collective gasp ripples through the room. My entire body goes rigid, every muscle tensing as the implications of her words sink in.

"There's more," Mitzy says, her voice cutting through my thoughts.

The room falls silent as Mitzy explains Protocol Zero and its true purpose.

Unease washes over me.

"How long have you been planning for this? And why weren't we informed?" I grind out the words, barely keeping my rising anger in check.

"We needed to monitor the activity," Mitzy continues, her voice steady despite the rising tension. "To let the breach run its course so we could trace it back to the source. If we'd acted immediately, we might have spooked them and lost our chance to uncover the full extent of the infiltration."

The rage that's been simmering inside me suddenly boils over. I slam my hands on the table, the sharp crack echoing through the room. "You knew? You knew, and you did nothing?"

Mitzy flinches at my outburst but holds her ground. "Blake, we had to—"

"No." I cut her off, my voice raw with emotion. "If you'd acted immediately, we could have caught Sophia. She wouldn't be missing now. She wouldn't be in danger."

The room falls silent. My words hang heavy in the air. Ethan steps forward, his hand on my shoulder, but I shrug it off.

"Blake, I understand you're upset, but—"

"Upset?" I laugh, the sound harsh and bitter. "Upset doesn't begin to cover it. You used her as bait. You put her in danger. And for what? To catch Malfor? Was it worth it?"

The silence that follows is deafening. I look around the room at the faces of people I've trusted with my life, and for the first time, I feel like a stranger among them.

"We had no choice." Forest's deep voice breaks the silence. "The risk was too great. If Malfor succeeded in infiltrating us undetected, the consequences would be catastrophic."

I face him, my anger giving way to a bone-deep weariness. "And what about the consequences for Sophia? What about her life?"

The room erupts in a cacophony of voices. Confusion, anger, and disbelief war for dominance.

No one has an answer for that. As the reality of our situation settles over the room, I can't help but wonder: in our quest to save the world, have we lost sight of the individuals we're meant to protect?

"What the hell, Mitzy?" Gabe's voice rises above the rest. "You're telling us you knew this was coming?"

"Yes and no," Mitzy cuts through the rising tension, making things even more unclear. She pulls up a new screen, lines of code scrolling faster than I can follow. "We implemented a Trojan Horse when we suspected a breach might occur. It's part of Protocol Zero."

My blood runs cold as the pieces click into place. "You used us as bait," I growl, my fists clenching at my sides. "You used Sophia as bait."

Mitzy holds up her hands, her eyes wide. "It's not like that. We've been expecting Malfor to make a move like this for months. We never suspected it would be Sophia, but we had to be prepared for the eventuality."

The anger bubbling in my chest threatens to overflow. "So you just let it happen? You let her walk into this trap?"

"We didn't know it would be her," Mitzy shouts back.

Before I can respond, a booming voice cuts through the chaos.

"Enough." Forest steps forward, his imposing frame casting a shadow across the table. The room falls silent under his stern gaze.

"The decision to keep the true intent of Protocol Zero secret was mine," Forest says, his voice leaving no room for argument. "We couldn't risk tipping our hand. If Malfor suspected we were onto him, we'd lose our best chance at bringing him down."

"With all due respect, sir," Ethan's voice is tight with controlled anger, "we're supposed to be a team. You cut us out of the loop."

Forest's expression softens slightly. "I know, and I didn't make that decision lightly. But sometimes, hard choices must be made for the greater good."

The weight of his words settles over the room. I want to argue, to rage against the injustice of it all. But a small part of me understands the logic, even as it tears me apart.

"So what now?" I ask, my voice hoarse with emotion. "How do we find Sophia?"

Forest's gaze meets mine, a mix of sympathy and determination in his eyes. "We use every tool at our disposal. The Trojan Horse, the badge data, everything. We find Sophia, stop Malfor, and end this once and for all."

TWENTY-SIX

Blake

____

As the team rallies around this new directive, I can't shake the feeling that we're playing catch-up in a game where the rules have suddenly changed.

Sophia is at the center of it all.

"Forest's right." CJ steps forward, his presence commanding attention. "We follow the data. Both from your badge and from the Trojan. We don't know Sophia's true intentions. She might be working for the Sentinels, or she may have been forced into this. Either way, she's our best lead to the entire Sentinel organization."

"Remember, this is still a rescue mission." Sam clears his throat. "Until we know otherwise, we assume Sophia is acting under duress."

The words are meant to be reassuring but twist in my gut like a knife. Because deep down, a part of me wonders if that's true. Or if the woman I thought I knew was just another lie.

As the team strategizes its next moves, I stare at the screen, tracing Sophia's digital footsteps. Somewhere in this data is the key to finding her, and I won't rest until we do.

"Blake." Ethan's voice pulls me back to the present.

"What?"

"I need you focused. Can you handle this?"

"I'm good." The question stings, but I understand the necessity. I straighten in my chair, pushing down the tumult of emotions threatening to overwhelm me. "What do you need me to do?

"Work with Mitzy." Ethan seems satisfied with my response. "You know Sophia better than anyone. If there's a pattern to her movements, you're the one who'll spot it."

I focus on Mitzy's station and scan the scrolling data across her screens. The familiar layout of Guardian HQ is overlaid with a maze of colored lines, each representing a different day's movements.

"Here." I point to a recurring pattern. "She visited the north server room every day at 1400 hours. That's when I usually hit the gym."

"What else?" Mitzy isolates the pattern.

We work silently for several minutes, the rest of the team's voices fading into background noise as I lose myself in the data. It's easier to think of Sophia as a puzzle to solve rather than the woman who's torn my world apart.

A flash of color catches my eye. "Wait, go back. There, in the drone storage room."

Mitzy rewinds the footage, zooming in on the grainy security feed. A figure slips into the room, emerging moments later with something clutched to their chest.

"Can you enhance that?" I lean closer, my heart pounding.

The image sharpens, revealing a familiar face. Sophia's eyes dart around furtively as she tucks something into her pocket. My breath catches. Even knowing what she's done, the sight of her sends a jolt through me.

"What did she take?" Gabe asks, peering over my shoulder.

"I can't tell." I shake my head, frustration building. "Whatever it was, she didn't want anyone to see it."

"I want a full inventory of that storage room, ASAP." Sam's voice cuts through the tension. "Mitzy, keep digging into those server logs.

"Come." Ethan tugs at my sleeve.

I follow him out into the hallway. Ethan leads me to a small conference room, closing the door behind us with a soft click.

"Sit." Ethan's voice carries the weight of command.

I lower myself into a chair, my body tense, ready for whatever's coming next. Ethan remains standing, his imposing frame backlit by the window. For a long moment, he stares at me, his expression unreadable.

He's going to berate me for losing my badge and not reporting it.

"I need to know if you can handle this." Ethan's voice is low and intense. "Because if there's even a shadow of a doubt, I'll pull you off this mission right now."

"You can't do that." The words burst out of me, raw and desperate. "I need to be part of this. I need to find her."

"What *you* need doesn't matter." Ethan's harsh tone cuts through my protests. "What matters is the safety of this team and the success of our mission. So I'll ask you again—can you handle this?"

I want to argue, to insist that I'm fine, but the truth is, I'm not sure. The image of Sophia sneaking through Guardian HQ, betraying everything we stand for, plays on a loop in my mind.

"I don't know." The words taste bitter on my tongue. "But I have to try. Don't make me sit this one out."

Ethan's expression softens slightly. He pulls out the chair across from me and sits, leaning forward with his elbows on the table.

"I get it, Blake. I do." Ethan's hard gaze holds mine, filled with understanding and compassion. "I've been where you are now. With Rebel."

The mention of Rebel's name sends a jolt through me. Ethan and Rebel are in a good place these days. It's easy to forget how their relationship started. I'd almost forgotten about that betrayal.

"That was different." I shake my head, refusing to see the parallels. "Rebel was trying to find her sister's child. Sophia—she was spying on us. Do you have any idea how much damage she could have done?"

"Don't jump to conclusions." Ethan's voice is firm but gentle.

"It's a long swim back, but you must keep your mind open to other possibilities."

"Nothing will convince me what Sophia did is justifiable." My fists clench at my sides, knuckles white with tension.

"Blake." Ethan leans forward, his gaze intense. "I thought the same thing about Rebel, but there was more to the story. There always is."

I stand abruptly, unable to sit still any longer. "This isn't the same. The harm Sophia could have caused… It's far worse than anything Rebel did."

"Maybe." Ethan stays seated, his calmness only amplifying the restless energy coursing through me. "Or maybe there's something we're missing. Something that forced her hand."

"Like what?" I whirl around, my voice rising. "What could justify this level of betrayal?"

Ethan's eyes narrow, his voice low and measured. "Think about it. What if someone had leverage over her? What if they threatened someone she cares about?"

"She doesn't have anyone." I sink back into my chair, my mind racing. "She would have told me. We don't keep secrets."

"We all keep secrets." Ethan's smile is sad. "Sometimes the people we're closest to are the ones we protect the most fiercely from our worst secrets."

I run a hand through my hair, frustration and doubt warring inside me.

"Even if that's true… How can I trust anything about her now? How do I know what was real and what was just—part of her cover?"

"You can't." Ethan's blunt honesty is both painful and oddly comforting. "Not yet. That's why we need to find her, to get answers."

"And if those answers aren't what we want to hear?" The question comes out barely above a whisper.

Ethan's gaze is steady. "Then we deal with it. As a team. But, Blake, you can't go into this assuming the worst. It'll cloud your judgment, make you miss things."

I take a deep breath, trying to center myself. "What do you need from me?"

"I need you to be objective." Ethan's gaze is unwavering. "To look at the evidence without letting your feelings—good or bad—cloud your judgment. Can you do that?"

The question hangs in the air between us. Can I?

"I can try." I finally meet Ethan's gaze. "I won't pretend it'll be easy, but I'll do my best."

Ethan studies me for a long moment. "Alright. I'll be watching you. The moment I think you're compromised—in either direction—you're out. Understood?"

"Understood." The word comes out stronger than I feel.

"Good. Now, let's get to work." Ethan rises, moving toward the door. He pauses, his hand on the doorknob. "We'll find Sophia, and we'll bring her home. You have to be prepared for all possibilities. The Sophia you knew might be gone, or she might be in more danger than we imagine. Either way, we need to find her."

The words settle over me, heavy with implication. I steel myself for what's to come as we return to the ready room. Whatever the truth is, whatever we find, I'll face it. Because the alternative—leaving Sophia out there, alone and possibly in danger—is unthinkable.

TWENTY-SEVEN

Blake

———

THE SHRILL RING OF ETHAN'S PHONE CUTS THROUGH THE TENSE silence of the ready room. His brow furrows as he checks the caller ID.

"It's Rebel." Ethan's voice is tight with anticipation as he puts the call on speaker.

"Ethan, you need to get to The Guardian Grind. Now." Rebel's voice crackles through the speaker, urgent and breathless. *"We found something."*

Ethan's eyes lock with mine.

"We're on our way." Ethan's already moving toward the door, and I'm right on his heels.

The short walk to The Guardian Grind feels like an eternity. The crisp autumn air bites at my skin, carrying the scent of fallen leaves and wood smoke. My mind races with possibilities, each step bringing us closer to… What? Answers? More questions? My stomach churns with anticipation.

The bell above the door chimes as we enter, and the familiar aroma of coffee and freshly baked pastries washes over us. For a moment, I'm transported back to happier times—Sophia behind the counter, her smile bright as she greets me. The memory fades as quickly as it came, leaving a hollow ache in its wake.

Rebel stands by the counter, her posture tense. Jenna and Malia hover nearby, their faces etched with concern—and barely concealed excitement?

"What did you find?" The words tumble out of me before I can stop them.

Rebel exchanges a glance with Jenna before leading us to the back room. The air grows thick with tension as we follow, my pulse quickening with each step.

"We were doing inventory," Jenna begins, her voice hushed as if sharing a secret. "And we found these."

She gestures to a small pile of objects on the table. My breath catches as I recognize them.

"Those are Guardian HQ issue." I pick up one of the small listening devices, turning it over in my hand. "How the hell did they get here?"

"Sophia." Malia's voice is soft, almost apologetic. "We found them hidden all over the café."

The betrayal hits me anew, a fresh wave of pain washing over me. I set the device down, my hand shaking slightly.

"That's not all." Rebel pulls out several bags of coffee beans, setting them on the table with a dull thud. "Look inside."

I tear open one of the bags, and the rich aroma of coffee fills the air. Nestled among the beans are small slips of paper, covered in a familiar, messy scrawl.

"It's Sophia's handwriting," I breathe, my fingers tracing the letters. The words are a jumble of numbers and letters, meaningless to my eyes.

"There's more." Jenna's already opening another bag, her movements quick and eager. "They're in all of them."

Soon, the table is covered in coffee beans and scraps of paper. The air buzzes with nervous energy as we sift through the messages, desperately trying to make sense of the cryptic notes.

"This has to mean something." Malia's voice is filled with hope. "She wouldn't have gone to all this trouble for nothing."

The door swings open, and Carter strides in, his face a mirror of my own concern. "I came as soon as I heard." He places a supportive hand on my shoulder.

"Perfect timing," Ethan says. "We need all hands on deck for this."

As we work to sort through the messages, the door opens again. Jinx enters, her laptop tucked under her arm, a determined set to her jaw.

"Ethan called me. Said you've got a code to break?" She sets up her equipment. "What do you have?"

With Jinx's arrival, the energy in the room shifts. There's a renewed sense of purpose as we gather around her makeshift workstation. Her fingers fly over the keyboard, lines of code scrolling across the screen faster than I can follow.

"It's not a straightforward cipher," Jinx mutters, her brow furrowed in concentration. "But there's definitely a pattern here."

As Jinx works her magic, the rest of us continue to sift through the physical evidence. Carter and I tackle another bag of beans while Rebel and Malia examine the listening devices more closely.

My phone buzzes with a message from Mitzy.

∿

Mitzy: Sophia visited the robotics department. A bumblebee drone is missing. It is not active. I hope she took it. It could help us find her.

∿

I relay the information to the others, a spark of hope igniting in my chest. "She's leaving breadcrumbs. She wants us to find her."

"Or lead us into a trap," Ethan counters, but there's less conviction in his voice now.

"No." Jenna shakes her head vehemently. "This is too elaborate for a simple trap. Sophia's trying to tell us something."

"Jenna's right," Malia chimes in. "Remember how Sophia always said the truth is in the details? She's giving us all the pieces. We need to put them together."

As the debate continues, Jinx lets out a triumphant "Ha!" Her exclamation draws all eyes to her screen.

"I've cracked the first layer," she announces, a hint of pride in her voice. "It's a list of locations and timestamps." Jinx interrupts my spiraling thoughts. "There's something else embedded in the code. A message, I think."

The room falls silent as Jinx works to decrypt the hidden text.

"Got it," Jinx says after what feels like an eternity. "It says: '*Not what it seems. Find the bee.*'"

"She took the drone." A smile fills my face. "She wants us to find her. She's telling us she didn't have a choice. And gave us a way to track her."

"If we can activate the drone," Rebel adds.

"I'll contact Mitzy," Ethan pulls out his phone. "Her team should be able to activate it remotely."

As Ethan steps aside to make the call, I find myself drawn to Sophia's locker in the corner of the room. Something tugs at my memory—a conversation we had months ago about hiding places in plain sight.

Acting on instinct, I run my fingers along the edge of the locker, searching for… There. A slight gap between the metal and the wall. I slip my fingers into the crevice, feeling the edge of something thin and flat.

I carefully extract a folded piece of paper. Sophia's handwriting scrawls my name across the front.

My hands tremble as I unfold the note. The others have fallen silent, watching me.

"*Blake,*" I read aloud, my voice barely above a whisper. "*If you're reading this, then everything has gone wrong. I'm so sorry. I never wanted to hurt you, to betray everything we stand for. But I had no choice. They're forcing me to do this. I can't tell you everything—it's too dangerous. But please, trust that everything I've done, I've done to protect what matters most. I'm leaving you clues where I can. Follow them. Find me. I love you. Sophia.*"

The letter slips from my fingers, landing on the table. The room is silent, the weight of Sophia's words settling over us all.

"So what's our next move?" Rebel asks, looking around the room.

All eyes turn to me, waiting for a decision. I take a deep breath. "We follow the clues. We find Sophia. And then we bring her home."

The room erupts in a flurry of activity. Jinx returns to her computer, diving deeper into the decrypted data. Rebel and Malia gather all the physical evidence while Jenna closes the café.

Carter pulls me aside, his hand on my shoulder. "You okay, brother?"

I nod, not trusting my voice. The emotional whiplash of the past hour has left me drained, but there's a new fire burning in my chest.

"We'll find her," Carter assures me, his voice low and determined. "Whatever it takes."

"Whatever it takes," I echo, the words feeling like a vow.

As we head back to HQ, I look around The Guardian Grind. This place, a symbol of new beginnings, feels like the starting line of the most important mission of my life.

Sophia's out there, counting on us to decipher her clues and rescue her. And I'll be damned if I let her down.

TWENTY-EIGHT

Sophia

THE CAR'S TIRES CRUNCH OVER GRAVEL AS WE PULL UP TO A PRIVATE airstrip. Rain lashes against the windows, mirroring the storm raging inside me. I glance at the driver, his face an impassive mask in the rearview mirror. He's been silent throughout the entire drive.

"Where are we going?" My voice sounds small, even to my own ears.

More silence. Not even a flicker of acknowledgment.

"Please," I try again, desperation creeping into my tone. "I need to know——"

"Get out." His voice is flat, devoid of any emotion, as if I'm nothing more than cargo to be delivered.

In a way, I suppose that's true.

Before I can move, he's out of the car, yanking my door open. His grip on my arm is brutal as he drags me onto the tarmac. Pain blossoms where his fingers dig into my flesh, the promise of a bruise to come.

The chill of the night air bites through my clothes as I stumble onto the asphalt. A sleek private jet looms before me, its engines already humming with impatience.

No questions, no explanations. Just a silent command to board.

Inside, the jet is a study in contrasts. Plush leather seats and polished wood paneling speak of luxury, but the cabin is eerily empty. No flight attendants, no amenities. The cockpit door is firmly shut, separating me from any human contact.

As the plane takes off, my stomach drops—not from the ascent, but from the finality of it all. I'm leaving everything behind. Blake, my friends, the life I built. With each passing minute, the distance between who I was and who I'm being forced to become grows insurmountable.

Hours blur together in a haze of discomfort. The cabin is cold, unnaturally so, as if the temperature has been deliberately lowered. There are no blankets, no food, no water. Just me, alone with my thoughts and the growing ache in my empty stomach.

I drift in and out of consciousness, my dreams plagued by Luke's terrified cries when he was taken from me and the image of Blake's face when he finally realizes what I've done.

When we finally land, the sun sets in an unfamiliar sky.

As I'm ushered off the plane, a man in a dark suit approaches. His face is as impassive as the driver's had been.

"Welcome to Montenegro." His accent is thick, Eastern European.

The words should be welcoming, but his tone is anything but. It's a statement of fact, cold and impersonal. We're halfway across the world from everything I know, and I've never felt more alone.

He gestures to another waiting car, as nondescript as the first. Once again, I'm treated like cargo, not a person.

No one speaks as we wind through narrow mountain roads, each turn taking us higher into terrain that feels as alien as my new reality.

Finally, we crest a hill, and I see it—a sprawling villa perched on the edge of a cliff overlooking the Adriatic Sea. But as we draw closer, the illusion of luxury fades, replaced by a growing sense of dread.

Tall, imposing walls surround the compound, stretching at least fifteen feet high. Razor wire coils along their tops, glinting menacingly in the fading light. Armed guards patrol the perimeter, their silhouettes stark against the darkening sky. Watchtowers loom at regular intervals, searchlights sweeping across the grounds.

On the sea-facing side, sheer cliffs plummet hundreds of feet to the churning waters below. The waves crash against jagged rocks, the sound carrying even to where we are—a constant reminder of the deadly drop.

This isn't a villa—it's a fortress. An inescapable prison disguised as a luxury retreat.

The car stops in a circular driveway. Before I can move, a new man appears, yanking my door open.

"He's waiting for you." His words are more of a growl than anything else. He yanks me out of the car, his grip on my arm as bruising as the first driver's had been.

I'm nothing more than a package to be delivered. Their callous disregard cuts sharper than any knife.

I'm led through ornate doors into a cavernous foyer. My footsteps echo on marble floors, the sound somehow ominous in the silence. At the far end of the room, a figure stands silhouetted against floor-to-ceiling windows.

"Ah, Sophia." Malfor's voice sends ice through my veins. "How kind of you to join me."

He turns, and I get my first real look at the man who's orchestrated my personal hell. He's shorter than I expected, maybe 5'5", but after spending so much time around Blake and his team of 6-foot-plus men, Malfor looks diminutive. Yet what he lacks in stature, he more than makes up for in presence.

His eyes, a pale, watery blue, hold an intelligence that belies their simpleton appearance. They bore into me, dissecting every nuance of my posture, every flicker of emotion I fail to suppress. Those eyes have seen countless cruelties and inflicted just as many.

Malfor's attire is a study in contrasts. An impeccably tailored suit hangs slightly askew on his frame. His tie is loose, the knot off-center. A single button on his jacket is undone. It's as if he's deliberately cultivating an air of dishevelment, a silent statement that he's above such trivial concerns as appearance.

"I trust your journey was—illuminating?" A cruel smile plays on his lips. "Realizing just how far from home you are?"

I struggle to find my voice, to remember the rules of this old, terrible game.

"Yes, sir," I manage the words, but they taste like ash.

Malfor circles me slowly like a predator sizing up its prey. "You know, Jonathan spoke quite highly of you. Said you were his favorite. His perfect, obedient little doll."

The mention of Greaves makes my skin crawl. I can't help but look up, meeting Malfor's gaze for a split second before I realize my mistake.

The backhand comes out of nowhere, the crack of flesh on flesh echoing in the cavernous room. Pain explodes across my face, white-hot and blinding. I crash to the floor, my hair spilling around me like a halo. For a moment, the pain is my entire universe.

"You dare look at me?" Malfor's voice cuts through the ringing in my ears, low and dangerous. "You will show proper respect. Eyes down. Kneel."

I struggle to my knees, my body responding before my mind can process the command.

"Better." Malfor's lips curve into a slow, predatory smile as he circles me, his gaze like a blade, slicing through any remaining shred of defiance. "Now, let me make something crystal clear. You are nothing here. Less than nothing. You will not speak unless spoken to. You will obey without question. You will bow, kneel, and scrape before your betters. Which, my dear, is everyone."

My thoughts race to Luke. The urge to ask about my son, to beg for any information, is overwhelming. I swallow the words, remembering the sting of Malfor's hand.

Malfor's fingers grip my chin, forcing my head up. His watery eyes peer into my very soul. "Ah, thinking of the boy, are we? If you're a good girl, if you please me, perhaps I'll allow you to see him. Not in person, of course, but... Well, let's not get ahead of ourselves."

He releases me with a shove, turning to bark orders at someone I can't see. For the first time, I become aware of others in the room.

Men in crisp suits stand at attention, their faces impassive. Among them move women in flowing, gauzy gowns that leave little to the imagination. Their eyes are downcast, their movements subservient.

"Take her to her room," Malfor commands. "Make sure she understands the—consequences of disobedience."

Rough hands grab my arms, hauling me to my feet. As I'm dragged away, Malfor's voice follows me. "Welcome to your new home, Sophia. I do hope you'll enjoy your stay. It's going to be a long one."

The journey to my "room" is a blur of opulent hallways and stern-faced guards. Everything is pristine, almost sterile in its perfection. It's a stark contrast to the darkness that clings to every corner, refusing to be chased away by the light. Even as the room brightens, the shadows only deepen, a reminder that no amount of light can erase the pervasive darkness lurking just beneath the surface.

We descend a flight of stairs, the temperature dropping with each step. The guards' grips tighten, their fingers digging painfully into my arms. They stop before a heavy metal door at the end of a long corridor.

With a brutal shove, I'm thrust into a cell. I stumble, crashing hard onto the cold stone floor. The door slams shut behind me, and metal bolts grind into place, their harsh clicks echoing through the small space, sealing my fate. The bitter scent of damp stone fills my lungs as the final lock snaps shut, leaving me with only the oppressive silence.

The "room" is little more than a glorified cage. Cold stone walls surround me, devoid of any warmth or comfort. A narrow bed—little more than a cot—sits in one corner. A small bathroom area offers no privacy, the facilities exposed for all to see. There are no windows, no sense of the outside world. Just four walls and the crushing weight of my new reality.

I curl up on the bed, my body aching from the rough treatment and Malfor's "correction." In the darkness, I allow myself one moment of weakness. Tears fall silently, mourning the life I've lost and the uncertain future ahead.

As I lie there, the full weight of my situation crashes over me.

I've betrayed everyone I care about. Blake, the team, all of Guardian HQ. The image of Blake's expression when he realizes what I've done… It's almost too much to bear.

I cling to the hope that they'll find the messages I left, that somehow they'll understand, that Blake will forgive me, and that he'll rescue me. But the thought feels like a distant dream. This fortress is impenetrable, and my situation is beyond hopeless.

The bumblebee drone, tucked safely in the lining of my jacket, is my lifeline. I've guarded it, knowing it's my one link to the outside world, my one chance at… What?

Rescue?

Redemption?

The weight of it is a constant reminder that, even here, there's still a sliver of hope.

But is it hope or delusion?

I assume I'm being watched. Malfor doesn't seem the type to leave anything to chance. With trembling hands, I reach into the hidden pocket I sewed into my clothes. The drone is there, no bigger than my thumbnail. It feels impossibly tiny, impossibly fragile against my palm.

I take a deep breath and go to the small bathroom area. If there are cameras, this might be the one blind spot. I cup the drone, bringing it close to my lips. My heart pounds so loudly I'm sure it must be audible, even through the thick stone walls.

"Find them," I whisper so softly I can barely hear myself. "Find Blake."

Rescue me…

The words feel foolish as soon as they leave my lips.

Can this tiny machine even hear me?

Does it understand commands?

I remember Mitzy's excited chatter about her invention, claiming it was revolutionary. But the specifics are lost to me now, washed away by fear and exhaustion.

As I release the drone and watch it flit toward the ceiling, a fragment of memory surfaces. Mitzy's enthusiastic voice: *"They're great for getting covert intel on the ground. No one pays attention to bugs."*

The drone disappears from view, seeking out any crack or crevice that might lead to freedom. I'm left alone once more, staring at the spot where it vanished, with Mitzy's words echoing in my mind.

No one pays attention to bugs.

Could it be that simple? In this fortress, could my salvation come from something so small and so easily overlooked?

The reality of what I've done crashes over me. I've pinned all my hopes on a device I barely understand, in a fortress halfway around the world from everyone I love.

The drone can't possibly fly back to the US, can it? Even if it could, how would it find Blake? How would it lead anyone here?

Maybe it doesn't need to make the journey all at once. Maybe it can gather information bit by bit, unnoticed by Malfor and his men. It's a long shot, but it is something to cling to rather than fall into an abyss of despair.

Hysterical laughter bubbles up in my throat. I choke it back, terrified of making noise. I sink to the cold floor, wrapping my arms around myself as if I could physically hold the pieces of my sanity together.

This is madness. All of it. I'm trapped in a nightmare I can't wake up from, and I've just sent my only tangible link to the outside world on an impossible mission.

Tears stream down my face, silent and relentless. This is a place where hope comes to die. The brave front I've been trying to maintain crumbles, leaving me raw and exposed.

Fear courses through me—fear for my life, for Luke's life, for the future that seems bleaker with each passing second.

What will Malfor do to me? What horrors await when the sun rises? The uncertainty is almost worse than knowing.

Almost.

I curl into myself, making my body as small as possible. As if by shrinking physically, I can somehow disappear entirely and escape this hell, if only in my mind.

But there's no escape.

No reprieve from this living hell.

The drone was my last act of defiance, my final grasp of hope. And now it's gone, leaving me utterly alone. The cold of the stone floor seeps into my bones, a physical reminder of the chill that's settled in my heart.

The Sophia who walked into Guardian HQ, who fell in love with Blake and dared to dream of a better life is gone. In her place is this hollow shell, trembling on a bathroom floor in a fortress of nightmares.

I am broken.

Shattered into a thousand pieces, with no idea how—or if—I'll ever be whole again.

And yet, some small, stubborn part of me refuses to let go entirely. It clings to the memory of the drone, to Mitzy's words:

No one pays attention to bugs.

It's not hope—I'm too far gone for that. But it's—something. A gossamer thread in a sea of darkness.

It's all I have left. A tiny, buzzing chance that, somehow, a little bumblebee might make all the difference in this world of monsters.

A harsh buzzing suddenly fills the room. Fluorescent lights flicker to life, momentarily blinding me. A voice, tinny and distorted, comes through a hidden speaker:

"Sleep well, Sophia. Tomorrow, your training begins."

The lights cut out as abruptly as they came on, plunging me into a darkness so complete I can't see my hand inches from my face. The promise of what's to come hangs heavy in the air, a suffocating blanket of dread settling over me. My breath echoes in the confined space, sharp and shallow, and each exhale is swallowed by the oppressive void.

I reach out, fingers brushing cold, rough concrete before I stumble into the hard metal cot. There's no comfort here—just a thin, lumpy mattress with no sheets, no pillow. Nothing to soften the harsh edges of this cruel reality. My body aches from the earlier punishment, and the cold bites through the thin fabric of my clothes, seeping into my bones.

I try to lie down, but the mattress offers no relief, only pressing against my bruises, making the pain throb deeper and more insistent.

The absolute darkness is a vile, living thing, wrapping itself around me, invading every corner of my mind. It smothers me. Its weight is so heavy it's hard to breathe. My heart races, a wild, panicked beat that thrums in my ears.

I close my eyes, not that it makes any difference, and try to sleep. But in this suffocating blackness, sleep is impossible.

The darkness is alive, whispering in my ear, twisting my thoughts into nightmares that aren't quite dreams. It closes in on me, a relentless, choking force that threatens to drive me mad.

I curl up tighter, pulling my knees to my chest, trying to find some small measure of comfort in my own warmth.

Restless, I toss and turn, my body trapped on this slab of metal, my mind caught in the clutches of despair.

Time loses all meaning. Minutes could be hours. Hours could be days. All I know is that the darkness is endless, and it's winning.

"Please," I whisper into the darkness, a prayer to whatever god might be listening. "Give me strength. Let me endure. Let me find a way back to my son, Blake, and the life I've lost."

But as silence engulfs me once more, I can't shake the feeling that my words fall on deaf ears.

In Malfor's domain, there is no room for hope.

Only survival.

And tomorrow, I'll learn just how much I can endure.

TWENTY-NINE

Sophia

SLEEP ELUDES ME. THE DARKNESS IS ABSOLUTE, PRESSING AGAINST MY eyes like a physical weight. I blink, desperate for any sliver of light, but there's no difference between eyes open or closed. It's like being buried alive, every breath a struggle, every heartbeat a reminder that I'm trapped and vulnerable.

The cold seeps into my bones, a relentless ache that joins the chorus of pain from earlier. Every slight movement sends jolts through my body, sharp reminders of the punishment I've already endured.

How long have I been left here?

Hours?

Days?

Time has no meaning in this suffocating blackness.

Nothing Malfor does is by chance. His tactics are precise and calculated to break me. I'm aware of this, and it should give me an edge, should help me resist, but his cruelty is perfection, a finely honed weapon that slices through my defenses with ease.

Knowing this is his plan does nothing to fortify me against it. Instead, the knowledge only deepens my despair because I feel myself failing, feel the darkness closing in.

I can't fight it.

Not here.

Not like this.

I try to hold on, to keep some part of myself separate, but the darkness is relentless. It gnaws at my resolve, whispering that there's no escape, no end to the torment.

I curl in on myself, quivering in fear, my mind slipping further into the abyss. I'd do anything—anything—to make it stop. To bring back the light, the warmth, the sense that I'm still human.

But there's nothing. No one. Just me, the darkness, and the knowledge that I'm losing and Malfor has already won.

The creak of a door shatters the silence. A sliver of light cuts through the darkness, and my heartrate skyrockets. Heavy footsteps approach.

"Good morning, my dear Sophia." Malfor's voice slithers through the air, dripping with false sweetness. "I do hope you slept well."

The overhead lights flicker on, momentarily blinding me. I blink rapidly, trying to adjust to the sudden brightness. When my vision clears, Malfor's face comes into focus, his smile all teeth, like a shark circling its prey.

I scramble off the cot, hitting the cold floor hard and kneeling before him, my heart pounding in my chest. The instinct to submit is overwhelming, ingrained from too many past encounters. I keep my eyes downcast, refusing to meet his gaze.

He steps closer, his boots echoing in the small, barren space. His fingers trail across my shoulders, and a shudder ripples through me before I can stop it.

"I have such an exciting day planned for us." His voice drips with false sweetness. He circles me, his presence a looming shadow. "But first, let's review the rules, shall we?"

His touch lingers, cruel and possessive, as he completes his circuit around me, each step a reminder of the power he holds and the nightmare that awaits.

My throat constricts, knowing what's coming. Malfor leans in close, his breath hot against my ear.

"If you disobey, if you try to run, if you even think about betraying me…" He pauses, letting the tension build, savoring my fear. "Well, let's just say little Luke will pay the price. Shall I describe again how creative I can be when it comes to punishment?"

The room spins as his words slice through me, dredging up the worst moment of my life with cruel precision—exactly as Malfor intended. The day my world shattered replays in vivid detail, each memory sharpened to a blade by his manipulation. He knows just how to twist the knife, to make sure the pain is fresh and raw, and there's nothing I can do to stop it.

~

Four Years Ago…

~

The small dormer room was stifling, the air thick with the scent of must and despair…

The only light comes from a single, bare bulb hanging from the low ceiling, casting harsh shadows on the cracked walls. The cot beneath me creaks as I rock back and forth, cradling my baby son in my arms. Luke's soft cries are the only sound in the room, a heartbreaking melody that echoes my own despair.

For months, I've been his only caretaker, the one constant in his fragile, young life. I've done everything to protect him, to shield him from the horrors of this place.

But nothing can protect him now.

Not after what I've done.

Refusing Jonathan's advances was a mistake—a fatal one. Every time I think the punishments can't get any worse, they do. Each new cruelty surpasses the last, a relentless reminder of the power he holds over me.

Luke whimpers, his tiny fists clenching in the fabric of my shirt, and I hold him tighter as if I can somehow keep him safe from what's coming. The room feels smaller, the walls closing in, and dread coils in the pit of my stomach.

The lock outside the door clicks, a sharp, metallic sound that sends a shiver down my spine. I freeze, my heart pounding as the door swings open. Jonathan stands in the doorway, his silhouette a dark, menacing figure against the dim light of the hall.

His gaze zeroes in on me, and the corner of his mouth twists into a cruel smile. "Sophia," he drawls, stepping into the room. "You've been very disappointing."

A chill runs through me at his words, but I force myself to remain still, to keep my grip on Luke steady. Jonathan's eyes drift to the baby in my arms, and a flicker of something dark crosses his face.

"You should know better than to defy me. Your performance was unacceptable." His voice is low, each word a blade cutting through the air. He takes a step closer, and I instinctively shift back, my body pressing against the cold wall. "You thought there would be no consequences?"

Luke's cries grow louder, sensing the danger, but there's nowhere to run. No escape from the punishment I know is coming.

Jonathan's hand reaches out, not for me, but for Luke. Panic surges through me, my arms tightening around my son, but Jonathan's grip is like iron. With a single, brutal motion, he rips Luke from my arms.

My son's cries turn into frantic wails, his small body thrashing in Jonathan's grasp. The sound shatters what's left of my resolve, and I fall to my knees, hands outstretched in a desperate plea.

"Please. Please don't take him. I'll do anything; just don't hurt him."

Jonathan's expression hardens, his eyes gleaming with satisfaction. "Anything?" He tilts his head, considering. "You should have thought of that before." He turns on his heel, walking out with Luke cradled in his arms as if the child weighs nothing.

The lock clicks again, sealing the door and, with it, my fate.

Luke's fate and his future.

His frantic cries fade down the hallway, a sound that tears at my soul, leaving me hollow and broken.

The dormer room, once my prison, is now a tomb. I collapse onto the cot, my body wracked with sobs, each breath a struggle as the weight of what I've lost crushes me.

But even as I drown in despair, a single, burning thought takes root in my mind.

I will get him back.

No matter the cost.

THIRTY

Sophia

Malfor's smile widens as he reaches into his coat pocket, pulling out a sleek, black collar.

"Strip." His voice is as cold and unyielding as iron. The word hangs in the air, leaving no room for hesitation or disobedience.

My fingers tremble as I fumble with my clothing, peeling away the thin fabric that clings to my skin. Each piece I remove is another layer of dignity stripped away, leaving me exposed and vulnerable before him. The air is cool against my bare skin, the chill biting at my exposed flesh.

Once I'm completely naked, Malfor steps closer, his gaze raking over me with a mix of cruelty and satisfaction. He lifts the collar, the weight of it heavy in his hands, before snapping it around my throat.

The metal is cold against my skin, the mechanism locking into place—a tangible reminder of my captivity. His fingers linger at the clasp, brushing against my skin with a touch that sends a shiver down my spine—a touch that is almost gentle but filled with the promise of pain.

"Clothing is a privilege," he murmurs, his lips curving into a sadistic grin. "One that you must earn."

I swallow hard, the metal collar pressing uncomfortably against my throat as I nod, knowing that anything less than full compliance will only worsen my situation.

Malfor turns sharply on his heel, and I follow, my bare feet padding silently across the cold floor. He leads me through the winding corridors of his fortress, each step echoing in the silence until we reach the outer walls.

The walls are high and imposing, a constant reminder of my imprisonment. Malfor's men stand in neat rows along the perimeter, their eyes tracking my every move with an unsettling mix of indifference and hunger. Their expressions are unreadable, but I feel their judgment, their silent approval of Malfor's control over me.

"The collar you wear is not just a symbol of your status but a deterrent to escape." Malfor barely glances at me as he speaks, focusing instead on his fingernails. He picks at a cuticle with disinterest, as if this conversation is a tedious chore, his voice detached and bored. "Approach the wall," Malfor orders, his voice leaving no room for hesitation.

I take a step forward, dread coiling in my stomach. The collar buzzes softly, a low hum that vibrates against my skin. I freeze, but Malfor's cold, unyielding gaze pushes me forward.

I take another step, and the buzzing intensifies. I bite my lip, trying to brace myself, but nothing can prepare me for the shock that follows.

The collar jolts, sending a sharp, electric pain through my body. I gasp, my muscles seizing up as I stagger back, but Malfor's voice cuts through the pain, relentless and cruel.

"Keep going. You don't stop until you touch the wall."

Tears sting my eyes, but I force myself forward. Another step, another jolt. The pain is unbearable, a searing, white-hot agony that travels through every nerve in my body. I can't stop myself from crying out, my voice cracking as the shocks increase in intensity with every inch closer to the wall.

I try to fight it, try to push past the pain, but my body betrays me. The closer I get, the more violent the shocks become, each one more punishing than the last. My legs give out beneath me, and I collapse onto the ground, trembling violently, tears streaming down my face.

But Malfor is unyielding. He stands there, watching me with a twisted smile, taking pleasure in my torment.

"Touch the wall," he repeats, his voice laced with sadistic pleasure. "Or I'll make you do it all over again."

I try to force myself up, try to reach out, but the pain is too much. My body refuses to obey, locked in a cycle of agony and fear. I can't do it—I can't reach the wall, and Malfor knows it.

He's teaching me a lesson, one I'll never forget. I'm nothing more than a plaything to be used and discarded at his will.

Finally, he strides over, his boots clicking on the ground with an air of finality. He grabs me by the hair, yanking me to my feet with a force that sends fresh waves of pain shooting through my scalp.

"This is only the beginning," he whispers in my ear, his breath hot against my skin. "Remember this pain because it will be your constant companion until you learn your place."

Malfor leads me back to my cell, the darkened corridor echoing with the heavy clang of his boots. My body aches with every step, each footfall sending jolts of pain through my bruised and battered skin. When we reach the small, windowless cell that has become my prison, he shoves me inside with a dismissive flick of his wrist.

I crumple to the ground, my body wracked with sobs. I'm too weak, too broken to even think of fighting back. All I can do is lie there, the taste of defeat bitter on my tongue, knowing that Malfor's lesson has been learned.

The door slams shut, the lock clicking into place with a finality that sends a shiver down my spine.

The darkness rushes in, thick and suffocating, pressing against my eyes until the lines between reality and nightmare blur. I crawl forward, my hands outstretched, feeling for the cold, hard surface of the cot. My fingers graze the thin mattress, and I collapse onto it, curling into myself, trying to ward off the biting chill that seeps into my bones.

But there's no escape from the darkness. It becomes a living thing, wrapping itself around me, squeezing tighter with every breath I take.

I try to keep my mind from unraveling, to remind myself that this is just another of Malfor's tactics—a calculated effort to break me. But knowledge does nothing to ease the terror.

When sleep finally comes, it is fitful and broken. The silence is oppressive, the darkness absolute, swallowing me whole. My dreams are filled with Luke's cries and the hollow sound of Malfor's voice, a taunting whisper that follows me even in the depths of unconsciousness.

Each day, the routine is the same. The door creaks open, and the sudden burst of light blinds me. Malfor's shadow looms in the doorway, his eyes cold and empty as he beckons me out of the cell.

My body protests as I force myself to stand, muscles stiff and sore from the previous day's torment. But there is no time to recover. No respite. He drags me from the room, his grip unyielding, and forces me back into the cruel world he controls.

The task is always the same—approach the wall. My collar buzzes as I near, a low hum that quickly intensifies into sharp, biting shocks. I try to brace myself for the pain, but it's impossible. Each step sends a fresh wave of agony through my body until I'm trembling, my legs barely holding me upright.

Malfor watches, his expression one of detached amusement as I struggle. His voice, calm and collected, cuts through the haze of pain.

"You know what to do. You can't stop until you touch the wall."

But I can't. I can't bear the escalating pain, the shocks that feel like fire searing through my nerves. My legs give out, and I collapse to the ground, gasping for breath, tears streaming down my face.

"Pathetic," Malfor mutters, but he doesn't let me stop. Not until he's satisfied that I've been sufficiently broken for the day. Then, he drags me back to the cell, tossing me inside like a discarded toy, and locks me in the darkness once more.

The cycle repeats day after day.

Each day, I brace myself for the agony, but it's a battle I lose every time. The collar buzzes as I approach the wall; its hum is a cruel whisper of what's to come.

The shocks start as a sharp sting, then quickly escalate, turning my nerves into live wires. The pain is blinding, each step a monumental effort as my body convulses in protest. I grit my teeth, trying to push through, but my legs buckle, and I collapse before I can reach the wall.

Malfor watches, arms crossed, his gaze cold and unfeeling.

"Again." His voice is a whip that lashes my spirit.

He never lets me rest or gives me time to recover. He drags me back to the starting point, and I try again, and again, and again, until my body is trembling, soaked in sweat, and my vision blurs with tears.

Days blend together, a relentless cycle of pain and failure. Each time I fall, Malfor's sneer deepens, his disappointment palpable, but he doesn't let me quit. Not until he decides I've suffered enough for the day, and he throws me back into the darkness of my cell.

Slowly, something shifts in me, a tiny ember of defiance that refuses to be extinguished. I brace myself differently, mentally fortifying myself against the pain. I focus on the wall, forcing every ounce of willpower into my legs, driving them forward even as the shocks sear through my body.

The pain is excruciating, but I fight through it, each step a victory in itself. Then, one day, something incredible happens.

I touch the wall.

My hand, trembling and raw, presses against the rough surface. Agonizing shocks still pulse through the collar, but I hold my ground, refusing to let the pain drag me down. Tears stream down my face, but they are tears of triumph.

Tears of joy.

I did it.

I finally did it.

Malfor's gaze sharpens as he steps forward, studying me with approval. A twisted smile curls his lips as he reaches into his coat and pulls out a small scrap of fabric. He tosses it at my feet.

"Congratulations." His voice drips with condescension, but I don't care. "You've earned this."

I stare at the cloth for a moment until the realization sinks in. He's offering me a reward. A small scrap of clothing, a pitiful token in exchange for the torment I've endured. But in this hellish existence, even this scrap feels like a victory.

I reach down, my fingers closing around the fabric, and for the first time in what feels like forever, I have something to cover myself with.

It's a small, pitiful comfort, but it's mine. I wrap it around my body, feeling the rough texture against my skin. It doesn't hide much, barely covering my chest and shoulders, but it's more than I've had since this nightmare began.

Malfor watches with a satisfied smirk. "Don't get used to it," he warns, his tone sharp. "Clothing is a privilege. One misstep, and I'll take it away again."

His words are true, but for now, I cling to this small victory. It's a reminder that even in the depths of despair, I can still fight and win something, however small. The pain, the darkness, the humiliation —they haven't broken me completely.

Not yet.

I'm done with that wretched wall and avoid it like the plague, but my torment has only begun.

The days blur together in a haze of fear and forced compliance. Every degrading task Malfor demands is punctuated by the sting of his lash, leaving angry red marks, welts, and cuts on my skin.

The pain is his sadistic signature, a brutal reminder that I belong to him, but it's the weight of his cold, calculating gaze that presses hardest on me.

When it's finally over, I collapse onto the cold floor, my body trembling with exhaustion and pain. My skin is bruised and tender to the touch. Each movement sends sharp stabs of agony through my muscles. The evidence of his cruelty is etched in every wince, every shallow breath, and the way my body betrays me with each trembling step.

THIRTY-ONE

Blake

——————

THE READY ROOM DOOR SWINGS OPEN UNDER MY TOUCH, THE familiar click of the latch echoing in the sudden silence. Every eye in the room turns to me. Exhaustion and determination fill their faces. The air is thick with tension and the acrid smell of too much coffee.

Alpha team huddles around one end of the long table, Max's imposing figure bent over a stack of reports. At the other end, Brady and his Bravo team pore over a map, their hushed whispers a constant undercurrent. My team is scattered throughout the room, each lost in their preparations.

I make my way to an empty chair, greeting Gabe and Walt. The dark circles under their eyes mirror my own, a testament to the sleepless nights we've all endured. As I sit, I catch sight of Mitzy and her tech team in the corner. Stitch's fingers fly over her keyboard while Jeb's eyes never leave the screens before them.

At the head of the table, Ethan stands with Sam and CJ, their hushed conversation breaking off as I approach. Forest Summers looms behind them, his presence a reminder of the gravity of our situation.

Sam straightens, his eyes sweeping the room. The low hum of conversation dies away as he clears his throat.

"Alright, people. Let's get started." His voice carries the weight of command, cutting through the tension. "We've been at this for days now, and I know we're all feeling the pressure, but we can't afford to rush this. We do this right, or we don't do it at all. Understood?"

A chorus of affirmatives ripples through the room. I force myself to nod, even as impatience gnaws at my insides. Every moment we spend here is another moment Sophia's in danger. But Ethan's right. We can't afford mistakes.

"Good. Now, status updates. Max, what's Alpha got?"

Max pushes away from the table, his jaw set in frustration. "We've run down every lead on Greaves. Nothing. It's like the bastard's gone completely off the grid."

"Europe's not looking any better," Brady chimes in, his fingers drumming a restless tattoo on the table. "Our contacts have been working overtime, but it's all smoke and mirrors. Greaves is covering his tracks well."

My fists clench involuntarily, nails digging into my palms. I force them to relax, focusing on my breathing the way Ethan taught me.

Control. I need to maintain control.

Ethan's eyes find mine, a silent question in their depths. "Blake? Anything new on your end?"

I shake my head, the motion sharp despite my efforts to remain calm. "Nothing concrete. We've been through Sophia's apartment, her locker, every place she frequented. No new messages, no hidden clues. Just—nothing."

The word hangs in the air, heavy with all our collective disappointments. I see the same frustration mirrored in the faces around me. We're all feeling it, this maddening sense of running in circles while time slips away.

But we can't give up. Sophia's counting on us. And I'll be damned if I let her down.

Stitch's eyes dart across her screen. She looks up, confusion etched on her face. "Mitzy, I'm receiving a data stream from one of our bumblebee drones." Stitch's fingers fly over her keyboard. "It's sending video."

The room erupts in a flurry of movement. Chairs scrape against the floor as everyone surges forward, the air suddenly electric with anticipation.

Sam's deep voice cuts through the chaos. "Find out where it's transmitting from."

The room falls silent, all eyes turning to the main screen as it flickers to life. A grainy image appears, and my breath catches in my throat. The main screen flickers to life, displaying a map with a blinking red dot.

"It's in Montenegro."

The atmosphere in the room shifts, tension ratcheting up another notch. Montenegro. We have a location.

"Show us," Ethan commands, his voice tight with barely contained emotion.

Stitch nods, tapping her screen. The map disappears, replaced by grainy footage. My heart leaps into my throat as I recognize the figure on the screen.

Sophia.

Her face is gaunt, cheekbones sharp under sallow skin. She stands at one end of what looks like a courtyard, her body tense, poised to move.

As she takes a halting step forward, her body suddenly convulses. A collective gasp ripples through the room. My knuckles turn white as I grip the edge of the table, the metal digging into my palms.

"What the hell is around her neck?" Gabe's voice is barely above a whisper.

Realization dawns, cold and sickening.

"It's a collar. A fucking shock collar.

We watch in horrified silence as Sophia takes another step, then another, each accompanied by increasingly violent spasms. She's moving toward a high wall, her progress agonizingly slow.

With each step, the intensity of her pain seems to increase. My nails dig into my palms, my whole body rigid with fury and helplessness.

Suddenly, a figure steps into frame. A short man in a rumpled suit with cold eyes that seem to bore through the camera.

Malfor?

Is it possible we're seeing him for the first time, the phantom given physical form?

"Mitzy—" Sam starts.

"On it," Mitzy interrupts, her fingers already flying over her keyboard. "Running facial recognition now. We'll find this bastard."

The footage continues, showing the same scene playing out day after day. Sophia, being led from a cell, forced to approach the wall, collapsing in agony each time.

"He's conditioning her," I growl, the words clawing their way out of my throat. "He's training her not to try to escape."

A low, rumbling cough cuts through the tension. Forest steps forward, his face grim. "That's not what's happening."

I whirl to face him, anger bubbling up. "What do you mean?"

Forest holds up a hand, silencing me. "Watch closely. It's not about the wall."

On screen, Sophia reaches out, her hand trembling violently, and touches the wall. Malfor's face fills the frame, his satisfaction palpable even through the poor quality of the video. He dangles something in front of Sophia—a scrap of fabric.

"He's breaking her, piece by piece." Forest crosses his arms over his chest.

And then we see it. The ghost of a smile tugging at her lips as she accepts the meager reward.

"Oh God," Ethan breathes, the horror of understanding dawning on his face.

Forest nods, his voice heavy. "This isn't about the wall. It's about fulfilling Malfor's demands, no matter how cruel or pointless. He's conditioning her to find joy in compliance, to crave his approval."

The room falls silent as the weight of Forest's words sinks in. This is beyond physical torture. This is the systematic destruction of a person's will and sense of self.

"It's the worst kind of dehumanization," Forest continues, his eyes never leaving the screen. "Because eventually, the victim begins to participate in their degradation. They find pride in pleasing their tormentor."

The room erupts in a cacophony of voices, but I barely hear anything. All I can see is Sophia's face, contorted in pain, yet still pushing forward.

Still fighting.

I stare at the image of Sophia, clutching that scrap of fabric like it's the most precious thing in the world, and feel something break inside me.

"We need to move," I say, my voice low and dangerous, barely recognizable to my own ears. "Now."

Ethan's hand lands on my shoulder, a steadying presence. "We will, but we do this smart. We do this right."

I force air into my lungs. Ethan's right. We can't let emotion cloud our judgment. Not when the stakes are this high.

"Stitch," Sam's authoritative voice cuts through the thick silence. "What else did the drone send us?"

Stitch tears her eyes away from the screen, visibly shaken. "Coordinates. And a rough map of the compound's interior. The drone's been gathering data this whole time."

"Good." Ethan nods, his jaw set. "That's our starting point. Mitzy, I want a full analysis of that compound. Brady and Max start working on infiltration scenarios. We need options."

As the room springs into action around me, I force myself to focus.

We have a location.

We have intel.

Now, we plan.

And then, we move.

Hang on, Sophia. We're coming for you.

As for Malfor? He'll pay for every second of pain he's caused. That's a promise I intend to keep.

The initial shock of the footage fades, replaced by a tense silence.

Gabe is the first to break it, his voice tight with skepticism. "How do we know this isn't some elaborate setup? Malfor could be forcing Sophia to lead us into a trap. He knows we'll come for her."

Walt nods, his brow furrowed. "It wouldn't be the first time someone's used a hostage as bait."

My jaw clenches, a retort on the tip of my tongue, but Ethan beats me to it.

"Valid concerns." Ethan scans the room. "But let's think this through. What are the chances Malfor could have hijacked one of our drones?"

Mitzy shakes her head, her multi-colored hair swaying. "Next to impossible. The encryption on those things is state-of-the-art. Plus, the data signature matches our protocols perfectly."

"Could be a perfect forgery," Brady suggests, arms crossed over his chest.

Jeb clears his throat. "Unlikely. The drone's been sending sporadic bursts of data for days now. We'd have spotted inconsistencies by now if it were a forgery."

Sam steps forward, his presence commanding attention. "Let's not forget, Sophia left us messages before she disappeared. She warned us about a potential trap. This could be her way of giving us the information we need while maintaining that warning."

The room falls silent as we all consider this.

Forest's gravelly voice cuts through the tension. "In my experience, the most effective traps often contain elements of truth. If this is a setup, it's a damned good one, but that doesn't mean we shouldn't act on it."

CJ nods, his expression resolute. "Forest is right. Trap or not, we can't afford to ignore this opportunity." He straightens, his posture shifting into what we all recognize as *command mode*. "Alright, people. We're moving forward with this, but we're doing it smart. Here's how we're breaking this down."

Sam turns to Mitzy and her team. "I want every scrap of data from that drone analyzed. Location, layout, security measures—anything that could give us an edge. Stitch, see if you can establish two-way communication with the drone. If Sophia's controlling it somehow, we need to know."

"She can't." Stitch shakes her head. "It's operating in full-autonomous mode. I doubt she's been in contact with it for days." She doesn't wait for a response, turning back to her computer as if that conversation's over.

"Alpha, Bravo, and Charlie teams, I want working infiltration scenarios. That compound looks like a fortress—I want options for every possible entry point." Sam turns to CJ and Mitzy. "I need the two of you to coordinate with our contacts in Montenegro. We'll need local support and potentially a cover story for why a team of American operatives is suddenly very interested in a private villa."

"On it," CJ confirms, already pulling out his phone.

Sam's gaze sweeps the room one last time. "Remember, people —Malfor threatens everything we stand for. Taking him down is a priority. Let's move."

We have direction now. We're going no matter what Malfor has planned or what traps he might have set.

THIRTY-TWO

Blake

The ready room has transformed into a war zone. Screens flicker with satellite imagery, 3D models rotate in mid-air, and the air is thick with tension and determination. Ethan and I stand before the main display, our faces bathed in the blue glow of data streams.

"Alright," Ethan says, his voice low and focused. "We need to approach this smart. Malfor's expecting us. How do we avoid playing into his hands?"

I take a deep breath, forcing myself to think tactically rather than emotionally. "We subvert his expectations. He'll be prepared for a frontal assault. We need to hit him from multiple angles."

Ethan's eyebrow raises, a glimmer of interest in his eyes. "Go on."

"A three-pronged approach," I continue, warming to the idea. "We create a diversion at the main gate, loud and obvious. The second team comes in from the sea, scaling those impassible cliffs. The third team comes from above. Either parachuting in or hang gliding." I point to the cliffs above Malfor's villa.

Ethan nods slowly, considering. "It's risky, but it might just work. The cliff climb is going to be a hell of a challenge, though."

"That's why we put our best climbers on that team. Gabe and I have the most experience with vertical ascents. We can do this."

Ethan shakes his head firmly. "You're too emotionally invested. I can't have you on the most dangerous approach. You'll be with me, parachuting in." Before I can respond, Walt calls out from across the room.

"Ethan, Blake. You need to see this."

We make our way to Walt and Rigel, who are hunched over an array of screens displaying satellite imagery. The images show Malfor's compound from various angles and at different times of day.

"What are we looking at?" Ethan asks, his eyes scanning the displays.

Rigel zooms in on one image, enhancing a section of the perimeter wall. "See these shadows? They're consistent with mobile gun emplacements. And here," he swipes to another image, "thermal imaging suggests automated defense systems on the roof."

"Damn," I mutter, the complexity of our task becoming even more apparent. "Any blind spots?"

Walt shakes his head grimly. "Not that we can see. This place is locked down tight. But," he pulls up another image, this one focusing on the cliff face, "we might have caught a break here. See these indentations? They could be handholds, possibly left over from the original construction."

Ethan leans in, his eyes narrowing. "Good catch. That could make our cliff approach more viable. Blake, what do you think?"

I study the image, my mind racing with possibilities. "It's something, but we can't count on it. We need to be prepared for a sheer climb."

"Agreed." Ethan nods. "Alright, let's get the team together. Time to put all this intel to use."

Minutes later, Charlie team is assembled in the VR training space. The VR world has been transformed into a precise replica of Malfor's compound, every detail meticulously recreated from the bumblebee's gathered intelligence.

"Listen up," Ethan's voice carries across the room. "We're

running full combat and rescue sims. I want everyone cycling through each approach—land assault, cliff climb, and aerial insertion. Gabe, Walt, you're on Team One, land assault. Rigel and Hank, you're on Team Two, cliff climb. Blake, you're with me on Team Three, parachute insertion."

As we don our VR gear, a surge of adrenaline rushes through me. This is it. Our first real step toward rescuing Sophia.

"Remember," Ethan continues, "Malfor's men will be using live ammunition. In this sim, if you're hit, you're out. Treat every engagement as if your life depends on it because when we do this for real, it will."

The first simulation begins, and it's a disaster from the start.

The simulation begins, and Ethan and I are suddenly in a plane, high above Malfor's fortress. The night sky surrounds us, and the compound below looks like a malevolent spider web of lights and defenses.

"Team Two, you're clear to start your ascent," Ethan continues. "Team Three, you have the go." Ethan's voice crackles in my ear. "Begin your approach."

Ethan and I jump; the rush of freefall sends my heart racing. As we near our drop zone, I deploy my chute. The sudden jerk as it opens feels all too real.

"Team One, begin your assault," Ethan orders as we drift silently toward the compound.

In the distance, explosions and gunfire rip through the air.

The diversion has begun.

As we near the roof of the compound, I spot movement below. "Guards on the roof, nine o'clock."

Time seems to slow as I assess our options. We're exposed, hanging in the air with no cover. If those guards raise the alarm, the entire mission is compromised.

"I've got this." I unholster my sidearm. Two quick shots, precise despite the sway of the parachute, and the guards crumple without a sound.

"Nice shooting," Ethan approves. "But we need to move faster. More will be here soon."

We land on the roof, quickly discarding our chutes and readying our weapons. Just as we prepare to enter the building, alarms blare across the compound.

It's a total shitshow from there on out.

Team One gets pinned down at the main gate, unable to provide effective cover. Team Two's climb is painfully slow, leaving them exposed to sniper fire from the walls.

Our parachute insertion goes smoothly, but without support from the other teams, we're quickly overwhelmed.

"Reset," Ethan calls out, his voice tight with frustration. "We need to rethink our approach."

We run the simulation again, and again, each time tweaking our strategy. But every attempt ends in failure. By the fifth run-through, the tension in the room is palpable.

"This isn't working." I toss my gear aside. "We're spread too thin. We need more manpower."

Ethan nods, his face grim. "You're right. It's time to bring in Alpha and Bravo teams."

The next day, the training room is packed with all three Guardian teams. Max, leader of Alpha, and Brady from Bravo listen intently as Ethan outlines our new strategy.

"Alpha team will take the walls," Ethan explains. "Your firepower should be enough to punch through their defenses. Bravo, you'll come in from the sky—HALO jump, full tactical gear. Charlie will take the cliffs. It's a hell of a climb, but it's our best shot at a surprise entry."

We run the simulation again, this time with all three teams. The results are better, but still not good enough. Alpha breaches the walls but gets bogged down in close-quarters combat. Bravo's aerial insertion is more successful, but they struggle to link up with the other teams. Charlie makes it up the cliffs, but barely half the team survives the ascent.

"Damn it," Max curses as we regroup. "We're still missing something."

The room falls into a tense silence, each of us lost in thought. It's Brady who breaks it, his voice thoughtful.

"What about a distraction? Something big enough to draw their attention away from our main assault."

"Like what?" I ask, intrigued.

Brady grins. "How about a 'malfunction' in one of their automated defense systems? If we could hack it, make it start firing randomly…"

Mitzy, who's been following our progress from the VR command suite, perks up at this. "That—might be possible. Give me a few hours with the data we've collected, and I might be able to create a virus that could do just that."

As the ideas flow, the energy in the room shifts from frustration to determined problem-solving. But then Max raises a question that brings us all up short.

"This is all well and good," he says, "but we're overlooking a crucial detail. How the hell are we going to find Sophia once we're inside? That compound is massive, and we can't afford to search room by room."

The question hangs in the air. We've been so focused on getting in, we haven't considered what happens next.

It's Mitzy who breaks the silence, her eyes lighting up with that familiar spark of innovation. "I have the perfect solution for that," she says, "but first, I've got some new tech that could help with our initial assault."

She moves to a large case in the corner of the room, opening it to reveal a high-tech exoskeleton. "This," she announces proudly, "is our answer to the wall problem. Exosuits that'll give you enhanced strength and agility. Should make scaling those walls a hell of a lot easier."

"For the cliff team," she continues, turning to another case, "I've been working with the RUFI. We can modify them for climbing—think mobile anchors. They'll reduce the risk of falling and help with the ascent."

"Help?" I look at the guys. "How?"

"They're more nimble than you. I can get them up the cliffs in increments, then pull you up on pulleys. Think of winches hoisting you up."

"I don't know about dangling from a RUFI. There's trust, and then there's trust." Gabe arches his brow.

"Trust me, it'll work. We'll run simulations on the rock wall at the gym. You'll see what I mean."

She then pulls out a piece of fabric that shimmers and shifts as she moves it. It's a bit disorienting and makes me sick to my stomach if I stare at it for too long.

"And for our air team, meet our new stealth material. It adapts to match the surrounding sky, making you nearly invisible during your descent."

The room bursts into excited chatter as we examine the new tech. It's impressive, no doubt about it, but I can't shake the nagging worry about Sophia's location.

"This is great, Mitzy," I say, "but what about Max's question? How do we find Sophia?"

Mitzy's grin widens. "That's where this comes in," she says, holding up what looks like a miniature version of our bumblebee drone. "I call it the Queen Bee. It's designed to seek out and lock onto the signal from Sophia's drone. Once it finds it, it'll lead us straight to her."

The room falls silent as we process this. It's Ethan who finally speaks, his voice filled with cautious optimism.

"Alright," he says, "let's incorporate all of this into our plan. We'll run more simulations to see how these new elements change things. But remember, people—no plan survives first contact with the enemy. We need to be prepared to adapt on the fly."

As we break to prepare for the next round of simulations, I feel a renewed sense of hope. We're getting closer. Each new idea and each piece of tech brings us one step closer to rescuing Sophia.

We spend the next several days running simulation after simulation, refining our approach. The casualties are still high, but we're making progress. By the end of the week, we manage a run where we extract Sophia with only one casualty—not great, but a vast improvement over our initial attempts.

As we gear down from our final sim of the day, Ethan addresses the teams. "Good work, people. We're getting there. But we're not done yet. I want everyone to study the compound layout and memorize every detail. We drill again at 0600."

The next few days blur together. We run combat drills, practice cliff climbing techniques with the RUFI, refine our HALO jump procedures, and put Mitzy's new exosuits to the test.

Every spare moment is spent pouring over intel, discussing contingencies, and preparing for every possible scenario.

Finally, after what feels like an eternity of preparation, Ethan calls us all together. The room falls silent as he surveys the assembled teams, his eyes hard with determination.

"Listen up," he says, his voice carrying to every corner of the room. "We've trained, we've planned, and we've prepared. Now it's time to execute. In 48 hours, we launch."

He pauses, letting the weight of the moment sink in. "This won't be easy. Malfor's compound is a fortress, and he's expecting us. But we have surprise, we have skill, and most importantly, we have each other. Watch your teammates' backs, stick to the plan, and we'll all come home. Any questions?"

The room is silent.

"Alright then." Ethan raises his right pointer finger and swirls it in a circle. "Gear up. We move out at 0200." As the teams disperse to make final preparations, Ethan's voice cuts through the buzz of activity. "Hold up, people. We've got one more briefing. Mitzy's team has some updates for us."

We reassemble, the atmosphere electric with anticipation. Mitzy steps forward, her usual excitement tempered by the gravity of our mission.

"Alright, folks," she begins, "we've made some final tweaks to our tech. Stitch, why don't you fill them in on the Trojan horse?"

Stitch steps up, her fingers dancing over a tablet as she speaks. "We've developed a virus that should give us access to Malfor's security systems. Once inserted, it'll create a backdoor for us to manipulate their defenses."

"How sure are we that this will work?" Max asks, his voice skeptical.

Stitch's grin is fierce. "Pretty damn sure. We've been testing it against simulations of their firewalls. It's not foolproof, but it's our best shot at giving you guys an edge."

Ethan nods. "Good work. What's the deployment plan?"

"We'll need to physically insert it into their main server," Stitch explains. "Once that's done, I can remote in and work my magic."

The room buzzes with murmurs as we process this information. It's a risky move, but if it works, it could turn the tide in our favor.

Jeb steps forward next, his face grim. "We've also been working on psychological profiles of Malfor and his key lieutenants." He taps his tablet, bringing up a series of images on the main screen. "Based on what we know, Malfor is likely to respond to our assault with overwhelming force. He's not the type to cut his losses and run."

"What about Sophia?" I ask, unable to keep the edge from my voice. "How's he likely to use her against us?"

Jeb's expression softens slightly. "It's hard to say for certain, but given his pattern of behavior, he's likely to use her as bait or a human shield. We need to be prepared for either scenario."

The weight of his words settles over the room. We all know the risks but hearing them laid out so starkly makes them feel more real.

"Which brings us to extraction," Ethan says, steering the conversation forward. "Once we locate Sophia, how do we get her out safely?"

Brady, from Bravo team, speaks up. "We've been working on a modified rappel system. If we can get her to the roof, we can have a chopper extract her while the rest of us provide cover fire."

"And if we can't get her to the roof?" I press, scenarios running through my mind.

"Then we fall back to Plan B," Ethan replies. "Overland extraction. It's riskier, but we'll have vehicles standing by just in case."

We spend the next hour going over every detail of the plan, refining our approach, discussing contingencies. By the time we're done, I feel like I could navigate Malfor's compound blindfolded.

As we break to do our final gear checks, I feel a hand on my shoulder. It's Gabe, his face uncharacteristically serious.

"We've got this," he says, his voice low. "We're going to get her back."

I nod, grateful for his support. "I know. Thanks, man."

The next hour is a flurry of activity as we make our final preparations. I check and recheck my gear, the familiar routine helping to calm my nerves. Around me, the other team members are doing the same, their movements precise and focused.

Finally, it's time. We gather one last time before heading to the transport. Ethan looks at each of us in turn, his gaze steady and determined.

"Remember your training. Trust your team. And no matter what happens, we all come home. Clear?"

A chorus of "Clear" echoes through the room.

THIRTY-THREE

Sophia

As evening approaches, a new face enters the room. A raven-haired beauty, her eyes are wary as she approaches with a first aid kit.

"This is Violet. She'll patch you up," Malfor orders. "Can't have my newest toy falling apart on me, can we?"

The woman's touch is gentle as she tends to my wounds. When our eyes meet, my pain and fear are reflected back at me. She moves quietly, her long, dark, wavy hair pulled back, framing a face that strikes a faint chord of recognition within me. She doesn't say a word, just kneels beside me, her hands gentle as they assess my injuries.

Her touch is skilled and methodical as she cleans the cuts and bruises left by Malfor's lash. Every so often, she pauses, her dark eyes flicking up to meet mine, a silent communication passing between us. I search her face, trying to place where I've seen her before, but the memory eludes me, slipping away like a shadow in the dark.

She applies a cool salve to the raw welts on my back, her fingers working quickly but carefully. The pain dulls slightly, though it doesn't fade entirely. Her gaze sharpens, catching the wince I can't quite suppress, and she offers the barest nod of acknowledgment.

"Thank you," I whisper when Malfor steps out briefly.

Her lips press into a thin line as she finishes bandaging a particularly deep cut. She leans closer, her breath warm against my ear as she whispers, "We're not allowed to speak."

I nod slightly, understanding the warning. She pulls back, her expression neutral, returning to her task with the same quiet focus. When she's done, she stands and gives me a final, lingering glance before turning away. The door closes behind her with a soft click, leaving me alone with my thoughts and the echo of her silent care.

Later, as I'm left alone to "rest," I replay a conversation I overheard earlier.

Malfor, discussing shipment details with someone. Information that could be valuable to the Guardians—if only I could get it to them. The thought of my former allies sends a pang through my chest.

Do they know what's happened to me? Do they care? Or do they see me only as a traitor?

That night, as I curl up on the thin mattress, I allow myself to remember Blake's arms around me, his laugh, and the safety I felt in his presence. The memory is a double-edged sword, comforting and tormenting in equal measure. I'm curious if he's looking for me and if he understands why I did what I did. The thought of him hating me is almost as painful as my physical wounds.

A soft knock pulls me from my thoughts. The woman who tended me slips into the room, a finger to her lips. She pulls out a phone and shows me a video. Luke, alive and unharmed, playing with some toys. My heart leaps into my throat at the sight of him.

"He's okay," she whispers. "I'm watching over him."

Tears stream down my face, relief and anguish warring within me. "Thank you," I choke out, my voice barely audible.

We talk quietly, sharing what little information we have. Two captives, bound by circumstance, finding a small measure of solace in each other's company. But Malfor, ever vigilant, isn't far away. We hear his heavy footsteps approaching, and the woman quickly hides the phone and slips out of the room.

Days pass in a haze of pain and fear. Violet returns each day to tend to my wounds, her gentle hands so different from Malfor's cruelty. We develop a system of communication through looks and subtle gestures, conveying what we can't say aloud.

One evening, as Violet changes my bandages, her hands tremble slightly. Her eyes dart to the door more frequently than usual, and there's a tightness around her mouth that wasn't there before.

"What's wrong?" I mouth silently when she meets my gaze.

She shakes her head minutely, but there's fear in her eyes. Something's changed, and not for the better. As she finishes her work, she presses something into my hand—a small piece of paper. I curl my fingers around it, hiding it from view.

That night, when I'm sure I'm alone, I unfold the paper. In tiny, cramped writing, it reads: *"Malfor plans to move you soon. Be ready."*

My heart races. Move me where? I swallow hard, trying to push down the panic rising in my throat. I have to stay calm, stay focused. For Luke.

The next day, Violet brings me food—a luxury I haven't been afforded often. As she sets down the tray, she leans close, pretending to adjust my blanket.

"Eat," she whispers. "You'll need your strength."

Whatever's coming, I need to be as prepared as possible. As I eat, I study Violet more closely. There's something in her eyes, a determination beyond mere sympathy for a fellow captive. She's risking a lot to help me, but why?

There's no time to ask because she's already slipping out of the room. Her visits are always brief—she can't afford to linger.

That night, Violet returns with her phone.

"We don't have much time," she says urgently, her voice barely above a whisper. "Malfor's out, but he won't be gone long."

She shows me another video of Luke, this time with a beautiful raven-haired girl of about seven years old I don't recognize. My son looks unharmed, playing quietly.

"Who is she?" I ask, my eyes fixed on the screen.

Violet's voice catches as she replies, "She's my daughter... Zephyr."

The name strikes me as unusual and beautiful. I look up at Violet, seeing the love and pain in her eyes as she watches the video.

"Your daughter?" I'm confused, with a hundred questions bubbling up inside me.

She nods, her eyes never leaving the screen. "Yes. I-I lost her a long time ago, but she's safe now—like Luke."

I reach out, grasping Violet's hand. "Thank you," I whisper fervently. "For showing me this. But, Violet, why? Why are you risking so much?"

Violet's eyes meet mine, filled with determination and fear. "Because I know what it's like to be separated from your child. Not knowing if they're safe or if you'll ever see them again. No mother should have to go through that."

Her words hit me hard, and tears well up in my eyes.

"How did you end up here?" I ask, unable to stop myself.

Violet glances at the door, then back at me. She takes a deep breath as if steeling herself. "It's a long story, but I think... I think you need to know."

She settles beside me, her voice dropping even lower. "Like you, I was taken years ago when I was barely more than a girl myself. They—they used me as a surrogate."

My breath catches in my throat. The horror of what she's saying sinks in slowly.

"Zephyr," Violet continues, her voice trembling slightly, "she wasn't supposed to be mine. She was a surrogate birth, a job, nothing more. But the moment I felt her kick inside me, I knew I couldn't let her be just another commodity."

She pauses, lost in the memory. I squeeze her hand, encouraging her to continue.

I listen intently, my eyes drawn to the beautiful raven-haired girl in the video. There's a glimmer of recognition in the way Zephyr moves, something about her spirit that echoes the woman's own quiet strength.

"The client contracted with Malfor for a child, but he wanted a son. When Zephyr was born, Malfor was not pleased. I was terrified of what would happen to her. The client... Something happened to him. I don't know the details, but I think Malfor might have had something to do with it. For whatever reason, Malfor kept Zephyr. I can only assume he has plans for her, plans that terrify me."

Her eyes fill with unshed tears, her voice choked with emotion. "I've tried to protect her, to give her love and comfort, even in this terrible place. But it's only a matter of time before Malfor takes her away from me. He's grooming her for something, and I can't bear the thought of what that might be."

My heart aches for her and for Zephyr. I can see the pain etched on her face, the desperate love of a mother trying to shield her child from a world of horror.

"When she was born, I tried to escape with her. But they caught me." Violet's voice breaks, and she closes her eyes as if trying to shut out the memory. "The punishment... It was severe. I thought I was going to die. I wanted to die."

I feel sick imagining the horrors she must have endured. "But you survived," I whisper.

Violet nods, her eyes haunted. "I survived. And when I didn't die, Malfor took me. He told me if I ever wanted to see Zephyr again, I'd do whatever he asked. No questions, no hesitation."

"So you've been here all this time? Working for him?"

"Yes," Violet says, her voice barely audible. "Tending to his 'guests,' doing whatever he asks. I'd do anything, endure anything, for Zephyr."

The weight of her words hangs heavy between us. I think of Luke, of the impossible choice I made to protect him. "And now you take care of her?"

Violet nods, a flicker of something like relief crossing her face. "It's the one mercy in all of this. I get to see Zephyr and care for her."

"But why help me?" I ask, still struggling to understand. "Why risk it?"

She looks at me, her eyes shining with unshed tears. "When I saw you, when I realized you were a mother too—I couldn't stand by and do nothing."

I'm overwhelmed by her story, by the strength it must have taken to survive all these years.

"How do you endure it?"

A soft smile touches Violet's lips. "Zephyr," she says. "The thought of her, the hope of being with her… It gives me strength. Even on the darkest days, when I feel like I can't go on, I remember her laugh, her smile. And I know I have to keep going."

Her words resonate deeply within me. I think of Luke, of how the mere sight of him in that video has renewed my determination to survive, to do whatever it takes to see him again.

"Tell me about her," I say softly, wanting to keep Violet talking, to strengthen this fragile connection between us. "You've done so much for her. You've given her hope and love in a place that offers neither."

Violet's eyes light up, a mother's love shining through despite everything. "She's—incredible. So smart, so kind. Even as a baby, she had this way of looking at the world, like everything was a wonderful new discovery."

She chuckles softly. "I used to sing to her, when she was inside me. Old lullabies my grandmother taught me. And you know what? Those same songs still calm her when she's upset."

I smile, remembering similar moments with Luke. "They remember," I say. "Even before they're born, they know us."

Violet nods, her expression turning serious. "Sophia, listen to me. What you did, infiltrating the Guardians… Malfor will use that against you. He knows more than anyone else, probably more than you realize. He talks… Sometimes he says things he shouldn't."

I feel a chill run down my spine. "What do you mean?"

Violet leans in closer, her voice barely above a whisper. "He has plans for you. I don't know all the details, but—he wants to break you, to turn you into a weapon. Maybe just for his own amusement, or maybe there's some larger plan. With Malfor, you can never be sure."

The weight of her words presses down on me, suffocating. I

want to say that I won't let him, that I'll find a way to make things right, but the words die in my throat. I know the truth—there is no making this right. This is the hand fate has dealt me, and for Luke's sake, I'll play it.

"Have you ever thought about trying to escape? To get Zephyr out of here?" My voice is small and hollow.

Violet's expression turns somber, and she shakes her head. "The one and only time I tried to escape, I nearly lost my life. Malfor… He's relentless. I can't risk it again, not when it could mean losing Zephyr forever. All I can do is stay here, be there for her, and hope for the best."

I understand her fear, but the thought of staying here, of accepting this fate, fills me with dread. "But what if there was a way? What if we could find help?"

She looks at me, her eyes filled with a mix of hope and despair. "I wish there was, but I won't risk it. All I can do is make sure Zephyr is safe. That's my only goal."

I nod, realizing the depth of her resolve. For now, we're both captives, bound by our love for our children. I can't help but hold onto the hope that there might still be a way out, a way to free Luke and Zephyr from this nightmare.

"So what do I do?"

Her eyes are filled with a mix of sympathy. "Behave. Do everything Malfor wants, without question. If you do that, if you prove yourself useful and obedient… Maybe, a few months from now, he might allow you to see Luke."

Hope and despair war within me at her words. The thought of seeing Luke again is everything to me, but the price—the price is my soul.

"Is that what you do?" I ask, searching her face. "Obey and hope?"

Violet nods, her expression a mask of resigned determination. "It's all we can do. For our children, we endure. We survive."

As she prepares to leave, I catch her arm. "Violet," I say softly, "thank you. For trusting me with your story. For everything. I don't know why fate brought us together, but I'm grateful it did."

She gives me a sad smile. "So am I. Remember what I said. Obey, endure, and maybe—maybe someday…"

As the door closes behind her, I lie back on the thin mattress, my mind racing. I think of Luke, of Blake, of the Guardians. I think of Violet and Zephyr, of the incredible strength it must take to hold onto even the smallest shred of hope in the darkest of circumstances.

I close my eyes, steeling myself for what's to come. Like Violet, I will do whatever it takes and endure whatever I must to see my son again.

It's not hope, not really. Hope implies a chance of something better. What we have is simpler and more primal. It's survival for the sake of our children. And sometimes, that has to be enough.

Malfor has made a grave mistake. His greatest miscalculation is underestimating the power of a mother's love, because a mother's love is the most powerful weapon in the world.

THIRTY-FOUR

Blake

THE CAVERNOUS HOLD OF THE TRANSPORT SHIP ECHOES WITH THE low murmur of voices and the metallic clicks of final equipment checks. We're outside Montenegro.

The night sky roils with an approaching storm. Distant flashes of lightning illuminate the choppy seas below. The air is thick with anticipation and the acrid smell of gun oil and nervous sweat.

CJ's commanding voice cuts through the ambient noise, silencing all conversation. "Guardians, listen up. We're T-minus thirty minutes. Let's go over it one last time."

I scan the faces around me—Alpha, Bravo, and Charlie teams are all gathered in one place, a rare sight that underscores the gravity of our mission. Each face is a mask of grim determination, eyes sharp with focus despite the long hours of preparation.

CJ activates a holographic display in the center of the hold, showing a 3D rendering of Malfor's compound.

"Alpha team," he zooms in on the perimeter walls, "you'll be our battering ram. Hit the main gate hard and loud. Create as much noise as you can. We want every guard in that compound scrambling to deal with you."

Max, the leader of Alpha team, steps forward. His voice is gruff but confident. "We've got enough explosives to make the Fourth of July look like a kid's sparkler party. Those bastards won't know what hit 'em."

CJ nods approvingly before shifting the hologram to show the airspace above the compound. "Bravo, you're our eyes in the sky. HALO jump from 30,000 feet, full stealth gear. Your primary objective is to neutralize their air defenses, specifically those guns on the towers, then provide overwatch and support for Charlie team's infiltration."

Brady, Bravo's leader, runs a hand over his closely cropped hair. "Understood. Weather will make the jump tricky, but nothing we can't handle. We'll be guardian angels with very big guns."

Finally, CJ turns to us. The hologram zooms in on the sheer cliffs at the rear of the compound. "Charlie team, you've got the most complex insertion. Two-hundred-foot climb up those cliffs, then a silent infiltration to locate and extract the primary target."

Ethan nods solemnly. "We're ready. The RUFI have the climbing route, and our exosuits are prepped for the ascent."

"Blake." CJ's eyes lock onto mine, his gaze intense. "Once inside, you're on point for locating Sophia. Are you prepared for what you might find?"

I swallow hard, forcing my voice to remain steady. "Yes, sir. Whatever condition she's in, we're bringing her home."

CJ holds my gaze for a moment longer before addressing the entire group. "Mitzy, give us an update on the bumblebee drone."

Mitzy's voice comes through the comms, clear despite the distance. "Drone is active and currently with the primary target. Once Charlie team is inside, we can provide real-time guidance to her location. Be advised, the drone's movements suggest the target is not stationary within the compound."

A ripple of murmurs passes through the group at this news. CJ raises a hand for silence. "This doesn't change the plan, people. We adapt and overcome. Any questions?"

The hold is silent, each Guardian mentally preparing for their role in the mission ahead.

"Alright," CJ continues, his voice carrying the weight of

command. "You've trained for this. You know your roles. Stay flexible, watch each other's backs, and complete the mission. Failure is not an option. Am I clear?"

A chorus of "Yes, sir!" echoes through the hold.

"Good. Alpha team, your transport leaves in thirty minutes. Get to your vehicle and prepare for insertion. Bravo, your bird takes off in ten. Charlie, you've got fifteen minutes before your boat drops you at the base of those cliffs. Move out, Guardians."

The hold erupts into controlled chaos as the teams gather their gear and move toward their respective transports.

Gabe places his hand on my shoulder, his usually jovial face serious. "We're getting her back."

Unable to find the words, I give a sharp nod. As I move toward Charlie team's area, I catch sight of the storm through a porthole. The waves are growing larger, and white caps are visible even in the darkness. The weather is going to make an already tricky mission even more challenging.

I join my team, and we begin our final equipment checks; a profound sense of calm settles over me. We've prepared for this. We're ready. And come hell or high water, we're bringing Sophia home.

The klaxon sounds, signaling five minutes until our departure. I take a deep breath, centering myself.

It's time.

Ethan gathers Charlie team around him, his face illuminated by the dim red lighting of the hold. "Alright, people, this is it." His voice is low but intense. "We've trained for this. We know what's at stake. Whatever happens in there, we all come home. Clear?"

A chorus of affirmatives echoes through our group. Our voices nearly drowned out by a particularly loud crash of thunder. We check our gear one last time. The exosuits hum with quiet power as we activate them.

We move to the side hatch, sliding it open. The storm's fury hits us full force—wind howling, rain lashing at our faces, the air thick with the smell of ozone. Lightning illuminates the churning sea below. The cliff face we're about to approach looms ominously in the distance.

One by one, we prepare to deploy into the RIB, the inflatable boat swaying slightly as it hangs from the winch. The tension is palpable as we secure our gear.

"Deploy RUFI," Ethan orders.

The three robotic units are lowered into the RIB first. Their waterproof bodies unfold, revealing compact flotation devices. They settle into the boat, immediately orienting themselves toward the shore.

We follow, climbing down into the RIB with practiced efficiency. The boat rocks beneath us, a stark reminder of the turbulent sea waiting below. Once we're all aboard, Ethan gives the signal.

The winch whirs to life, and the boat begins its slow, steady descent toward the angry waters. The storm's roar is deafening as we brace ourselves for impact, the sea waiting to swallow us whole.

We hit the water with a jarring splash, the icy spray stinging our faces despite the protection of our gear. The waves immediately begin tossing us about, but the RIB is designed for these conditions.

Ethan guns the motor, and we surge forward, cutting through the tumultuous waters. The RUFI, secure in the boat with us, scan the surroundings, their built-in sonar guiding us through the treacherous sea toward the distant shore.

After an eternity of battling the elements, the cliff face looms closer. Ethan skillfully maneuvers the RIB, bringing us alongside a small, rocky outcropping at the base of the cliff.

"Comms check," Ethan's voice crackles in my ear.

We sound off one by one to confirm our comm links are operational.

"RUFI, begin the ascent," Ethan commands.

The robotic units spring into action, their limbs reconfiguring for climbing. They scurry up the rock face like crabs, displaying unsettling speed, pausing every few meters to drill in anchors and attach climbing ropes.

"Alright, team. Let's move." Ethan hits the base of the wall.

We begin our ascent, and the exosuits immediately prove their usefulness. Their enhanced strength makes pulling ourselves up the ropes almost effortless despite the weight of our gear and the relentless battering of the wind and rain.

The climb is brutal. The cliff face is slick, and the wind threatens to tear us from our precarious holds. But the RUFI prove their worth, scurrying up the rock face with inhuman agility and setting anchors for us to follow.

We ascend in a leapfrog pattern, with three RUFI and six men working in perfect synchronization.

Suddenly, a shout of alarm cuts through the howling wind. I look up just in time to see the RUFI immediately above me lose its grip on the slick rock face. For a heart-stopping moment, it plummets toward me.

"Hold on," Ethan yells unnecessarily.

The RUFUS's tether to its companions snaps taut, arresting its fall mere meters above my head. It swings wildly in the wind, struggling to regain purchase on the cliff.

"Blake, guide it back," Ethan orders, his voice steady despite the precarious situation.

I grab the RUFUS's frame and steady it against the rock face. Its limbs reconfigure, finding new holds, and it resumes its climb within moments.

"Nice save." Gabe's voice comes through the comms, a hint of his usual humor breaking through the tension. "I was not looking forward to being pancaked by a robot dog today."

"Cut the chatter and stay focused," Ethan reprimands. "We need to pick up the pace, but safety first. This cliff isn't going to beat us."

We continue our ascent, now hyperaware of every handhold and brace against every gust. The storm's fury intensifies the higher we climb as if Malfor himself is commanding the elements to repel us.

Finally, after what feels like hours, we near the top. Ethan signals for us to hold position a few feet below the edge, out of sight of potential guards.

"Charlie team, this is Command," CJ's voice crackles through our comms. "Alpha team is in position and ready to begin their assault. Bravo team is on final approach for HALO insertion. What's your status?"

"Charlie team is in position," Ethan replies, his breathing heavy from the climb. "Ready on your signal."

"Copy that, Charlie team. Bravo team, you are cleared to jump. Charlie team, hold for Bravo's insertion. On my mark, we initiate Phase Two."

We wait, clinging to the cliff face, the anticipation building. After a few tense minutes, Brady's voice comes through: "Bravo team on the roof. Ready to neutralize air defenses."

"All teams, execute." CJ's voice is filled with grim determination. "Operation Honeycomb is a go. I say again, Operation Honeycomb is a go."

In the distance, a series of explosions light up the night sky. The assault has begun.

THIRTY-FIVE

Blake

My HUD flickers with constant updates. Altitude, windspeed, team positions, and RUFI status—a data stream that would be overwhelming if we hadn't trained for this exact scenario.

Through it all, I focus on the top of the cliff, where our real mission begins. The wind whips around us, carrying the scent of ozone and sea spray, a stark reminder of the storm raging around us.

CJ's voice crackles through our comms, steady despite the static. "Alpha team, status?"

The sound of distant explosions punctuates Max's reply, the bass rumble reverberating through the ground beneath our feet. "We're engaged at the main gate. Heavy resistance, but we're holding. These bastards fight like they've got something to prove."

"Bravo?"

"HALO insertion complete," Brady reports, his voice slightly breathless from the high-altitude jump. "Air defenses neutralized. You're clear to proceed, Charlie."

"Copy that," Ethan responds, his voice low and focused. "Charlie team, we're green. RUFI, take point. Let's move."

The three RUFI spring into action, their sleek forms barely

visible as they crest the cliff edge. We follow closely behind, the wind nearly knocking us off balance. Taking cover behind a low stone wall, we survey the compound before us.

It looms like a dark monolith against the stormy sky, its windows glinting ominously in the flashes of lightning. In the distance, muzzle flashes light up the night, accompanied by the staccato rhythm of gunfire. Alpha team is keeping Malfor's forces busy, as planned.

Ethan signals silently, and we move out. The RUFI take the lead, and their advanced sensors scan for threats as we approach the villa. Our steps are careful and methodical, with the RUFI adjusting their pace to match ours. The rain pelts us relentlessly, but our gear keeps us dry and focused.

We reach the villa, its ornate stonework marred by bullet holes and scorch marks. One of the RUFI identifies a broken window on the ground floor—our entry point.

RUFI-2 takes point, slipping through the window first to secure the immediate area. The smell of ozone grows stronger as we follow, glass crunching beneath our boots despite our best efforts for silence.

The interior is dark, lit only by the occasional flash of lightning from outside. Our night vision kicks in, bathing everything in an eerie green glow.

"Mitzy, we're in," Ethan whispers into his comm. "Guide us to Sophia."

Mitzy's voice comes through clear and focused. "Routing to your HUD. She's in the east wing, sub-basement level. Be advised, I'm detecting multiple hostile signatures between you and the target."

"Copy that," Ethan responds. "Charlie team, move out. RUFI, maintain perimeter scan. Blake, you've got point with RUFI-3."

I take the lead alongside RUFI-3, my rifle at the ready. We move like shadows through the compound, our black tactical gear and the RUFI's adaptive camouflage blending seamlessly with the darkness. The exosuits enhance our speed and agility, allowing us to cover ground quickly and silently. The smell of damp stone and mold grows stronger as we descend, the air growing noticeably cooler.

RUFI-3's sensors highlight two heat signatures ahead. I raise a fist, signaling the team to halt. Two guards moving in our direction, unaware of our presence. I lock eyes with Gabe, a silent plan forming between us.

When the guards round the corner, Gabe and I strike. RUFI-3 provides cover. My suppressed rifle coughs once, twice. The guard on the left drops without a sound. Beside me, Gabe's target falls just as silently.

"Hostiles neutralized," I report, my voice barely above a whisper. "Moving on."

We progress deeper into the compound, the sounds of the battle outside growing more distant with each step. The interior is eerily quiet, most of the guards drawn to the commotion at the walls. Our footsteps and the soft whir of the RUFI's servos echo softly off the stone walls, the only sound besides our controlled breathing.

My HUD flashes, indicating we're nearing our target. A heavy steel door blocks our path, and an armed guard is standing watch. Before he can react, RUFI-3 launches a non-lethal stun projectile, incapacitating him instantly. I move in to secure the guard while Ethan examines the electronic lock.

It's high-tech, well beyond anything we've encountered so far. "Mitzy, we need access," he murmurs into his comm.

"Working on it," she replies. Seconds tick by, feeling like hours. Finally, a soft click echoes in the corridor. The door swings open, revealing a dark room beyond.

Heart pounding, I step forward, RUFI-3 at my side, its sensors sweeping the room for hidden threats. A figure huddles in the corner, barely visible in the dim light. My throat tightens as I speak, barely trusting my voice.

"Sophia?"

Sophia looks up, her eyes wide with shock and fear. She's thinner than I remember, her face gaunt, but there's fire in her eyes. She hasn't given up.

"Blake?" she whispers, disbelief coloring her voice.

Mission accomplished.

I'm across the room in an instant. Sophia looks up, her eyes wide with disbelief and hope. I pull her into my arms, feeling her fragile form against me. Despite her weakened state, her grip on me is fierce and desperate.

"Sophia," I whisper, my voice thick with emotion. "We're taking you home."

For a moment, she clings to me, her body shaking with silent sobs. Then, suddenly, she pulls back, her eyes wild with panic.

"No," she says, shaking her head vehemently. "We can't leave. Not without Luke."

Luke?

I exchange confused glances with the team.

"Who's Luke?"

THIRTY-SIX

Blake

______

THE AIR CRACKLES WITH TENSION AS SOPHIA'S FACE HARDENS, HER jaw set with a fierce determination that sends a chill down my spine. There's no confusion in her eyes now, only an unwavering resolve that burns with an almost feral intensity.

"Luke's my son." Her voice is low, raw, each word weighted with years of fear and desperation. "Malfor has him. He's being held hostage."

"Your son?" The revelation hits like a thunderbolt, electrifying the air around us. The comms erupt with a cacophony of surprised exclamations and sharp intakes of breath, the shock rippling through our team like a shockwave.

"Holy shit," Gabe mutters, voicing what we're all thinking.

"Your son?" I repeat, the words feeling foreign on my tongue. My mind reels, struggling to process this seismic shift in everything we thought we knew. "Sophia, why didn't you tell us?"

In a blur of motion, she grabs my arms, her grip surprisingly strong, fingers digging into my flesh with an urgency that borders on pain. Her eyes, wide and wild, bore into mine with an intensity that steals my breath.

"I couldn't. He threatened to torture and kill him if I said anything. You have to understand. Everything I did… It was all for Luke. I can't leave without him. I won't."

The weight of her words, the depth of her sacrifice, strikes me like a tidal wave. I look at Ethan, seeing my shock mirrored in his eyes. He nods grimly, understanding the gravity of the situation, but we both know questions are for later. Right now, every second counts.

"Sophia," Ethan says, his voice calm but urgent, cutting through the tension like a knife. "Do you know where Luke is being held?"

Sophia's eyes never leave mine as she speaks, her gaze burning with a mother's desperation. "Upper level, north wing. At least, that's where he was when I last saw him." Her grip on my arms tightens, fingernails biting into my skin. "I'm not leaving without him. Do you understand? No matter what happens, I will not leave unless Luke is with me."

The intensity of her words leaves no room for doubt. This isn't a request; it's a declaration carved in stone. She means every word, every syllable etched with the fierce love of a mother willing to burn the world down to save her child.

Once again, I look at Ethan, seeing the gears turning in his mind as he processes this new information. The air around us seems to thicken, the stakes rising with every passing heartbeat.

"Command, this is Charlie Team Lead," Ethan speaks into his comm, his voice tight with controlled urgency. "There's a secondary extraction target. Repeat, secondary extraction target. Name's Luke. Sophia's son. Currently held in the upper level, north wing of the compound. How copy?"

There's a moment of stunned silence, the tension stretching like a rubber band about to snap. Then CJ's voice comes through, strained but professional. "Charlie team, this is Command. We copy your last. Standby for updated mission parameters."

As we wait for new orders, I turn back to Sophia. "Why didn't you tell me?" I ask, unable to keep the hurt from my voice. "I could have helped you."

Sophia's eyes flash with fierce protectiveness. "I couldn't risk it. Malfor threatened to kill Luke if I breathed a word about him to anyone. Every message I sent, every clue I left... I was terrified they'd figure it out and hurt him." Her voice breaks slightly. "Blake, you have to understand. Everything I did, every betrayal—was all for Luke. He's all I have."

Her words wash over me, heavy and undeniable, the magnitude of her sacrifice crashing into me.

I pull her close again, feeling her trembling in my arms. "We'll get him," I promise, my voice low and fierce. "Both of you. I swear it."

She nods, tears glistening in her eyes but a new strength in her posture. "Thank you," she whispers, the words a prayer and a battle cry rolled into one.

CJ's voice crackles through the comms again. "Charlie team, new mission parameters confirmed. Primary objective is extraction of both Sophia and the child, Luke. All other objectives are secondary. Proceed with caution."

Ethan turns to Sophia. "Can you move?"

"Yes." Sophia straightens, a new strength flowing through her at the prospect of rescuing her son.

"Alright, team," Ethan says, "new formation. Blake, you and RUFI-3 take point with Sophia. Gabe, you're on rear guard. The rest of you, flanking positions. Stay sharp. We're in uncharted territory now. Let's move out."

There's a shift in our team's energy. The stakes have just gotten exponentially higher, but so has our resolve. We came here to save one life. Now, we're fighting for two.

As we move through the dimly lit corridors, every shadow seems to hide a potential threat. The air is thick with tension, our breaths coming in short, controlled bursts. Sophia moves with a renewed purpose. She's weak, clearly malnourished, but there's a fire in her eyes that burns brighter than any physical pain.

Her son?

I still can't believe it.

We're coming, Luke, I think to myself as we ascend toward the upper levels. *Hold on, kid. Your mom's coming for you, and she's bringing an army.*

A son?

As we near the north wing, the resistance intensifies. The sharp crack of gunfire echoes through the corridors, the acrid smell of cordite filling the air. Malfor's men have finally realized the diversion at the gates is just that. They're regrouping, desperate to stop us.

We take them out efficiently, but each engagement slows us down. Every second lost is another moment Luke remains in danger, and I can see the fear and determination warring in Sophia's eyes.

Finally, we reach the room where Luke is supposed to be held. Sophia's breathing quickens, her eyes wide with anticipation and fear.

"Ready?" Ethan asks, his hand on the doorknob, muscles coiled tight.

Sophia nods, her whole body tense.

Ethan tries the handle, but it's locked. He nods to Gabe, who steps forward with a lockpick set. Within seconds, we hear a soft click.

"We're in." Gabe steps back.

Ethan pushes the door open slowly, his rifle at the ready. We file in, eyes scanning for threats. But the sight that greets us isn't what we expected. The room is empty, except for a small bed and scattered toys.

"No," Sophia whispers, her voice breaking. The single word carries the weight of a thousand shattered hopes. "No, no, no. He was here. He has to be here!"

She rushes into the room, her movements frantic, desperate. She overturns furniture, throws open closet doors, her actions growing more frenzied with each passing second. "Luke?" Her voice echoes off bare walls, a mother's anguished cry. "Luke, baby, where are you?"

"Sophia, we need to—" I move to pull her back, acutely aware that we're exposed, vulnerable.

She whirls on me, eyes blazing with a fury born of fear and desperation. "I'm not leaving without him. I won't—"

Suddenly, Gabe's voice cuts through the tension like a knife. "Movement. Back stairwell."

We all turn, weapons raised, to see a woman hurrying down a hidden staircase. In her arms is a small boy, his face buried in her shoulder, and behind her, a little girl follows, eyes wide with fear.

Sophia's reaction is instantaneous, primal. "Luke!" The name tears from her throat, a sound of pure emotion that seems to freeze time itself.

She breaks free from my grip with a strength born of desperation, launching herself toward the stairs. The woman turns, startled, her eyes widening in shock and confusion as she takes in our armed group.

"Who-who are they?" she stammers, clutching the boy tighter.

Beside me, Ethan goes rigid, his eyes widening in shock.

But there's no time for explanations. Hearing his mother's voice, Luke lifts his head, his small face lighting up with recognition and hope.

"Mommy!" he cries out, his voice piercing the tension like a ray of sunlight breaking through storm clouds.

What happens next seems to unfold in slow motion. Sophia reaches for her son, her arms outstretched, tears streaming down her face. The woman, seeing the raw emotion in Sophia's eyes, hesitates for just a moment before setting Luke down.

The little boy flies into Sophia's arms as if propelled by an unseen force. They collide in a tangle of limbs and tears, Sophia clutching Luke to her chest as if she'll never let go again. Her voice, choked with emotion, fills the air as she murmurs reassurances to her son, each word a balm to years of separation and fear.

"It's okay, baby. Mommy's here. I've got you. I've got you."

For a moment, the world seems to stand still. The gunfire outside fades away, the danger momentarily forgotten in the face of this raw, primal reunion. My eyes sting, and the lump in my throat makes it hard to swallow.

But the moment of peace is short-lived. I glance at Ethan, expecting to see relief, but instead, I'm struck by the intensity of his gaze as he stares at the woman. His face is a mask of shock and disbelief as if he's seen a ghost.

His voice is low and tight as he speaks into his comm. "Command, this is Charlie Lead. I need an immediate ID check. The woman with the boy...."

The words trail off, lost in the chaos of the moment. But as I look between Ethan and the mysterious woman, I can't shake the feeling that our mission has just become even more complicated.

THIRTY-SEVEN

Blake

THE TENDER REUNION BETWEEN SOPHIA AND LUKE IS SHATTERED IN an instant. The sharp crack of gunfire splits the air, and time seems to slow. I react on pure instinct, my body moving before my mind can process what's happening.

"Get down!" I roar, launching myself at Sophia and Luke. We hit the ground hard, the impact knocking the wind from my lungs. Bullets whiz overhead, so close I can feel their heat. The acrid smell of gun powder fills the air, mixing with the metallic tang of fear.

RUFI-2 engages the guard with cold efficiency; its mechanical movements are deadly accurate despite the chaos around us. The guard falls, but I know it's just the beginning.

"Charlie team, this is Bravo Lead." Brady's voice crackles over the comms, tight with urgency. "We've got multiple tangos converging on your position. You need to exfil now."

Ethan snaps back to attention, his eyes clearing of the daze that settled over him at the sight of the unknown woman.

"Copy that," he responds, his voice sharp with renewed focus. "Charlie team, move out. Command, we've got four to extract. Back to the cliff face."

We form a protective circle around our charges: Sophia clutching

Luke to her chest, the boy's face buried in her neck, the mystery woman, her eyes wide with a mixture of fear and determination, and the little girl, clinging to the woman's hand as if it's a lifeline.

Our progress is agonizingly slow. Every step feels like a mile, and each corner is a potential death trap. Malfor's men seem to materialize from the very walls, their gunfire a constant, deafening roar.

We're pinned down in a wide corridor, caught in a vicious crossfire. Bullets chip away at our cover, showering us with debris. The air is thick with smoke and the desperate cries of our team trying to coordinate over the chaos.

"We're not going to make it like this," Gabe shouts, his voice strained as he returns fire.

Just as hopelessness threatens to overtake us, the world explodes. The ceiling behind us erupts in a shower of concrete and steel. Through the newly created hole, in drops Bravo team, their exosuits gleaming despite the dust and debris.

"Thought you could use a hand." Brady grins, his rifle already blazing. The tide turns in an instant, Bravo team's firepower giving us the edge we desperately need.

"Move, move, move!" Ethan bellows, his voice cutting through the chaos.

We make a break for it, the RUFI taking point, their sensors alerting us to threats before we can see them. I've got Sophia and Luke, her arms wrapped around her son in a grip that would take an army to break.

Ahead of us, Gabe struggles with the woman. She's got the girl in a vice-like grip, both stumbling as Gabe tries to urge them forward. The little girl's face is buried in the woman's neck, trembling with fear.

"Ma'am, please," Gabe pleads, his voice strained as he tries to keep them moving while returning fire. "We need to move faster. It's not safe here."

The woman shakes her head vehemently, clutching the girl tighter. "I won't let her go," she chokes out between ragged breaths.

Suddenly, Sophia's voice rings out, sharp and clear despite the chaos around us. "Violet. It's okay. These men are here to rescue us. You can trust them."

The woman—Violet—hesitates, her eyes darting between Sophia and Gabe. For a moment, I think she might still refuse, but then she gives a shaky nod.

"Zephyr, sweetheart," Violet says, her voice trembling as she kneels to her daughter's level. "Mommy will be right behind you. Can you be brave for me?"

The little girl—Zephyr—nods, her eyes wide with fear but trusting in her mother's words. Ethan steps forward, his movements surprisingly gentle as he takes Zephyr's hand.

"Zephyr, my name's Ethan. You'll be safe with me," Ethan assures Violet, his voice softer than I've ever heard it.

Violet reluctantly lets go of her daughter, allowing Gabe to guide her forward. Ethan takes charge of Zephyr, his movements protective yet oddly tender.

The reconfigured group moves faster now, but I can't help noticing how Ethan keeps glancing back at Violet, a mixture of confusion and recognition in his eyes.

"Keep moving," I shout, urging the group forward as another burst of gunfire erupts behind us. "We're almost there."

The journey back is a hellish gauntlet of gunfire and near-misses. We move as one unit, our formation tight, protecting our charges at all costs. Bravo team works around us, providing suppressive fire as we escort our rescues out.

The exosuits prove their worth, allowing us to move quickly despite the added weight.

A bullet grazes my arm, the sharp pain barely registering through the adrenaline. Luke whimpers, and Sophia's soothing whispers somehow cut through the chaos.

"It's okay, baby. Mommy's got you. We're going to be okay."

As we near the cliff face, the power of the storm hits us like a gale-force wind. The wind howls a banshee's wail that threatens to knock us off our feet. Rain lashes at us, reducing visibility to mere feet. It's as if nature itself is conspiring against our escape.

"There," Ethan shouts, pointing toward the cliff edge where we left our descent gear.

Relief floods through me, but it's short-lived. A fresh wave of Malfor's men emerges from the compound, their gunfire intensifying.

"Cover us," I yell, making a dash for the gear with Sophia and Luke.

Bravo team lays down suppressing fire as I work frantically to secure makeshift harnesses around Sophia and Luke. My hands shake with adrenaline and cold, the wet ropes slipping in my grasp.

"You're doing great," I tell Sophia, meeting her eyes. The fear there is palpable, but beneath it burns a fierce determination. She nods, tightening her grip on Luke.

I look over to see Ethan working on the little girl's harness, his movements mechanical and distracted. His gaze keeps drifting to Violet.

"Ethan," I call out over the howling wind. "You good?"

He starts, as if pulled from deep thought. "Yeah—yeah, I'm fine." But there's turmoil in his eyes. Violet bears an uncanny resemblance to someone, but in the chaos of the moment, I can't place who.

Gabe works on securing Violet, his voice a constant stream of reassurance as he straps her into a harness. She's calmer now, but her eyes never leave her daughter.

"We need to move. Now," Walt interrupts, his voice sharp with urgency.

As if to emphasize his point, a bullet pings off the rocks near us, sending fragments flying. The little girl cries out in fear, and the woman's head snaps up.

"Zephyr!" she screams, struggling against her harness. "Let me go to her!"

"Ma'am, please," Gabe pleads, struggling to keep her still. "You need to stay calm. We're getting you both out of here, I promise."

"Everyone hooked up?" Ethan calls out, his voice barely audible over the storm and gunfire.

A chorus of affirmatives rings out. I move toward Sophia and

Luke, my heart pounding so hard I can feel it in my throat. I reach for Sophia, intending to secure her to my harness, but Sophia's hand on my arm stops me.

She looks up at me, her eyes blazing with an intensity that takes my breath away. Despite the chaos around us, despite the bullets whizzing past and the howling wind, time seems to slow for just a moment.

"You take Luke," Sophia says, her voice steady and sure. "I trust you with his life."

After everything she's been through, everything she's endured to protect her son, she's willing to entrust him to me? The faith in her eyes is almost more than I can bear.

I nod, unable to speak past the lump in my throat. With quick, efficient movements, I secure Luke to my harness. The boy wraps his arms around my neck, his small body trembling against mine.

"It's okay, buddy," I murmur, hoping he can hear me over the storm. "I've got you."

Sophia gives Luke a quick, fierce hug before Walt helps her into position. Around us, the team is pairing up with their charges. Ethan has the little girl secured to his harness. Gabe is with Violet, speaking to her in low, reassuring tones as he double-checks her harness.

"On my mark," Ethan shouts, his hand raised. The gunfire intensifies, Malfor's men making one last desperate push to stop us. "Three... Two... One... MARK!"

We step off the cliff edge into howling oblivion, the storm enveloping us as we begin our descent. The world becomes a blur of wind, rain, and the terrified cries of our charges.

Luke's arms tighten around my neck, his face buried against my shoulder. I can feel his rapid heartbeat, or maybe it's my own, pounding in time with the adrenaline coursing through my veins.

Through the chaos, I catch glimpses of the others. Sophia, her face set in grim determination as Walt guides their descent. Ethan, somehow managing to look both fiercely protective and deeply troubled as he shields Zephyr from the worst of the wind. Gabe and

Violet, the woman's eyes locked on her daughter even as they plummet through the air.

Bravo team remains on the ground, protecting our descent. The cliff face rushes past us, a blur of wet rock. Every few seconds, a bullet pings off the rocks nearby, a stark reminder that we're not out of danger yet.

Suddenly, a particularly strong gust of wind slams us against the cliff face. I twist, taking the brunt of the impact to shield Luke. Pain explodes across my back, but I grit my teeth and keep going. Luke whimpers, and I tighten my hold on him.

"Hey, Luke," I say, "have you ever seen any superhero movies?"

He nods, a flicker of interest in his eyes despite the fear.

"Only superheroes get to scale down cliffs like this." I gesture to the daunting drop before us. "Guess what? Today, you get to be a superhero too."

For the first time, a small smile tugs at Luke's lips. "Really?"

"Really," I confirm, grinning back at him. "And you know what? I bet you're going to be even braver than Captain America."

To my left, Walt struggles with Sophia. She's weak from her captivity, barely able to hold on. Walt has her secured tightly to him, practically carrying her down the cliff face.

"Stay with me, Sophia," I hear him growl. "Don't you dare give up now. Your boy needs you."

On my right, Gabe is managing our mystery woman. She seems to be in better shape than Sophia, but the terror on her face is apparent every time lightning illuminates the sky.

"Don't look down," Gabe advises her. "Just focus on me. One step at a time."

The RUFI move around us, their mechanical bodies unaffected by the wind and rain. They set anchors, adjust ropes; their tireless efforts the only thing making this insane descent possible.

I keep talking to Luke, turning each terrifying moment into an adventure.

Suddenly, another massive gust of wind slams into us. My grip slips, and a moment of heart-stopping terror fills me. Luke and I swing out over the abyss. The boy screams, the sound piercing even through the storm's fury, but it's not a cry of fear. The little shit is having the time of his life. I play it up and milk it for everything I've got.

"Whoa, did you feel that?" I say as a gust buffets us. "I think Thor's trying to help us fly."

Luke giggles, his fear momentarily forgotten. "Thor doesn't fly, silly. He has a hammer."

"Oh, right." I laugh. "My mistake. Maybe it's Iron Man then?"

We continue our descent, each meter gained a victory against the storm and gravity. The sounds of combat from above grow fainter, replaced by the crash of waves below. We're close now. So close.

Throughout the perilous journey down, I keep the superhero narrative going. When we pause for the RUFI to reset our ropes, I tell Luke we're using our 'Spidey-sense' to find the safest path. When the rain lashes at us, I say it's Aquaman trying to give us a boost.

Despite the danger, despite the storm and the sheer drop below us, Luke relaxes his death grip, and he looks around with curiosity rather than fear.

"Are you a superhero?" he asks as we near the bottom.

I smile down at him. "Nah, I'm just a regular guy. But you know who the real superhero is?" I pause for effect.

"No."

"Your mom. She's the bravest, strongest person I know."

As we continue our descent, I can't help but reflect on the weight of Luke's words. The innocence of a child, coupled with the harsh reality of what he and Sophia have endured, makes our mission feel even more crucial. We're not rescuing hostages; we're reuniting a family.

After what feels like an eternity, my feet touch solid ground. I stumble, my legs shaky from the descent and the weight of Luke. Around me, I hear the others landing, their breathing heavy and ragged.

"That was awesome! Can we do it again?" Luke looks up at me, his eyes shining.

"Maybe next time, buddy." I can't help but laugh, relief and amusement washing over me. "Bravo team is coming down now, and we don't want to be in their way."

One by one, the rest of my team touches down. Walt with Sophia, who collapses to her knees the moment she's on solid ground. Violet looks shell-shocked but alive.

The rest of the team, including the RUFI, are all accounted for.

"COMMAND, CHARLIE TEAM IS ON THE GROUND," ETHAN CALLS IN our progress.

"Copy that, Charlie team. Bravo is on their way." CJ's voice crackles through our comms. "What's your status?"

Ethan looks around, taking a quick headcount. "All packages secured. Requesting immediate evac."

The storm surges, the wind driving sheets of rain against the cliff face, and the water below churns, slamming against the rocks. There's almost no ground—except for a jagged outcropping of rocks that juts out from the base of the cliff. The sea crashes against it, sending sprays of cold salt water into the air.

I glance back up at the looming cliff we just descended, barely able to make out the figures of Bravo team on their way down. The compound is lost in the storm above, but the faint sound of ongoing combat continues. Alpha team is giving Malfor's men a run for their money and will be the last to exfil.

"Charlie team, this is HQ." CJ's voice comes through, thick with static. "Exfil chopper is en route. ETA three minutes."

Those three minutes stretch into what feels like an eternity. We take up defensive positions, eyes locked on the cliff top, muscles tense, waiting for any sign of pursuit.

The distant sound of an approaching helicopter reaches us.

It emerges from the darkness like a ghost, its rotors slicing through the night air, hovering just above that jagged outcropping of rocks. A single line drops down, swaying in the storm's fury.

My heart pounds, and my muscles tense.

The wind howls, the storm almost mocking our situation as I

tighten my grip on Luke, the kid trembling in my arms. His small hands clutch at my gear, knuckles white. Earlier, when we were scaling down the cliffs, I joked with him about playing superhero. It got him to laugh—just a little—but now, with the water crashing against the rocks below and the storm battering us, his fear creeps back in.

"One line, everyone clips in. First four with the rescuees." Ethan's voice crackles through the comms, steady as ever, cutting through the chaos. "We go in pairs. Move fast. Stay together."

I glance toward the jagged rocks jutting out ahead—the only place solid enough to get a foothold. The water surges, slamming against the base of the cliff, the spray soaking through my gear. I shift Luke in my arms, forcing my voice to stay light.

"Remember, we're still playing superhero, right? Gotta make a quick dash and catch that rope." His wide eyes meet mine, and I give him a quick wink before nodding toward the outcropping where the helicopter lines whip violently in the wind. "Then we fly through the air."

"Fly?" Luke tries to put on a brave face, but he trembles in my arms.

"On my go," Ethan orders.

Heart pounding, I crouch low. "Hold on tight, buddy," I murmur, feeling Luke cling tighter as the chopper's spotlight cuts through the storm.

"Go!" Ethan's command snaps through the storm.

I push off, my boots finding purchase on the slick rocks as I sprint toward the lines. Luke's weight makes every step feel precarious, but there's no time to think, just react. The sea roars beneath us, the wind yanks the line back and forth, and I lunge forward, grabbing the rope with one hand while keeping Luke secure with the other.

Luke clings to me, his arms tight around my neck. His heartbeat pounds against my chest, matching the rapid thrum of my own.

The rest of the team clips in, one by one, until it's Ethan's turn. He's the last to attach, taking position as the final link on the line.

"All set, HQ. Get us out of here," Ethan signals through the comms, voice steady, despite the chaos around us.

The helicopter winch whirs to life, the line pulling taut as we begin to rise, slowly at first. The ground drops away beneath our boots, jagged rocks and surging water growing smaller as we ascend. All ten of us—six team members and four rescuees—dangle beneath the chopper in a single line, the wind battering us from all sides.

Luke tightens his hold on me, his head pressed against my chest.

"It's just like flying, remember?" I murmur, though the wind rips the words from my mouth before I can tell if he heard me.

We rise higher, the storm pressing in, but the winch holds steady. Slowly, we're reeled toward the safety of the helicopter. I focus on the weight of Luke in my arms, the tension in the line, and the rhythmic hum of the rotors above us.

Finally, as we near the belly of the chopper, a hand reaches out, pulling us in. One by one, each team member and rescuee is hauled into the safety of the aircraft. The storm rages outside, but inside, there's a sense of calm—a breath we've been holding for too long, now finally released.

We're safe. All of us.

For now.

THIRTY-EIGHT

Blake

—————

THE RHYTHMIC THRUM OF THE PLANE'S ENGINES VIBRATES THROUGH my body as I make my way to the rear of the plane.

Sophia's huddled on a bench, a blanket wrapped tightly around her shoulders. Luke is fast asleep beside her, his small hand clutching her shirt. Our eyes meet, and for a moment, the world stands still.

"Blake," she whispers, her voice barely audible over the engine noise. Her gaze is distant, likely filled with painful memories.

In an instant, I'm across the compartment, kneeling before her. Her face is gaunt, and there are dark circles under her eyes, but a fierce light in them takes my breath away.

"Are you okay?" I ask, my voice rough with emotion. "Did they hurt you?" Silly question. Malfor did far more than hurt her.

Sophia shakes her head, tears welling in her eyes. "I'm fine. I'm so sorry. I never wanted to betray you, to betray the Guardians. I had no choice. They had—"

"Luke," I finish for her, glancing at the sleeping boy. "Your son."

I settle on the bench opposite her, leaning forward with my elbows on my knees. "Why didn't you tell me?" We've had this conversation before, but it was in the heat of a battle. I have so many questions.

"I told you."

"Tell me again." I place a hand on her knee rather than pulling her into my arms. That's what I want, but my senses tell me it's too soon for her. "Tell me about Luke."

She takes a shaky breath, her hand absently stroking Luke's hair. "I couldn't tell anyone. Malfor threatened to kill him if I... If I..." Her entire body shudders.

Again, I want to hold her, but she needs to do this alone.

"I want to explain everything. You deserve the truth."

"I'm listening." I steel myself for her words.

Her eyes cloud with painful memories as she begins her story, her voice low to avoid waking Luke. "It started long before Malfor took Luke. It started with his conception."

"What do you mean?"

Sophia's hand absently strokes Luke's hair as she continues. "When I was first taken, they put all of us on birth control. Pills for the women, condoms for the men we... serviced. They were meticulous about it, but I was part of the 1% where it failed."

My fists clench at the mention of the things she endured. Fury bubbles up inside me, but I force myself to stay quiet, to let Sophia continue.

Gabe notices our conversation. He jerks his chin toward Walt, and the two of them slowly approach. We're all curious. Not in a morbid way, but because the things that happened to Sophia impact our next steps.

Greaves and Malfor are both going down for the atrocities they've committed.

"When Jonathan Greaves discovered my pregnancy, I thought..." Sophia's voice breaks. "I thought he'd force me to get rid of it... Get rid of Luke. But he didn't. He kept me healthy and treated me well. It was as if I was somehow... special. I received the best medical care and was treated exceptionally well. I didn't have to..." She pauses, unable to continue. We all know what she means. "Anyhow, Luke was delivered, a healthy baby boy."

Luke stirs at the sound of his name. Violet, who's been hovering nearby, steps forward. "Here, let me put him down."

Sophia nods gratefully, and Violet takes Luke and settles him on a makeshift bed of jackets. Once he's settled, Sophia continues, her voice even lower.

"For the first year, I wasn't forced to... serve others. Just Jonathan. He allowed me time with Luke. It wasn't freedom, but it was... bearable." Her eyes cloud over. "Then, one day, something changed. I still don't know what happened, but suddenly, Luke was taken from me. Used as a weapon to control me."

My fists clench, and fury bubbles up inside me. I force myself to stay silent and let her finish.

"I was loaned out again, forced to serve other men. My access to Luke became increasingly restricted with each passing year." Sophia's voice is hollow, her eyes distant. "Then Malfor showed up on Jonathan's yacht."

Ethan, Hank, and Rigel join us, settling in a loose semi-circle around Sophia.

"Malfor?" Ethan leans forward, his face grim. "What did he want?"

"Jenna," Sophia says. "He wanted the girl who got away. He and Jonathan concocted this plan to get Jenna back, but it wasn't just about her. They decided to use me. Not to get to Jenna, but to infiltrate Guardian HQ."

The implications of her words settle over the group like a heavy blanket.

Walt breaks the silence, his voice gruff with emotion. "So the rescue from the yacht, that was all—"

"A setup," Sophia finishes, her eyes finding mine. "An elaborate series of events to place me exactly where they needed me—on Guardian HQ grounds. Once Malfor got involved—I don't know all the details—he took Luke from Greaves. From me."

The implications of her words felt like a dagger to the heart. Our entire relationship, the foundation of trust we'd built, suddenly feels like it's built on lies.

"So, us… Was any of it real?" I hate how vulnerable I sound, but I need to know.

Sophia reaches out, grasping my hand. Her touch is warm and familiar, sending a jolt through me. "Please believe me. My feelings for you—they're real. They've always been real. That's why this was so hard. I fell in love with you while being forced to betray everything you stand for."

I want to believe her. God, I want to believe her so badly. But the doubt gnaws at me, and it's relentless.

"I tried to leave clues," she continues, pleading. "Malfor was watching me the whole time. I left notes in the coffee beans at the Grind. I was so scared Malfor would figure it out, but I had to try something."

"We found them."

The plane's intercom crackles to life. "We're beginning our descent. Please secure all loose items and prepare for landing."

The announcement stops that conversation. We move to secure equipment. As I help Sophia with Luke, I can't help but notice Ethan glancing at Violet, his brow furrowed in thought.

The landing is smooth. We're home, but nothing feels the same.

The next few hours pass in a blur of medical checks, preliminary debriefings, and hushed conversations. Sophia and Luke are whisked away for thorough examinations, while Violet and her daughter, Zephyr, are taken to a secure area for questioning and care.

Debriefing occurs immediately. I lean against the wall, arms crossed, watching my team gather around the long table.

Watching Sophia.

She sits at the foot of the long conference table, her fingers absently tracing the wood grain. Her eyes, red-rimmed, dart to the door where Luke sleeps just outside, watched over by Guardian personnel.

Violet perches on a chair nearby, her posture tense, ready to bolt at a moment's notice. I know who she reminds me of.

The resemblance to Rebel is uncanny. Questions burn in everyone's eyes. But those will have to wait. Right now, we have a debrief to get through.

The leadership team files in quietly: Sam, his usual stoic expression tinged with concern, CJ, thumbing through a tablet with furrowed brows, Mitzy, her eyes glued to a laptop she carries, Forest, his massive frame filling the doorway as he enters, and Skye, Forest's sister and head of Medical. Her keen eyes assess everyone in the room.

Sophia's earlier revelations hang heavy in the air between us. I can't help but feel a mix of relief, hurt, and uncertainty as I watch her.

Sam clears his throat, breaking the uneasy silence. "Alright, let's get started. Sophia, I know you've already shared a lot on the flight, but we need to go over everything again. Every detail could be crucial."

Sophia nods, her hands clasping tightly in her lap. "I understand. Where should I begin?"

"From the beginning," Forest rumbles, settling into a chair that creaks under his weight. "How did Greaves and Malfor orchestrate this whole thing?"

As Sophia takes a deep breath to begin her story, the door opens, and the rich aroma of freshly brewed coffee wafts into the room. Jenna enters, carefully balancing a tray of steaming mugs, followed by Carter, who carries a box of croissants and scones.

"Thought you all could use some fuel," Jenna says softly, setting the tray on the table.

Carter places the box beside it, then steps back, leaning against the wall next to me.

"How are you holding up?" My twin keeps his voice low, speaking just loud enough for my ears only. His eyes, mirror images of my own, search my face with concern.

I exhale slowly, my shoulders sagging under the weight of the past few days. "Still standing." I shake my head, grateful for my brother's steady presence. "But the ground keeps shifting under my feet."

"I bet." Carter nudges me with his shoulder, a gesture we've shared since childhood. "You've had one hell of a week, bro. Sophia, Luke, all these revelations…"

"Understatement of the year," I mutter, raking a hand through my hair.

Carter's gaze drifts to Jenna for a moment, his expression softening. "Not that you need me to say it, but take one day at a time. You may have had the rug pulled out from under you, but I think you should give it a chance."

My throat tightens, and my words are momentarily stuck behind the lump in my throat.

"I thought I knew her. I thought what we had was real."

"Hey." He grips my shoulder firmly. "From what I've seen, it was real. Complicated as hell, but real nonetheless."

"Thanks, bro." His words hit home, and some of the tension in my muscles eases.

"That's what brothers are for, right?" Carter grins, lightening the mood. "Now, let's grab some of that coffee before it gets cold. Something tells me we're going to need it."

Grateful murmurs fill the room as people reach for the offerings. Sophia wraps her hands around a steaming mug, letting the warmth seep into her palms. The familiar scent of coffee from The Guardian Grind brings memories of our time there—both genuine and manufactured—flooding back.

"It started long before the yacht." She takes a deep breath as if fortifying herself. "Greaves has been planning this for years. When Malfor came into the picture, things escalated quickly."

She pauses, her brow furrowing. "A few months ago, something changed with Malfor. He became twitchy and urgent. It had something to do with an asset they lost, and he was on edge about it."

Mitzy's head snaps up. "That's about the time we took Citadel down. We rescued a lot of women in that operation."

"That's when Malfor sent me that text telling me to stay away from Sentinel." Stitch tightens her grip on the edge of the table, her knuckles whitening as the realization sets in.

"Greaves finally found Jenna," Sophia continues. "He wanted to take her, but Malfor forced him to wait. They needed a connection to Guardian HRS and came up with a plan to take her. Those girls you rescued…" Sophia turns her attention to Carter. "They knew you were a detective and that you were interested in Jenna. They took those girls because they knew you'd reach out to Blake. Blake would bring in the Guardians, and the Guardians would shelter me inside HQ."

"That's a fucked-up plan with a million ways it could've gone sideways." Sam taps his chin. "They depended on a lot of things going the right way."

"Maybe, but it worked." Sophia's expression falls, and her eyes cloud over. "I was ordered to get close to one of the Guardians…"

I shift against the wall, my jaw clenching. Sophia's eyes flick to me, then away, guilt etching lines around her mouth.

"Which I did, and I'm sorry for that." Tears slip down her cheeks, and this time, when she looks at me, her gaze holds. "I never wanted to hurt you. I never expected to fall in love with you. That's why I left those messages. It was the only thing I could think of that Malfor wouldn't know about. I hoped it might reduce some of the damage he forced me to…"

"Those notes you left were crucial." Mitzy's fingers pause over her keyboard. "We already initiated Protocol Zero after Mia Chen's rescue, so we were well situated for such an attack."

"Protocol Zero?" Confusion flickers across Sophia's face.

"It's a failsafe we put in place to protect Guardian HQ in case of a breach." Sam leans forward, his elbows on the table.

The conversation continues, with Sophia detailing every aspect of Malfor's operation she can remember. Time passes, the coffee gets refreshed, and still, we press on. Violet remains quiet, her eyes distant, lost in her memories.

After a few hours, Sam, Skye, CJ, and Mitzy excuse themselves, moving to a corner of the room for a hushed conversation. When they return, Sam's attention turns to Violet.

"Violet, we want to hear your story too. Anything you can tell us about Malfor's operations is important," Sam says gently.

Violet flinches at the sound of her name. Her gaze snaps to

Sam. She opens her mouth to speak, then closes it, shaking her head.

Skye leans forward, her voice gentle. "It's okay, Violet. You're safe here. Take your time. But first, we have something for you. Are you up for a visitor?"

Violet's brow furrows in confusion, but she nods hesitantly.

The door opens, and Rebel steps into the room. She's older than Violet but has the same fiery red hair and high cheekbones. Her eyes scan the room before landing on Violet, widening in disbelief.

"Oh my God." Rebel breathes the words. "Vi?"

"R-Rebel?" Violet stands so fast her chair falls over backward. "It can't be…"

The room falls silent as the two women gaze at each other, years of separation hanging between them like a tangible weight. Then, with a choked sob, Rebel rushes forward, enveloping Violet in a fierce embrace.

"I thought I'd lost you forever," Rebel whispers, her voice thick with emotion. "My little sister…"

I look on, moved by the reunion but feeling like an intruder in a deeply personal moment.

Violet clings to Rebel, her body shaking with silent sobs. Tears stream down both their faces as they hold each other, years of pain and longing pouring out in this moment of reunion.

Ethan stands and moves to Rebel's side. He places a supportive hand on her back, his eyes glistening with emotion as he watches the sisters reunite.

After what seems like an eternity, they pull apart, tear-streaked faces breaking into watery smiles. Rebel cups Violet's face in her hands, studying her as if memorizing every detail.

"You've grown so much," Rebel says softly, her voice catching. "I've missed so much…"

Violet manages a shaky laugh, wiping at her eyes. "I never thought I'd see you again."

"Where's your…" Rebel's voice catches, her eyes meeting Ethan's with gratitude and regret. "I tried finding your child. I did things I wish I hadn't done." She swallows hard, tears threatening to spill over. "But I never stopped looking. Never."

The sisters cling to each other, years of separation dissolving in a flood of tears and whispered words. A knot forms in my throat as I watch them, an ache blooming in my chest.

My thoughts drift to Sophia and Luke, their presence a harsh reminder of how drastically my world has shifted in mere days. Everything I thought I knew is turned upside down.

Sam clears his throat gently. "I hate to interrupt but, Rebel, your experience might be invaluable here. Would you be willing to stay and help Violet tell her story?"

Rebel nods, keeping an arm around her sister's shoulders as they sit down. "Of course. Whatever I can do to help."

With Rebel's reassuring presence, Violet begins. Her voice grows stronger as she recounts her years in captivity, the horrors she witnessed, and the bits of information she managed to glean about Malfor's operation.

"The security was tight." Violet's voice is stronger now, growing more confident. "But there were patterns, routines. I started to notice things, especially in the last few months."

CJ leaned forward, his interest piqued. "What kind of things?"

"Guard rotations, delivery schedules. And there was a room… A room no one was allowed to enter except Malfor and a few of his top men."

Forest exchanged a glance with Sam. "Sounds like it could be his command center."

Violet nodded. "That's what I thought. I never got close enough to confirm, but—"

"It's a good lead," Sam said. "Anything else you can remember?"

As Violet delves into more details, the weight of recent revelations presses down on me, making the air in the conference room feel thick and heavy. I glance at Sophia, noticing the fatigue etched on her face. She keeps glancing toward the door.

I make an executive decision.

I push off from the wall, cross to where she sits, and crouch beside her chair. "Hey. You okay?"

"I—I need some air." Sophia shakes her head, her eyes squeezed shut.

"Why don't we take a break? I'm sure you want to check on Luke." I help her to her feet. "I'll take you to him."

Relief flashes across her face. She nods, pushing back from the table.

"Thank you."

We excuse ourselves quietly, slipping out of the room as the debriefing continues. Luke is curled up in a small cot in a neighboring room, and a Guardian agent sits nearby, watching over him. The agent nods to us and quietly excuses herself, giving us privacy.

Sophia kneels beside the cot, gently stroking Luke's hair. The boy stirs, his eyes fluttering open.

"Mommy?" he mumbles sleepily.

"I'm here, sweetie," Sophia whispers, gathering him into her arms. "Everything's okay."

Watching them, I'm struck by a memory of our descent down the cliffs of Malfor's estate—the way Luke clung to me, how we distracted ourselves by talking about superheroes as we navigated the treacherous path—it feels like a lifetime ago.

A complex blend of emotions swirls in my chest. Relief that they're safe, lingering hurt from the deception, and a growing warmth as I observe the love between mother and son.

"Hey, buddy," I say, crouching to Luke's level. "How are you holding up?"

"When are we gonna play superheroes again?" Luke's face brightens.

"Maybe later, champ. Right now, the grown-ups need to talk about some important stuff. But how about a high five for being such a brave kid?"

Luke grins and enthusiastically slaps his small hand against mine. The simple gesture warms my chest. He's a cute kid.

Sophia watches our interaction, a mix of gratitude and something deeper in her eyes. "Luke, why don't you thank Blake for helping us."

Luke regards me solemnly for a moment before a shy smile spreads across his face. "Thank you for helping us, Mr. Blake."

"Just Blake is fine," I say, my heart melting a little at the boy's politeness. "And you're very welcome. I'm glad you and your mom are safe now."

"Hey there." Rigel knocks on the door. "Sorry to barge in, but they have a few more questions for Sophia."

I stand, offering a hand to help Sophia up. She hugs Luke tight.

"Sweetie, I have to go for a bit. Will you be okay waiting for me here?"

Luke's lower lip trembles slightly, and I surprise myself by speaking up. "I can stay with him if that's okay. We could find something fun to do while you finish up."

Relief washes over Sophia's face. "Would you? That would be wonderful."

I crouch to Luke's level as Rigel leads Sophia to the conference room. "So, buddy, what do you like to do for fun?"

Luke's face brightens. "I like to draw. And play with Legos. Do you have any Legos?"

I chuckle, surprised by his enthusiasm. "I'm not sure, but let's go on a treasure hunt. Maybe we can build our own Guardian HQ out of whatever we find."

We set off down the hallway, Luke's small hand in mine. His excitement is contagious, and I get caught up in his childlike wonder. We rummage through supply closets, finding colored pencils, paper, and even a battered old box of building blocks.

Luke and I are lost in a world of imagination for the next hour. We build towering skyscrapers out of blocks, draw fantastic creatures with too many eyes and not enough legs, and create elaborate stories about superhero squirrels saving the day.

Luke's laughter fills the room. It's a sound I never knew I needed to hear, and it stirs something profound within me. I've never given much thought to having kids of my own, but watching Luke's face light up as he shows me his latest creation makes me think that maybe, someday, it might not be such a bad idea. Luke's energy starts to fade. His words become punctuated with yawns, and his eyelids grow heavy.

"How about we take a little rest, buddy?"

Luke nods sleepily, crawling onto the cot. To my surprise, he curls up against me, his tiny body warm and trusting. Within minutes, his breathing evens out, and he's fast asleep.

I sit there, hardly daring to move, marveling at the strange turn my life has taken. Just days ago, I was a Guardian focused solely on the mission. Now, I'm cradling a sleeping child, my heart full of emotions I can't quite name.

The minutes pass, marked only by Luke's steady breathing and the fading light outside the window. I'm lost in thought when soft footsteps approach.

Sophia appears in the doorway, exhaustion etched on her face. Her eyes soften as she takes in the scene before her. A soft smile plays on her lips as she takes in the sight of Luke and me surrounded by our creations.

"Looks like you two have been busy," she says, her voice warm.

Luke stirs, then jumps up when he sees his mother. He runs to show her his drawings. "Mommy, look. I drew our new home."

As Sophia kneels to admire Luke's artwork, our eyes meet over his head. So much is left unsaid between us, so many questions and complications. But for now, in this moment, there's a fragile peace.

"*Thank you,*" Sophia mouths silently to me.

I nod, offering a small smile in return. "Anytime." A lump forms in my throat, and getting my words out is challenging. "Sophia, I…"

"We have a lot to talk about, I know." She cuts me off gently. "But can it wait until tomorrow? I'm exhausted, and—"

"Of course." I carefully shift Luke so I can stand. "Get some rest. We'll talk when you're ready."

Despite everything, my feelings for her haven't changed. They're complicated now, tangled up with hurt, betrayal, and uncertainty, but they're still there.

With a deep sigh, I clean up the scattered toys and papers.

Tomorrow will come soon enough, bringing the next chapter in our ongoing struggle against Malfor and his sinister plans.

I head to my quarters, a small bachelor pad outside Guardian HQ, a space I've barely thought about in weeks. As I unlock the door, the familiar scent of my apartment hits me—a mix of old books and a faint trace of coffee.

Everything is exactly as I left it, almost eerily so. The bed is made with military precision. The dishes are in the rack by the sink. Not a thing is out of place.

I run my hand over the smooth countertop, realizing with a start that it's been weeks since I've slept in my bed. The thought of crawling under those cool sheets alone fills me with profound loneliness. I've gotten used to Sophia's warmth beside me.

Memories of our time together flood my mind. The curve of her smile in the dim light, the feeling of her skin against mine, the way she whispers my name in the dark. My body responds to these thoughts, a familiar tension building.

I shake my head, trying to clear it, but the physical reminders of our intimacy persist. Our exploration of each other, both tender and passionate, the roles we'd played, the trust we'd built—it all seems so distant now, yet my body remembers every touch and every kiss.

Sighing, I strip off my clothes and step into the shower. The hot water cascades over me, but it does little to wash away the ache of desire and loneliness.

Under the steady stream, I allow myself a moment of release, Sophia's name on my lips, as the tension within me finally ebbs.

Afterward, I fall into bed, my body heavy with exhaustion. The sheets are cool against my skin, a poor substitute for the warmth I've grown accustomed to.

The soft click of my bedside lamp signals the end of one of the longest days of my life. As I lay my head on the pillow, my last thoughts are of Sophia's smile and Luke's laughter.

What will happen between us? Can we rebuild what we had, or has too much changed to salvage what we once had?

THIRTY-NINE

Sophia

THE FAMILIAR SCENT OF FRESHLY GROUND COFFEE BEANS ENVELOPS me as I work behind the counter at The Guardian Grind. It's been weeks since I've returned to work, and the routine feels both comforting and strange. My hands move automatically, preparing drinks I could make in my sleep while my mind wanders to other things.

Other things being specifically Blake.

The bell above the door chimes, and I look up. It's Blake entering with his team. My heart skips a beat, just like it always does when I see him. Our eyes meet, and he gives me a small smile that doesn't quite reach his eyes. The distance between us, once nonexistent, now feels like a chasm.

"The usual?" I ask, already reaching for their preferred cups.

"You know us too well," Gabe replies with a wink.

As I prepare their orders, I steal glances at Blake, hoping to catch his eye. Hoping for him to see me. To engage with me the way we used to, rather than this stilted distance that's crept between us.

He's deep in conversation with Ethan, probably discussing their latest mission. I miss being part of those conversations, miss being part of his world in that way. But things are different now.

I'm different.

I hand over their drinks, careful to avoid brushing Blake's fingers as he takes his cup. The brief flash of disappointment in his eyes tells me he noticed too. We're both trying to give each other space, but it feels wrong.

Everything feels wrong.

As they leave, Blake turns back. "See you this afternoon? For Luke's climbing lesson?"

"We'll be there." Warmth spreads through my chest at the mention of my son, but Blake is only seeing Luke. He doesn't seem excited to see me. That kills me a little on the inside.

The door closes behind them, and I'm left with Blake's unique scent lingering in the air, and a hollow ache in my chest. I want to run after him, throw my arms around him, and beg him to come home.

But I can't.

Not yet.

There's too much unsaid between us, too many hurts to heal.

I glance at the clock. A few more hours, and I'll see him again. Maybe I'll find the courage to bridge this gap between us, and we can start to rebuild what we've lost.

The cavernous gymnasium echoes with the sounds of squeaking sneakers and clanking metal. I stand at the base of the towering rock wall, my neck craning as I follow Luke's ascent. The wall spans the entire length of the football-field-sized room, stretching over 100 feet toward the ceiling. The smell of chalk and sweat hangs in the air, mingling with the faint scent of rubber from the mats below.

"You're doing great, bro!" Blake's voice rings out, encouragement laced with genuine excitement. He's right beside Luke, guiding him to the next hold.

"Thanks, bro!" Luke chirps back, his small face scrunched in concentration.

Below them, Gabe and Hank man the belays, the safety system that will save my son's life if he falls.

Only Luke never falls. He has an inborn gift for climbing like a monkey.

My heart swells at Luke and Blake's interaction. In the weeks since our rescue, they've formed a bond I never dared hope for. The easy way they've slipped into a brotherly rapport both warms and aches my heart.

"Remember, always keep three points of contact," Blake instructs, demonstrating the technique. "Two hands and a foot, or two feet and a hand."

Luke nods thoughtfully, mimicking Blake's movements. They're about twenty feet up, and my muscles tense with each inch they climb higher.

"You've got this, buddy," Blake encourages as Luke reaches for a tricky hold. "Trust your strength."

I watch, breath held, as Luke stretches his tiny arm, fingers grasping. For a heart-stopping moment, I think he'll fall, but then his fingers curl around the hold, and he pulls himself up.

"I did it!" Luke's triumphant yell echoes through the gym.

"That's my bro." Blake high-fives him, pride radiating from his smile.

They continue their ascent, Luke growing more confident with each move. I slowly relax, trusting Blake's careful guidance and Luke's natural agility. The way Blake watches over Luke, anticipating his needs and offering support without hovering, speaks volumes. He'd make a fantastic father. The idea brings a bittersweet pang to my chest.

As they near the thirty-foot mark, Luke pauses, looking down at me with a mischievous grin. "Mom. Watch this."

Before I can respond, he turns to Blake. "Hey, bro, can I fly like a superhero?"

Blake's eyes meet mine for a split second, a crooked grin spreading across his face. "Go for it, buddy."

My heart leaps into my throat as Luke pushes off from the wall. I gasp, torn between horror and amazement. For a terrifying moment, he's airborne, arms spread wide like wings. Then the auto-belay system catches, and he's gliding down in a controlled descent.

My son is all smiles as he touches down on the mat, unhooking himself with practiced ease. He bounds over to me, eyes shining with excitement.

"Did you see me? I flew like a superhero." He throws his arms around me in a crushing hug.

I laugh, relief and joy bubbling up inside me. "You sure did, baby. You were amazing."

Over Luke's head, I catch Blake's eye. He rappels down, a soft smile as he watches us. At that moment, I'm struck by how right this feels—the three of us together, almost like a family.

As Luke chatters excitedly about his "flight," I hold onto that feeling, hoping against hope that, somehow, we can make this work. That we can build something real and lasting from the pieces of our complicated past.

The rest of the afternoon passes in a blur of coffee orders and stolen glances at the clock. As my shift winds down, Jenna arrives with Carter in tow, their faces lit with matching grins.

"We've got a proposition for you," Jenna announces, leaning against the counter.

"Oh?" I raise an eyebrow, wiping my hands on my apron.

Carter's usual stoic demeanor softens. "We want to take Luke to *Insanity* to play with the other kids. Forest has installed a new VR arcade, and it's opening night. It should give you and Blake some time to... talk. It's a sleepover, by the way. Luke will be gone *all night.*"

I swallow hard, a mix of gratitude and nervousness swirling in my stomach. "That's—that's really thoughtful of you guys."

Jenna reaches across the counter, squeezing my hand. "You two need this. We've all seen how you've been dancing around each other."

I nod, blinking back sudden tears. "Thank you."

As I hang up my apron and gather my things, a plan begins to form. It's been so long since Blake and I have been alone. I need to make this count.

Quickly, I send him a text, asking him over for dinner. I don't tell him Luke won't be there because I'm afraid Blake won't come otherwise. The tension between us is growing by leaps and bounds every day.

And it needs to stop.

FORTY

Sophia

The kitchen in my new apartment still feels foreign, but my hands move with purpose as I prepare dinner. The rhythmic chopping of vegetables and the sizzle of meat in the pan ground me, giving me something concrete to focus on instead of the nervous energy thrumming through my veins.

I've chosen to make Blake's favorite—a spicy stir-fry that reminds him of a mission in Thailand. The scent of ginger and lemongrass fills the air, and for a moment, I'm transported back to easier times. Times when the biggest worry was whether I'd remembered to stock his preferred brand of beer.

A knock at the door sends my heart racing. I smooth down my shirt, take a deep breath, and open the door.

Blake stands there, looking as nervous as I feel. His eyes roam over me, a flicker of something—desire? longing?—crossing his face before he schools his expression.

"Hey," he says softly.

"Hey." It's so awkward. I step back to let him in. "Dinner's almost ready."

He follows me to the kitchen, the heat of his gaze burning into my back. The air between us is charged, crackling with unspoken words and suppressed emotions.

"Where's Luke?" Blake's gaze casts around the room.

"He's at a sleepover."

"A what?"

"Jenna and Carter took him to *Insanity* to play with the other kids. Forest's unveiling his new VR kid-friendly suite."

"Oh…" His eyes widen.

As we sit down to eat, the silence stretches between us, thick and heavy. I watch Blake take his first bite, his eyes closing in appreciation.

"This is amazing, Soph." The use of my nickname sends a shiver down my spine. "Just like I remember."

I smile, warmth blooming in my chest. "I'm glad. I wanted tonight to be... special."

"We need to talk." Blake sets down his fork, his intense gaze meeting mine.

"I know." My throat suddenly closes off.

He reaches across the table, his hand hovering over mine before gently grasping it. The touch sends sparks of electricity racing up my arm.

"I've missed you," he says, his voice rough with emotion. "But I... I don't know how to do this after everything that's happened."

"I need you. In whatever way we can make work."

He shakes his head, frustration evident in the set of his jaw. "It's not that simple. There's Luke to consider…"

"You always said our dynamic was private." I turn my hand in his, intertwining our fingers. "Blake, I'm so sorry. For everything. I—"

"Stop." His tone carries a hint of that commanding edge I've missed so deeply. "You don't need to keep apologizing."

I swallow hard, fighting back tears. "I can't help it. Things still feel... off between us. I want us to be like we were before."

Blake's jaw tightens, his eyes darkening with barely restrained emotion. "I don't know if that's possible. With Luke, things are different. Not to mention everything you've been through."

I shake my head, my heart pounding. "Luke has nothing to do with what we share. I miss you. I miss your touch, your kisses, your commands, your dominance. I crave it on a cellular level. I want it back."

Blake's expression tightens, conflict clear in his eyes. "I was wrong before. Pushing for that kind of relationship was a mistake, given everything." He stands, pacing the small kitchen. "A power dynamic might be more damaging than I ever thought. It could interfere with your healing. I was wrong to push it before, too caught up in my cravings to consider the implications such things would have on you. It's my job to watch over you and protect you. Forcing dominance was wrong."

"No." I push to my feet, anger flaring hot in my chest. "Don't you dare make that decision for me. I know what's in my best interest. Being separated from you, this rift between us only grows wider each day. I need this. I want this." My voice breaks. "Please. I need it now more than ever."

Blake shakes his head, his jaw clenched. "I'm not sure if that's something I can give anymore."

"Why?" The word comes out as a strangled cry. Fury and desperation war within me. I lunge forward, my fists connecting with his chest. "Why are you pulling even further away from me?"

Blake's hands close around my wrists, holding me back. The familiar grip and how his body towers over mine triggers something primal within us both. I struggle against his hold, my fury and desperation driving me to push harder.

"Let me go!" I demand, even as my body betrays me, leaning into his touch.

Blake's eyes darken, his breath coming in short gasps. He spins us, pushing me up against the wall, my wrists now pinned above my head in one of his large hands. His other hand grips my hip, holding me in place.

For a heartbeat, we're frozen, staring at each other, chests heaving. I look into his eyes, seeing them blown wide with lust and desire. For a moment, everything hangs in the balance, and then something shifts in his gaze.

A switch flips.

Blake's mouth crashes down on mine.

The kiss is heated and desperate, with weeks of longing and love poured into a single point of contact. I arch against him, my initial resistance shattering under the onslaught of sensation. Blake's grip on my wrists tightens as he deepens the kiss, his tongue sweeping into my mouth, reclaiming what was always his.

I moan softly, the sound swallowed by his kiss. Blake's hand at my waist slides up to tangle in my hair, tilting my head to give him better access. He breaks away only to trail heated kisses along my jaw and down my neck.

"Blake," I gasp, my body trembling against his. "Sir…"

At the honorific, Blake stills. He pulls back slightly, his forehead resting against mine. The internal struggle flickers in his eyes, the fierce control he exerts barely containing the animalistic fury simmering just beneath the surface.

"I've missed you so much," he whispers, his voice rough with emotion.

"I've missed you more." The words carry the weight of everything we've been through, everything we are.

Blake's eyes darken at my words. He releases my hands from above my head, steps back, and pulls me with him to the center of the room. For a moment, we stand there, the air thick with anticipation.

Then Blake releases me completely, taking another step back. His gaze is intense, filled with love, desire, and that commanding presence I crave.

He points to a spot on the floor before him. "Kneel," he says, his tone leaving no room for argument.

My breath catches in my throat. This is it—the moment everything changes—the moment we rebuild what we've lost. Without hesitation, I sink to my knees, looking up at Blake with all the love and submission I feel.

The air between us crackles with the weight of the past and the yearning for our future. Blake's eyes darken as he drinks in the sight of me, his presence towering, overwhelming, but oh so necessary.

His hands go to the hem of his shirt, and in one fluid motion, he peels it off, exposing his body's raw, chiseled perfection. The low light casts shadows across the hard planes of his chest, the ridges of muscle etched into his abdomen.

My heart races, each beat echoing the primal need that simmers beneath my skin. I can't tear my gaze away—every scar, every line, every ripple tells the story of the man I love, the man who has fought for me and suffered for me.

Blake reaches for his belt, the clink of the buckle loud in the otherwise silent room. His movements are deliberate, almost slow, as if savoring the anticipation that coils tighter between us. The leather slips through the loops with a hiss, and he tosses it aside, his eyes never leaving mine. He unbuttons his jeans, the sound of the metal snaps tearing through the silence, each one sending a jolt of heat through me.

His gaze is heavy and intense as he drags the zipper down. The metallic teeth part with a soft rasp, and the denim slips lower, revealing the taut lines of his hips.

My breath hitches, my pulse pounding in my ears, and the air is thick with the scent of him—earthy, masculine, intoxicating.

"Show me." The command is a low rumble that sends a shiver down my spine. "Show me how much you've missed me."

His words are a match to dry tinder, igniting a blaze of desire that consumes me whole. Without breaking eye contact, I lean forward, my hands trembling as they reach for him. Anticipation hums through my veins, the electric connection between us stronger than ever, as I prepare to give him everything—every ounce of love and devotion.

I know exactly what he's asking for and am more than willing to comply.

"You're so beautiful on your knees." His breath catches as he looks down at me. He reaches out to run his fingers through my hair.

The praise washes over me, soothing hurts I didn't even know I had. I lean into his touch, a soft sigh escaping my lips.

"Tell me what you need." Blake's voice takes on that commanding edge I've missed so much.

"You," I whisper. "However, you'll have me."

"I love you." Blake's gaze softens as he looks down at me, his hand gently cupping my cheek. "That's never changed."

The tension between us shifts, transforming into something deeper, more profound. He cups my face in his hands, tilting it to meet his gaze.

"I love you, too. Always." Tears prick at my eyes as I lean into his touch.

The last of the walls between us crumble. His resistance shatters. We have a long way to go, challenges to face, and a new life to build…

And then he's pressing his cock against my lips. I open and take him inside, savoring his taste. He tastes like home, like everything I've ever wanted. Blake groans, thrusting his hips forward, driving himself deeper into my mouth.

"*Fuuuuck*, I've missed this." His hands tighten in my hair as he guides me, showing me exactly what he wants.

I revel in the knowledge that I can still please him. I run my tongue along his length, lingering on his sensitive spot before sucking hard.

Blake's grip on my hair tightens. "Harder," he groans.

I do as he commands, taking more of him into my mouth, sucking harder, the vibrations of his moans spurring me on. I take him deeper, my tongue swirling around him in long, wet strokes.

His moans intensify. He's close. "God, Soph, that's it, baby, just like that." His hips buck, matching the rhythm of my mouth.

Knowing I have this much power over him, that I can bring him to the edge, is better than any drug. I redouble my efforts.

"*Fuuuuck*, I'm going to…" Blake's voice trails off as his orgasm overtakes him. I wrap my arms around his thighs, holding on tight as his pleasure ebbs.

He helps me to my feet, pulling me into a tight embrace. We stand there, holding each other, our heartbeats synchronizing. The world falls away, leaving just us—two souls finding their way back to each other.

"Now, what do you need?" he asks.

"You," I whisper back, my voice barely audible. "I need you."

His lips twitch in a small smile, his eyes softening with understanding. "That's never changed, sweetheart." He leans down and presses a feather-light kiss against my forehead before pulling me up into his embrace. His strong arms encircle my waist, drawing me close as he savors the feel of my body against his.

As Blake's fingers sift through my hair, I lean into the touch, my body responding instinctively to his touch. His praise washes over me like a cool breeze on a hot summer day, soothing my soul and settling my nerves.

"It's my turn now." He lifts me into his arms and carries me to bed. "I've missed your taste."

Never in my wildest dreams did I think I'd be here again, in Blake's arms, feeling the fire I thought had been extinguished. But here we are—survivors of a hellish experience, finding solace in each other's arms.

Blake's kisses trail down my neck, his breath leaving hot tingles in their wake. His hands roam my body, reacquainting himself with every curve and valley.

I cling to him, reveling in the sensations I once thought I'd never experience again. I can't help but smile, feeling safe in his arms once more.

Blake lays me down gently on the bed, his eyes never leaving mine. I can see the hunger in them, but there's also something else —a tenderness I've never seen before.

He settles himself between my legs, his hands gentle as he undresses me. But his eyes undress me first, stripping away the hurt, the betrayal. I'm left bare before him—body, mind, and soul.

His lips find mine again, more insistent this time, and I can't help but respond. Our tongues dance together, familiar yet new, as if relearning each other's bodies. His hands roam my body, memorizing every curve, every valley.

Blake's kisses trail down my neck, sending shivers down my spine as he goes. He pauses at my collarbone, planting open-mouthed kisses along the sensitive skin. I arch my back, silently begging for more.

He chuckles softly, his warm breath on my skin sending goose bumps down my arms.

"Impatient, are we?" Blake asks, his voice a deep rumble in his chest. But he doesn't wait for an answer, instead continuing his journey down my stomach, his tongue making slow, wet circles around my bellybutton.

I moan, my nails digging into the sheets above my head. It's been so long since I've felt this alive, this wanted. Blake's hands slide up my thighs, fingertips gently brushing the inside of my thighs. I can feel the heat radiating from between my legs, my body aching for his touch.

He teases me mercilessly, tracing the outline of my underwear with his fingertips.

"Blake," I whine, my voice barely above a whimper.

He looks up at me, a wicked glint in his eyes, and I know he's enjoying this—enjoying the control he has over me. It should infuriate me, but instead, it only adds fuel to the fire within me.

Finally, mercifully, he slips a finger between my legs, finding my slick core. I gasp, my back arching off the bed. He doesn't relent. Instead, he adds a second, then a third finger, stretching me, preparing me for what's to come.

The room around us vanishes, and it's just us, tangled in the sheets, lost in each other. Forgotten worries melt away as we pick up where we left off, two halves of an intertwined whole. Blake's lips find mine, and I welcome the familiarity of his touch, the heat between us consuming us both.

As we move together, our bodies are in sync, and I realize some things are just meant to be. Blake and I may have taken a circuitous route to get here, but we made it.

Looking up at him, I see our future in his eyes—challenges, yes, but also love, strength, and unwavering commitment. The final barrier between us falls away, leaving only the foundation of our bond stronger than ever.

"What are you thinking about?" Blake asks, his hand gently stroking my hair.

I take a deep breath, gathering my thoughts. "Everything. The past, the future. Us."

He shifts slightly, propping himself up on one elbow to look at me more directly. "And what do you see when you think about our future?"

"I see hope," I say, my voice thick with emotion. "I see us building a life together. I never thought I'd have this. A family, a home, love. After everything that happened, everything I did—"

"Hey," Blake interrupts gently, "we've been through this. You did what you had to do to protect Luke. I understand that now. We can't change the past, but we can build our future."

"How did I get so lucky?"

"I think we're both lucky. We found each other against all odds. Twice." Blake's laugh rumbles through his chest.

We lie there in comfortable silence, basking in the simple pleasure of being together. The weight of our past, the pain and betrayal, still lingers, but it no longer feels like an insurmountable obstacle.

We have a long way to go, a new life to build, but in this moment, wrapped in Blake's arms with his steady heartbeat echoing my own, we'll make it.

We drift off to sleep in each other's arms; as long as we are together, we can face anything the world throws at us. For the first time in years, I fully embrace hope.

This is our new beginning. Our happily ever after. And it's more beautiful than I ever could have imagined.

Enjoyed Blake and Sophia's story?

Come join us for an exclusive bonus scene with Blake and Sophia.

You can read Blake and Sophia's bonus scene here.

elliemasters.com/RescuingSophia_BonusScene

~

Craving more high-stakes romance and pulse-pounding thrills? Dive into the world of "The Starling," where art theft meets forbidden passion.

Experience a daring new adventure in the Guardian HRS universe. Vivianne Faulks and Paul de Gaulle's electrifying dance of deception will leave you breathless.

Don't miss this sizzling story of secrets, desire, and danger. Grab "The Starling" now and let the game begin!elliemasters.com/TheStarling

Cara's Protector

Rescuing Barbi

Charlie Team

Rescuing Rebel

Rescuing Stitch

Rescuing Mia

Jenna's Protector

Rescuing Sophia

Delta Team (Coming Soon)

Rescuing Ember

Military Romance

Guardian Personal Protection Specialists

Sybil's Protector

Lyra's Protector

The One I Want Series

(Small Town, Military Heroes)

By Jet & Ellie Masters

EACH BOOK IN THIS SERIES CAN BE READ AS A STANDALONE AND IS ABOUT A DIFFERENT COUPLE WITH AN HEA.

Saving Abby

Saving Ariel

Saving Brie

Saving Cate

Saving Dani

Saving Jen

Rockstar Romance

The Angel Fire Rock Romance Series

Becoming His Series

THIS SERIES MUST BE READ IN ORDER.

The Ballet

Learning to Breathe

Becoming His

Dark Captive Romance

A STANDALONE NOVEL.

She's MINE

Books by Jet Masters

If you enjoyed this book by Ellie Masters, the LIGHTER SIDE of the Jet & Ellie writing duo, and aren't afraid of edgier writing, you might enjoy reading BDSM themed books written by Jet, the DARKER SIDE of the Masters' Writing Team.

The DARKER SIDE
Jet Masters is the darker side of the Jet & Ellie writing duo!

Romantic Suspense
Changing Roles Series:
THIS SERIES MUST BE READ IN ORDER.
Command Me
Control Me
Collar Me
Embracing FATE
Seizing FATE
Accepting FATE

HOT READS
A STANDALONE NOVEL.

Down the Rabbit Hole

Light BDSM Romance
The Ties that Bind
EACH BOOK IN THIS SERIES CAN BE READ AS A STANDALONE AND IS
ABOUT A DIFFERENT COUPLE WITH AN HEA.
Alexa
Penny
Michelle
Ivy

HOT READS
Becoming His Series
THIS SERIES MUST BE READ IN ORDER.
The Ballet
Learning to Breathe
Becoming His

Dark Captive Romance
A STANDALONE NOVEL.
She's MINE

About the Author

Ellie Masters is a USA Today Bestselling author and Amazon Top 15 Author who writes Angsty, Steamy, Heart-Stopping, Pulse-Pounding, Can't-Stop-Reading Romantic Suspense. In addition, she's a wife, military mom, doctor, and retired Colonel. She writes romantic suspense filled with all your sexy, swoon-worthy alpha men. Her writing will tug at your heartstrings and leave your heart racing.

Born in the South, raised under the Hawaiian sun, Ellie has traveled the globe while in service to her country. The love of her life, her amazing husband, is her number one fan and biggest supporter. And yes! He's read every word she's written.

She has lived all over the United States—east, west, north, south and central—but grew up under the Hawaiian sun. She's also been privileged to have lived overseas, experiencing other cultures and making lifelong friends. Now, Ellie is proud to call herself a Southern transplant, learning to say y'all and "bless her heart" with the best of them.

Ellie's favorite way to spend an evening is curled up on a couch, laptop in place, watching a fire, drinking a good wine, and bringing forth all the characters from her mind to the page and hopefully into the hearts of her readers.

FOR MORE INFORMATION
elliemasters.com

facebook.com/elliemastersromance
x.com/Ellie__Masters
instagram.com/ellie_masters
bookbub.com/authors/ellie-masters
goodreads.com/Ellie_Masters

ELLZ BELLZ

ELLIE'S FACEBOOK READER GROUP

If you are interested in joining the ELLZ BELLZ, Ellie's Facebook reader group, we'd love to have you.

Join Ellie's ELLZ BELLZ.
The ELLZ BELLZ Facebook Reader Group

Sign up for Ellie's Newsletter.
Elliemasters.com/newslettersignup

Connect with Ellie Masters

Website:
elliemasters.com
Purchase Direct:
elliemasters.com/shopify
Amazon Author Page:
elliemasters.com/amazon
Facebook:
elliemasters.com/Facebook
Goodreads:
elliemasters.com/Goodreads
Bookbub:
elliemasters.com/Bookbub
Instagram:
elliemasters.com/Instagram

Final Thoughts

I hope you enjoyed this book as much as I enjoyed writing it. If you enjoyed reading this story, please consider leaving a review on Amazon and Goodreads, and please let other people know. A sentence is all it takes. Friend recommendations are the strongest catalyst for readers' purchase decisions! And I'd love to be able to continue bringing the characters and stories from My-Mind-to-the-Page.

Second, call or e-mail a friend and tell them about this book. If you really want them to read it, gift it to them. If you prefer digital friends, please use the "Recommend" feature of Goodreads to spread the word.

Or visit my blog https://elliemasters.com, where you can find out more about my writing process and personal life.

Come visit The EDGE: Dark Discussions where we'll have a chance to talk about my works, their creation, and maybe what the future has in store for my writing.

Facebook Reader Group: Ellz Bellz

Thank you so much for your support!

Love,

Ellie

Dedication

This book is dedicated to you, my reader. Thank you for spending a few hours of your time with me. I wouldn't be able to write without you to cheer me on. Your wonderful words, your support, and your willingness to join me on this journey is a gift beyond measure.

Whether this is the first book of mine you've read, or if you've been with me since the very beginning, thank you for believing in me as I bring these characters 'from my mind to the page and into your hearts.'

Love,
Ellie

THE END